TOO MANY EYES

AND OTHER THRILLING STRANGE TALES

BY

PATRICK LOVELAND

A Stay Strange Publishing Publication
Edited by Christopher Smith Adair
The work published herein © Patrick Loveland
Introduction © 2019 Sam Lopez
This book copyright © 2019 Stay Strange Publishing
Cover Design and Illustrations/Interior Illustrations © 2019 Patrick Loveland

First Edition 2019
Published in the United States of America.
staystrange.com • patrickloveland.com • csmithadair.com

ISBN—978-1-7333349-0-7

"Iris and Kayyali Beyond Trolltown," first published in *Hellfire Lounge #5: Purgatory Potpourri* (edited by R. Allen Leider, Bold Venture) / "Not Cavities" first published in *The Sirens Call #29* (edited by Gloria Bobrowicz, Nina D'Arcangela, Julianne Snow; Sirens Call Publications) / "Ley Lines" first published in *Crime Factory Issue 18* (edited by Cameron Ashley, L. Scott Jose, Andrew Nette, Jimmy Callaway; Crime Factory Publications) / "Whoever Fights Monsters..." first published in *Monster Brawl!* (edited by Sirens Call Publications) / "The Bulb" first published in *Stomping Grounds (Short Sharp Shocks #2)* (edited by Neil Baker, April Moon Books) / "Ghosts of the Spires" first published in *Ill-considered Expeditions (Short Sharp Shocks #3)* (edited by Neil Baker, April Moon Books) / "PIE" first published in *Altered States II: A Cyberpunk Anthology* (edited by Jorge Salgado-Reyes and Roy C. Booth, Indie Authors Press) / "R-Day for Mr. D" first published in *The Sirens Call #28* (edited by Sirens Call Publications) / "HalcyonnoyclaH" first published in *The Stars at my Door (Short Sharp Shocks #5)* (edited by George Ilett Anderson and Neil Baker, April Moon Books) / "Beluga" first published in *Dark Designs: Tales of Mad Science* (edited by Thomas S. Flowers and Duncan Ralston, Shadow Work Publishing).

CONTENTS

FOREWORD by Sam Lopez

FOREWORD

"The horror! The horror!"

These horrors that flashed through Kurtz's skull as he lay dying time in the bleak novella *Heart Of Darkness*, however ghastly or hideous, certainly corpse-pale in comparison to the monsters found in Patrick Loveland's short story collection, *Too Many Eyes*. His malformed beasts and death-greased leviathans are my favorite kind of monsters. I've grown callous to the hooded psycho killer, the genius-yet-fractured manslayer, the garden-tool-wielding maniac seeking revenge for a heinous deed committed years ago. I like my monsters oozing, tentacled, and foul mouthed from a place more hellish than the darkest, deepest Lovecraftian grotto. Patrick serves those kinds of abominations in this compendium in all of their diseased and virulent contempt.

When dark author Patrick Loveland first asked for Stay Strange to publish his first horror anthology, I was honored. But what did I know about book publishing? Stay Strange is a noise music collective, not a book publisher. But the deeper I got into reading Patrick's writing and the color of his words as they dripped gory off the pages, I began noticing the similarities between his stories and the sinister nuances of harsh music. Both tell a story, both paint a picture, and in Patrick's case, just like a good audio thrashing, leaves the reader shocked, disgusted, and on the verge of nausea.

The past, present, and future of horror are wrapped in these pages like a mummified cadaver. Some horror lies dormant, readying itself for the opportunity to awake, in a fury, from some malignant nightmare. Other times the horror is right there at your doorstep: dismemberment and devourment, the only things on its mind. And the worst horror is the horror that takes it time to get here. Manmade, emotionless, and vicious. Programmed to sink its steely and scalpel-sharp teeth right into your core.

Thank you, Patrick, for giving me the creeps and staring at me with those probing, unflinching Too Many Eyes!

–Sam "Stay Strange" Lopez, 2019

YESTERDAY AND TODAY

Ekwiiyemak (The Place Where It Rains)

Cuyamaca Mountains, California—1889

The heavy rain outside had slowed and stopped as I was sopping up the last of my "free" supper at John's Peace saloon—it was free so long as you bought at least one drink. Beer was my choice, as it had been for years. I'd cut down from my strong drinking days, so I kept it to two glasses of John's own premium brew.

After the involuntary plantation work of my youth and the war just after, I'd spent years drifting. Plenty of the places I'd drifted between had been well stocked on firewater and rotgut, which I'd gladly poured down my gullet in exchange for laughs and, when needed, something resembling courage. Later on, I'd also developed a habit of drinking strong stuff to quiet my meaner memories and get some sleep. Sometimes that benefit conflicted with dark dreams the coffin varnish had cooked up from the memories, and it canceled out anyway. Eventually, I just gave harsher spirits up, along with a few other things that had seemed more fun and satisfying in my younger days. So beer it was.

It was John's proprietary beer that kept me coming back to John's Peace instead of one of the other saloons in this fine mountain town. His beer was strong, but even stronger beer wouldn't bring out my ugly side—or trouble my sleep—like the whiskey or mezcal I used to prefer.

Having finished said beer and plate, I wiped crumbs off my face with a bandanna from my back pocket, dropped a few coins on the table, then got up and weaved through starved and half-drunk gold miners who'd just come in

2

from long shifts. Watching them eat and drink with such a passion almost made me hungry again.

I stepped out of John's onto the wooden walkway that ran along Main Street down a gentle, curving slope toward the southeast—where Main became the road out of town, and the snaking southern route out of the mountains. I took out my pipe and pouch, packed the former and lit it with a match, then enjoyed the smooth, invigorating smoke. The town and surrounding woods were prematurely dark from thick clouds overhead but it would still be a lovely evening soon, if the rain stayed gone.

A cutting gust of wind blew through the town from the south and I caught something else in its natural howl—a strange wailing that seemed to come from somewhere down the mountain. It was only barely different from the wind itself, so I decided both sounds were one and the same.

I started toward Lou, my horse, who was hitched just down the walkway at a post. As I walked, I looked around at Youthful—the town I'd called home for several years now. Situated in the mountains northeast of San Diego, Youthful had been a gold-mining town since its creation over fifteen years before. But if my long-term plans came to fruition, I was hoping to change that.

Lou was real nervous, stepping around in place as he pulled a bit at the hitched reins. I reached out to comfort him—

Distant cracking sounds came from the same direction as the wailing, but the wind made it hard to tell how distant.

Lou reared up some and let out sounds of fearful confusion, so I stroked his mane.

"It's okay, boy. It's alright."

The wind was strong enough I just assumed it was heavy limbs being knocked off of trees and dropping to the forest floor—or even older trees being knocked down and cracking against stronger ones. The wind died down some and there were no more cracks, so Lou calmed a bit.

"There's nothing to be scared of, Lou."

I'll admit I was a touch spooked myself, so soothing Lou maybe had a mutual benefit. I stroked his mane and gently patted him until he calmed down even more.

"That's good, Lou. That's real good."

I caught sight of someone coming down the exterior steps from a second-floor room above a saloon across the muddy street, their gaze fixed down toward where the strange sounds had come from—and I'll be damned if it wasn't *Shiv O'Shea*....

She saw me too and stopped halfway down the stairs and raised her hands and laughed. I started across the puddle-dotted street toward the stairs, finishing off my pipe and tucking it.

Charlotte "Shiv" O'Shea was a mighty singular individual. We'd been caught in a crossfire between bandit gangs in a small town in New Mexico around twenty years before. We'd covered each other as we skinned out, taking turns moving and shooting as we made it to some horses. After we rode out, we'd camped overnight, drank, and patched each other up. We got real close that night....

We'd separated the next morning, as that seemed to be her way, but I'd come across her every few years since then. In Utah, Idaho, and Montana territory towns and posts I'd encountered her—even Alaska and other unforgiving regions. Other than gun-fighting and other (possibly) unlawful pursuits, she was also somewhat famous for being the only survivor of a frontier outpost massacre way back. She never had told me that whole story.

"I knew it was only a matter of time, lady...," I called out and laughed.

Shiv laughed too and said, "Ain't that the truth!"

I noticed Shiv's old horse, Willie, tied to a post near the base of the stairs. He had some special gear strapped to him on his rear and sides that I couldn't identify. Also one of the newer bolt-action rifles from Europe, complete with a telescopic sight for long shots.

We met at the bottom of the stairs and hugged, slapping each other on the back.

Shiv said, "I haven't seen you since...."

"Oregon," I said, feeling a dull ache of regret as I did.

"Damn. Guess that's true."

Shiv always wore an open crown, flat-brimmed black hat, riding gloves, and dark men's riding clothes—which took getting used to for some, on account of her being shapely enough and real good looking. She wore her wavy auburn hair either short like a city man would, shaggy, or in two thick braids when it was longer, as it was today. She talked like an Irishman trying not to sound like she was, and looked to be the child of one and maybe a Celestial—from a hint in the shape of her bright green eyes. She was tall, strong, and quick too.

She looked real relaxed.

I lowered my voice some and said, "Saloon girls ain't never safe around you, huh?"

"Hey, you know me," Shiv said and winked. There was just a hint of a blush in her freckled cheeks.

I'd discovered her freeness of affections years before quite by accident, and her only response had been that she just felt a warm body with you on a cold night was real fine either way. I'd never been overly religious or anything like that so it hadn't ever bothered me much, but I knew it could get her into trouble in this town, as I'd seen it do before in other places.

I could feel from the embrace that she still kept a Bowie knife on the small of her back, and I'd seen a long Gasser 1870 black-powder cartridge pistol on her thigh. She also had a Colt Single Action Army on her right hip front with its handle angled for grabbing with her left hand. In the past, I'd also seen her wield a ball-tipped cudgel that curved forward some—an obvious Indian weapon but I never could make out the region or tribe—but I didn't see that anywhere

4

obvious. That mean-looking weapon had always gone away after use as quick as it'd been produced.

Shiv had always been full of surprises.

She said, "So hey, what brings you to this high place, Blake?"

I looked around and said, "It's *Tate* now. *Absalom Tate.*"

Shiv glanced around too and said, "You workin' a graft, eh?"

"No, no—nothing like that. Legitimate. I bought some acres up here a handful of years ago and I planted dozens of apple trees. Gonna make this town an *apple* town. Gold mines run dry eventually, right?"

She narrowed her eyes and said, "Apples?"

I watched her scrutinize my face, something I'd seen her do to others many times to ferret out honesty. It felt strange having her do it to me, but I'd survive it.

Shiv nodded and said, "Apples it is."

"That's what I said, that's what I meant. Growing apples and reading is about how dangerous I like it now."

"I get you. Hey, I'm just glad you found somethin' safe and productive to do with your share of that mess in Oregon, 'specially after it put Bristly Pete in the bone orchard."

"Yeah, well...he always was a might slow. So what brings you up here? Catch the gold bug?"

She took out a white chainless pocket watch and checked it.

Shiv said, "More like hunting...."

She looked down the gentle slope to the southeast out of town, then at Crocker's general store and said, "You think that general store is stocked on kerosene?"

I frowned and said, "Coal oil? Imagine so. You take up bounty hunting again, Shiv?"

She started across the street toward the general store next to John's Peace. "Not exactly, no."

I looked down the slope out of town and saw a flickering light coming from around the bend. I said, "Stagecoach might have some if the store don't."

"Stagecoach?" Shiv said, stopping in the street.

She took a collapsed spyglass from a little case on her belt, flipped it to full length, and examined the stagecoach. She collapsed it and started for the general store again without another word.

"Shiv, what's going on?"

I looked down at the approaching coach and noticed a few things, now that Shiv's odd behavior had caused me to focus. Two limping horses pulled it—should be four. Only one lit lantern—other looked broken, even from a distance. No driver—no one visible at all.

"Shiv?"

I looked toward the general store but she'd already made it inside.

5

The stagecoach creaked and rocked as the two exhausted horses pulled its whole weight up Main in the dim rainy afternoon light. Townspeople were starting to notice the coach, ghostly as it appeared and limping along as it was. People stopped on walkways, slowed their pace to watch the coach shamble as they crossed the street, and walked to windows inside establishments to gawk.

I hadn't decided to approach, but realized I'd already started walking down Main toward it. I also drummed the grip of my Schofield revolver on my right thigh, without having thought about it. Maybe I'd had too much of John's beer after all.

I heard a belch behind me and glanced back—Julian Beksinski, a huge Polish miner, had come out of John's Peace and stood scratching his ribs under his grimy overalls as he surveyed the town. He caught sight of me and looked toward where I was heading and saw the advancing coach, then stepped off the walkway frowning.

Turning my attention back southward, I saw Sheriff Dean Morris storming around a corner a few streets down, coming from his office and jailhouse with a new lever-action shotgun held as tight as his face. The coach had come down Main far enough that it was between Morris and myself, though still closer to him.

"What's the situation, Tate?" Fausto Esposi asked from back on the other walkway near Shiv's horse. Esposi was a tailor and retired army man, originally from Chicago, who'd fought in the Victorio Apache campaign in New Mexico— where he'd earned himself a medal and a limp.

"I'm not sure myself."

As the stagecoach neared a bakery next to the general store, I noticed that its structure and wobbling wheels shuddered and creaked in time with a damaged axle. Drexler, the baker, stepped out of his shop with eyes narrowed—

Drexler jolted backwards as the axle snapped free on one side and came down through the front right coach wheel, splintering it.

The whole coach sagged forward toward me and I stepped back too.

The horses collapsed from the added weight, one just exhausted—the other's torso and gut were open, and it must have been dragging its innards for some time. The tired horse was better off, but I saw wounds on it as well.

After just watching the horses rest and die for a moment, Drexler stepped toward the badly injured one and looked it over. It was a goner, no doubt. Probably both would be soon.

All the coach window shades had been pulled down. Fluid leaked out of the lowest corner of the coach interior, where it had collapsed into the mud. There was red in it but it was mostly black, and I felt a shiver as I caught sickly, unnatural hues in it too like real bright green and bluish purple. Those strange colors made me a little queasy to look at and almost seemed to—for lack of a better word—*glow* a bit. A powerful stench I was just taking in now, coming from the stagecoach, might've also helped to twist my stomach up.

6

Something moaned inside the coach and my hand went to my Schofield. I skinned my pistol and cocked the hammer, then creeped closer, aiming at the door.

"I got you covered," Sheriff Morris said from the other side of the coach, aiming his shotgun at the door opposite mine.

"Yeah, go ahead," Esposi said from behind me and I looked back—he didn't wear a gun in town but he'd found a wood-splitting axe somewhere and had it raised and ready. I admired Esposi's courage for a moment then turned back toward the coach.

More of that nasty fluid leaked from the lowest coach door corner and as I grabbed the handle and flung it open, the colored mixture of thicker fluid and gallons of caught rainwater poured onto the muddy street. Some fingers, a lower leg, and a stew of unidentifiable human insides slapped down into the puddles as the last of the mixture drained out.

The roof had been pried open somehow and the ceiling was open to the sky, a jagged hole four feet across. Parts of limbs, organs, and less recognizable chunks were strewn about with empty 10-gauge shells, all gleaming from the thick residue of whatever that black and bright-colored fluid was that had mixed with the blood and rainwater.

The moans had to have come from the upper half of the coach driver, now still and staring with his one remaining eye toward me. That moan must've been this pour soul's death knell, but the staring eye seemed locked on my own. I broke the gaze and saw that his jaw also looked to be dislocated.

The sheriff wrenched open his door on the far side of the cabin and the blood left his face as he aimed his shotgun with trembling hands. Our wide eyes met and I shook my head.

I caught the stench again, stronger now that the cabin was open, and held back a retch. I grabbed my bandanna and covered my mouth and nose, then holstered my pistol so I could tie the cloth into a mask. I took in the grisly sights in the cabin, and heard Esposi vomit onto the street behind me.

Sheriff Morris said, "Tate.... What the *hell* happened to this coach?"

"Couldn't say...."

The driver had dropped his short side-by-side shotgun and its barrel end was against my side of the coach interior. I went to pick it up but was surprised to find that the barrel was still hot. I leaned in and grabbed it by the grip, then pulled it out. I opened the breech—one round fired, one not. The gun's warmth made me real uneasy and I stepped back and looked down the darkening route the stagecoach had arrived from. It hit me that the cracks I'd heard only minutes before must've been from whatever desperate battle this coach had been host to and victim of.

The coach shifted and lurched forward some. I stepped back a few steps to see and—

The maimed horse was moving. Maybe it wasn't dead like I'd thought.

7

The horse rose up from the pile of its own innards with its mouth wide—its teeth somehow black now, and almost see through like broken, pitted shards of some dark, cloudy gemstone—and flopped toward the other horse. Its head swung down and those terrible teeth sunk into its partner, gouging a fist-sized chunk from out of the other horse's neck. The more intact horse grasped for strength it just didn't have as it tried to get to its feet again and escape its cannibalistic attacker.

I could see tight black boils with bubbles of bright green and purple form and multiply around the eviscerated horse's mouth and eyes as it limped after its prey. The two horses pulled the coach forward bit by bit as they fought their harnesses. The attacking horse's eyes went all black and its head and neck started to bulge and change. It clamped onto the other horse's neck, this time not letting go. The other horse tried to cry out until all that came were gurgling sounds, and it collapsed.

A shot rang out, startling everyone out of a stupor this awful display had put us in.

Drexler had fired a Derringer he'd pulled from a vest pocket, striking the attacking horse in the back of its pulsing neck. The horse wailed and whipped back toward Drexler, its boil-covered maw dangling bumpy black tentacles it'd had to pull out of the other horse's neck. It flopped around and crawled toward him. He fired the other Derringer barrel, striking its right eye. It didn't stop but sickly black fluid spurted and bubbled out of its head. Drexler stepped back and stumbled, thumping down on his butt and still aiming his empty gun. The horse creature kept coming toward him—

Beksinski grabbed its reins, wrapped them around his hands, and used all his strength and weight to keep it from getting those teeth and tentacles into the baker. The horse dug in and pulled Beksinski with it, still focused on doing Drexler grievous harm.

A shot boomed from the general store doorway and the horse-thing's head busted open and it collapsed.

"No, *thank you!*" Shiv called out in taunt.

She held her Gasser 1870 and a big can of kerosene with hose and pump nozzle. The horse's headless body kept moving and Shiv stepped toward it, firing twice more into its swelling gut as she advanced. She holstered her smoking pistol and took the kerosene nozzle with that hand, then pumped the lever and sprayed the fluid all over the busted-open horse and the coach.

Shiv said, "What kind of general store keeps its kerosene in a locked shed out back—that they can't find the *keys* to? Gonna owe 'em for the door, I guess...."

I didn't know *what* I was seeing—it made me even sicker than the strange fluid had, and I almost felt hypnotized looking at the creature—but my old friend seemed practically undaunted. She took out a friction match, lit it, and flicked it into the horse's open gut—just as a few new clouded eyes and black-toothed mouths opened impossibly in the seeping mess of organs.

Fire consumed the thing that had been a horse, then jumped to the stagecoach. Beksinski let go of the reins and flopped back into a puddle.

"Shiv!" I yelled, but the fire roared between us.

The other horse near me shuddered and its abdomen bulged. I saw those same black boils forming on its mouth and nose, then its eyes pulsed black.

I tried to fire the coach shotgun into its head—but the hammer hit the primer with an impotent thud. The horse writhed and bucked against the ground, knocking me back. It wailed and shook as it came for me—Beksinski grabbed *its* reins now, and held it back long enough for me to produce my Schofield and fire it twice into the monster's head.

Sheriff Morris appeared and fired a shotgun round into it too, and its head slapped down into the mud. But the wailing hadn't all stopped—there was more of it, muffled as it came out of the dead horse's torso. It kept moving toward me as it bulged and swelled.

Shiv had heard the shots and came around the main blaze to add the other horse to it. She pumped and sprayed the kerosene all over the sickening abomination. Before she could grab a match, embers from the coach had lit it up.

Beksinski let go of the reins and helped Esposi pull me farther from the fire. The three of us collapsed and just watched the creatures writhe and wail as the blaze whirled and ate at them. They screeched too.... I'd never heard anything so harrowing and unnatural.

Townspeople ran for blankets and water. Some beat embers away from the other buildings on Main while others threw buckets of mud and water onto the flames.

I turned my attention to Shiv, who was just watching the creatures and coach burn, hate and satisfaction in her eyes the likes of which I'd never seen.

Sheriff Morris rode in front, his lantern throwing a circular cone of light ahead. Beksinski and Shiv had similar spotlight lanterns, and the three created a good overlap of light ahead. Esposi and I had regular, wide-area lanterns that filled in the gaps to the sides and rear of our riding path—which I was mighty thankful for, after what we'd seen a short time earlier.

After forming a group to deal with the scorched remains of the horses and coach back in town—as per Shiv's instructions that involved digging a pit and covering the remains in the contents of a heavy sack she gave them that resembled one for flour—the sheriff had formed this small posse out of those who'd done their damnedest during the horse madness. The sheriff knew Esposi, Beksinski, and myself were ready for the worst and I'd vouched for Shiv, even if her display of unbridled damage dealing and courage had spoken for itself. She'd even told Morris that she was in the area on government business and didn't need our help. Morris wasn't having any of that, and I was a bit ruffled by it myself.

After we'd stopped by Esposi's place for his pistol and repeater, we headed down the mountain route the stagecoach had taken on its way up. From the warmth of the driver's gun barrel when I'd found it, the driver had last fired it pretty close to town, but we'd gone a ways and seen nothing other than signs of the trailing entrails and other viscera from what had been the worse-off horse.

I was pretty certain four of us weren't at all sure what we'd do if we found the source of the horror back in town, myself especially. Shiv was another story, all focused and calm—other than what seemed like excitement under the surface.

At least we were well armed—other than what Esposi'd grabbed for himself, I'd taken the coach driver's shotgun and acquired some rounds for it from the general store, and always had my Schofield on me. Beksinski had a cut down double-barrel with no stock and a real short barrel, plus an ancient looking LeMat cap-and-ball black-powder revolver. Morris had a pistol and the lever-action shotgun.

Also, Shiv had made us each carry a kerosene tank with pump and spray nozzle and had helped fit us with straps so they could be worn on our backs, with the nozzle ends in our belts. She'd even hooked them up at a bit of an angle toward our non-shooting-hand sides so we could pump the kerosene by reaching back over our shoulders.

We rode slow enough to scan the road, unsure what we'd find. Our lights danced around on the muddy road and the pines and oaks of the mountain forest I usually loved. Recent events had me seeing strange shapes in the darkness out past the reach of our lanterns.

As we'd made our way southward, Beksinski had relayed to us a fact he'd learned from a local Indian. This area south of our town and closer to one of the other goldmines south of a lake there was called *Ekwiiyemak*. He said he'd been told it meant either something to do with clouds or "The Raining Place," a meaning related to it being more precipitous up here in the mountains, or something like that. Getting a meaningful translation in English secondhand, especially from someone who didn't speak it that well to begin with, was never that easy or effective.

Now when it came to Shiv, I had more questions than patience. I caught up and did one of our old whistles in a way she'd understand. She slowed enough to allow Esposi to take her spot and continued scanning the woods all around as we kept pace.

"What's on your mind?"

I said, "What was it you said we're after again? Rabid bears, was it?"

"It's like rabies, but it can infect any animal of a minimum size."

"How'd you get this duty? I saw those papers you showed the sheriff, but I didn't catch how you got involved."

10

Shiv looked at me, then back at the road and other riders ahead.

She said, "You remember that frontier outpost way back you asked me about once?"

"Yeah, and I've heard others talk about it over the years as well."

"This infection caused that too. Later, there were more awful infection massacres like that one, and once the government made the connection, they sought me out."

I thought on that, then said, "And they let you do this work alone?"

Shiv said, "I'm not always alone. Hadn't had time to contact any of my fellow hunters for this one. Got the hints of it too late."

"I have to be honest with you, Shiv...."

"Yeah?"

"Back in town.... That sure didn't look like no rabies I ever saw."

She looked at me and said, "You'll have to trust me."

I just nodded and we rode in silence a bit.

Then I said, "Can I ask you one other thing?"

"Sure."

"Are you an angel or something?"

Shiv laughed real loud and Beksinski glanced back at us.

"Why, Absalom Tate—are you gettin' flirtatious with me? It's been years, boyo. You still got what it takes?"

"*Years.* Yeah, that's why I ask. You're the spitting image of the day I met you. That was almost *twenty years* ago, Charlotte."

Shiv lost her smile and looked real sad at that.

"I age graceful, I suppose. I'm surely no angel."

"Not a *vampire* either then, are you?"

Shiv smiled again and said, "A what?"

"I read these penny pamphlets called *Varney the Vampire* some years back that a Brit trader sold me and—"

Sheriff Morris raised his hand and called back, "Woah, woah—we got something!"

We all slowed to a stop near some signs of struggle ahead and pulled up our tied bandanna masks—Shiv had said there was something like spores or pollen the infection could leave that shouldn't be breathed in. Bandannas were good enough, she'd said, but then she pulled up a special mask of her own with some tubes on its sides along her jawline that she'd slid glass ampules into. I'd wondered if maybe we should all have had those....

Morris got off his horse and approached a big chunk of mangled human corpse with an open torso, one arm, and about half its head, its guts spilled like it'd been flung and landed on the side of the road. Cases from the stagecoach were busted open and sprayed with blood—and that thick black fluid with the sickly bright spots. More torn and broken limbs, innards, and organs had been strewn about, some half sucked into the muddy road.

Shiv said, "Burn everything black you see. Red too," already pumping her gas can over her shoulder. She sprayed it from atop her horse on some nasty parts of the road before flicking a match down at the gore. Esposi, Morris, and I did the same, but Beksinski seemed distracted.

Sheriff Morris said, "So, these infected bears came down here and just savaged the stagecoach?"

"Looks that way," Esposi said.

I looked at Beksinski, who'd mostly just been staring off to our left since we got here.

"What's on your mind, Julian?"

He gestured up toward a meadow on the brow of a hill below a lesser peak to the southeast. There was a house there in the meadow.

"That was Halverson's house."

Esposi said, "Was?"

"He die two weeks ago."

I said, "So?"

Beksinski said, "He live alone...."

The rest of us looked at the house again—there were slivers of light through a few windows and a thin wisp of dark smoke from a weak fire. Shiv took out her scoped newer rifle and aimed it at the house, then lowered it slowly.

"That's where I'm goin'."

Morris said, "You mean *we*."

"Sure, why not?"

We rode a bit farther down and went left onto a half-overgrown horse trail, then up its gentle slope under a foreboding canopy of oak and pine that made me really value our lamps. Coming out of the tree cover into the meadow, I felt fresh sprinkles coming down and saw a misty low-lying fog was clinging to treetops all around, and rolling through the meadow around the house.

As we approached, Shiv slid off her horse and snuck toward the house without bothering to tie Willie to an available hitch post a little closer to it. She stalked around to the side of the house while we got off our horses and tied them to the hitch.

I could see the windows were shattered and had all been blocked or boarded up from the inside. One corner of the house had been half collapsed inward, but still held roughly intact. Slivers between the internal barricading showed flickering from a dying fire inside. The collapsed part and other gouges and splintered areas of the barricades made me real uneasy, then moaning from inside increased that feeling.

Sheriff Morris said, "Hey, who's in there?"

There was only more moaning and some coughing inside, then, "*Nhnnnnggh-izz*at you, Sheriff?"

"That's right! Who are you?"

"Doesn't matter who! *Nnngk....*" the man inside retched and coughed then said, "You gotta blow up Bright Moon Mine, Sheriff!"

"That's been abandoned for years—"

"We went in thar t'see if thar's gold that maybe got missed afore e'rybody left it be! We brought some dynamite in thar—" then he coughed again.

Esposi got closer and pressed his face against a larger opening in one of the damaged barricaded windows to peek in.

"*Hnnnngk....* We foun' somethin'.... Not gold...."

His voice was getting weaker.

Sheriff Morris said, "Is that you, Cyrus Benton?"

"Maybe...."

"Where's your damn gang, Benton?"

"In the *mine....* Don't you worry. They'll come again when it *rains.* You gotta blow it...."

After a long pause, Morris said, "You still there, son?"

The breathing got louder inside and the moans became deeper and sounded more tortured.

"Get away from the house!" Shiv yelled as she came around from the back, spraying kerosene on the walls and roof. She flicked a match onto it, setting the east side, roof, and south side ablaze in a violent burst of flame.

Wailing like we'd heard from the horses arose from inside. Morris, Beksinski, and me backed away. Esposi was still trying to get a look inside when a stalk of bumpy, pulsing tentacles busted through the barricades near his head and grabbed him, pulling him hard against the boards.

Beksinski reached Esposi in two big strides, ignoring the flames creeping toward the front of the house. He tried to pull Esposi away but couldn't. Then he slammed his foot against the outer wall and pulled with everything he had.

I could see the tentacles burrowing into Esposi's back and spine through his clothes. I ran to help and with our combined strength, we pulled Esposi away from the boards some and—

Esposi's eyes were wild and he looked like he was trying to scream, but the creature that had been the tortured man inside the house had inserted a thick, muscular tongue of layered tentacles into Esposi's mouth. The head of the awful thing inside the house had too many eyes and its pulsing bulk was covered in the tight black boils I'd seen on the horses. I could see its shape was wrong too—it had started as a man, but had become something *else,* like the horses had.

Me and Beksinski pulled even harder, but I could feel Esposi's insides fluttering and bulging—then sucking *inward.*

The creature wrenched Esposi back against the boards and I shifted focus, grabbing Beksinski and pulling him away from the house as the flames licked at the eaves above us. Esposi writhed against the wall and boards—

Until the creature broke a hard appendage like a fleshy insect leg out through the gaps in the boards, sunk it into Esposi's shoulder, and pulled his

13

body down away from its grotesque tentacle stalk. With no small effort, it removed Esposi's body from its tangle of sucking tongues with a sickening pop sound as it broke free. His body crumpled and slapped down looking half as substantial as it had moments before.

With me and Beksinski out of the way, Shiv and Sheriff Morris opened fire, driving the vile beast farther into the burning house. After its retreat, Shiv sprayed more kerosene on the front of the house and the whole thing went up while the thing wailed, chittered, and screeched inside.

Morris, Beksinski, and myself stumbled away from the inferno and unhitched our terrified horses, then pulled them to a safer distance. Shiv stood where she'd doused the front of the house and stared at it, pouring sweat from the heat. After she'd had her fill, she turned and strode back to us. She whistled and Willie came galloping to her, not afraid like our horses.

Shiv stood with her back to the burning house, a looming silhouette.

She said, "I know what needs doin' now. You all should go home and forget about this."

Sheriff Morris said, "Like *Hell!*"

I said, "That fuckin' thing ate his insides.... He was alive the whole time, an' it *sucked* his guts out."

"Like jam in jar...," Beksinski said, looking queasy and unsettled for the first time since this had started.

I stepped toward Shiv—but stopped when she cocked her head half toward me and her face caught the fire light behind her. Her eyes were hot and cold at the same time. I wasn't sure she even recognized me.

"Shiv, that weren't no rabies."

She blinked twice and seemed to see me again.

She said, "Go home, friend."

"What are you after, O'Shea?" Sheriff Morris said.

She turned her face into the dark again and said, "There's a debt being paid back, older than you can understand. I hope you never have to."

Beksinski snorted and said, "I know what I saw. Today, I fight the *gloom* that took Fausto."

Morris said, "If there's a kind of rabies that does that.... I'm gonna seal it in that damned mine."

I looked past Shiv at the fire and the charred husk of Esposi's body in it.

I said, "Well...what good are apples with no people left to eat them?"

A light rain fell as we neared the mine entrance. It had been excavated from between two splayed crags. Rusting, termite-eaten mine carts rested on tracks that ran to the mine opening and disappeared into its inky black tunnel mouth.

We'd tied our horses' reins to trees and sturdy bushes a healthy distance from the tunnel mouth and out of its line of sight around a bend in the trail near its sign marker. I didn't want something coming out after we'd gone in and having a meal too easily available—assuming we hadn't already filled their bellies....

Shiv went in the mine first and we followed, all still wearing our masks and kerosene tanks—and armed to the teeth. She'd switched her scoped rifle out for a shotgun, and of course one unlike any I'd ever seen.

The shotgun resembled a side-by-side double-barrel, but it had three—the third above the other two in a triangular arrangement. A "triple-barrel," I guess you could say. It was finished with some kind of glossy black lacquer, but had engravings all over its wood and metal surfaces that reminded me of finely detailed scrimshaw whale-tooth carving. There was a fitting built into its stock that held a long glass cylinder that had colorful fluids inside and a thin metal tube from that to the closed breach, and the rounds she'd loaded into it and wore on a bandolier over her chest were a little thicker than twelve or even ten gauge as well.

The government—if that's really who Shiv was working for—must have been dealing with this bear rabies infection a while if they'd devoted weapon engineering to its eradication.

She'd also helped us secure our smaller hand lanterns on our chests with the straps she'd rigged up for the tanks, so we'd have our hands free. She'd definitely done this before, for certain, but I still wasn't sure that made me feel better about it.

We'd barely made it twenty feet inside before discovering most of the mine was flooded. Shiv just waded into the murky water and was knee deep in only a few steps. She took some sort of explosive charges out of a satchel she'd grabbed off of Willie, pressing each one against the mine ceiling as she went. Little poofs of air came out of the charges and they stayed in place. They looked like two concentric glass spheres, each chamber filled with a different colored fluid. I had a worsening feeling about our survival chances with every one of those odd charges she placed. I'd never known Shiv that well, but the extent of my possible misjudging of her nature or ignorance of her true heritage was really coming clear today.

"What're those for?" I whispered.

She mumbled something, almost to herself, that sounded like, "Just in case...."

I didn't like the sound of that.

Our lanterns threw ominous shadows from the upper parts of rusting half-sunk mine equipment onto the walls as we trudged through now waist-high watery muck, and I wished I could see the damn tunnel floor. We'd only taken one forking path and I already felt lost. There was dripping and creaking and beams sighing, but no rabies monsters—not yet.

15

We kept trudging on, heads constantly jerking and scanning—all except Shiv. She moved with purpose, aware but always wading forward.

We were pretty deep in the mine, the water almost to my ribs, when we came across a narrow, angled chasm that had opened in the mine wall and ceiling.

Shiv examined the chasm and said, "This way."

She started in before we could get a good look. As we followed her in I saw from the dancing lamp light that the chasm ascended at a gradual incline. The kerosene tanks on our backs made the chasm a tight fit, big ol' Beksinski especially. Within twenty feet we were almost out of the mucky water, which I was thankful for—until I saw the *boils*....

The craggy chasm surfaces became dotted all around with the tight little sacks—same as before, only in the rocks instead of flesh—starting the size of lady bugs, then larger on up to silver-dollar sized as we advanced.

Shiv said, "Keep those masks on, boys."

The boils were the size of oranges by the time the chasm opened up. Shiv snuck out of its confines and covered us with her shotgun as we slid out after.

We'd ended up in a cave system and this part we'd stumbled onto was a decent-sized chamber. At the edges of our lamplight I could see smaller chambers and tunnels snaking off into the darkness.

There were parts of the boil-covered cave walls—some of the black and sickly colored sacks the size of halved cannonballs now above and around us— and stalactites and stalagmites that seemed roughly carved into something like statues. Statues of what, I couldn't say, but their creation looked deliberate.

There were also tools, guns, and torn clothes scattered around in the ankle-deep water on the cave floor. Those must've been from Benton's boys.

But none of that worried me as much as what had been exposed in the cave wall across from the chasm opening—a huge black ball, like the mother of all black boils. It must've been almost thirty feet across, estimating from the rough third of it I could see that wasn't obscured by the rock it was ensconced in. Its surface was bumpy too, like even it was covered in boils of all different sizes. I could swear that things didn't look right near it—like the light and shapes were warped near it, and it was hard to look at. The whole chamber seemed to look wrong like that too, the longer I looked at it....

I whispered, "That...sure don't *look* like rabies."

Sheriff Morris said, "What is that, O'Shea?"

"Madness and death, is all."

Shiv took out her Colt SAA, cocked it, and fired into the center of the exposed part of the black ball. It rippled and pulsed, thick fluid pumping and spraying out with the bright sickly colors in it.

Wails and screeching came from the side tunnels I'd seen on our way in and Beksinski, Morris, and I looked at each other with wide eyes.

Shiv said, "I s'pose I shoulda asked before now.... How many boys in Benton's gang, Morris?"

16

"Nine or t-ten—I thought we were after *bears*."

She said, "Shit, I was hoping for half that number.... They're gonna be big this time."

Shiv took one of her glass-in-glass charges from her satchel, adjusted something, and threw it into the spurting black ball where she'd just shot it. The charge traveled a ways inside—the liquid wasn't opaque, but was almost too thick to see through—then it must have exploded. But instead of blasting outward, the surface of the black ball shrunk away as it was sucked inward toward its center. The ball went into itself and *vanished*.

At that very moment it struck me how little I understood—about Shiv, about this "*infection*," about *anything*. I couldn't think clearly and just stared at the big empty cavity in the cave wall where Shiv had lanced that sickly abscess. It was just gone....

The wails got louder just as that happened, sounding more sorrowful than angry for a moment—but then the wailing got even angrier and I saw what we were really fighting and understood what Shiv meant about "big" now, nonsensical as it had seemed a moment before.

Three awful things came for us—two from the left tunnel, one from the right—and big they were. They distorted the light and looked wrong like the ball and the rest of the chamber had—but even worse, like the wavy haze over a fire or the air above a real hot road on a sun-beaten day. I couldn't see the things clearly, even looking straight at them. What I got were glimpses through whatever that haze or messed-up trick of the light was, and they were gruesome.

If they'd been men, I'd have started shooting on sight—but they *weren't*, and I couldn't do anything but stare at the monsters now with my hands shaking around the shotgun I held.

They'd sure started out as Benton's gang, but all his boys who made up each of the three abominations had been stuck together somehow into one clump of body—and with no obvious start to one man or end of another. The biggest one had to be made up of four men, and maybe one less for the other two creatures. The three things moved with no regard for the original bodies they were made up of, one even climbing across the cave ceiling like some insect or monkey might.

I could almost make out an arm or part of a face, but everything between was tangled up and misshapen. Those cloudy black eyes I'd seen on the horses and Benton were all over the bodies, and in between those there were those damned black and sickly boils, all different sizes. And the bulk of their bodies all those orbs and sacks were in was almost see through, like a tadpole could be. The guts and bones inside looked all wrong too. Everything was twisted up, bulging, pumping, swollen—

"Shoot 'em, god-*dammit*." Shiv said, then aimed her triple-barrel at the one coming across the cave ceiling and fired.

The gun flashed with strange light and where the shot should've just blasted into the monster's see-through meat, it went in like a slug shell—then

17

sucked a big ball-shaped chunk of the thing's body into the spot where it'd stopped inside. The three-foot orb of warped innards and bones vanished like the mother boil had, but left a hollow of gaping flesh instead of rock.

I still couldn't shoot....

Then I thought of my apple orchards just waiting back at my big patch of land for me to tend to tomorrow morning, after some flapjacks, eggs, and a big mug of hot coffee.

I'm not dying today.

I figured Shiv could handle the one still coming across the ceiling with that impossible gun of hers, so I aimed at the other one coming from the left tunnel and fired one chamber. The buckshot hit hard and tore into it, but the thing kept coming.

Shiv fired another two shots at the ceiling crawler. Two more big, ball-shaped holes got sucked out of it and it dropped to the cave floor. She opened her strange shotgun's breach and started reloading it, swapping out the glass fluid tube in the stock for a fresh one too.

Beksinski and the sheriff started shooting too, now that we had. Morris used his repeater on the one rushing out of the right tunnel and Beksinski fired with his LeMat at the one I'd just shot, his cut-down shotgun ready in the other hand.

I fired my other barrel, shredding deep into its center area. It stumbled but kept shambling toward us.

Beksinski fired one more LeMat round then seemed to just wait for a long moment. When the creature was only two strides away, he aimed his shotgun and fired both barrels into its thickest bunch of eyes and boils. It collapsed, flopping toward us and rolling over itself some.

"Ha!" Beksinski said—followed by something in Polish—celebrating maybe as he holstered his LeMat and went to reload his shotgun.

I wasn't as confident, and broke open my shotgun to reload too.

Morris wasn't doing enough damage with his repeater, so I slid the shells into my gun and snapped the breach closed. Shiv had reloaded too and we both aimed at the one going for Morris—

Shiv was struck hard by the creature she'd downed from the ceiling and flung across the cave trailing thick streams of blood. She smacked into one of the weird stalagmite statues, breaking it off its base, and they both rolled away into the dark of the right tunnel.

"Shiv!"

But there was no time for rescue as the one from the ceiling lunged for me and Beksinski. He tried to get out of its way but collided with me in the process and we both stumbled. Beksinski fired both barrels into the thing, almost cutting it in half at one of the narrower parts left from Shiv's triple-barrel. It didn't go down, but it sure shrunk back and retreated toward the darkness of the left tunnel.

I gained my footing and aimed at the one near Morris—

18

It already had him on the ground, a stalk of those nasty tentacles—same as the ones the Benton monster'd had in Esposi—coming out of one of its black-toothed mouths and shoved down his throat, pumping in and out while it held him down and sucked out his insides.

His eyes were crazed, and the creature sounded like it was...*moaning.*

I shot Morris in the head with one barrel, then aimed for the denser clump of boils and eyes near where the stalk came out and fired the other. It shrunk away some and screeched from other jagged mouths, but kept eating the dead sheriff's guts.

"Shiv!" I called again, but heard nothing from the dark over that way.

"We go!" Beksinski said.

He pushed me toward the chasm entrance as he holstered his guns.

"Wait—*Charlotte!*" but I heard no answer as the big miner forced me toward our only escape route. He sprayed kerosene from his tank in between pumping it over his shoulder and pushing me. He doused the one having its way with Morris last.

"Shiv dead, and we *will* be!"

I was still looking back as I started into the chasm and saw Beksinski strike a match and throw it, lighting up what seemed like the whole chamber with roaring fire. Then he came into the chasm after me, pushing me down it toward the flooded mine. I could hear wailing and screeches from those foul fucking things back in the chamber, and just hoped that meant they were dying.

I kept going a bit and caught that Beksinski wasn't pushing me the last few steps.

"Tate...."

His bulk, the tank, and the angle of the chasm had conspired to get him good and stuck. I slid back to him and worked on releasing his tank straps.

A wail from down toward the chamber we'd just left got me working even faster and I got one free and he could almost get it off—

Beksinski jerked and shifted, and the lantern on his chest shattered against the chasm wall and went out.

I reeled back, sliding away from his side.

In the flickering light of my chest lamp, I could see the back of Beksinski's head jerking back and forth—then a few of those cloudy black eyes just by his face. It had its sucker things down his neck and in his belly.

I dropped the empty shotgun that was still in my right hand, took out my Schofield, and squeezed my gun arm around and over my body in the tight chasm to shoot. This time, the monster knew what was coming and lowered itself some to avoid the shot—but mercy was once again my goal, not damage to *it.*

I shot the back of Beksinski's head—twice to be sure, and it came apart enough that I was. I hated doing it, but it needed doing.

The creature didn't seem to care—as long as its meal was still warm maybe, I suppose—and pulled his big body back down the chasm into the dark.

19

I worked my own body around so my Schofield arm was pointing down toward the chamber area and backed down the chasm, trying to ignore the awful sounds of predation and pleasure coming from the darkness that direction. I couldn't figure how much of that inhuman moaning was from the eating, or maybe something even more obscene—sickening, either way.

The water at the bottom of the chasm got deeper as I retreated, chilling my body and my spirit. It was waist deep in no time, and I reached the flooded mine ready for an ambush....

But there was only mucky water, darkness, and rusting half-sunk mine equipment.

I held my pistol toward the crooked chasm mouth and pumped my kerosene handle. I switched hands and held it in my left as I sprayed the whole chasm entrance with kerosene, then slung the long nozzle and lit a match.

I hesitated, the events having unfolded so fast it was just now sinking in I was really alone. Then I heard those moans in the dark chasm over the sizzling of the match. I threw it into the chasm mouth and everything above the waterline burst into flames. Having no idea how long the flames would last on rock, I started rushing through the high water holding my pistol ready.

The water was only knee high when I heard the wailing behind me. I could see the gray light of the tunnel entrance and kept going, but I could hear swirling and splashes coming up fast—faster than *I'd* been, which was bad for me.

I was ankle deep when Shiv's glass-in-glass charges started going off, starting all the way back at the angled chasm entrance but catching up fast. After each explosion, I could hear a slamming sound and the tunnel shook.

You better believe old "Absalom Tate" ran, and with a quickness.

I chanced a look back as I made it out of the tunnel—and past the first charge Shiv had placed—and caught a grisly but satisfying sight.

The abomination that had made gruesome meals of Morris and Beksinski was close behind me, but not close enough. Shiv's charges, like almost everything she'd carried since I'd run across her in town this time, defied all natural laws I'd taken as true.

Behind the monster that was chasing me the charges flashed, then the tunnel walls, mine support materials, and rusting equipment were pulled toward the site of each explosion.

The charges were closing the mine tunnel into itself.

And just my luck, that fucking unholy mess of a thing was still in it, and I wasn't. The last charges flashed as I backed away further. The tunnel flashed one last time, and closed around that loathsome creature. Some of its putrid fluids spurted out the tiny hole left as the tunnel closing crushed it—but were sucked back in and the tunnel mouth rolled into itself like the solid rock was dough being kneaded. Then it stopped, and looked truly solid again.

I just stared at the sealed tunnel entrance and shook for a long time, rain pouring down now and soaking the upper half of me that hadn't already been.

If it weren't for the tracks and decayed mine carts and other equipment around, you would never think there'd been a mine there....

Heavy *slurch*-ing and flapping sounds, then wails and chittering from above drew my attention—

The biggest of the Benton Gang monsters had made it out somehow—stupid as it sounds, it hadn't dawned on me until that minute that the caves to the left and right of that mother boil chamber could've had some open way out somewhere—and was perched unsteadily atop the two splayed crags the tunnel entrance had been at the base of.

Unsure if it had seen me, I backed away at an angle from the sealed entrance, hoping to reach the tree line to that side before—

One of its sets of eyes fixed on me and the whole creature shifted. It was still real damaged, but seemed to have reconstituted in patches somehow. Nothing really surprised me now, and for a moment I felt weary enough to accept that I was going to die by viscera suction.

It began climbing down and that feeling changed.

I fired three shots as it came down for me. It winced and shook, but didn't stop.

As I backed away down the muddy road toward the bend our horses were hopefully still hitched near, I watched all that see-through nastiness in the creature's fused bodies pump and quiver. Its descent exaggerated the foul wrongness of the unnatural thing's makeshift physical build. Organs that had had one purpose in the separate Benton Gang boys' bodies looked to all just have a singular purpose now, working in concert toward vile aims.

From above I heard what struck me as a familiar whistle.

The rain pattered on my face, forcing me to blink and squint as I looked up. As my eyes closed and opened again, I saw a far more human form rise up on top of the crags where I'd first seen the creature perched.

And strike me down if it wasn't Shiv O'Shea herself....

Drenched in blood, clothes torn, satchel hanging by threads, and hat missing, but that was her. She stared down like an eagle at the climbing monster that was coming for me, and produced a weapon in each hand. They weren't guns, but what looked to be her Bowie knife and that odd Indian spiked-ball cudgel she always had hidden somewhere.

Her eyes followed her prey and she crouched. Just before the monster reached the ground at the base of the crags, she rose up again and dropped.

Shiv plummeted down onto the creature, attacking without hesitation.

Her big knife plunged into the thing's back in the same spot over and over, then she brought the cudgel down at the same spot a few times too.

As the asymmetrical thing writhed and screamed in a ghastly manner, it twisted its bulk around with swollen, deformed limbs—that didn't look at all like they'd been parts of the Benton Gang men's bodies to begin with like some parts did.

21

One of its warped limbs struck me bluntly and threw me away and onto my back.

I lifted myself up with my left arm and aimed my Schofield at the monster—

"Save your shots!" Shiv yelled.

She hacked at the spot she'd been focused on a few more times with her knife, then threw the cudgel away and used that hand to dig in her satchel. Shiv took out a last glass-in-glass charge and sunk her knife into the thing's back for stability.

Ignoring the creature's bucking and deadly swipes, Shiv plunged the charge into the channel she'd cut, pulled her arm back out of its sucking insides, then threw herself back off its back and slapped to the muddy ground on her back and ass.

I just watched it claw at itself, stunned and oblivious.

"*Now* you shoot!"

Just as the thing turned back toward me, I aimed and fired my last pistol round at the charge in its bulk—

It exploded, bursting the beast outward, only to suck straight back in an instant later with even more force. The last monster vanished as its mother boil had—into thin air.

I let myself flop back down into the mud. I'd been through many awful situations, but never one so horrible or exhausting.

Shiv hauled herself to her feet and limped over to retrieve her cudgel, then made her way to me.

She looked down and said, "You always were good in a fight."

"Not good enough, though, I reckon...three men dead and all."

"In my defense, I told you all not to come."

"True."

She sheathed her knife but held the cudgel in a way that wasn't quite fully relaxed.

"What happened here today?" she said, and I couldn't read the look in her eyes—but I didn't like it.

"I don't know you very well, do I, Shiv?"

"You do...and you don't."

I blinked a few times, thinking, then said, "Rabid bears.... Couldn't stop 'em. Others got bit and we had to burn 'em."

She studied my face and smiled—I liked that a lot more.

"You're a good man, 'Absalom Tate.' Maybe I'll come back this way some time and try a few of your bound-to-be-famous apples. I'm sure they'll be world class."

"Damn right."

Shiv chuckled and walked away toward the horses around the bend. I craned my neck to watch her go, then relaxed and looked up at the pouring black sky.

"You are damn right...."

After a while, I rolled over and got to my feet. I limped around the bend, exhausted but watchful.

Lou stood where he'd been hitched, alone and restless. Shiv had taken the other horses.

I sidled up to Lou and stroked his mane, getting a confused but more relaxed neigh and whinny in reply.

"Yeah, I couldn't say, Lou. She's always been a wanderer."

PATRICK LOVELAND

The Ballad of Chihuahua Puente

Undisclosed Location, US Occupied Vietnam—1967

Colonel Northrop set a closed file on his immaculate desk in front of Doctor Spencer Boyd, an army psychiatrist.

"He's being held away from the other patients at Twelfth Evac in Cu Chi Base Camp."

Boyd shifted in his seat and frowned a bit without intending to.

"Why the hospital and not the stockade?"

"I'll get to that."

"I...I still don't understand why you need me, sir," Boyd said.

"It's not as cut and dry as I'd like it to be, Major."

Northrop was humorless on a good day, but on this day, Boyd noticed he had somehow become even more serious.

Boyd said, "Sounds pretty clear. Combat stress, sir."

"You haven't understood me. If this is just combat stress, then we're gonna have even more problems than VC and NVA soon. No, it's something else."

"Sir, I don't understand."

"I told you what we _suspect._ I didn't tell you how little we actually know. _Please,_" the colonel said, and nodded toward the closed file.

Boyd opened the file folder and scanned the text walls and photographs of wounds and weapons he had no context for. Nothing jumped out at him, but he kept scanning and tried to look gravely impressed.

The colonel said, "This soldier stumbles out of the jungle ten feet from a patrol—luckily it was one of ours. Lucky for him, anyway. He might've gotten what he deserved if it'd been VC. So, he comes out of the jungle in the rain—"

"It's a wonder he wasn't shot, sir."

"He was. Just tagged his shoulder, though. So, he comes out of the jungle with no gear and with an empty, locked-open forty-five in one hand and a Ka-Bar ready in the other."

"'Kay bar'?"

"Jesus, Boyd.... Weren't you in Korea? Big fuckin' combat knife. Not standard for us.

"Anyway, his uniform was all torn up and hanging and he's half drenched in blood. One of the boys said it looked like he'd had more on him but the rain washed *half* off. Probably exaggerating some...but still. And only *some* of it was his."

"And his was from being shot?"

"No.... From this," the colonel said and flipped the file a few pages to a paper-clipped photograph of a dark, shiny, somewhat curved object and continued, "It was halfway in his gut. That and his grazed shoulder have kept him in the Twelfth with one guard posted at all times and two whenever possible."

Boyd couldn't make out what the strange object was and looked it, so the colonel said, "Best assessment is it's either some kind of root or branch that got eroded all smooth like that and he fell on it, or some kind of gook villager weapon from the Stone Age or something.

"I'd have it here to show you but...apparently, it came apart just after this picture was snapped, almost like it reacted to the flash. Disintegrated, which made the weird old root story make sense to some."

"Some, sir?"

The colonel looked uncomfortable now and said, "There was a thorough debriefing of this sapper, Puente...and no shortage of discussion after."

"By Intelligence?"

The colonel studied Boyd's face but said nothing.

"Then now I really don't understand why I'm here," Boyd said, careful not to sound too questioning while questioning.

"This soldier went out into the jungle with eight others on as close to a standard mission as tunnel-rat crews get, and comes back alone, covered in blood, and with a whopper of a story. I'm just glad his squad was a bit short or we might've lost a few more boys.

"'Intelligence' has their own interests and feel as satisfied as they can about whatever it is they asked him...and they can believe whatever it is they want to..." the colonel drifted off for a moment then continued, "...I believe this man is insane and killed his fellow soldiers."

Boyd nodded acknowledgement of finally getting his answer.

"No, you don't get me yet. This man had no prior issues. Model soldier. No family history from what they could find. This normal young man quite possibly killed eight other soldiers for absolutely no reason we could get out of him."

"Could it have been a VC or NVA patrol?"

"Too far south for NVA and if it was a VC massacre, why the story? Why was he so messed up...and why the blood?

"We sent a platoon to the coordinates where his mission started and then had 'em check a pretty big area around there. Nothing.

"Only, they couldn't check the one place they probably would have found his coffin nails—the tunnels. His team's explosives did their job, for better or worse."

Boyd noticed the colonel's hand closing into a fist on his desk and trembling a bit, so in a much more deferential tone said, "And you want—"

"I want you to get this motherfucker to admit what he did and I want it *on tape.*"

Boyd watched UH-1 Huey helicopters land and take off from afar as his jeep was driven by an MP up Highway 1 toward Cu Chi Base Camp. Those "choppers"—as they were commonly referred to by the troops since Korea— turned his stomach, a constant reminder of where he was.

Boyd was a career military and psychiatry professional, but this place was not Normandy, or Midway, or the Elbe River. Boyd saw no hope for glory here and definitely not a decisive, "clean" victory. He hoped for one, as they all did, every victory against communism a bolstering of democracy. He just couldn't see how they would do it fighting an enemy disguised as the people they were supposedly liberating and protecting. He just had this sick feeling it would end up unfinished like Korea...or worse.

The colonel was his only concern for the moment, though, he knew. He was an honorable man but he was also determined and could badly damage Boyd's career with very little effort.

The MP stopped the jeep a touch roughly and Boyd looked at him sideways. The MP stared straight ahead.

"*Thank* you," Boyd said as he stepped out of the vehicle with a heavy satchel in his hands.

The MP gave a curt nod and said, "*Sir.*"

Boyd turned back toward the MP and said, "What's the problem, soldier?"

The MP kept looking forward and said, "Sir?"

Boyd decided to let him off the hook in the interest of time—he didn't want to be here any longer than necessary.

"Carry on."

The MP looked down at an M1911 pistol on Boyd's left hip.

"You up for using that sidearm, sir? This ain't the officer's club."

"You'd be surprised how many times I have, *Private.*"

The MP started to look up at Boyd's glaring eyes but thought better of it and locked his gaze forward again.

"*Carry...on.*"

"Yes, sir."

The MP drove off through the mud in the jeep, its tires splashing through small puddles and spraying up here and there.

Boyd walked with his satchel into the base, its weight due to an all-metal tape recorder the Northrop asked him to record Puente's "confession" with. Boyd was still unsure what he could get out of the young soldier that Army Intelligence or CIA spooks or whoever had grilled him hadn't.

He checked in at 12th Evac, then passed nurses' hooches and operating-room Quonset huts until he reached the one Puente was being held in.

A crack and boom sounded and the ground shook, sending Boyd stumbling to a crouch near the hut entrance and almost into the legs of a nurse who was leaning against an outer-hut wall sucking down a cigarette like it was the only thing keeping her alive. He stood and sheepishly regarded her with a nod.

She chortled mirthlessly and said, "Howitzers. Brilliant, placing them across the road from a hospital, right? Hey, at least I get to watch the bugs bounce on my bunk's critter nets after they wake me up at night."

Boyd ignored her nervous griping and lack of respect and entered the Quonset hut.

The screaming, moaning, and back-and-forth of surgical-team communication were nothing new to Boyd, but it never got much easier to be confronted with them. He advanced down the hut, hugging the downward-curving right wall all the way down. As he reached the end, he saw that they had cordoned off the back-left corner of the long hut and created a makeshift cell with chain-link fence, complete with a locked fence gate and razor-wire hoops at the top that were bunched up against the curving ceiling at their lowest sections.

Two stern-looking MPs—one white with ginger hair, the other black with two inches of groomed afro peeking out from under his MP emblazoned helmet—saluted as he presented papers from his satchel's front pocket. They glanced at the papers, still saluting, so he returned it and they stood at attention.

"He's asleep, sir," the ginger said.

"I'm not asleep, just bored and in pain," a voice croaked from within the darkened corner. "Goddamn I wish they'd quit firin' those fuckin' guns...," he said and moaned.

The MPs parted as Boyd stepped forward and he got a look at Specialist Angel Puente, who was curled up on a cot with a blanket loosely resting on his lower body. He seemed to be clutching his swollen abdomen, but after what the

29

colonel told Boyd about what they took out of there, he realized that made sense. He was small with dark hair and black eyes that flashed in the dim light as they picked up a dangling lamp over one of the surgery bays behind Boyd.

Boyd said, "I'm here to ask you some questions, Puente."

"Man, that's a switch," Puente said.

"I think you mean *sir.*"

"Hey, I'm either gonna get strung up, hanged, or shot...so either take that hog leg out and shoot me now or relax. You wanna talk...or be polite?"

Boyd was tempted to end the conversation just as Puente suggested—bullet in head—but he thought better of it.

"Let's talk, Specialist."

"Sure, why not? Oh, we need cigarettes, though."

"I don't smoke."

"That's a tragedy. No smokes, no talk."

Boyd said, "I thought you were bored."

Puente chuckled and said, "More comfortable than bored, actually, now that I think about it."

The ginger said, "I have cigarettes, sir."

Puente said, "What brand?"

"Pall Mall."

"That works. Oh, and we have to go outside."

"Outside? Or you won't talk?" Boyd said.

Puente raised his eyebrows and nodded.

Boyd walked about twenty feet from the door of the Quonset hut and set two folding chairs down several feet apart in the mud. He sat down and took the recorder out of his satchel and set it up on his lap.

Puente shuffled toward one of the chairs, smacking the sealed pack of cigarettes against his palm repeatedly. Puente put the pack between his teeth, took ear plugs out of each ear at once, and flicked them into the mud. He sat and took the pack out of his mouth then opened it.

Puente looked around and waved his hands in mock desperation until Boyd realized he needed a light. Boyd looked at the ginger MP who returned the look for a moment before catching on. He took a Zippo lighter from a pocket and threw it to Boyd, who lit Puente's cigarette and pocketed the lighter.

Puente took a long drag and moaned as he exhaled slowly.

"So good, man."

Boyd cleared his throat and waited for Puente to take a few more drags before asking him anything.

Puente said, "What do you need?"

"On April Ninth—"

"Naw, fuck that. What do you want to know? I've gone through the record-keeping shit. What do *you* want to know?"

"You aren't in control here, Specialist."

"I don't want to be. Just get it going," Puente said and winced a bit before massaging his distended gut.

"You went into the jungle with your squad to recon a tunnel of unknown size and clear or destroy as needed."

Puente snorted and said, "Yep."

"You came back injured, alone, and covered in blood."

Puente's hand shook as he took another drag and his playful defiance washed away for a moment. He seemed to look through Boyd.

"I'm never going underground again.... Not even on the day I die. My mom'll cry but I'm gettin' burnt to ashes, man. Anything to stay up top."

"Puente, what happened?"

"My story ain't gonna change, 'cause it's true. I don't give two shits who believes it. I know I'm screwed anyway."

Boyd put on a smile and said, "I barely skimmed the reports. I'm here on orders. I just need you to tell me your story and that should be the last time you have to, I'd say."

Puente hit his cigarette one last time and flicked it into the mud. He grabbed another from the pack with his teeth and leaned toward Boyd. Boyd lit it and they both leaned back in their chairs.

Puente said, "So we get to the spot they gave us and there's a VC tunnel alright. Sergeant Rabeneck says, 'Get in the hole so we can get back, Chihuahua.'"

"Chihuahua?" Boyd asked.

"Yeah, that's what they call...called me. I'm Puerto Rican but they thought I was Mexican—plus I'm small—so I got Chihuahua all the time and it stuck."

Boyd said, "Go on...."

"Rabeneck says get in the hole, so I get in the hole. I squeeze down in through an opening the dinks hid in the jungle floor. Seabrook hands me down my revolver—"

"Revolver? What about your forty-five?"

"Forty-five? Oh, that thing wasn't mine.... Forty-fives are too loud and bright for underground—at least for me. I heard of 'em collapsing worse-made tunnels too.

"I always went underground with my Model Ten revolver, bayonet, flashlight, and a few speed-loads for the pistol in my thigh pockets."

"Mmhmmmm...," Boyd intoned.

"*Mhmm?* What the fuck is that?"

Boyd cleared his throat and said, "Well, you could do a lot of damage with all that ammo, yes?"

Puente studied Boyd's face as he went for another cigarette from the pack. Boyd reached for the ginger MP's lighter but Puente gestured that he needn't

31

bother. Puente lit it with its burnt-down predecessor, then flicked the butt into a mud puddle and it fizzed out.

Puente said, "You're not very good at this."

"No? I've been told different."

"Maybe you are if you care.... But see, I don't think you want to be here. *I* think that *you* think I'm crazy already."

Boyd said, "From what I read in the report, at one point you were all down in the tunnels—which is odd in itself—but you and Keebler were the only ones with experience in them. I'm sure there's a lot you could accomplish with inexperienced men in such mazelike, confined—"

Puente flicked his lit cigarette at the tape recorder and Boyd flinched at the showering embers then reached for his holstered pistol. The MPs went for their pistols too but Puente just shook his head and laughed to himself.

"You can fuck off, square," Puente said.

Boyd remembered the colonel and relaxed his grip on his pistol then waved for the MPs to as well. They did but were still staring Puente down.

Boyd said, "Alright, I apologize. I came to you.... And I'll hear you out." He took out the lighter and continued, "Here, have another cigarette...," and tried unsuccessfully to strike it aflame a few times.

Puente mulled it over as he watched Boyd fail repeatedly then leaned forward and said, "You gotta cup it," and he shielded the lighter from wind with one hand while bringing a fresh cigarette to his teeth once again. Boyd succeeded. Puente used the flame and leaned back.

"Yeah, you're here on orders alright. Hey, you think I could get some cold rum or vodka to drink, that being the case? I'd say more morphine but that shit gives me nightmares."

Boyd just looked at him, expressionless.

"Whatever, okay."

"So...," Boyd said.

"So, Seabrook hands me down my revolver...."

Puente took his pistol and turned on his red-filtered "anglehead" flashlight with the other hand. He preferred red light underground. If for no other reason than that it might scare the VC somehow like a mad old demon coming down the tunnels. He set down the light, holstered the revolver, and took out his bayonet.

He picked his light back up, pointed the glowing red beam down the murky three-foot-high tunnel, and made a quick scan for deadly bugs, snakes, or other vermin. He knew that everything underground could kill him and would, given half a chance.

As Puente crawled down the tunnel, he kept close watch for traps and prodded anything suspicious with his bayonet. He heard Keebler coming down after him with a wired phone and compass. Puente preferred taking point and relaying info.

They crawled down the tunnel, Puente calling out positions of air ports and Keebler repeating the info into the wired field phone. Puente liked to think of the wire phone like a real elaborate, powered version of a string and two cups.

The entry tunnel opened up into a small chamber about five feet high and across. As Puente crawled across the floor of the chamber, he noticed the sound change in a spot. He brushed off the floor, revealing an abnormally well-hidden trapdoor.

Puente whispered, "Hey, Cookie. Mark this one special. I'm gonna leave it be for now, 'cause I got a feeling."

Keebler nodded and relayed the compass reading and position over the wire phone.

Puente continued on, leading them through a hammock-rigged barracks and almost tumbling into a punji-stick trap in a tunnel just past the sleeping chamber. After motioning for Keebler to stay at the punji trap, Puente continued up the tunnel, came to its end at another secret jungle-floor entrance, and returned to Keebler. They made their way back to the barracks chamber and Puente led them down a different, downward-sloping tunnel, his bayonet prodding as he constantly looked for traps.

Instead, he found signs of tunnel damage and possible instability. It was strange though, he thought, because it looked like the tunnel had expanded, not collapsed naturally. But there were no signs of explosives that could maybe explain that. He also saw a damaged trapdoor in the tunnel floor a few feet down.

Something glinting down the tunnel past the trapdoor caught Puente's eye and he readied his revolver. He made his way down the tunnel, coming to a concealed hiding spot.

The barrel of a severely cut-down Mosin rifle glinted in the frozen hand of a dead VC. His head was half gone out the back and top.

Keebler said, "What is it, man?"

"Dink topped himself with like a sawed-off Mosin that's like a huge pistol—probably broke his wrist when he fired it, not that he cared right then."

Puente chuckled but more to cover his growing discomfort with this more-spooky-than-usual tunnel than because he was amused. He looked up at the tunnel ceiling, trying to imagine how deep they were, and noticed another trapdoor.

Puente hooked his light on the upper part of his chest holster and took his bayonet back out. He prodded around the edges of the trapdoor and it seemed safe enough but wouldn't budge upward at all. Taking a chance, Puente stabbed up into the trapdoor near its center and there was a meaty thunk. As he slid it down, blood streaked down the blade but it wasn't fresh. He wiped the blood off on his dusty pant leg, sheathed his bayonet, and shouldered the trapdoor upward, rolling another VC out of the way into a conical air raid shelter construction.

The VC body he had stabbed and rolled out of the way was one of three huddled in the shelter, all dead. These looked to be from starvation though.

"That was reckless, man," Keebler said and he seemed to be getting spooked too.

Puente said, "Yeah, this ain't right...," and he crouched back down into the tunnel. "Let's head back and check that one special trapdoor. The one here probably just leads to a well and other stuff like this."

Keebler nodded but didn't seem enthusiastic.

They made their way back to the chamber with the special door and Puente examined it a few ways before knocking on it and getting an echo. Puente started prying it up with his bayonet—and threw himself back against the chamber wall as a large venomous centipede crawled out.

"Shit!" Puente said and laughed as the insect skittered away.

Puente crawled through the trapdoor into another downward sloping tunnel and descended. It curved back up a bit and he came to a larger trapdoor. Keebler followed and sent the readings through the wire.

Puente went to work looking for traps. When he was satisfied it was safe enough, he worked it open and kicked up dust as he crawled into a larger chamber than the rest that was filled with communications equipment, gas masks, maps, and dossiers.

Puente said, "I knew it."

The ceiling was almost six feet high but he remained crouched and crawled to the far side of the chamber and noticed that side's trapdoor was open. Keebler came into the chamber behind him.

Puente aimed his red light down the tunnel and saw what at first looked like a cave-in but after a moment he realized there was also a large, rough opening that was definitely not Viet Cong or Minh construction. More like their tunnel collapsed down into a natural one like a cave or sinkhole. Something about the cave-in mouth troubled Puente but he tried to ignore it. It made him think of the expanded tunnel they had seen earlier.

"Hey, Cook', tell 'em there's a caved-in tunnel...but it's also like it collapsed down into a cave or something—"

Keebler interrupted, "I'm still trying to get to them about this intel stash...."

"Well then, we make a note and go back up. There's something wrong here—"

"Got 'em!" Keebler's eyes jumped back and forth, glinting in the red light as the phone squawked in his ear.

Puente said, "What?"

"They're in a firefight—Lewis and Caffrey are fuckin' dead—the rest are trying to come down!"

"No-no-no...this is bad, man."

"No shit, it's bad!"

"And Rabeneck'll barely fit down here.... Fuck."

Keebler scoffed and said, "Like that's our biggest problem."

"Shut up. Let's get up to 'em."

Keebler headed into the tunnel they'd entered from and crawled up the slope. Puente went to enter and looked back at the other tunnel across the chamber in the dim red light and shuddered, then followed Keebler in.

As the two tunnel rats neared the trapdoor into the five-by-five first chamber, they could hear muffled M14 and M16 fire. Keebler opened the trapdoor and hefted the wire phone up into the chamber and dropped it and the compass on the floor. He hurried to the mouth of the low tunnel they had entered the system from and shined his red light down it, revealing a jumble of sliding, clawing soldiers.

Puente climbed up into the chamber and took his revolver out of its holster and kept it pointed at the chamber ceiling as he crouch-walked to the mouth and stood ready next to Keebler.

The first to reach them was Corporal Ahearn, who was dragging their cylindrical 40-pound "cratering" explosives. They helped him out of the tunnel and he spun to face it and backed up some, rifle at the ready. Seabrook was next and did the same. Unck was pulling Rabeneck through behind himself and Tack was practically pushing him from behind.

Unck reached his arm out as he got closer to the mouth, and Keebler and Puente reached in and helped Unck heave himself and Rabeneck out of the tunnel, causing Tack to tumble into the chamber after them and collapse against Keebler's legs. Ahearn and Seabrook joined Puente by the tunnel and they all aimed down it, waiting for the first VC to drop down.

Instead, they got three US M26 hand grenades thrown down in a strung bundle and missing their safety pins. The spoon levers were flung off by their strikers with a metallic sound.

Puente and Ahearn tackled Unck and Rabeneck, and Seabrook did his best to push Keebler and Tack out of the way as he dived away from the tunnel mouth.

The grenades exploded, shaking and collapsing the tunnel entrance.

Seabrook hauled himself up and checked Keebler, who was fine—then Tack, whose upper arm and back had been hit with shrapnel. In the red light it was hard to spot for a moment, but blood poured and pumped out of the back of his upper arm and he already looked dizzy.

Seabrook said, "Shit. It hit an artery," and tried to apply pressure as the others looked on. Seabrook couldn't keep the blood from coming out and Tack moaned and mumbled nonsense until he died while they watched, unable to do anything. Caffrey was the closest thing they'd had to a medic and he was dead up top on the jungle floor. Seabrook slumped down on his haunches, bloody hands shaking.

There was a muffled boom, then another and Puente realized the directions and distances were consistent with a local triangular formation of secret jungle entrances he'd come across before. He said, "They're sealing the other openings.... Trapping us down here."

Rabeneck spat dust out of his mouth and said, "You don't know that. We can still—"

"No, he's right—trapped for sure," Keebler said.

"Bullshit!"

Unck said, "I think they'd know, sir."

"I'm in command now, so shut up, Private. Chihuahua, Cookie—look for another way out. We made a map with Keebler's readings. I know there are more tunnels."

Puente stared at Rabeneck who returned it and said, "Now, Specialist."

"There's only one other way," Puente lied, and Keebler didn't argue.

Keebler entered the tunnel that led to the dead VC in the ambush spot and conical air raid shelter and Puente followed. They quickly reached the damaged trapdoor they hadn't felt the need to enter on their first visit and Keebler used a bayonet to prod the edges and look for signs of traps. Keebler started sniffling and rubbed his eyes as he worked. After deciding it was safe, Keebler pried the trapdoor up and open. He tried to lower his light into the downward sloping tunnel but his arm jerked and he dropped it.

"Keebler?" Puente said.

Keebler coughed hard and couldn't stop then started vomiting too before collapsing onto the tunnel floor and convulsing.

"Keebler! Shit!"

Puente tucked into a rough fetal position and turned around in the tunnel, then hauled it on hand and knees back to the five-by-five chamber. As he scrambled back up into the chamber, Rabeneck said, "Goddamit, Puente—"

"*Gas!*" Puente exclaimed and crawled to the special trapdoor, dug for it, and flung it open. Puente dived in, rolling into a ball and making it almost halfway down in an instant. But he tumbled awkwardly out of the ball shape and started clawing his way down the slope until he reached the trapdoor for the intel room. He opened it but stopped in its square-ish threshold and turned back.

He said, "Last guy—close it tight behind you!"

From up the tunnel and muffled by other moving bodies now in it, he heard Unck yell, "No shit!"

Soon they were all in the intel room and Seabrook helped Puente move some of the larger communications equipment over against the trapdoor and fill in gaps with maps and dossiers.

Rabeneck said, "I thought you said there weren't any other tunnels, Chihuahua."

"The other one probably led to the surface eventually, if it wasn't completely caved in, next set of bunkers down past the well. This one's caved-in and there's just some cave there."

"Sounds like our best chance then."

Seabrook laughed and Ahearn said, "A cave? What's your plan—we go deeper into this pigfuck?" Unck chuckled too now and Ahearn continued, "Look, there's gasmasks on that rack—six of 'em. Only five of us. I say—"

"I'm the only sergeant here now, Corporal! Are you undermining my authority?" Rabeneck gripped his forty-five in its holster and popped its securing strap.

"No, sir." Ahearn said, but Rabeneck took his pistol out anyway.

Seabrook said, "He backed down, sir."

As Rabeneck went to raise his pistol, they all heard a low, distant chittering sound from the open tunnel opposite the sealed up one.

Puente didn't like the sound at all, and by looks of it, Ahearn, Unck, and Seabrook felt the same way.

But Rabeneck said, "See, there's animals down there.... It must be a cave that opens up near the river."

"Sir—"

"Shut up, Seabrook. Okay, Puente, you're first 'cause you're the tunnel man. Then the rest of you. I'll be in the rear so none of you can run away."

Puente crossed to the tunnel and crawled inside, not eager to cross Rabeneck in his current unstable state. He shuffled down to the strange opening at the base of the VC tunnel cave-in and peered down it with his red light.

The opening didn't look right and it was less a cave at that point and more like another tunnel—only, larger and with very odd and inexplicably shiny surfaces. Almost like it was bored out with a huge tool or eroded to achieve the same effect over a greater length of time. Its angle was steeper than any of the VC tunnels but the irregularity of its formation led to nodules here and there and Puente used them as hand and foot holds as he descended—

Puente's left hand slipped and his body dropped. He caught another hold with his right hand and left foot and held strong, but pebbles and dirt showered the dark tunnel below him.

"*Careful*, shithead! If you fall, we'll be screwed tryin' to get out of this clusterfuck!" Rabeneck called down.

"Yeah, yeah...."

He made it down about thirty more feet before noticing water seeping into the tunnel from slit rings in the tunnel surface. Puente decided they could be from the water table. The water made the descent harder but it became less steep a bit lower so he was able to make it to a large cavern opening. His light didn't penetrate far enough to hit a rock wall of any kind in the distance, leading Puente to realize it was quite large.

The cavern opening was intersected with a few thick, bumpy pillars that had the shiny look of the tunnel and were also hard to pin down as natural or deliberately formed. Water flowed down from the cavern ceiling and seeped down the pillars, causing a constant trickling sound all around.

There was a slimy-looking luminescent moss or fungus on the pillars with even brighter flowering plants on them. He flicked his light off to see how strong the luminescence was and discovered it was bright enough to see by after a moment, if barely.

The click his light had made was louder than he'd hoped. He crouched near a pillar and waited for signs of movement or approach. He didn't see anything, but he heard....

From deep within the cave past the glow of the moss, Puente heard what sounded like singing. It was faint, but sounded deliberate—warped and odd, but deliberate.

Puente stepped farther in and realized there were dozens—maybe hundreds—of the pillars, and they got thicker the higher the ceiling got, which was almost higher than he thought possible. He kept walking into the cavern a good ways, unconcerned with the others now and driven by fascination and a dreamy quality the light from the moss gave off. The song from the depths also pulled at him, and its gradual increase in clarity and eerie beauty soothed him more with every few steps.

The cavern floor seemed to drop away at an angle he could only just make out in the dim moss light, and the water seeping down the pillars all around filled this deep depression like a wide bowl with no visible bottom. Only there, in that huge bowl of cavern floor, were there no pillars.

What Puente saw instead was impossible.

"What was it?" Boyd asked, unsure he believed any shred of this, but curious how the young sapper's defense story would play out, given the grave circumstances he faced in the near future.

Puente stared through the muddy ground outside the Quonset hut near the base of Boyd's chair. He sat there, unresponsive until his seventh cigarette of the session burned down into his fingers and he flinched before flicking it into the mud.

"What was it, Specialist?"

"Not *it*.... Them. There was one huge one, but the rest were all over it and around it down in the water too. The big one was hard to see clearly 'cause it—you know how things look right above something that's real hot?
Like...shimmery? It was like that, only crazier, 'cause the light was distorted by it. The smaller ones were longer and moved around easier, but they had the same look to 'em. Like kinda see-through sacks of glowing balls and slime with long spider legs and—what do you call them? Tentacles? Yeah, those. And

there was nothing, uh, symmetrical about 'em. You could barely look at any of 'em straight 'cause of the way they messed up the light, but the big one was in its own storm of messed up.

"And all of these things were making these sounds.... I'd thought it was singing, but I think it was maybe them talking to each other. Like maybe dolphins or insects or—shit, I don't know. Might have just been the sounds of 'em movin' around all weird like that."

Boyd couldn't believe Puente was saying all this with a straight face and decided he had almost lost patience for humoring him.

"Okay, Puente, where were the others?"

"I guess turning off my light and being quiet as a habit from being in the tunnels saved me, 'cause what was left of the squad all turned on their lights at the base of the spooky tunnel and started calling for me. Some of the smaller, longer creatures dropped off of the big one and crawled out of the water too and went for them. There were shots from their rifles for a few seconds, then screams and moans...then nothing."

Boyd had returned to analytical mode after being sucked in a bit by the more realistic parts of Puente's story, if he was being honest with himself. He just wanted the whole crazy story on record for the colonel to be enraged by and to be done with this whole thing.

"And the blood all over you?"

"That's where it gets weird," Puente said and Boyd couldn't stifle a chuckle at that but Puente ignored him.

"I snuck back through the cavern but the water that was seeping down the steep tunnel made it slippery and I fell. On the way down I grabbed for holds and I must have grabbed like a hatch button, 'cause the tunnel opened up below me and I went down a kind of slide thing. I was gonna climb back up but there was this kind of pumping and vibration down the tunnel and my attention got swept away again with it, I think 'cause there was more of that moss. The moss ended a ways down and it got real dark and I fell off a short ledge 'cause it was vibrating so hard—and I saw why. These glowing machines...."

Boyd fought the urge to shake his head and laugh in Puente's face.

"Anyway, I fell into a pool of glowing red liquid and it sucked me through into a river—only I don't think that river was *here* because when I surfaced, there were too many moons. Then I turned in the thick liquid as I trod the surface and saw a mountain that shouldn't be there—it *isn't* there, *here*. It had lights and symbols glowing in its surfaces and above its rocky edges, and there were more of the creatures on a surface near the peak, doing somethin' I couldn't see. Then it was like the sky cut open in a circle above them and...and...."

"And what?"

Puente took another cigarette out and Boyd lit it for him, feeling almost sorry for him after this display of complete, utter delusion.

39

"I swam back down and eventually found the tube or whatever I was pulled through. Out of sheer cojones I clawed back up through and into the machine room then back up to the cavern opening and tunnel mouth. I lost my revolver and bayonet in the liquid bridge thing, so I took Rabeneck's forty-five off what was left of the middle of him and Seabrook's Ka-Bar from the floor near some of the shredded parts of him."

"Why was the pistol empty when they found you?"

Puente took a drag and let it out.

"One of the smaller creatures came for me while I was setting the forty-pound charges in the tunnel to the intel room and up in the five-foot room.

"I'd grabbed one of those gas masks and gone to work after my head had cleared from being away from the moss and machines and monsters.

"So, it came for me and I stabbed it a few times and emptied the pistol into it. Instead of blood, glowing muck with its own tentacles and weird marbles spewed and squirted out of it and stuck on the walls, floor, and ceiling of the five-foot chamber. Then it stuck me with one of its spider legs and the end broke off in me. Fucker. It died, though, even if its splatter stuff didn't. I finished up, ran the slash wire all the way through to the well, climbed up it, out, then blew the tunnel with the wired phone as a trigger. I must've kept the pistol in a pocket or something, 'cause I don't know why I was carryin' it. That last part when they found me is real hazy...."

Boyd couldn't contain his incredulity any longer and laughed, his head shaking back and forth. For someone so earnest and clearheaded, Puente was somehow powerfully delusional or believed memories based on some form of hallucination. In other circumstances, Boyd would have kept his composure, but the sheer intensity of Puente's conviction was too humorous for him.

Puente didn't get angry, though. He just took another drag off his cigarette and as he exhaled said, "Yeah, laugh it up, Doc. It's the honest truth. You should be thanking me for trapping those shit sacks down there."

Boyd said, "Oh, by all means, *thank you.*"

"So, we done? I need more meds for my gut."

"If you are incapable of telling me what actually occurred in the tunnels, whether unable or unwilling...."

Puente just shook his head and mouthed a silent "fuck you" to Boyd.

"Then, yes. We're done."

"Sweet Lord, thank you," Puente said then stood up from his chair and shuffled toward the Quonset hut door as Boyd recorded some notes.

The ginger MP said, "Gimme back what's left of my smokes, Puente."

Puente went to hand him the pack but dropped it as he doubled over and clutched his swollen gut, moaning long and low.

"Mnnnhnn—gimme a nurse, asshole."

The two MPs each hooked one of his arms over one of their shoulders and hurried him into the hut calling for a nurse. Boyd surprised himself by hoping Puente felt better. Before he could feel too bad, though, he heard a scream from inside the Quonset hut. Boyd stood and set the tape recorder down on the seat Puente had been using.

Boyd crossed to the Quonset hut door in time to see Specialist Puente come apart.

His head, upper chest, and left arm went with the ginger and his right arm went with the black MP as Puente's entire chest and abdomen bulged and burst open spherically all around the surgery area. Screams from nurses, surgeons, and patients alike sounded all over the hut as small translucent sacks of glowing spheres covered with long insectoid legs and wriggling tentacles sprang to life and attacked, each one undulating and clawing toward the closest thing to them.

The small monsters made dissonant, atonal sounds as they moved that layered together paradoxically into something almost like a strained, haunting opera vocal.

Boyd could barely make out what they were doing because they were indeed very hard to see clearly, light distorting around them as they contorted and whipped and flailed at their confused and helpless victims. In only a few seconds, some people were in pieces, alive or otherwise. The MPs didn't have time to defend themselves and were taken down still holding parts of Puente.

Boyd backed away from the door fumbling for his pistol. He got it out as the first creatures were clawing and pulling themselves out of the hut. He fired two shots at one and missed then focused on the closest one to him and hit it twice in four shots, but instead of dying it just slowed down some and sprayed glowing muck into the mud.

Boyd backed into one of the folding chairs and fell over it. He crawled backwards through the mud, not sure if he should use his last bullet on one of the creatures or himself.

That soul-piercing song the creatures made together was all he could hear or think about, and he dropped the pistol, then closed his eyes and covered his ears.

A crack and boom sounded and the ground shook, the oblivious Howitzer operators firing it into the distance.

The creatures stopped in place, shuddering and pulsing. Boyd watched as every one of the fearsome, impossible creatures pierced the muddy ground with their sharp appendages and forced themselves down into it and out of sight.

Boyd collapsed back into the mud with a slap, breathing harder than he had in years. He just hoped that they were going back deep down and not hiding under the surface, ready to rise again and commit slaughter.

A squeaking mechanical sound caught his attention and he turned his head against the ground and raised it a bit to look back toward the hut.

Even half sunk into the mud, the metal tape recorder was still going, its microphone exposed and its tape full of Specialist Angel Puente's story, the last moments of his life, and the awful, almost beautiful songs of the creatures he had unwillingly birthed in the process.

41

Boyd said, "There's your fucking tape, Colonel...," and let his head slap back down into the muck.

7

Pizzapokalyps

New Alps, California—1989

A heavy-metal track by a band called Venom growled and thundered out of Ramsey Salazar's car stereo as he sped down South Grade Road in a 1971 Plymouth GTX, a six-rack insulated pizza bag secured on his passenger seat with a three-point safety belt. The stereo and seatbelts were the cherry quality Plymouth's only aftermarket additions, unless you counted a special rig Ramsey hooked up on its roof when making deliveries—a translucent panel with his place of employment's logo on it lit from inside with a slowly pulsing strobe, built onto a repurposed bike rack.

Ramsey slowed his slick Plymouth, lovingly nicknamed "Emily"—after the blind lady in *The Beyond*—and turned right onto Derand Drive.

This part of New Alps had always bothered Ramsey. It was generic. Square. Just your basic two-story houses that could be in any suburban sprawl—only they were here in New Alps, a small town in the mountains east of San Diego. Seemed out of place.

Ramsey eased Emily to a stop and unzipped the pizza bag. Two large barbeque-chicken pizzas. He wasn't a fan of that kind, himself. But part of what made his workplace so popular was the creator and owner's tactic of "borrowing" any new or different pizza style he heard about being done in other places.

He got out, carried the boxes to the porch, and rang the doorbell. An elderly woman in a robe and slippers answered the door. She looked down at the pizza box and cringed.

The black food boxes were two-color printed with scenes suggesting—but not exactly showing—mutilation and torture.

"Why do you have to put that nasty, evil *junk* all over your boxes, Ramsey?"

He recognized her now. She'd been his homeroom teacher in the ninth grade.

"It's a heavy metal–themed pizza place, Mrs. Slattery. It's kind of our thing. Some boxes are horror, some are like fantasy, some are more like Viking stuff...."

"Well it's ghastly. If your food wasn't so darn good, I'd stop ordering from you." She shook her head and reached out for the boxes. She started to close the door then noticed Ramsey was still standing there.

"Yes?"

Ramsey raised his eyebrows.

"Oh, a tip? How about taking that gory filth off your boxes. Goodnight, Ramsey Salazar...."

Ramsey drove back into what served New Alps as a downtown area. It was mostly short strip malls and restaurants along New Alps Boulevard—which itself ran in a curvy rough parallel to Interstate 8.

Ramsey usually loved his job. Free pizza. Got to wear his black boots and jeans and DIY homemade Obituary and Sepultura shirts and the like.

But something about running into Mrs. Slattery had soured his mood.

Pizzapokalyps was the "happening spot" in New Alps, as his parents might've said if they'd still been above ground to see it.

Emily was all Ramsey had to remember his mom and dad by. Then before his grandparents had also passed, they told him to sell the car many times. Emily the Plymouth was a "rolling college fund" in their view but he'd never committed to the idea of more schooling after high school anyway.

Ramsey pulled into a lot Pizzapokalyps shared with a few other businesses. Most of the closer spots were all taken. Good for business, especially on a Tuesday night. The owner—Hank "Reaperman" Scott—would be in a good mood.

Ramsey got out and carried the pizza box as he approached the front doors.

A big neon sign glowed red above the door on the edge of the roof: PIZZAPOKALYPS—the neon outlining the letters in that sharp and hooked metal-band logo style, like Sepultura had used for *Morbid Visions* and *Schizophrenia,* before switching to the newer, cleaner logo for *Beneath the Remains.* It also kind of reminded Ramsey of all the neon trim in the wedding-room scene in *Big Trouble in Little China.*

45

"Piece by Piece" off of Slayer's *Reign in Blood* album could be heard playing inside as he walked between rows of short tables out front. Tables full of joking, drinking, eating people. Hank would be on a good one for sure.

Ramsey opened the double doors and walked through the lively, dimly lit dining area. He caught Angela following him with her eyes from behind the bar as she finished pulling a pint of Coors for a leering customer. She smiled, so he nodded and returned it before going into the kitchen.

Trevor was making the pizzas in the back. He took a personal-sized pie out of an oven and set it on a counter. He checked the other ovens and looked over at Ramsey.

Trevor smiled. "Duuude...."

"I just fucking left less than an hour ago. Where's Hank?"

"He took off early again."

"Jesus...."

"Right? *And* he forgot to order more pizza sauce last week too! Luckily we had some in the storage room." Trevor chuckled but saw Ramsey wasn't laughing. "What's up, man? Tabitha?"

"Nah."

"Hey, she'll get bored of Scott too, eventually. And Slaughterotika was *your* band, man. You guys made all those Gwar-style costumes and shit together. Fucked up, bro."

"You're kinda making it worse right now, man. I'm fine, okay?"

"If you say so. But hey—think about what I was saying before. Abominomicon. Let's do it. Your crushing chords and *throat*. My filthy down-tuned bass. Just wretched, *vile* lyrics. Even crazier foam costumes than Slaughterotika. Come on, man."

"Sure, man. Let's jam some more."

"Fuck yeah. Hey, I was thinking, also. You want to watch *Aliens* again later? I been thinking about it and even though it's not the same kind of scary as *Alien*, it's still pretty rad."

"Totally. Best movie ever made. That, the first one, and *The Thing*. Those movies kick the shit out of all that Star Wars junk, man."

Trevor cringed. "Hey, that's harsh. They're just different."

"I guess so. Anyway, my *Aliens* tape is almost worn out, though. Have to keep messing with the tracking now, I watched it so much."

Trevor chuckled and shook his head, then sobered a moment.

"Oh, wait. Some orders came in right after Hank took off. Twenty-eight-ninety-eight Green View Road and twenty-four-oh-six Derand."

Ramsey grabbed a smaller insulated pizza bag.

"Derand? I was just there."

"*And so shall you be again.* Hey, you want a piece of this?" Trevor said, lifting a drippy slice of his extra-saucy, extra-cheesy personal pizza to his eager mouth.

"Nah, feel more like a burger or rolled tacos."

46

Trevor took a big bite and breathed in and out until he could chew. Mouth full and smacking, he said, "Traitor...."

King Diamond, Motörhead, and Megadeth came up on Ramsey's mixtape as he drove to the Green View Road stop. Polite, probably stoned guy. Good tip. Back to Emily and onward.

Just before he got to the Derand turn, Ramsey noticed a large moving or storage truck parked on the side of South Grade.

He turned onto Derand and cruised up it. As he passed Mrs. Slattery's house, he saw some shadows moving, backlit against the curtains.

Emily eased to a stop a few houses up from the Slattery place. He pulled the handbrake and left her running in neutral, the truck and shadows he'd seen giving him a twisting of unease in his stomach.

Ramsey got out and carried the pizzas to the front door. Nice enough woman. Okay tip.

As he walked back to his car, Ramsey thought he heard a weird sound from down the street. Emily's V8 engine was not quiet, and his music inside was blaring too. But this was something else. He kept walking down the street.

Ramsey realized the noises were coming from the Slattery place.

He walked across the driveway then up to the front door he'd so recently been chastised at. He got on his tiptoes to see through a few small windows near the top of the door. Boring décor. Darkness.

Strange thumping sounds seemed to come from the second floor. Ramsey crept back to the driveway and looked up at the second-floor windows.

Crashing and wailing sounds came from a second-floor room and he could see a flurry of movement. More thumping and a high-pitched sound—

Something busted out through the second-floor windows, flopping and twisting as it rolled down the slanted overhang and slapped down on the driveway. Ramsey recoiled from its steaming, writhing form.

Oily fluid dripped and poured off its vaguely human form as it hauled itself up to its malformed feet, large pools of it forming and streaming down the driveway. Its drooling, oozing, pulsing body was yellow and red with chunks of something caught in the continuous gooey avalanches of the thing's body. A swirling cloud of fumes surrounded the creature and when its scent reached Ramsey, he was confused. It wasn't the rotten, vile stench he expected from the sight of the thing. It smelled delicious. Like pizza. Barbeque-chicken pizza.

"Wh-what the *fuck*?"

The monstrous thing whipped its head toward him—it had Mrs. Slattery's face. It *was* Mrs. Slattery. But she was larger, warped, and made up of bubbling, self-regurgitating pizza.

47

The pizza monster took a few slurching, gloopy steps toward Ramsey with three leglike pizza appendages and he backed away toward the street. The high-pitched sound started again and Ramsey looked back up at the busted window.

What he saw peering down from the window looked like a humanoid robot or something. Its head was a matte opaque spheroid with a thick, short antenna springing up from its rear and angled forward some over the ball's back half. Struts and shocks supported that over its armored body. A container on its back looked like fused-together scuba tanks. Tubes ran from the tanks to a large gun or nozzle that stretched down from where a person's forearm would be.

Ramsey just gawped, frozen in place by these utterly bizarre beings.

The robot/android thing aimed its gun arm down at Mrs. Slattery's pizza-fied form. With the force of a fire hose, thick fluid struck Mrs. Slattery's gooey body. The monstrous pizza woman wailed as the fluid burned and ate away at her limbs and body like a powerful acid.

The pizza monster tried to stumble away down the driveway on what was left of its weird limbs—but another droid appeared from a side yard back near the front door and sprayed it with its own nozzle-arm. The monster wailed even harder, retreating toward Ramsey.

He stumbled back and fell on his ass as the creature rushed toward him.

A third droid appeared from the side yard closer to Ramsey and sprayed. The combined assault ate large chunks out of the thing's form. The creature thrashed whiplike tendrils of thick molten cheese around at the droids, but couldn't reach them.

The first droid stopped spraying and dropped from the window, landing on digitigrade legs. All of the droids' other arms ended in circular saw blades. The other two droids quit spraying too as the first one took a few heavy steps toward the oozing, thrashing pizza monster. Its blade arm extended almost to the ground, then the droid pulled it back and cut the air on its way to the beast as it swung. A bright light crackled out of the spinning blade disc and it went through Mrs. Slattery's form in an instant, flashing and blurring as it cut.

(Ramsey couldn't help but think of the circular blade arm as a pizza wheel, a hand tool they used to slice the pies up at Pizzapokalyps.)

After a moment, the abomination's corroded trunk, head, and warped upper limbs slid off its lower half on a cleanly severed slice along the droid's pizza-wheel strike path. All of it slapped down and Ramsey saw sickly colored fluorescent organs and fluids spilling out of the monster's two halves while its limbs retracted, rigidly quivering against the body sections.

Ramsey ran for Emily, still idling up the street. He reached the car and got inside. The street ahead was a dead end. He shifted into reverse, peeled out, and dropped the handbrake.

The Plymouth reversed hard on smoking, squealing tires. Ramsey looked back at the Slatterys' driveway. Zooming past it, he saw one of the droids aiming a shoulder-mounted gun at Emily and firing.

A brilliant bolt of odd-colored light buzzed just over the hood—the engine sputtered and almost stopped running then roared back to life, sending him barreling in reverse toward the intersection of South Grade Road.

Ramsey skidded backwards onto the road, shifted into first, floored it. The Plymouth hit 70 mph in no time. Something glinted in his rearview mirror.

One of the droids was following him, tracks on its weird cyber legs combined with its pizza-wheel arm rolling it so fast it was keeping pace and aiming a shoulder gun at Emily.

Ramsey grabbed the pizza bag from his passenger seat, rolled down his driver window, and flung it back toward the droid. It slowed to avoid the bag and he floored it again, pushing Emily up into almost triple digits on the speedometer. He was almost back to downtown New Alps in less than three minutes.

Ramsey turned into the Pizzapokalyps lot and parked by the back door. He killed the engine, got out, and rushed into the kitchen.

"You're not gonna believe me, but...."

Trevor wasn't listening. He looked terrible.

The pizzas were burning and Trevor was hanging from an oven handle. His other hand gripped the prep table.

"You okay, man?"

Trevor moaned. He let go of the handle and leaned over the prep table, dripping sweat onto some poorly kneaded dough. Ramsey saw Trevor's personal pizza plate, now empty. Ramsey looked at a large plastic tub they used for pizza making, only about one-third full of sauce. He cringed.

"Trevor."

"Wuh'sssup, bro?"

"You said we ran out of sauce. Where are the containers of the sauce you found?"

Trevor pointed toward the trash and recycling area. Ramsey crossed to it and lifted one of several empty cans. The label around the can exterior was faded beige and generic. Old bar codes, gibberish letter codes, and a date were all it had on it. The only readable thing on it was a date: "BEFORE APR-1997"

He rubbed away some old grime enough to see that it actually read:

CDC--APR-1977 (L.CANAL-P.HUT)--MUTAGEN
RE-EVALUATE OR DESTROY BEFORE APR-1997

"Trev...?"

He half-moaned, "Nhnn-yeah?"

"How long did you say you were using that sauce today?"

"Pretty much the whole shift sso far.... Hnnnnngk—"

Trevor doubled over and grabbed his gut. His sweat was thicker now, like grease, and it poured down his face. He convulsed hard and his body bulged and swelled. Steam vented from slits forming in his skin. Then it sloughed off, revealing self-regenerating cheese and sauce like Mrs. Slattery had. Trevor's

49

pizza form had small rafts of pepperoni sliding down the falls of oozing melting cheese and molten sauce.

Ramsey backed away toward the dining area, so transfixed by Trevor's transformation that he didn't hear the screams and sounds of struggle in the restaurant behind him. He stepped backwards through the doors and spun around slowly in a daze, taking in the carnage inside Pizzapokalyps.

Everyone who had eaten their pizza had changed like Trevor.

They were eating their own families and friends. Those who weren't being devoured by large, jagged crimson-toothed mouths that had flapped open in most of the pizzabominations were being melted by their acid-like melting cheese and sauce.

"R-Ramsey!" a female voice cried out.

Angela was fighting off two creatures that had climbed onto her bar. Her arms were already melted down to the muscle and bone all over as she held back the warped limbs of the creatures with a bottle of bourbon and a corkscrew.

Ramsey just watched as ropes of the monsters' cheese and flowing pesto sauce met her face, head, and chest and ate away at them. Her skull opened and her brain didn't stand a chance. Angela's arms lost all strength. The creatures descended upon her behind the bar. Sounds of crunching and wet chewing replaced her cries.

Inhuman wails from the kitchen snapped Ramsey back into the moment and he backed away toward the entrance.

Pizza Trevor howled as it slammed its way out of the kitchen. It was larger than the other creatures and its big, undulating mass barely resembled a human now. It was a lopsided ball of goo on several warped pizza limbs and tentacles of bubbling cheese draping down all around from its bulk. Several baseball-sized eyes had opened all over it—irises blue like Trevor's had been, but where the whites would be they were bright dayglow green with licorice-thick red veins pulsing in them.

The monster shambled toward another of its kind, grabbed it with tentacles and warped appendages, and pulled it against itself. The smaller creature struggled but the Trevor thing absorbed the smaller thing's body into its own bulk. The smaller one's mushroom-and-olive-shedding head was melted into the larger mass.

Ramsey bolted for the front doors, busted out through them. He ran between rows of smaller tables with pizza parents and pizza children eating each other. An unturned woman who'd only had a salad tried to fight off her pizza husband.

One creature lashed out at Ramsey as he ran toward the parking lot, its anchovy-oozing tentacle just missing. He looked back toward the pizza parlor as he kept running—

His lower body slammed into the side of a sheriff's car, slapping him onto its hood and knocking the wind out of him. He flopped onto the asphalt.

Two deputies got out of the vehicle.

"You better not have dented my vehicle, Salazar!"

Ramsey tried his best to breathe.

The other one pulled his pistol. "What the *hell*?!"

The first deputy saw the chaos outside Pizzapokalyps and pulled his revolver too. He called some codes into his handheld radio and got a confused response. "Just get the fuck over here! We're at the weirdo pizza place!"

They approached the patio, calling out orders. The pizza creatures noticed the men and rushed them. They fired until their useless pistols were empty. Other pizza things converged on them and took them to the ground.

With a moaning and crashing sound, the big Trevor thing busted its way out of the front of the pizza parlor. It must have consumed all the other pizza creatures in the dining area. It ambled toward the sheriffs on several oddly shaped limbs.

Big T ignored the dying deputies and attacked the lesser pizza things. The monster moaned as it ate. In between disgusting sounds of absorption and perverse pleasure, Ramsey heard that high-pitched whining sound again.

The droids from before were perched up on the roof by the flickering, half-busted Pizzapokalyps neon sign.

The droids on the left and right broke away in unison, dropping off the roof and taking up positions out of sight as the one still up by the neon signs started spraying its powerful stream down onto the monster. The monster wailed and spun around, having trouble finding the spray source. It spotted the droid on the roof and took a few steps toward the building.

The other droids appeared from the sides of the building and combined their powerful hosing with the first droid's.

The powerful spray ate away at the creature's bulk as it had before—but this creature's form regenerated as fast as they could subtract from it. The monster ignored the spray and got closer. Warped, spasming tentacles spilled from its bulk. The slippery tendrils uncoiled and the creature flung them at the droid on the roof. It pulled the futuristic machine down and lashed at it with its many tentacles, taking it apart like it was a cheap robot toy.

The other droids on its flanks stopped their useless spraying and extended their pizza wheel–arm blade weapons. They ran at the looming beast, their slicer arms spinning up—

They bolted past each other on either side of the monster, their weapons flashing as they leapt. They landed almost exactly where the other had just been at the start of their attack.

Large wounds opened on the creature's sides, dayglow organs and muck spilling out onto the asphalt. The abomination hunched down and howled...before sucking its innards back in and sealing up the big cuts.

The thing whipped its longer drippy pizza tentacles out at the two remaining droids. It caught them both, then reeled them in towards its pulsing body. It latched more sizzling tentacles and malformed appendages around

51

their struggling bodies, then wrenched them away, cutting through them with ease. It flung their parts all over the patio and parking areas.

Ramsey had caught his breath but couldn't move. All he could do was watch as the fifteen-foot pizza monstrosity slowly turned, scanning the area with its many glowing eyes.

Something struck Ramsey below his ear where his jaw met his neck with a wet piercing, then he felt an itchy tingling in that spot and an overall rush of clarity and focused calm.

–Hey, hesher kid!–

Ramsey looked around. One of the droids' upper halves that had skidded across the pavement away from Big T was pointing a half-mangled shoulder gun at him and angling its opaque dome helmet/head toward him.

"Wh-what?"

A female voice said, –You were in shock. I injected you with some combat stims and a nano-comms unit.–

"N-Nana what? This is unreal...."

–I get that this isn't your normal tractor pull or rodeo night in these parts, but I need you to focus, alright?–

"Hey, fuck you!"

–Calm down, hesher.–

"What do you want, robot asshole?"

–Actually, I'm a human female asshole, and I commanded those "robots" you just watched getting wrecked. I need you to—–

"How? There were three of them?"

–VR interface, preprogrammed macros, constrained AI assist.... But that doesn't matter—this outbreak is way more dangerous than we'd anticipated. I need you to—–

"What? Like a video game or something? And who is 'we'? Come on...."

–How about you focus? Your town will be firebombed in about twenty minutes if we don't get this handled, understand? They'll call it another freak wildfire and no one will think twice.–

Ramsey could tell she meant it. "Okay, what *can* we do?"

–I'm in a truck back near where you delivered one of those infected pizzas. When I'm jacked into the droids, I don't move, so I'm still a ways away. I can get some heavier weaponry there, but I need you to buy me some time, got me?–

"Yeah, I get you."

Big T rotated its hellish pizza-fied form toward Ramsey and he hauled himself to his feet, strangely calm and ready.

–Grab the shoulder unit that's pointing at you.–

Ramsey crossed to the sparking, twitching droid's upper body and took hold of its shoulder weapon. With a beep, it detached and Ramsey cradled it.

Two sheriff trucks lit up the parking lot red and blue and set off warning sirens as they rolled up. The deputies got out and brandished shotguns and rifles. After a long moment of disbelief, they started firing their weapons at the creature that loomed before them.

The monster didn't appreciate their annoying bullets and pellets and stormed toward them on its weird pseudo-legs.

Ramsey bolted toward Pizzapokalyps, ran in, and rushed through the kitchen on his way to the back. He hopped into Emily and dropped the droid shoulder gun on the passenger seat. He rolled down his window and tweaked a cheap dial he'd installed on the Pizzapokalyps logo delivery lightbox, causing it to flash at a seizure-inducing interval. His mixtape started belting out Celtic Frost's "Circle of the Tyrants" and he readied himself.

"I'll buy you some time...but you better get here real fuckin' quick!"

–Already on it, hesher—just make sure you go *west* down...New Alps Boulevard, it's called on the map.–

"West on New Alps, got it."

Ramsey put the Plymouth in gear and peeled out, curving around from the back of Pizzapokalyps then slowing to catch Big T's attention. He caught a glimpse of it devouring the last deputy, who was screaming and still firing his shotgun. He rolled his windows all the way down and turned up his stereo even louder.

"Hey, Pizza the Hutt—come get it while it's hot, motherfucker!"

The feeding beast turned its pulsing dayglow eyes toward Emily and Ramsey, let out a heinous belch that ejected a deputy's bloody booted foot toward a car in the parking lot, then started shamble-galloping after the car.

Ramsey dropped the hammer, screeching his tires on his way out of the parking lot and hauling ass down New Alps' main drag toward the distant Pacific Ocean.

Special Squadron Commander Erin Kemp jacked out of her VR droid-control interface and keyed a command that lifted a coffin-like hood over her control bay up and away from her body. A wheelchair she'd designed herself rolled up and she hefted herself over onto it. She used thought commands to guide the chair to the front of the now-empty droid-transport-and-supervision truck. She'd rolled up to its seatless driver area, docking her chair into a control station.

All of their tech was beyond bleeding edge, and with good reason, considering what they were tasked with defeating. She just hoped it would be enough.

"Good luck, hesher...."

She started the truck up, made a U-turn, and drove the opposite direction Ramsey had escaped earlier as fast as the vehicle would allow.

The beast stayed on Ramsey's tail as he tore down New Alps. The loping thing got closer than he was comfortable with a few times, its many strange lower limbs working with unsettling amounts of coordination—Ramsey pictured a many-eyed octopus riding atop several deformed giraffes of different heights, only it was all one thing and all pizza.

Just before reaching the intersection of New Alps Blvd and Saloon Road, he felt the tingling in his ear and jawline from the "nano-comms," whatever the fuck that meant.

–Coming in hot, hesher! Keep going through the four-way!–

Ramsey looked to his left and saw the droid truck speeding toward the intersection from the south. The roof of its long storage compartment came apart, the opening sections sliding away into special compartments as a mounted gun that looked like a bigger, meaner version of the droids' spray-nozzle arms rose up on hydraulic supports. The gun swiveled toward the monster and locked on. The fire hose comparison really fit now, the thick liquid blasting forth and striking the monster with enough force to slow it down and eat away at it faster than the droids could.

Emily blew through the intersection and Ramsey threw her into a long skidding stop down New Alps as Kemp braked hard enough to come to a screeching stop in the droid truck, directly perpendicular to the pizza monster's path.

The gushing fluid hurt and confused the big creature, and it seemed to have stopped moving to concentrate on regenerating.

Ramsey looked back down the boulevard and watched the monster getting hosed down hard. "What is that shit?"

–A cocktail, but mostly? Super-concentrated pineapple juice.–

"No way."

The abominable half-dissolved creature locked most of its eyes on the truck and it rushed the vehicle on its remaining legs, glowing organs spilling out and trailing behind as it galloped.

–Oh shit....–

Big T threw itself into the truck's side with incredible force and it toppled over, slamming down on the pavement and sending the pineapple juice–acid stream arcing and cascading down. Inside the truck, Kemp shook her dazed head. She saw something above her in the passenger area and she smiled.

Outside, the thing climbed onto the truck's side panel. As it regenerated, it oozed tentacles down onto the vehicle's cab, cutting into it. The sizzling, bubbling cheese tendrils slid down the mirrored windshield and covered it.

–We've got to blow the juice tanks, hesher!–

Ramsey threw Emily into reverse and backed up until she was facing the truck.

"I-I'm gonna drive my car into the van and jump out at the last—"

–Fuck no—that's a real classic! Better plan!–

54

There was a bright flash from the driver's area of the truck and all of the tentacles oozing down onto it were instantly severed. Then a blur of motion as something crashed out of the truck's cab—

Kemp had somehow ejected herself out of it and landed rolling in a special high-speed wheelchair. She'd come out at a bad angle but she rode it out and threw her weight, righting it and rolling into a skid. She wore a harness on her upper body that gave her an exo-armored version of the pizza-wheel droid arms. She flung the pizza monster's sizzling body and blood off of the circular blade and the delicious-smelling pizza filth ate into the street's surface.

–Take that droid gun I gave you and aim it at the juice guns!–

"I don't think it's powerful enough to—"

–My transport plane is circling at high altitude! I'll keep the monster near the truck and you aim the gun's laser pointer at the juice gun!–

Ramsey grabbed the gun and tried to aim it out his driver-side window but it wavered too much from Emily's rumbling.

Kemp gripped a support handle on her chair with her free hand, raised her pizza-wheel weapon, and drove her wheelchair around the truck. When Big T tried to get down to the street or swipe at her, she sliced its tentacles and limbs and kept rolling evasively.

–Do it!–

Ramsey pulled the parking brake but forgot to throw Emily into neutral, so she stalled and died. "Fuck!"

He got out and ran closer to the truck, then aimed the droid arm at the big juice turret and held its little red dot as steady as he could with his shaking hands.

Kemp used her free hand to press a command on her chair.

Ramsey caught a silent flash over the mountains to the north in his peripheral vision. A moment later, the truck disintegrated into a ball of liquid pizza-killing acid that exploded outward spherically and engulfed Big T in an instant. Ramsey was thrown back onto the street and hit his head.

The smell of pineapple-topped pizza hung in the air as Ramsey came to. He shook his head to clear it and looked around. The monster was gone. The truck was gone. Kemp was—

"Hey, hesher!" She rolled around the last smoldering wreckage of her truck and up to Ramsey, who sat up and laughed.

"Holy shit...."

A vertical takeoff–style aircraft like a really big Harrier jet swooped over the intersection and landed near the truck wreckage.

Kemp leaned down closer to Ramsey.

"So, it looks like you're in need of new employment. Lucky for you, the new job I can offer you also has a lot to do with pizza."

Iris and Kayyali Beyond Trolltown

Oregon—Present Day

"You mean Istanbul?" Iris asked, raising a thick, pink-speckled blue plastic tray up a bit to catch the mysterious stew that a pleasant-looking churchgoer was ladling out.

"I mean Constantinople," Kayyali responded from within a thick, partible parka hood.

It bothered Iris that Kayyali almost never pulled his hood down, but that wasn't the only thing that did or anywhere near the worst. She didn't much like Kayyali, but they had both escaped from a rough situation and ended up looking out for each other. She didn't much care what he thought of her either but she suspected it was similar for him.

In a pidgin language they both knew but she was positive these church people wouldn't, Iris said, <<How old *are* you anyway?>>

"Don't hold the line up," Kayyali said.

Iris took a few steps down the food line and an almost maniacally grinning pastor gently placed two warm dinner rolls, a pack of sealed plasticware, and a couple of wrapped butter pats on Iris's tray as Kayyali prepared to accept his stew. She balanced the tray in one hand and picked up an apple juice from an ice bath at the end of the line.

She tried to ignore an old lady posted just past the ice bath who was handing out religious pamphlets, but Kayyali cleared his throat in a way she knew meant she was being rude. Iris clamped the offered pamphlet casually between the top two fingers on her apple juice hand. She strode out of the way

58

of Kayyali's path and that of three dozen homeless or otherwise downtrodden wretches still making their way down a row of banquet tables the churchgoers were using for their Christlike generosity fest.

Iris wondered what the fenced-off square of gravel lot was used for when it wasn't the scene of a food line. Ten-foot-wide canopies lined almost the entire square inner border of the lot, which Iris decided was good because it was a misty evening and rain couldn't be far behind. In the short time they'd been in the Pacific Northwest of the United States, she'd picked up on some of the subtle idiosyncrasies of their cold, wet weather.

She and Kayyali were not so long ago in a place far to the north capable of having much colder weather, but there wasn't snow as far as the eye could see here, at least. No energy-sealed cages here either....

They had escaped a large underground facility in a region of the Arctic they had never bothered to pinpoint after finally gaining their freedom. They never planned on returning, since the rest had made it out too and didn't need rescuing. *Most* of the rest had made it, would be more accurate.

Kayyali was one of the less obvious "deviations" in terms of outward appearance, as was Iris. That's how they had come to traverse mountains, ride freight trains, and walk in the open when many of their fellow "Deviants"—as they called each other as a play on their former captors' clinical label—had to move by night for more than one reason. She and Kayyali weren't much fond of the sun either, but they could stand it when necessary.

Even now, though, Iris looked up from the questionable contents of her tray and watched as the fine churchgoers gave Kayyali sideways looks and the ladler's hand shook as she did her volunteer duty. He nodded and thanked her politely and advanced to receive his rolls and such and the pastor's grin was only half as maniacal for Kayyali.

Kayyali looked *more* normal than your average Deviant, but he was covered in scar tissue, some of it overlapping in almost obscene looking folds and crevices. Also a bit unsettling, his eyes were a pale blue-gray which contrasted strongly with his dark-olive skin and they seemed slightly clouded over, but his vision was perfect.

Kayyali took a pamphlet from the last churchgoer and followed Iris to a plastic table and chair set along the fence line perpendicular to the food line and under the canopies. They sat and started to eat.

"So, maybe we should think about finding a more permanent setup...again. I hear there are whole chunks of mostly unused underground city in Moscow," Iris said.

Kayyali frowned like he was trying to think of a better way of saying what he was thinking but went ahead anyway and said, "Your black skin and homosexuality would not go so well there, from what I remember. Even among the cast-downs and throwaways. My past there would make it even worse. Even living in the shadows below would not keep you safe, I don't think."

Iris watched the line of homeless and poor zip up coats and throw up their hoods as it started sprinkling.

"Paris then? I hear there's a lot of underground there."

Kayyali thought a moment and replied, "I say that we stay fluid until maybe the rest find a new home and then we join them. Also, our scouting has been fruitless thus far, but we could still find something down here...or even farther south. It is important to remember, though, that underground only meets one requirement," then he switched to the pidgin the Deviants had developed in captivity to communicate secretly, as a well-bundled hobo cradling a plate approached and sat near them.

"*We are...monsters to these people. That is why the bad ones like them took and studied us. We are as different to each other as all of us are to them, but what we share is that difference and it binds us. We should be with our own, and only our own.* It just might take some time," he finished in English.

The bundled hobo seemed to notice their cautiousness and said, "Name's Rich. I'm nothin' to worry about. Just here to eat."

"Your name is Rich? Ironic, right?" Iris said and chuckled.

Rich sighed and said, "Yeah, hilarious."

Kayyali gently elbowed Iris. She scowled at him but stopped upon receiving what she always thought of as his all-business face. She sheepishly looked back at Rich and said, "Hey, no offense."

Rich said, "Not worried about it."

A round of yelling met with cautious complaints near the open fences of the lot entrance drew their attention away from Rich's unfortunate name and Iris's insensitivity.

Eight or nine scraggly, mean-looking men strode into the lot with purpose. They looked like freight-hoppers and wore packs and hobo ensembles of denim and warm layers and coats. The only thing that was the same on all of them was a black bandanna around each of their necks, at least on the ones where that area was visible. More black bandannas were worn around legs, arms, or curling out from a jeans back pocket, and the meanest-looking one in the front wore another tied as a thick headband from his brow line up to almost the top of his head. They moved down the food line, pulling back hobos' hoods, getting real close, and examining everyone. No one was happy about it, but no one protested real strongly.

Rich let out a soft "shit" to himself.

Kayyali asked, "What is happening?"

"FTRA shakedown or some shit. They don't usually make their presence so obvious."

"FTRA?" Iris asked.

Rich said, "You don't look new to riding the rails. You never heard of 'em? They're kinda like...bikers without bikes? Gang'uh burnouts, racists, tweakers, and scuzzy bastards who ride the rails too, only they're like king shit riders. Hey, just don't piss 'em off, for both our sakes, huh?"

The gang of unwholesome freight-riders ignored over-gentle protests from the church group as they made their way past the food line and along the line of plastic tables and chairs under the canopies. Unsatisfied by the hobos and vagrants on that side, they followed the corner around toward Rich, Kayyali, and Iris, the only ones sitting on the back row.

The leader sauntered up to them and stopped, so the rest of them did too. Some of them kept scanning all around while the others looked hard at the three diners because the leader was.

Headband, as Iris decided to think of him, bent over and cocked his head to get a look at Kayyali under his hood and winced a bit. Noticing this, one of the minions stepped forward to pull the hood off of Kayyali's head but Headband grabbed the grungy man's outstretched arm.

"I can see it ain't the kid, fuckin' moron," Headband growled then pulled the minion away from Kayyali and handed him back his arm as he straightened back up. Kayyali nodded in acknowledgement of what could be perceived as something like politeness.

Headband said, "We're lookin' for a young guy." He made a point of looking at Iris and winking as he said, "*White....*" then to Kayyali and Rich, "...leather jacket with that punk shit all over it—bright green Mohawk if he's stupid enough to still have it. He's our problem an' not worth a shit of trouble for nobody else."

Rich said, "I haven't seen 'im."

Headband glared at Rich but his tone was calm and even as he said, "Well, if you do, you'll send it on down the grapevine, right?"

Iris was pretty sure Headband was really high on something but didn't care to guess what. These types didn't scare her, but she knew all too well what happened if too many more normals found out about her and Kayyali's *special attributes.*

Plus: she knew Kayyali had a strict no-show policy on their true selves unless absolutely necessary. In fact, Iris hadn't actually seen Kayyali's true form for herself and she wasn't sure she wanted to. In any other circumstances Iris wouldn't give two shits about that or someone's opinion of her actions, but even the Examiners—the name they had for the pseudoscientific paramilitary goons who had held them—seemed to be afraid of, or at least nervous around, Kayyali, and that wasn't an easily earned honor.

"W-will do," Rich stammered. Kayyali nodded his answer and Iris did the same after a long moment.

"Sounds *great.* Enjoy your food," Headband said and strolled away with his gang in tow. They made their way out of the gravel lot and were quickly out of sight in the thickening sprinkles.

Rich spat at the ground and said, "Pieces'uh shit."

"But they seemed so *nice*," Iris said.

"Hey, you guys sleepin' out?" Rich asked.

"Yes," Kayyali replied.

61

"I can't recommend that, 'specially with those jackasses roamin' around. Might wake up dead. I can get you into *Trolltown.*"

Kayyali and Iris just looked at him.

"It's a shanty camp under a big river overpass a little ways into the woods. Don't worry, it's just a name—no real monsters there."

"Oh man, I'm glad you said that. I was worried," Iris said, deadpan enough that Rich took a second to decide how to take it.

"Cute. Anyway, if I'm with you, should be fine gettin' in."

They looked at each other and Kayyali nodded his approval. Iris thought a bit longer, then nodded and said, "Sure. Thanks."

Rich said, "Wealth isn't always about money, I guess."

Iris wasn't sure what that meant but he was half-smiling as he said it so she decided she was forgiven.

After finishing their meals, Iris and Kayyali slung their packs and followed Rich through the rain-battered town and into the forest on its eastern edge.

A little less than a mile into the woods, Iris noticed the sound of cars on a highway. A quarter mile after that, she heard the sounds of a river. Just a bit farther and they could see both. The highway rose and curved away from them over the decent-sized river, and, in the dark under the bridge overpass and behind a high fence which stopped a ways into rushing river water, Iris could make out the shanties, tents, and draped cloth and tarp of what could only be "Trolltown."

Rich led them through knee-high overgrown grass to a cutout in the fence that had been reattached with zip ties to create a kind of hinged action across the top, allowing it to be used for entry without looking like it could.

"It's like a doggie door...," Iris said.

Rich said, "It serves its purpose. Not too worried about people's feelings or conceptions here if it's functional." He crouched down and went through it then stood and held it for them. After Kayyali and Iris were through and up, Rich let the door of fence patch fall back into place. It made a tinny scraping and tinkling sound as it made contact, which set Iris's teeth on edge.

They followed Rich through more tall grass the short distance into the "town square" at the rough center of the makeshift housing Iris had seen from their approach. She noticed a kind-looking—possibly Native American—woman lighting candles placed in cheap Chinese paper lanterns hung in about a dozen spots. The lanterns were almost all different and some even had the shape of cute, cartoonish animals and must've been for children. Another resembled a jack-o'-lantern. Their multicolored glow was comforting in the darkness under the overpass, if Iris was being honest with herself.

Iris heard a generator being pull-started somewhere out of sight on the other end of the camp and once it kicked on, roots reggae music started playing and strings of bluish-white Christmas lights strung between the tops of tent poles and hooks on shanty walls came on in sections and twinkled a little over head level all around the camp. She smiled, which was rare for her, and caught a little gleam in Kayyali's murky eyes as he looked around at the lights.

Rich was out of sight in what must've been his tent for just a moment and upon returning he produced a large bag of what looked like juice with big chunks of fruit half-dissolved in it.

He said, "We got dinner out of the way..." In his other hand was a stack of bright blue and red plastic cups. "...so let's get to dessert!"

Of course, the bag of juice was powerful fermented fruit alcohol, also known as "pruno." It was actually a pretty drinkable batch and/or recipe in general and Iris and Kayyali—not wanting to be rude—drank their fair share. They drank with Rich, the Native American girl Hope, the generator starter Dave, a dwarf called Chicago, and a colorful band of more nameless misfits and loners. A rare fun time was had and Iris almost wished these normals *were* real monsters so that she and Kayyali could finally settle down...again.

Something woke Iris up from a dream about an alternate Trolltown filled with those real monsters and some of her own creature friends from "The Bottle"— their former home and prison. She'd had worse hangovers, but she definitely didn't feel spectacular.

The rain was steady and the sound mixed with the running river to create a soothing effect, so for a few moments she just watched Kayyali sleep a few feet from her across Trolltown's square—they opted for using their own sleeping bags since the townies had made a fire anyway. The fire was just brilliant embers now and most of the Chinese lanterns had flickered out, as had the generator, so the Christmas lights were out too.

In the faint light of the last few lanterns and the embers, Iris could make out Kayyali's face fluttering a bit under his draped parka hood almost like the layered wings of an insect spreading out and folding back together—but it was layers of flesh, not little wings and there was a strange glow from somewhere deep within that was mostly obscured by all the folds. She was no beauty when she showed herself either, but she could only imagine what his real face was like. The Examiners had always taken Kayyali into sealed surgery and observation theaters to study him so Iris and the others had never seen his truer form. She looked around to see if any normals could see this but everyone was down for the count.

A shriek and tinny clang of thin metal colliding drew her focus. *The doggie door?*

Iris crawled to Kayyali and shook him awake. His face fused entirely upon waking to look like the scar pattern Iris was used to seeing and his eyes blinked open.

"What?"

"I heard that gate door open and close," Iris said.

Kayyali locked eyes with her and, despite their differences, his trust in her instincts negated any need to question her further. He threw open his unzipped sleeping bag and only stopped to rub his temples and groan before hauling himself up to his feet. Without having to discuss it, they both rolled their bags up and attached them to their packs in case they needed to leave quickly.

They took heavy foot-long flashlights from sheaths on the sides of their packs and headed for the fence without turning them on. They didn't actually need them to see in the dark but they made for good truncheons when necessary.

As they approached the fence line, they half-crouched and went silent. There was no one in sight, but that just made them more cautious. The steady-falling rain just past the fence line went from soothing to the opposite due to its ability to interfere with their heightened sense of hearing.

Kayyali abruptly stopped, so Iris did. She smelled what he must have: blood. They looked at each other and scanned the area again. Iris noticed a patch of bright, artificial green amidst the tall grass and made a gesture to get Kayyali's attention, then pointed at the green.

They advanced carefully and stopped again at the sound of a tortured moan. Closing the final distance revealed a young white man with "punk shit" all over his leather jacket and a bright green currently limp Mohawk he was apparently stupid enough to still have.

The "kid" started moaning and crying into the long grass as he clutched his abdomen with bloody hands. Kayyali touched his shoulder and said, "Do not be alarmed," which had the opposite effect and sent the kid flailing and crawling away from them back toward the hinged section in the fence.

As the kid forced himself up to a crouch to get through the doggie door, a suppressed gunshot was heard out in the dark woods. The bullet grazed the fence, just missed the kid's shoulder, and ended up going between two of Kayyali's ribs only to hit one on the other side of his ribcage interior before ricocheting more languidly into his left lung. Iris dropped all the way down to the grass out of instinct, as did the kid, but his dropping was only half intentional. Kayyali sunk roughly onto his butt in the grass and breathed in repeatedly like he'd only had the wind knocked out of him.

From the woods Headband yelled, "Do *not* help that kid! He's our business! I'll burn that whole place!"

"Fuh-hngk-f-fuck *you!*" the kid forced out, flinging blood spittle from his lips.

"That you, Jake? Hey, is it gettin' hard t'breath yet? And walk? If you'd just taken it in the head like you should'a, I could've made this a *lot* less painful."

Jake the kid tried to curse Headband again but just coughed and moaned instead.

Iris crawled to Kayyali and grabbed his arm gently but firmly to get him to look at her. He smiled mirthlessly and nodded.

"I'm fine."

"I figured. So let's get out of here already," Iris said.

Kayyali gestured toward Jake and said, "And him?"

"What *about* him? He's a dead punk we don't owe shit."

Iris heard rustling and cracking from the tree line through the sounds of rain and river.

"Are you a *monster*?" Kayyali asked of Iris.

"What the hell?"

"Yes or no?!" he now demanded.

"No!"

"You act like one!"

Iris said, "It's a fucking *word!* I'm not normal.... What's the difference, old man? If I showed myself, it would be a small difference...."

"And yet for him it could be everything. Not to mention...how can we blame what you call normals for hating us if we truly are *monsters*, in flesh or otherwise."

Iris listened to the sounds of approach and hated Kayyali real hard for a moment before rising to a crouch, crawling to Jake, and hooking her arm under him.

"I s'pose you won't give us a pass on the no-show, huh?"

Kayyali shook his head.

"Okay, but if we're doing this, you need to get off your old ass."

Kayyali got to his feet as Iris half-dragged/half-assisted Jake's stumbling toward Trolltown square. He followed her to their packs, put his on and helped her with hers, also re-sheathing their flashlights.

Rich came out of his tent rubbing his eyes and kneaded his crotch like he was heading to the river to piss. He saw them in the dim light of the last lanterns and fire embers and said, "Jesus! What's goin' on? Is that blood?!"

Iris said, "That gang is here for their kid." She nodded to her charge.

"Y-you've gotta go!"

Kayyali coughed and said, "We know. Is there another fence opening on that side?"

"Nobody comes from that direction so we just go over or around the fence. Shit—I'll help you but get him *out* of here."

They all rushed as best they could through Trolltown to the far fence. Kayyali effortlessly hopped up onto it and climbed with one hand while pulling his rolled sleeping bag out of its straps. He placed it across the top of the fence and straddled it.

Iris climbed onto the fence one-handed as well while handing Jake up to Kayyali like a sack of groceries. Rich went slack jawed upon witnessing their incredible and unexpected agility.

Kayyali noticed and said, "We get good exercise on the road."

"I guess you do...," Rich said.

Iris was up and over the fence in an instant, then dropped the twelve feet to the grass on the other side into a crouch. She rose back up and took Jake's half-conscious bulk from Kayyali like it was almost nothing. Kayyali dropped too and his legs absorbed the shock but as he came up he coughed and groaned.

Iris said, "Are you—"

"Let's go."

Without acknowledging Rich again, they rushed through the rain for the tree line ahead of them, Iris with Jake's arm hooked behind her neck and her fingers down in his belt loops.

Just before they reached the eastern woods, they heard yelling and sounds of struggle back in Trolltown so they stopped. Kayyali must've been thinking but Iris couldn't see his face in his dark parka hood. Then he turned, grabbed her flashlight from the side of her pack, crooked his elbow to grab his own, and flicked them both on.

Kayyali waved the bright flashlights back and forth over his head as a flight deck worker would and whistled high and loud like you might to a distant dog. He started flicking the lights off and on as he waved them and fluttered the whistle too, trying not to go unnoticed.

A bullet whizzed through the rain and hit a tree about ten feet to their right.

Kayyali turned off the lights and headed into the deep shadows of the tree cover and Iris followed, but he stopped several feet in, turned back, and watched Trolltown and the overpass. Iris wasn't entirely sure what he was up to but she trusted him enough not to ask.

After less than a minute, she could see several of the black-bandanna-wearing gang members hopping the high fence and helping each other over, then a few ran across the overpass between a late-night driver here and there.

When all nine of them were in view, Kayyali turned and advanced through the dark forest. Iris realized he was trying to lure them away from the relative innocents in Trolltown, but she wouldn't have bothered so it had taken her a bit to get that.

Headband taunted from a distance behind them but the rain and fluttering trees masked the words. Kayyali just silently trudged forward as Iris followed and helped Jake do the same.

"What's your plan?" Iris asked.

"From my memory of the local maps, there is a town with a hospital this direction. We just have to stay ahead of them."

"They'll c-catch ush-hngk...," Jake spat out.

"Kayyali, if we keep our hands tied, he's probably right."

"And?"

"So I say we set him down for a minute, take out the trash, then go to the hospital."

Kayyali said, "Not while he is awake, which we must *keep* him if he is to live."

Iris scoffed and shook her head.

"You can leave if you like. I will take him there."

Iris stopped and said, "No foolin'? You *shall release* me? Oh thank you, infallible *master.*"

Kayyali stopped and looked back at her with a dark—even in darkness— expression on a face which fluttered at the scar-seams.

"If you want to make this petty and personal, I will oblige you. Just not now...and not here."

Jake swayed at the end of Iris's loosened grip and mumbled, "Can we knh-keep goin'?"

Iris weighed her options. She really wanted to drop this punk kid and go some rounds just to see what Kayyali was made of once and for all. It occurred to her, though, that she might not win and—if she was being honest with herself—she would probably get really lonely without him if she *did*, condescending asshole or not.

A train horn sounded in the woods behind them in the distance to their left. Iris and Kayyali looked at the trees in the direction of the sound then locked back on each other. They nodded in silent agreement and rushed forward and to the left of their original path.

After a few minutes of hurried hiking, they could see tracks through the trees. They made their way to the border between the trees and gravel of a slight rise the tracks were installed upon.

The freight train was coming but fast.

Jake mumbled, "Too nhn-fasht.... Goin'toofast...."

"Maybe for you, kid," Iris said.

They let the train engine car pass and—since it appeared to be a long one— they waited in the downpour edge for a good spot to hop on nearer to the end.

Kayyali and Iris started to run at pace with the train and Kayyali leapt up and onto the ladder at the rear of a freight car. Iris matched pace with the speeding train and handed Jake up to Kayyali who climbed one-handed to the roof of that car with Jake on his back. Iris jumped on and climbed up to join them.

"NnhWhatthafuckwasthatshitt....," Jake drawled out but Iris doubted he'd remember much of this part and assumed Kayyali had decided the same if he was alright with that little show of ability.

67

A bullet ricocheted off the side of the freight car they were resting atop and Kayyali and Iris saw Headband and several of his crew standing at the edge of the gravel track rise near where they had just waited.

Headband fired again, grazing a round off of the freight car's upper lip, so Iris and Kayyali dropped against the roof surface. Jake was already there.

Iris groaned in annoyance more than anything else. They let the train go a bit farther before looking again. The train curved to the right, giving them a clear view of the last snaking length of its hind section.

Headband, most of his crew, and whatever larger gang they belonged to had apparently earned at least some of the fear and respect they seemed to have garnered from the freight-hopping hobo community: they hopped the second to last car and the reversed rear engine car at speed by grabbing any available hand-and-foot holds and enduring the joint-ripping force of it. One of the gang wasn't as legendary and ended up severed and messy in the wheels.

"So...do we just 'stay in front of them'?!" Iris yelled over the machine roar of the train and the now pounding, diagonal rain.

Kayyali watched Headband and his gang crawl and climb all over the last two cars and thought. He looked down at the barely conscious Jake, then back at the end of the train.

Headband—also known as Splitter to his "Freight Train Riders of America"/"Fuck The Reagan Administration" cronies—climbed confidently onto the rain-slick roof of the empty rear engine car—*rain and speed be damned*—with suppressed revolver in hand.

Too bad about Dank gettin' lunched by the train, but Jake needs to bite it or the rest of us are all lookin' at decades inside. He took a headcount: *Chonch, Popper, Tits, Monk, and Zippy made it on.*

Splitter could just make out Jake—AKA Vanilla—and the two good Samaritans' dim forms through the darkness and rain several cars down. He was feeling his sweet smoke real strong so he ran across the engine roof and jumped for the next car. He landed just right and strutted into the wind and rain across the last freight car toward his prey.

With only a few stops to crouch for balance from the train rocking and such, he made it across two more cars before realizing the three soon-to-be-victims hadn't moved yet. They must not have seen him even though he was only two cars down now. *This won't be nearly as fun if they just sit there and eat some bullets real easy. And they better not think they can reason with me or some shit. Not an option. Better make that clear.*

Splitter fired a round toward Jake and the two hobos without really trying to hit them. They grabbed Jake and helped him along toward the front of the train. *That seemed to get 'em energetic!* He hooted and called out nonsense words to spook his prey and hurried along atop the cars after them. He looked

68

back and saw Monk and Zippy right behind him and Chonch, Tits, and Popper not far behind.

One of the prey must be hit—other than Jake who already was. They're movin' pretty slow.

Splitter gained on the trio and heard Monk and Zippy close behind him. The train went around a bend and rocked pretty hard so they all crouched down and grabbed handholds. Splitter looked up from his holds and could swear he only saw two of his prey now: Jake and the bigger hobo. Splitter narrowed his eyes and studied the cars ahead, remembering something his awful uncle and surrogate father used to say about wounded, scared animals being the most dangerous.

The hobo with Jake started descending out of sight a couple cars down between two boxcars, hefting Jake down with less difficulty than Splitter would've expected, *but I've got the gun, so fuck him.*

Splitter, Monk, and Zippy made it to the cars Jake and the hobo went down between but didn't see them down in the junction. Splitter leaned over the sides and saw the boxcar toward the front of the train had a mangled lock and was partially open. *How the fuck did he get it open? He's carrying Jake, this train is hauling ass, and that's the hardest one to pop—even when it's sittin' still. I still have the advantage, what with this hunk of deadly on me.*

"Awright—let's get these shits, boys."

Splitter tucked the suppressed pistol in his waist and started climbing down to the car junction well with Zippy and Monk ready to follow.

Chonch led Tits and Popper down the rain-battered freight car roofs. They were going slower due to Chonch and Popper having a touch of trouble getting on the train intact. *Hell, I think my shoulder almost popped out and Popper tweaked his ankle somethin' fierce. Splitter's losin' it, jumpin' a train this fast! Jake's gonna die from his gut shot any-damn-way! Now we gotta grease two unknowns for no reason along with him.*

Splitter started to climb down between two boxcars a few cars up and Chonch wished he could ask Splitter what was going on. The wind and rain whipped up real powerfully and Chonch couldn't see for a moment—Popper yelled, "How the *hell?!*"

Chonch tried to rub the water out of his eyes and opened them on a smiling black woman in hobo clothes.

"Hi," the woman said with a gleam in her eyes.

She broke apart into a whipping flurry of glowing, warped insects, fish, and birdlike beasts of varying sizes. These abominations swarmed around Chonch but only to pass him. He looked back in time to see the woman reform with more eyes running up along her temples and more holes running up her nose. Her mouth broke open, a gaping chasm of obsidian shark teeth, and she tore

69

into Popper's neck where it met his shoulder and came away with most of it in a meaty spray.

Tits jolted and threw himself back to avoid being next but slipped on the slick surface of the roof and fell back off the train and down into the wheels.

Chonch was too confused and terrified to scream, but that didn't stop Popper.

Splitter was climbing across the sliding channel for the graffiti-covered boxcar door when he heard something like a scream back down the train a few cars. *I better not have lost another idiot to this train. This is what we do. Can't let it get out that my crew can't even ride some freight.*

He made it to the opening and swung himself into the inky black interior of the boxcar. He steadied himself and immediately took out his revolver and his Zippo lighter. He flicked the lighter a few times with no results while Monk and Zippy were climbing into the car behind him. Monk took out a wrench he carried and set it in the door channel so they couldn't get locked in by the train shifting. They took out their own pistols to play the backup role. They didn't have suppressors, but in here that shouldn't matter.

The lighter ignited and flickered, throwing shadows up around the crate-and-palette-filled boxcar. There were narrow channels between the ceiling-high contents and Splitter tried to peer into darkness past his flame to the left and right.

Jake moaned quietly to the left.

Ha!

Splitter aimed the pistol toward the source of the sound and crept toward the far end of the car. He saw two hobo packs against the far wall and Jake's legs along the boxcar floor like he was lying down, *and hopefully bleeding out.*

The big hobo stepped into view at the end of the channel. His hood was down enough that Splitter couldn't see much of his face, but his eyes were reflecting the flickering lighter in a strange way. It was eerie and made Splitter anxious to be done with this.

The big hobo said, "You can't have him."

Splitter chuckled through his fear and said, "If I were askin' that might mean somethin'," and he aimed his revolver between the almost glowing eyes in the dark.

"So, I am correct to infer...," the hobo started as he stepped down the channel and pulled back his hood to reveal a heavily scarred head and face, "...that you intend...," he opened his parka, lifted it a bit, then let it fall down his arms and off his body, "...to do me harm?"

His cutoff shirt sleeves revealed more of the thick, heavy scarring shared with his head, and dense, intricate tattoos all up and down his arms.

Without answering, Splitter shot the big hobo between the eyes dead on.

The large man's head was thrown back and his body swayed around once like it was going to topple—but his head snapped back laughing and he threw his arms wide out from his sides.

The shock of just that caused Splitter to drop his lighter and they were back in almost total darkness. Then there was a metallic sound back by the door as the wrench was removed and the door slammed shut.

The big hobo unraveled then flapped and spread open, filling the boxcar with an otherworldly and ineffable luminescence followed by a neon-and-tar mixture of organic chaos which poured into the space Splitter, Monk, and Zippy were taking up.

Were taking up.

Iris heard and saw enough coming out of the cracks from her hanging position outside the door to decide for certain that she didn't need to ever see Kayyali's true form for herself. Plus, she finally got some *real* food, so things might be looking up for them.

The nurses and doctors gave Iris and Kayyali suspicious and fearful looks as they deposited Jake's unconscious but still-living form onto a gurney. Most of them wheeled him into the trauma ward and got right to work, but one nurse tried to intimidate them into waiting for the police and gestured to the armed guard near the entrance who was already watching them closely. Kayyali gave her his all-business face from within his draped parka hood and politely explained that they were leaving but the police should have more than a little interest in what Jake could have to say about crime and gangs in the area.

Iris and Kayyali walked out of the emergency area unmolested and kept going until they were across the street and past the periphery of the hospital lights.

Kayyali stopped and looked back so Iris did the same.

Iris said, "He'll be fine. *In good hands* and all that."

"I didn't think you cared."

"Well, not much. It is nice not to be a 'monster' for once, though. That was pretty cheap, though...."

"It got you moving, right?"

"Sure. Hey, anyway.... You gotta admit that was more than a little fun. We should be like...monster vigilantes or something."

Kayyali smiled and shook his head.

"Maybe.... If we don't kill each other first."

7

PATRICK LOVELAND

Not Cavities

Midwestern United States—Present Day

Little Taneeka Sumner fought back tears as she pulled with all her strength at a carrying strap connected to her blue jack-o'-lantern bucket, the thin black plastic cutting at the insides of her clenched fists. Reese's Pieces packs and Smarties rolls dropped to the damp sidewalk from the struggle.

On the other end was an older boy named Richie Jenkins, a mean smile on his skull-painted face. Richie's friend Max looked on, smoking a cigarette and laughing through his own ghoulish face paint.

Halloween was Taneeka's favorite holiday and she'd looked forward to it all year. The dinosaur costume her dad had worked so hard on by himself—because her mom had passed away from breast cancer a few years before—was getting crumpled as she fought the huge boy. Her best friend Nancy tried to pull Richie's hands off the candy bucket—because Max had already taken her orange pillowcase for himself—but he was too strong.

One of Taneeka's feather patches fell off in the melee and she lost it. She kicked Richie in his left shin—he just growled and pushed her. She fell onto her bottom, crumpling her costume's tail. Then he elbowed Nancy away.

Nancy said, "Hey! You're so mean!"

"Give it back!" Taneeka pleaded, sure now that she couldn't fight him.

Richie leered down at her and said, "Hell no! My candy now!"

Max said, "It's bad for you anyway!"

Taneeka said, "You're just...*a-assholes*!"

74

The boys feigned surprise.

Richie said, "How could you say that? We're doin' you some good...."

Taneeka stifled sobs in her chest as Nancy re-engaged, but Richie batted her attacks away with little effort.

Richie heard squeaking noises behind him and looked back over his shoulder. Taneeka and Nancy looked too.

Max turned and said, "What the hell?"

A small old woman in dark, threadbare knit clothes approached, pulling a ratty rolling suitcase almost as big as she was behind her by a telescoping handle. Her stringy salt-and-pepper hair was held down by a visor hat.

She eased to a stop and turned her head toward them, raising it enough so that her dark eyes glinted under her visor bill.

"Hello, children."

Richie said, "*They're* kids—we're older."

The woman looked up at the sky and hummed to herself, ignoring the boy. Taneeka looked up too, through the clawlike branches of trees that had discarded most of their leaves onto the street, lawns, and bushes.

The woman said, "What a lovely night for an occasion such as this...."

Max said, "This weather sucks."

Richie said, "Yeah, worse than you at *Call of Duty.*"

"Hey...."

Taneeka watched the old lady take in all the decorations and costumes of the holiday on the nearby houses and sidewalks. She could've sworn she saw the woman's bag bulge a bit.

"You okay, lady?" Max asked, watching the woman swoon a bit.

She said, "You boys are quite contrary, aren't you?"

"So what? You could just leave," Richie said.

"You boys aren't in keeping with the spirit of the season. Samhain is but once a year...and only just begun. After sun downs once again tomorrow you'll have to wait for the feasts of Imbolc to feel as close to the—"

"What's 'sewing' got to do with this?"

Max chuckled and said, "And shit, lady—this is just how we do our tricks!"

"Right?" Richie agreed.

Richie dangled and swung the candy-filled bucket over Taneeka, mocking her and screwing up his painted face for effect.

Richie said, "Yummy yummy...."

Taneeka just glared at him as tears formed at the edges of her eyes.

The old woman said, "Boys...."

Richie and Max looked at her.

"If you eat any of that candy, you'll lose your teeth."

Richie laughed and said, "How? *Cavities?*"

The woman raised her head enough so they could see her dark eyes under the visor.

"No.... Not cavities."

Richie said, "Whatever, Your Creepiness. Let's get out of here, man."

Max followed Richie across the street and they were off down the far sidewalk.

Nancy helped Taneeka to her feet and Taneeka tried to keep her crumpled tail from coming off, but it detached and her tears finally came out. She stamped her feet and groaned.

Nancy said, "Stupid boys!"

Taneeka started walking down the sidewalk toward her house.

"You want to get bags or something and get more candy? Maybe your dad will come with us, since he wanted to anyway...."

Taneeka choked up and said, "I don't c-care about candy anymore! My dad made my costume and he's gonna be so mad at me!"

"Oh, I doubt that," the old woman said behind them.

Taneeka kept going but Nancy stopped and looked back.

She said, "Thanks for trying."

The woman just nodded, her eyes more natural again and her smile more warm than the creepy ones she'd given the boys.

"Goodnight," Nancy said, then started after Taneeka again. She caught up and said, "Hey, maybe there's a good movie on—I saw this real old one last year called *The Worst Witch*. It was super good."

Taneeka sniffled and tried to smooth her breathing out and fight off her sobs.

"Yeah, okay. Oh, and if my dad's not too mad, I think we might have some ice cream."

Nancy smiled and said, "Cookie dough?"

"Or peanut butter cup."

"Awesome."

Nancy looked back and didn't see the old lady down the street anymore. She was a bit relieved—nice as she'd been to the girls, Nancy hoped she'd never see that lady ever again.

Richie held Max's foot, boosting him over the gates of the local elementary school. After climbing over and dropping down, Max reached through the gate and boosted Richie up and over. They reached through the gate and grabbed their stolen candy, then started into the school. It was Taneeka and Nancy's school, and Richie would take particular trollish pleasure consuming those brats' sweets in their own stomping grounds.

Max said, "So, you get nasty with Tricia yet?"

"Nah, she's a bitch, man. She's like Mormon, and won't give it up."

The boys crept through the school's walkways and recess areas. Drenched and soggy decorations drooped all around, the rains earlier having been so sudden and more intense than the scattered showers of the days prior. They reached the outdoor lunch area, a rough trapezoidal stretch of asphalt bordered on its longest side by the locked-up school cafeteria and auditorium building.

"Hey, maybe if you go to church or whatever with her she'll—"

"Hell no—she'd just want to wait till marriage then or some shit."

The boys laughed.

The school's teachers and administrators had had barely time enough time to cover the Halloween Festival games and booths once the rain had started beating down. In the large open area bordered by pushed together lunch tables that had been moved to make room for the festivities, there were themed prize booths, a Nerf gun–monster-shooting gallery, a "Ghost Funk Dunk" tank, and a large apple-bobbing tub—all hastily draped with black tarps.

Richie led Max to one of the rows of pushed together tables and they sat down. Richie turned his stolen pumpkin bucket over, spilling out its contents onto the slick surface. Max did the same with his pillowcase. They sorted the candies by type—fruity, gummy, chocolate, peanut buttery, etc.

"Daaaamn.... Those stupid little girls were workin' for it," Richie said and they chuckled.

Max said, "Alright, first one?"

"Kit Kat, for sure."

"Naw, it's all about Witches' Teeth."

Richie cringed and said, "What, candy corn? Them shit's will rot your teeth in a hurry."

"All this shit will," Max said and Richie raised his eyebrows and nodded in reluctant agreement.

The boys unwrapped their sweets and dug in.

Richie said, "Damn, dude—close your nasty-ass mouth when you chew...."

"Whatever, bitch."

They sat and chewed, Richie making little sounds of appreciation and Max half-heartedly trying to fight his habit of smacking his open mouth.

In between Max's smacks, Richie heard a squeaking sound. He stopped chewing to hear more clearly. He put a finger over his mouth to silence Max, but his friend kept chewing.

"Max—stop that."

Max stopped but frowned in confusion.

The squeaking was coming from back the way they'd come in at the school gates. Richie dropped his Kit-Kat and stood up, then started toward the front of the school.

Max looked at all the candy and said, "Dude, what if it rains?"

"That's what the wrappers are for, man. Come on...."

Max got up but he took his candy corn with him, chomping on it as they sneaked back through the school. Richie started around a corner that was in view of the main gate—

77

The old woman was there, limping as she wheeled her luggage toward them. Richie stopped in place, but Max kept going and came around the corner before Richie could stop him with a groping right hand.

Max said, "What the *fuck*?"

Surprise or sneaking abilities out the window, Richie came around the corner too.

The lady stopped and looked up, enough so they could see those black eyes under her visor.

"You and that mouth...," the woman said.

Richie said, "What are you gonna do about it, bitch?"

"Well, let's just see, shall we?" she said, then set the telescoping handle down on the wet pavement, hobbling around and hunching over her luggage bag.

"Wait.... How did you get over the fence?"

"Neither here nor there. This should be your main concern...."

She fumbled with small, weird-looking locks on her luggage bag.

Max looked at Richie, then back at her and said, "Bullshit—what if we call the Po-Po?"

"Police? Feel free to."

The boys took out their mobile phones and activated their screens—the displays were awash with psychedelic distortion, and useless.

"Nothing? Okay, let's continue."

As the boys exchanged a worried look, the woman went back to her locks.

Richie said, "Wh-what's in the bag?"

She finished unlocking her bag and chuckled.

"Not 'cavities '...."

The woman made a strange chirping whistle, and the luggage bag started bulging and straining. She unhooked the locks and stepped away from her bag....

The tattered suitcase flap rustled and broke open—it spilled several humanoid creatures the size of small monkeys out, only they were inky black and gray and almost see through in parts, lopsided and warped in all different ways, and had too many piercing, glinting eyes.

The boys turned and ran. Richie looked back just before the lady and creatures were out of sight, and saw a few of them jumping onto the roof of the building that ran along to his right—and the woman was smiling, ear to ear.

The horrible little things that had come out of the luggage bag made chirping sounds as they ran behind the boys and along the rooftop. They jumped from roof to roof above, staring down at Richie as they sailed overhead. He'd never been as scared as those beady eyes made him.

"How do we get out?!" Max called back to Richie.

"Just keep going!"

Richie rounded the next corner into the lunch area with the shrouded festival booths and games in time to see two of the creatures throw themselves down onto Max ahead. Max yelped and spun, maybe trying to throw them off—but the motion sent him careening into the covered apple-bobbing tub. It tipped and crashed onto its side, spilling water and apples across the asphalt as Max slipped and flopped down onto his side, hard.

Richie cried, "No!"

The little creatures climbed up Max's body as he tried to fight them off.

Richie tried to get to Max, but slipped in the spilt water and slapped down onto the asphalt too—

Then he felt small hands gripping his ankles and calves like tiny vice-grips. He rolled over and pulled himself along the asphalt, but the little monsters climbed around his legs then up his body. Then two others pulled his hands and arms away, flopping him down onto his back with a splash.

But then that didn't matter.

The creature crawling up his chest opened its mouth, exposing what looked like hundreds of tiny interlaced molars.

"Those teeth have a special purpose, boys," the woman said as she limped up to them.

"Please, don't do this!" Max said.

"No, 'this' is going to happen. You boys imposed your will on those little girls. Because you were bigger—because you were *stronger*. My friends aren't bigger...but they *are* stronger, and they are certainly meaner. They're going to do the same to you."

Richie started, "Don't—" but little fingers clawed into his mouth from top and bottom, holding his jaw wide open. The creature on Richie's chest rested there a moment, then leaned in and seemed to smell his mouth.

The old woman looked down with her black eyes.

"They won't kill you, but they have to eat.... There's only one thing they can stomach."

The creature opened its own mouth wide and bit down on one of Richie's lower incisors—its own teeth made short work of crushing it into shards.

The pain almost blinded Richie, but he could see just enough through the haze to watch the little monster chewing his tooth into a boney mush and swallowing it as it made stomach-turning sounds of appreciation. He could hear one doing the same to Max and he tried one last time to throw the creatures off with no success.

Then the tooth-loving thing leaned in for another.

Taneeka and Nancy heard a knock at the front door. They were lying on their stomachs on the living-room floor, watching *The Worst Witch* and eating their ice cream. Taneeka stuck her spoon into the ice cream and got up, then walked to the front door. She picked up a big candy bowl on a small table next to the door.

Her father approached and gently grasped her shoulder.

He smiled and said, "Oh no—I'm not letting you walk into a trick trap or something."

She smiled up at him and said, "Okay."

He opened the door and looked out.

"Weird...," Nancy said from back in the living room.

Taneeka looked back and saw the movie had been interrupted by a news story about two boys having been taken to the hospital due to a disturbing hazing incident. They advised children and teens to be kept inside for the rest of the night.

Taneeka's dad opened the door wide and stepped out.

"Must have been knock and ditch or something...," he said.

He walked down their front steps and looked up and down the streets and sidewalks, but didn't see anyone.

Taneeka set the candy bowl down and stepped out onto the porch.

At the foot of the steps nestled next to their flickering candle-lit pumpkins, was an orange pillowcase and blue jack-o'-lantern bucket.

Both full.

7

Ley Lines

Middle of Nowhere, California—Present Day

Special Agent Blakely Tran knew the man on the surveillance monitor playback was their guy as soon as she saw him. Well-worn straw cowboy hat with a curled-up crease, a few inches of reddish-blond beard, T-shirt with what had to be Frank Zappa with pigtails printed on it and the sleeves cut off, heavy tattooing from the backs of his hands up to his exposed shoulders. Average size, but well built, and he moved with confidence—possibly ex-military, Blakely decided.

She and SA Hank Monroe had canvassed the truck stop, asking Burger Time, Spanky's, and Tubeway sub shop employees if they'd remembered anyone sticking out for any reason the night before, with no results. She and Hank agreed from the lack of decomposition that they'd come across the latest victim less than a day after the deed was done, and that the killer worked at night under ultraviolet lights for stealth. Strange patterns on the ground around the victims in a mixture of blood and fluorescent pigments had supported that conclusion.

They'd had no luck until Taco Party. Its night manager remembered two customers acting strangely the night before. One she described as a "hoo-billy," and the other looked like a college kid who'd just come off a bus for a dinner break. She remembered the hoo-billy carrying the other out of the bathroom area, explaining that his friend was sick. He helped the kid out to his truck. It seemed strange, but she hadn't actually seen the kid get off the bus, so she couldn't be sure.

Blakely watched their man carry the college kid from the bathroom area with the kid's arm hooked over his own shoulders. The young man's legs barely worked. Part of her wished she could show this manager woman what that hoobilly had done to the college boy.

Hank said, "Must've tased him or punched him up pretty good...."

"Yeah...," Blakely said.

The college kid wriggled and their man's hat dropped off his head—a strange tattoo on the top of his buzzed skull struck Blakely. He picked his hat up and put it back on.

"Pause it."

The manager did what she asked.

"Scrub it back a bit...."

Their man's hat came back off. The tattoo on his head was a triangle with inward-curving sides and sharp points. Near each point was a wide-open eye.

Blakely said, "You said he was reading?"

"Yeah, he ate, then just sat and read. I took his tray and noticed he was like mumbling to himself as he read, almost like it was a Bible...but it was an old paperback with highlighter in it. And there was monsters and space stuff on the cover."

That almost sealed it for Blakely.

They'd already gone back and found an angle on a camo spray-painted Hilux 4×4 parked outside that he'd carried the poor college kid to, complete with license plate number. The off-road truck even had a camper shell, perfect for hauling his two-part, screw-together *pikes*, Blakely thought, her teeth grinding together.

Blakely stepped out of the Taco Party's back office, making her way toward the glass front doors. She heard Hank thank the manager and head after her. She exited the restaurant and looked out at the night-cloaked desert surrounding this lit-up oasis. Her gaze drifted out into the black open desert east of the oasis and highway it serviced. A pale blue, glowing bubble could be seen in the inky expanse—the local forensics team's scene-preservation tent.

Blakely walked to their assigned truck, opened the passenger door, and took out a small tablet. She went into an e-reader app and purchased a favorite old book.

"Thank you, Burger Time Wi-Fi...."

Hank came out after her and said, "This place is a few restaurants, gas stations, and some maintenance sheds and restrooms for both. Not a single residence—not even a motel. Halfway between the Bay Area and SoCal, inland from the central coast...."

"Yeah, kinda spooky, just sitting here in all that darkness. Like a dream place."

"Uh, I was gonna say, why here?"

Blakely said, "Run that plate while I drive us back. I think I know why, but I need to check something."

"*Grady Lee Chisum*. Last known address in Wasco, northern Oregon—that's right near Locust Grove, where one of the first victims was found. And also puts him near southern Washington, with a few of the others," Hank said.

Blakely drove through the open desert, lights burning away the darkness ahead. She stayed in the tracks that multiple vehicles had made in and out of the area since the early morning, when an illegal off-roader had noticed the victim seemingly standing upright in the middle of nowhere, and ridden up on his dirt bike.

"He was a combat medic—Navy corpsman—attached to multiple Marine units in Afghanistan. Saw a lot of combat. Lives saved. Then Big Chicken Dinner...."

"Huh?"

Hank said, "Bad Conduct Discharge."

"Fabulous...."

Blakely parked near the thirty-foot-diameter tent and they got out. They showed their IDs and entered the scene. Blakely could get used to a lot of things, but not what this Chisum got up to....

The college boy's body was upside-down, run through with a twelve-foot pike, which was half buried to keep the body up. Head was severed and impaled atop his severed hands and resting on the soles of his feet. Hole drilled in forehead, containing a third eyeball, from unknown victim. The ankles were bound with his own Achilles tendons, and other sinew threaded through the hands to keep them in place. Blood removed. Organs—other than intestine—removed and placed around symbol-engraved ball at buried base end of pike in a sealed plastic torus in a solution of several herbs, honey, and spring water; large intestine still attached to rectum, length of it and small intestine coiled down to the desert sand.

Blakely crossed to a large ultraviolet-light rig on a tripod and flicked it on. The fluorescent pigments glowed now, dots with curving lines radiating from them. They hadn't been able to find a pattern in the markings, but they were very deliberate and different at each of the many murder scenes.

Blakely said, "They're *menhirs*, all of them. In the Ashpoole sense."

"What, like the long, buried rocks? Ash-what?"

"Morgan Ashpoole. Welsh expat, moved to New York, then some small town on the coast of Oregon. Wrote in the late fifties, sixties, and a bit into the seventies. In his novella *Ley Lines*, horrifying totems or statues appear with no explanation at certain points where all these energy paths intersect. Like translucent jumbles of animals and people parts frozen together. He called them 'menhirs,' 'cause they're about the same size and shapes as the real thing."

"And?" Hanks said.

Blakely took out her tablet and brought up the story. On the title page, there was an intricate map of the Pacific Northwest, with dozens of points dotting it, and curved lines crisscrossing between them.

"Jesus, every one of the scenes is on one of those points," he said.

Blakely looked at the three-eyed horror Chisum had left.

"He's trying to make something happen...."

Hank said, "What?"

She just shook her head.

Hank drove them southeast toward the desert east of San Diego. They'd come across a marriage license for Chisum and a young woman named Jolene. She was still using the Chisum last name, but living in a tiny town called Ocotillo, almost a thousand miles from Grady's last address. Blakely was rereading the *Ley Lines* novella on her tablet.

"So, what happens in the story? I mean, how's it play out?" Hank asked

"Once all the menhir things have appeared, they unfreeze, wriggle out of the ground, and roam the countrysides and towns as monsters, savaging and eviscerating everybody. Eventually, they ascend to meet their goddess, Mu'shihk'sa—she's the most powerful of this ancient alien civilization in another part of the cosmos called 'The Matrons' that show up in different ways in all his stuff. They got so advanced technologically they, like, *made* their own version of Heaven and peaced-out into it, leaving this universe behind."

"So, what's that tattoo and the third eye on the bodies mean?"

"In Ashpoole's stories, that symbol wards off powerful evil and/or alien forces. It's used in different ways across his body of work. I'm not sure what it means to Chisum."

"Tran, how'd you get into this guy's shit? Sounds kooky."

"I was kind of a goth-y teen. My friends were into Ashpoole, so I checked him out."

Hanks chuckled and said, "What, like raccoon makeup and oversized sweaters?"

"Pretty much," she said.

"I guess I can picture that. I was more into baseball and *Magnum, P.I.* reruns."

Blakely chuckled and said, "I would've *hated* you."

"Likewise, Wednesday Addams."

Blakely smiled, shook her head, and found her place on the tablet screen again.

They made it into Ocotillo around 9 a.m. Hank took the off-ramp down onto a short stretch of Imperial Highway called S2, which ran north-south under the 8—with the town north of the 8 and almost perpendicular to it—then elbowed west off toward dozens of huge wind turbines and foothills. She could count the nonresidential establishments on a hand. The rest were trailers and small houses with waist-high chain-link fences around patches of desert sand.

As they did a quick run through to get an idea of the layout—and because Hank seemed amazed this place had its own name, being the size it was—Blakely noticed a completely rusted-out tractor half-submerged in the ocean of sand in one yard. They also passed abandoned shacks, disintegrating water towers, and what must have been a gas station and garage at one point—now an open-air husk with some very impressive graffiti on the exposed inside wall of what was once the mechanic's big work area.

The motel in town was a set of trailers with window AC units in every available opening other than the doors, so they agreed to drive to El Centro or Alpine maybe, after their business here was concluded. They pulled up to a small diner where Jolene was listed as employed and went in.

A young woman carrying hot plates said, "Seat yourselves," and continued to one of only two occupied booths. Dark hair, dark brown eyes, cute—JO on her name tag. They sat and turned over their coffee cups. Jolene came back and started pouring coffee as they showed her their IDs.

"Feds? Why're you here?"

"You're Jolene Chisum?" Hank asked.

"*Saunders.* Haven't been able to change my name back yet, though."

Blakely said, "But you're still married, right?"

"Grady won't sign the papers."

"Have you had any contact with Grady recently?"

Jolene narrowed her eyes a bit.

"None. Coffee's on me. After that, you can leave."

Hank said, "But we have a few—"

"You're welcome," Jolene said, already turning away. She walked back to the register and sat on a padded stool in the path of a circulating fan, then opened an old *National Geographic* and focused her attention on it.

They'd decided against pulling the obstruction card for the time being, left the diner, and driven to a hill on the other side of the freeway that off-roaders used to access the trails that snaked between even more huge wind turbines all around the hills in this area south of town.

Seven hours later, Blakely gazed through Hank's huge, door-mounted binoculars while he slept in the passenger seat. Blakely sat with the windows down in a few layers of sweat from the course of the breezeless day. She watched the diner for signs of Grady, or Jolene leaving work.

Hank snored himself awake and he readjusted in his seat.

"Anything?" he asked.

"Nope."

"We should drive to Julian and get some decent food for dinner, and maybe some apple pie."

Blakely said, "Aww...did you wake up hungry, sport?"

"Hey, Wednesday, why don't you step out for a clove—might soothe you some."

"Hey, I only smoked Dunhills, thanks very much. I'd—wait...."

"What?"

"She's leaving."

Jolene walked down Ocotillo's main road with a six-pack, past the Sleepy Snake Saloon, then took a left on Mesquite Road, heading for what they knew was her address at the corner of Mesquite and Shell Canyon Road. Less than ten minutes after Jolene was out of sight, a camo Hilux 4×4 got off the freeway and headed up the main drag.

Blakely turned the engine over and sped down to the asphalt toward town. As she barreled under the 8 overpass, Hank checked his Glock. She tore around the corner of Mesquite. Grady's Hilux was parked at an angle in the dirt between the road and Jolene's yard fence, so Blakely jammed their vehicle at an angle into its bumper—Grady'd have to go through the fence to get away.

She took her Glock out as she got out of the truck, and the two agents crouch-jogged up to the truck, each clearing a side of the interior. Blakely looked toward the house and saw the door was ajar—

Jolene screamed somewhere in the house. Hank hopped the fence with gun raised and rushed the door—Blakely caught up as he put his back against the door's right frame. She did the same on the left. She nodded and Hank raised his knee and kicked backwards, slamming the door inward. Blakely cleared one side, Hank the other, and they advanced through the living room. Hank was rushing and as they took positions on the next room's doorframe, she wasn't sure he'd checked his corner. Then Jolene screamed again and he stepped through before Blakely could check hers and entered the bedroom—

A shotgun blast hit his vest, dropping him to the floor. Blakely was already stepping through and raising her pistol toward the direction of the blast when something struck her head—

Stars, planets, nebulas...black space between. Warmth, pulsing, vibrations.... Roaring? Singing?

Blakely had come to high and tripping on something nasty—things were pretty and mean at once. Hank's screaming was the singing, and sounded distant but hit thick walls. She looked around, her vision dancing and blurring. Glowing paint on the walls of a...mine tunnel? Generators powered black lights along the path, lighting up a hand-painted cosmos.

She was bound at the ankles and wrists, in a large workbench-lined alcove. Tools hung above the benches, and she shuddered, images of all the victims she'd examined filling her head. Hank's screams and gurgle-interrupted moans shook her insides even more.

A silhouette shambled from the shaft that ran toward Hank's screams. Grady shuffled toward her, awkwardly. Grady was higher than she was, covered in blood, and shirtless. The monster she'd been hunting seemed almost vulnerable. Then she saw the reflections of the glowing black-lit star chart on a long blade in his right hand and remembered what he was. Blakely shut her eyes.

"Yeah, you're awake."

Blakely's panic forced an idea into her head. She opened her eyes and locked onto Grady's.

"*Your desire is that the locks of time and space be opened?*" Blakely belted out, tapping into her high-school late-night reading sessions, tabletop roleplaying games, and drama classes. The drugs made it easier.

"Wh-what?"

"*You've made the offerings—is transport what you desire? We have observed your menhirs being constructed, and admire your purity.*"

"We can join you?"

Hank's screams reached a peak, then synced with a crunching sound, and ended. Blakely shut her eyes for a moment, then they fluttered open and she said, "*Is there another?*"

"Well, yeah...," he said, then turned toward where Hank's screams had just quieted.

"Jo!"

The crunching sounds stopped. "What?!"

"It worked! They came for us!"

Blakely saw something in Grady's rear waistband—one of their Glocks. "*Untie me, ch-child.*"

"Huh?" he asked, dazed, then nodded and cut her ankle bindings. Blakely raised her wrists to him—

"What the fuck are you doing?" Blakely heard Jolene say, closer than before.

Grady hooked his blade between her forearms.

He said, "She's one of them!"

Blakely looked toward Jolene's approaching silhouette and she became clearer—as did the "Witness Protection" sawed-off in her hands.

"Grady, step away."

Grady was tripping too hard to hear her and cut Blakely's wrists free—

Blakely whipped Grady around and fumbled for the Glock. She freed the pistol and raised it toward Jolene as she pulled Grady against herself.

Before Blakely could give a command, Jolene fired—

The blast slammed into Grady's head and upper chest, and Blakely's forearm. Blakely tensed and her thumb pressed into the release button on the Glock. Her magazine dropped from the gun, thudding into the tunnel dirt. Grady's body collapsing brought her to the ground too, his bulk weighing down on her.

"I told you I was done with him, you stupid bitch," Jolene taunted. "He kept doing my work for me, and all I had to do was send him eyes in little vacuum packs...."

Blakely couldn't take her eyes off the smoking shotgun barrel, just seconds from exploding at her now. Then she remembered—one in the chamber.

"Now, when the God Mothers really come—"

Blakely fired toward Jolene's head, but hit her neck. Jolene's blood sprayed and pulsed out. She racked the shotgun's pump action and tried to aim toward Blakely—she fired, peppering Blakely's shoulder and throwing her back onto the mine-tunnel floor.

Blakely awoke in a hospital bed, her right arm and shoulder wrapped and aching. Bea Arthur and Rue McClanahan argued on a *Golden Girls* rerun displayed on a TV mounted high in a corner of the room. She looked at a small rolling table that was next to her bed and retrieved the remote. A *Magnum, P.I.* episode started and her remote hand drooped and rested on her lap.

She didn't have the heart to turn it off.

PATRICK LOVELAND

Whoever Fights Monsters...

San Francisco, California—Present Day

"I mean, he's gotta be deformed or scarred up or something.... He'd have to be, if he thinks that weird mask makes him look *less* creepy," the bundled homeless man said, a mouthful of a double burger Blakely had given him rolling and squishing around in his mouth.

His mouth made her picture a tumble dryer, only toothy, alive, and breaking down decayed flesh and viscera instead of pulling moisture out of cloth. Then she heard crunching and screaming rising from the deep darkness at the end of the living tumbler and realized it was a tunnel.... Special Agent Blakely Tran blinked a few times and swallowed, doing her best to look with it and attentive while clearing her head enough to actually hear the man's ongoing thought stream.

"...and the weird fake eye rolls around, almost in sync with his big real one on the left, which you can see through an opening on that side. The fake one's almost like one of those compasses that's like a ball in fluid, you know what I mean? 'Cept it moves all around somehow like a real eye."

She nodded affirmative like she was paying attention, but she was really looking at a digital recorder in her raised left hand and the seconds ticking up as the man ate and spoke. She wondered how much of the smacking sounds and little appreciative moans he'd make here and there were making it onto its little storage drive.

To take her mind off that, she looked down at a half-empty bag of burgers she'd been carrying through the misty San Francisco morning and this tent city near its eastern bay shore. Would the mist or the spreading grease spots weaken the bag enough first, spilling writhing guts and ichor all over the stained concrete?

Blakely blinked a few more times and tried again to focus on her interview. She was finally starting to accept that she'd come back to active field duty too soon.

She said, "Okay, so he looks weird, I get you. When was the last time you saw him around here?"

After a thoughtful look and a few more smacks of his mouth he said, "Like yesterday? Yeah, late yesterday. Unhooked and drove off."

"Unhooked?"

"Yeah, left his trailer. I told you that. He's got a real old truck and camper trailer. Sometimes he just parks both and walks off. Sometimes, he drives it all off. This time, he unhooked and just drove the truck away."

Blakely scolded herself for missing solid info. The man they were after wasn't to be treated casually. The bodies he left were always a weird mess. She needed her edge. He was known as the "Ganesh Killer" but that name had been around long enough that most didn't remember why. All Blakely knew was that a witness years before had glimpsed a large man near the scene of one of the grizzly crimes and had called him Ganesh for some reason.

"So the trailer's still here somewhere?" Blakely asked.

The homeless man pointed toward one of the large supports for an overpass the sizable, almost welcoming tent city had formed under.

"Okay, thanks for the information," Blakely said and started to walk toward the support.

"Hey, got another burger?"

She stopped, dug her hand into the bag, and handed him two more burgers. He smiled big as he chewed the last of the first burger, already unwrapping a second as he cradled the third.

Blakely started walking and said, "Hey, you done?" to her new partner SA Maurice Saunders, who was down a row of tents holding his own burger bag while finishing an interview. He thanked his subject, then followed Blakely toward the overpass support.

Saunders said, "You got something?"

"I think I just might."

"Feels like we're closer than Vacaville, at least."

"We would've had him in Vacaville...."

"Yeah-yeah, I know. I've apologized enough, I think. Do you ever lighten up, Tran?"

"Almost never."

As they came around the cylindrical pillar, they found the parked camper trailer. It was old and its funky pastel and earth-tone paint scheme was faded and there were rusted spots all over. Its window shades were drawn and Blakely had a feeling that was for good reason.

She pictured the strangely scorched and burned remains he'd left so many times. Wasn't from fire, and she'd known that before the local MEs and their own FBI labs decided that. It was more like acid, but they still weren't sure what substance could do what had been done to the remains this killer left. Nothing about this killer was what someone like her would call remotely normal. For one thing, serial killer didn't cover it—more like serial mass murderer, or maybe even executioner.

There was never just one body—usually at least five or six on up to seventeen at the most, all in these scorched chunks and with a lot missing. Curved slices of head and face, the meat on the inner surfaces boiled and charred. Sometimes there were severed limbs and torso chunks with nothing in between. The people didn't seem to have any connection to each other either.

She'd toyed with the idea that maybe these were some kind of cartel hits, done this way to cause superstition. But there was also a trail of possibly connected killings dating back decades with very similar remains. These were from all over the country, sometimes with almost a decade in between. She'd even found some similar occurrences in other countries using some special contacts, but her superiors just wanted to deal with the here and now and catching him.

Blakely took a step toward the trailer's door and reached toward its handle. She could feel something like strong static electricity—

"You should leave him alone," a raspy voice said from against the pillar to their right.

Blakely stopped and looked at the homeless woman. She was bundled well and had the hood of her sweater over her head, strings pulled so it was tight around her face. She was sitting on a folding chair, cigarette in one hand and boiling something with a small butane camping stove propped on an overturned milk crate.

"Who? *Who* should we leave alone?" Blakely asked.

"The one who owns that trailer."

"Why?"

"He's not your concern."

Saunders said, "This guy is a killer—"

"*Saunders*," Blakely cut him off.

The woman took a drag, then leaned over her coffee or whatever it was and stirred it with a metal chopstick.

"I'm sure he's a lot of things. Doesn't mean you shouldn't leave him alone."

Blakely chuckled and said, "Do you have a *reason* for saying that?"

"He's not of this realm. Whatever he's doing here...it's not for you to judge."

Blakely and Saunders exchanged a look.

"Also, I'm pretty sure you need a warrant to look in there with no probable cause."

94

Blakely chuckled again and said, "Well, look at you."

"If you know something you're not telling...," Saunders said.

"I just told you all you need."

"You have a wonderful day, ma'am," Blakely said, gesturing for Saunders to head back to the bulk of the tent city and started that way herself. The woman just followed Blakely with her eyes until they were around the pillar and out of view.

Saunders said, "I'd heard this about you.... You let obstruction slide too much."

"That woman didn't know shit. Probably needs meds she can't afford or doesn't want to take. She believes something about our guy that's straight nonsense...and you want to lock her up?"

"She knew more than she was saying, I'd bet—"

"Agent Tran!"

They stopped and watched the burger wrecker Blakely had been interviewing last hurry toward them with another bundled-up homeless guy.

"Tell 'em, Scott...."

Scott said, "I seen that big guy who's got the truck and trailer."

"Tell 'em *where*."

"I seen him on Broadway a lot. Around there, anyway."

Saunders said, "Down by the Presidio? By the Embarcadero? Where on Broadway—be *specific*."

"By the strip clubs. Sometimes I stay in this residence hotel with a buddy. It's at Columbus and Kearny, just south'a there. I seen him around there four or five times."

Blakely said, "Wait, by the strip clubs...or that hotel?"

"I think...uh.... The strip clubs, pretty sure."

Saunders said, "Great info."

Blakely started for their car.

Burger Wrecker cleared his throat and said, "Uh...."

She stopped and looked at him. He was looking down at her hand.... She remembered the bag of burgers and tossed it to him.

"Hey, try to save one for later...."

The two men tore into the bag and Scott had one unwrapped and in his mouth already.

Blakely and Saunders had gone to their hotel downtown and changed out of their suits into casual clothes, then driven to eastern Broadway and walked up and down in the area most concentrated with strip clubs. Restaurants, an old video game arcade, and a museum dedicated to the Beats broke up the stretches of clubs with large neon signs and circulating bulbs in attention-grabbing metal housings. Girls in street clothes had offered to watch adult films with one or both of them in the back of adult video stores on the same strip. They'd politely declined. Having had no luck, they'd grabbed coffees and returned to their car.

They watched the people streaming up and down the damp sidewalks, not a large, masked weirdo killer type in the bunch.

Blakely said, "So, Saunders...."

"Yeah?"

"What else have you heard about me?"

Saunders looked over at her from the passenger seat.

"Huh?"

"You said you'd heard the 'obstruction' thing about me. What else do people say?"

"Come on...."

Blakely looked at him and said, "You opened the door."

Saunders sighed and said, "You took down the 'Ley Lines' killers in a crazy mine hideout they had near Ocotillo down south. Lost your partner. Got hurt. This is your first field work since."

"Succinct. Accurate. Well done."

"Hey, you asked."

Blakely watched a middle-aged man across the street take one of the video store girls up on her offer, letting her lead him inside by the hand. She looked back to the sidewalk on their side of the street. A good-looking dark-haired young man passed by the strip clubs and porn shops, making his way toward the old school arcade tucked between them. She noticed he had two different colored eyes—light blue and dark brown. She also noticed a couple tourist types double-take and share a surprised look upon seeing the young man's eyes. He ignored them or hadn't noticed.

Blakely thought, *He must've had to get used to people staring.... People don't much like different. Go play your* Moon Patrol *or* Paperboy *and fly free, young man.* She chuckled at her own silliness, but then thought about how this kid couldn't walk down the sidewalk looking mostly "normal" without getting looks, but their by-all-accounts-weird-looking huge suspect only caught the attention of the local homeless. She tucked the thought away, unsure if it held any significance.

"Anything else people say?"

"Uh, something about all that made you carry a nonstandard sidearm. That's it."

Blakely set her coffee in a cup holder and pulled the back of her hoodie up, producing a large pistol from a holster on the small of her back—a Colt Government Model .45. She cleared the magazine and chamber then handed it to Saunders, grip first. He examined it.

Saunders raised his eyebrows and said, "Beauty. You carry that cocked and locked?"

"Not much good if I don't. Sometimes you only have one hand," she said, loading the ejected round back into the magazine. Blakely reached her hand toward Saunders. He handed her pistol back grip first.

"Got tired of the Glock, huh?"

"Pretty much," Blakely said, then inserted the magazine and returned it to cocked and locked condition. She slid it back into its holster and covered it with her sweater.

"Hey, I'm starting to think our burger-loving friends may have accidentally misguided us."

Saunders said, "Yeah?"

"Yeah, I say we check out this hotel the one guy mentioned."

"Agreed."

Blakely started the car and drove them the short distance to the Hotel St. Paula. It was the upper three floors of a four-story building on the corner of Columbus and Kearny. A Chinatown-style donut shop and a couple bars made up the first floor.

They sat and watched the area around the building. Vehicles and people streamed through the busy intersection.

After a while just sitting and watching, Saunders said, "So, hey. Why did you switch to that .45 anyway?"

Blakely thought for a moment then said, "You ever watch *Magnum, P.I.*?"

"Nah, I was more into *Airwolf* and *Knight Rider*, as far as rerun shows go. *A-Team* was cool too."

"Eighties shows with vehicles," she said and chuckled softly. "You would've liked Magnum's Ferrari, at least. Well, Robin's or Higgins's, I guess. Anyway, that partner I had in Ocotillo.... He hipped me to *Magnum*. I got a collection of it and I've been going through it since. It's cheesy here and there, but it's actually pretty great, if I'm being honest."

Saunders smiled, scrunched his face, and said, "Okay.... What's that have to do with your sidearm?"

"Huh? Oh, nothing."

She opened her door.

Saunders said, "What's up?"

"Might as well get a feel for the place."

Saunders got out too, then followed her across the street and down around the donut shop on the corner. They passed an Indian restaurant and spa, almost missing the hotel's entrance—a steep stairwell directly to the second floor. The décor was dingy and the lights were dim. A barred security office seemed to double as the reception desk. A large, imposing-looking man with icy blue eyes eyed them knowingly from within the office, doing his best to ignore a scraggly bathrobe-wearing man's droning complaints from just next to the office window.

In a thick Slavic accent the man said, "Jerry, please. There are patrons."

Jerry eyed Blakely and Saunders then stepped aside, shutting his mouth but still blatantly staring at them.

"Would you like a room?" the man in the office said, trying to smile but it didn't suit him. His faded name badge read ARKADY.

Blakely went into her front jeans pocket for her Fed ID and noticed Arkady tense and reach under his desk. She slowed down, telegraphing more and producing it for his consideration. Saunders did the same. Arkady relaxed his half-hidden arm, but didn't change his now-guarded expression.

"Federal agents. Have you seen anyone matching this rough description," she asked, producing a folded faxed copy of a suspect sketch—large, hooded, odd mask resembling normal features.

Arkady snorted and said, "That look like half our tenants."

Saunders said, "You might want to think about that then."

"What does that mean?"

Blakely tucked the drawing back in her pocket and said, "We'd just like to take a look around then, if you don't mind."

Arkady nodded, still looking hard at Saunders.

Blakely looked down the hallways that stretched from the corner the office occupied to her left—where she noticed some communal bathrooms—and straight down past it on the right, following the outer wall of the building. She looked back and noticed a stairwell continuing up in square turns near the steps they'd come up, and decided to go up those.

"Saunders, make a sweep of this floor. I'll check upstairs and meet you back down here."

Saunders nodded but didn't seem happy as he walked past the office down the hall to the right. As Blakely mounted the stairs to the third floor, she caught Arkady picking up his phone and dialing. She also caught part of what Jerry was complaining about this time—something about "those new fuckers."

The second proper hotel floor was almost gloomier. Soft orange lights barely illuminating puke-green carpet and burgundy walls. She walked down the hallway stretching forward along the exterior wall, passing a short alcove ending in an open window with a fire escape. She kept going, passing closed doors to rooms, then came to another fire escape. As she passed it, she could see the lights circulating and blinking from the strip clubs up on the corner of Broadway.

The corner of the building was an angled section all the way up, so she came around two less sharp corners into the north hallway. She could tell from examining the layout that the building must have two air shafts from the first-floor level up to the roof. The bases were usually like narrow courtyards and vented all the rooms on each side of the internal hallways with natural air access, due to a lack of functional AC.

Due to that old venting design, the place had a constant unsettling murmur that sporadically broke into loud muffled laughter, yelling, and sometimes obvious sounds of rough fucking. She assumed the place wore a few hats, prostitution and flop house for the usually homeless who wanted to burn government checks for a few days of comfort and warm shelter—shitty shelter, but warm all the same.

Blakely looked down the first long, room-flanked hallway running down to the south side and a door at its T-intersection—the south hall she could've headed down on either floor. She followed the north hall a bit farther and reached another, parallel hallway even longer and also flanked by rooms on either side. Not seeing anything worse than dilapidated décor and musty-looking communal shower and toilet rooms, she turned back—

Jerry was standing at the corner of the first long north-south hallway, staring wide-eyed at Blakely. If it weren't for his slight frame and bathrobe, she would've been terrified. As it was, he was still quite unsettling.

He whispered, "Hey, you here to clear *them* out?"

"Who?"

He winced and motioned with his hands for her to stay quiet. She raised her eyebrows and mouthed a silent "Who?" this time. He waved her toward him. She took a few steps and he raised his hands, stopping her at the opposite corner from his at the end of the central hallway.

Jerry jabbed a finger southward and said, "Group of real odd ones stayin' here the last few weeks.... I know this place ain't much, but these fuckers are cree-py. Maybe on some new street shit, I don't know."

Blakely was close enough to the hallway that she looked down its length while listening to Jerry.

She could see one of the doors down near the south end open a bit, only black visible inside. Then she saw what looked like two small circles in the darkness glinting off the hallway ceiling bulb, reflecting it strangely. She took a half step back, letting only her left eye remain in line with the mouth of the dim hallway. The circles moved, catching the light again—eyes. The doorway creaked open a bit more and another set of the weird eyes caught the light, and now silhouettes of the people were barely visible. Then Blakely saw someone doing what she was doing—staying just out of obvious sight at the far end of the hallway, only one of its eyes partially visible.

Blakely couldn't tell if that eye could see her, but she felt a wave of pure ineffable fear wash over her. This could be like all her other recent hallucinations or whatever they were—"Power of Suggestion," and all that. *Or...what if those "Ley Lines" killers did something to me...?* She felt a chill, but steeled herself.

She whispered, "We're not here for this. Your local vice cops can handle this...."

"Yeah, lotta good they've been."

Jerry shook his head and headed back around the hall corner out of sight. Blakely realized she didn't want to walk past the mouth of the hallway. She stepped back, closed her eyes, then opened them and walked past it as casually as she could.

"Jerry," she whispered.

As she came around the corner, she saw Jerry entering his room, then closing his door. *Shit.* Blakely kept going down the hall toward the stairs slowing a bit as she reached the junction with the south hallway. She saw a form in her peripheral vision as she passed toward the stairs.

A tall, subtly misshapen woman with mottled, sickly skin and a mess of thickly clumped hair leaned against the hallway wall with her back to Blakely—had to be the owner of the eye she'd seen looking down the hall, hidden like she was. Just before Blakely's vision was obscured by the stairwell corner, the woman looked back toward her without turning, her eyes catching the lights the same way as the silhouettes in the dark rooms.

Blakely caught herself skipping down the steps two and three at a time, a feeling of dread and impending attack hastening her descent. She felt like a scared seven year old again and couldn't look back up the stairs as she rounded them down onto the first hotel floor and Arkady's strangely welcoming presence in the security office.

"Seems clear," Saunders said to her left and she couldn't help jolting back. "You alright, Tran?"

"Yeah-yeah, let's go."

They stepped toward the steep stairwell down to the street and their descent was blocked by a blonde woman in a skirt-suit and a man even larger than Arkady in a dark turtleneck and jacket behind her.

"Hello, officers. What brings you here this evening?" the woman said in an ever-so-pleasant tone and Slavic accent.

Saunders waited for Blakely to speak but noticed her uncharacteristic silence and said, "This was a routine check as a part of an ongoing investigation," half-lying impressively. The woman glared at him but kept her face in a façade of pleasant cooperation.

Blakely sized up the woman and muscle and glanced back over her shoulder toward the security office, noticing Arkady had left it and was standing behind them back by its door, one of his hands behind his back. She had seven shots in her Colt and figured she'd need all of them if things got hectic.

Smiling, the woman said, "Surely, you need a warrant to be here?"

Blakely said, "Not in the halls and stairwells. Your offices, your storage rooms, your *tenants'* rooms—sure, warrant needed."

"Are the hallways and stairwells to your satisfaction, officers?"

"Agents. Federal agents. Clear a path, or you'll be charged with obstructing justice. Or would you like me to pat down you and your men here? I can't imagine they're unarmed, and who knows what we'd find on their persons. Or yours, for that matter."

The woman said nothing and narrowed her eyes. Blakely took a step toward the woman and lifted the back of her hoodie, grasping the Colt's grip.

In Russian, Blakely whispered, <<*If you don't step out of my way, I'll put one in your fucking head....*>>

100

The woman lost her composure for a moment and from her expression Blakely could feel Arkady confirming the woman's suspicions of Blakely being armed and ready from his view of her back and pistol. The woman blinked a couple times, then stepped up out of the stairwell, motioning for her muscle to let them by.

Blakely descended past the big man flattened against the wall, who eyed them with a barely contained murderous glare. Saunders met his look as he went around him, then hurried down after Blakely to the sidewalk. She was strutting past the donut shop already.

Saunders almost ran into a huge, rancid-smelling man stepping out of the shop, then picked up his pace to catch up to Blakely. He looked back as he rounded the corner after her and saw that the man's hood draped down over his big head as he fed a handful of donut holes from a bag into his mouth somewhere under the shade of the hood.

"Hey, Tran!" Saunders said, hoofing it after her.

"What?"

"Seriously—what just transpired in there?"

"Honestly?"

"Yeah-the-*fuck,* honestly!"

Blakely unlocked the car door with the remote, opened the driver door, and sat down inside. Saunders got in the passenger seat and stared at her.

"Tran, what happened?"

"We almost got merked and snuck by the Russian mob, I'm thinking.... Or an affiliated group?"

"Oh, *bullshit!* They wouldn't kill two federal agents for no good reason!"

Blakely looked at him and said, "I think they have a damn good reason."

"We're here looking for a serial killer, Tran! This has nothing to do...with...with...."

She looked back toward the corner below the hotel and saw what Saunders saw.

The huge, bundled man who Saunders had almost collided with had the large hood of his coat almost obscuring the strange mask he wore over his face. He was real big naturally, but Blakely could make out obvious bulky parts from things under his thickly layered clothing.

"Oh, fuck you...," Blakely said, starting to doubt her grasp of reality again.

Saunders said, "You see him too, right?"

They watched him shovel donut holes up under his mask, giving the illusion he was pushing them into his neck, due to the mask's face-emulating attributes.

"I'd ask you the same."

Saunders said, "What's going on here?"

She shook her head and said, "I don't know."

Their target finished the last of the donut holes, crumpled the bag into a ball, and tossed it toward a trashcan, where it bounced off the lip and rolled

101

away. Unfazed, the hooded figure jumped up, grabbing nooks in the building's outer wall and hauling himself up, then hooking the lowest level of the fire escape and climbing onto it. He climbed the outside of the fire escape with surprising and unsettling agility, and they lost sight of him as he climbed onto the roof.

Blakely heard Saunders groan then exhale sharply and watched him rub his face hard with both hands. She had no idea what he was thinking. He dropped his hands to his lap and said, "Trunk?"

They locked eyes.

"You sure?"

"Whatever's going on, this hotel needs new management. New tenants too, I'm thinking...."

Blakely couldn't stop her nervous laugh from escaping and turned the car key, radioed in a call to the SFPD using Fed codes, then shut the car off and got out. She and Saunders went to the trunk, opened it, put on gloves, tactical vests with ammo holders, FBI lanyard badges over those, and took out their big guns—a tactical shotgun for Saunders and a semi-auto 9mm carbine for Blakely. They checked their weapons and shut the trunk, lowering them as they hurried back to the entry stairwell past the donut shop.

Saunders covered Blakely as she ascended the stairs from the street, then she took overwatch position as Saunders followed her up.

"Office is empty," Blakely said.

They could hear yelling on the floor above as they swept their weapons around down the empty hallways. The voices were loud enough that tenants were poking their heads out of their doors or standing in the hallways. Blakely covered as Saunders started up the stairs, then followed a moment later.

As they reached the third floor, Blakely could hear that the argument was coming from the central hallway Jerry had warned her about. She kept going down the hallway near the outer wall that Jerry's room was on and stopped, taking overwatch around the crook of the hall. Jerry opened his door to see what the noise was about and almost jumped at the sight of the heavily armed Blakely and Saunders in the hall.

He said, "Fuckin' A...," and pumped a thumbs up a few times as he backed into his room again then shut and locked his door.

Saunders bounded up to and past Blakely with his shotgun angled down and to the side, but ready. He took position at the next crook, aiming down the north hallway as she leapfrogged past him and took position at the corner where Jerry was when he'd followed her up earlier. She crouched low, weapon angled at the floor and all but her right eye tucked behind the edge. She hand-signaled for Saunders to tuck in high behind her. He did, and also looked down the hall with one eye from a few feet above her.

The Russian woman was standing near the end of the hallway, Arkady and the other muscle behind her. The odd tall woman Blakely had seen looking down the hall at her earlier was once again leaning against a wall facing away.

She looked like she was too heavy to stand upright, but not from fat. The women argued in Russian. The odd woman's voice was gravelly and deep—Blakely felt the fear again, just from hearing it.

Saunders whispered, "You speak some Russian, right?"

"Yeah. The mob bitch is mad these weirdos are attracting attention.... Something about a deal above her head she'd rather not have to honor."

Saunders looked around from his tucked position and said, "Where's our guy?"

The argument grew in intensity, the mob woman becoming more animated and making swift pointing and swiping motions toward the big, strange one. The big one barked a couple strange things that were beyond Blakely's knowledge of Russian, or weren't in it. The mob woman stepped back, then pulled out a large, short revolver. The big woman whispered, hissing something unintelligible, and Blakely could have sworn the lights in the hallway dimmed. The big one pushed off from the wall with a thick, ropy arm and rose up from her slouching position.

The mob woman fired her revolver, cracking the other woman's head open partway and dropping her sizable form to the hall floor.

Blakely and Saunders both called out, "Federal agents!"

Saunders sidestepped to the other corner with his shotgun raised and took cover again; they both aimed their guns down at the mob woman and her muscle. Arkady and the other man pulled out Skorpion machine pistols and Arkady stepped forward and put himself between his boss and the agents.

Blakely started, "Drop your weapons! We won't hesitate to fire...!" but her words were drowned out by inhuman yowls of sadness and anger from within the rooms lining the hallway. The doors were flung or broken open and almost two dozen misshapen men and women with those odd reflective eyes and heavy, slouching bodies burst out of the rooms. They hissed and wailed as they filled the length of hallway closer to the Russians.

Arkady and the other two opened fire on the group, their bullets tearing into the closer ranks while the woman chose targets for her other five revolver shots. Before Blakely or Saunders could think of what to do next, the Russians were out of ammo and the rest of the slavering horde descended upon them, literally tearing them apart.

Saunders looked at Blakely. She shook her head, confused and unsure what to do. They'd witnessed a murder, but the savagery these beastly people were committing in return was more than she could process. The savages at the far end of the hallway were *sharing* the pieces they'd wrenched out of sockets or ripped from abdomens and chests....

Saunders said, "Wh-what do we do?"

Blakely stood up, still in cover, and fired her carbine twice into the ceiling near the end of the hallway above the ghastly human-shaped things—hoping with that angle to prevent stray rounds going through and hitting someone who

103

didn't deserve to get shot. Most of them stopped and looked back at them, eyes glinting as their jagged, blood-smeared-and-oozing maws hung open.

Blakely said, "Federal agents! An army of police and feds are on the way—surrender or we will have to use *deadly force*!"

Emboldened by her words, Saunders said, "Hell yeah, we will...."

The beasts' eyes all shimmered and flashed as they examined the two agents at the end of the hall. Then Blakely saw the savages the Russians had shot picking themselves up from the bloody hallway floor and turning toward them too. Then the big woman who'd been shot in the head did the same, hauling herself up and slouching over and leaning against the wall again. She was taller than any of the others, and her head was still broken open. Her reflective eyes were too far apart now to look even close to natural, but they both locked onto Blakely's and she bellowed a rumbling, guttural call to her fellow savages. They returned it like coyotes might, but there was nothing canine about these people—they looked human enough, but they were something *other*. Blakely's acceptance of that was being fought by her fears for her own sanity, but she knew.

The savages halfway down the hall started toward them, then the next closest group, all howling those otherworldly calls.

Blakely yelled, "Stop or we fire!"

She heard shattering glass and splintering wood from one of the rooms closest to them on their right. It sounded like something huge crashing in from one of the long airshafts between rows of rooms—

The door of that room broke open and apart, the large form of their Ganesh Killer busting out through it and standing fast on his big legs. The savages stopped in place and the big woman down the hall actually gasped in a moment of obvious recognition.

Saunders said, "Freeze!" but it sounded almost more out of confusion than authority to Blakely.

Ganesh turned halfway back toward Saunders and raised his gloved hand in his direction. A pale green light flashed from its open palm—

Saunders was thrown back against the other wall of the north hall like he'd been two-hand pushed, and he was knocked unconscious. Blakely looked from Saunders to Ganesh—who had turned at the waist and raised his other hand toward her. She glimpsed his real eye through the hole in his "normal face" mask, big and black as a shark's. The intricate fake eye in the mask almost looked more normal, rolling as the homeless interviewee had said, in sync somehow and in a liquid-filled encasement.

"No!" Blakely said, lowering her carbine and raising her other hand out of instinct.

Ganesh paused, maybe out of surprise, then turned back to the hall full of savage crazies. He pulled what looked like a foot-long spike with a clear ball at the top from inside his coat, raised his arm, and flung it down into the floor in front of him with a *thunk*. Fluid in the ball atop the dagger bubbled, then

104

swirled with black streaks and flashed even brighter than the glove. Blakely saw and felt waves of distortion emanate from it. As the visible energy rolled out from the ball in all directions, it bathed the savages at the front of the mob. They started wailing but it sounded more pained than angry.

After the energy flowed through them, the human savages came apart—what looked human about them, anyway. Their bodies jerked and spasmed, then grew outward, the decayed human bodies they'd been wearing shredding and spraying their putrid fluids all over the hall. Where there'd been arms and legs, there were many appendages of less obvious purpose tucked and folded against the warped trunk of body. These stretched and unfurled, breaking ribs and throwing out organs. Some were like segmented limbs but less symmetrical in shape and placement, and some thinner and longer with more fluid movements like slithering tentacles. The creatures' heads kept the flashing human eyes, but as the chunks and flaps of human flesh came free, more eyes were visible—one obvious above and between the two that had almost passed for human, and smaller ones on the bumpy folds of what was under the cheek flesh that was sloughing off.

Blakely's mind was already near gone from all of this, but the part doing her the most damage was the triangular eye placement. The Ley Lines killers had drilled out the foreheads of their victims, placing a third eyeball from another set of victims into the hole. A powerful wave of apophenia or possibly recognition of some unknowable connection hit her and she slid down the corner of the wall to her knees, then dropped onto her lower legs and just watched the madness in the hallway unfold with her carbine resting in limp hands on her thighs.

As the arcane energy rolled through the hallway, each of the creatures writhed and burst out of their human disguises like squishy, crunchy cocoons. Almost two dozen amorphous otherworldly beasts clicked and hissed and wailed as their sickening rebirths were completed. No two were exactly alike. Even the eye arrangements were off from creature to creature, but the three major ones were always present.

The big "woman"'s transformation was the most painful, and once she was done, she stood tall and stretched all of her various limbs and shook. She was covered with glowing runes and pictograms Blakely didn't recognize from human history. She also had glowing ampules of different colored fluids stitched into the glistening surfaces of what served her as a torso.

Through the haze of draining sanity, it occurred to Blakely this bigger creature must be some sort of sorceress or witch. Blakely almost laughed, thoughts of tabletop roleplaying sessions in her adolescence filling her head. She also realized why they'd always found such odd body parts in the wake of Ganesh's slaughter—the cast off disguises of these things he must be *hunting*. Blakely's head swirled, filling with so many strange thoughts and ideas....

105

The witch creature wailed her loudest wail yet, and flicked some warped appendages toward Ganesh. The disoriented creatures found purpose again, starting down the hallway toward the hulking killer.

Ganesh crossed his hands over his bulky chest and into his big coat, then took out two glowing, rune-etched weapons—a three-foot parang-style machete and a forward curving, ball-tipped war club carved from one large piece of something like jade. He crouched halfway, assuming a ready stance.

As the first few creatures rushed at Ganesh, he dodged their swipes and whipping attacks, ducking, sidestepping, and rolling. He hacked at them with the parang and smashed their heads and chests with the ball of his club—the creatures came apart or crumpled inward, then disintegrated. They screeched as they exploded in clouds of glowing ash—then these sucked into their own centers, vanishing.

Blakely counted seven gone in the first fight. She decided Ganesh was good at this.

The Witch must have felt the same, and started chanting, then flicking and swishing several of her larger limbs and their digits around. The movements cut the air with glowing curves and angles, a sigil burning impossibly in the air for just a moment upon completion of her gesticulations. What happened next pushed Blakely all the way over the edge she'd been teetering on for what seemed like an hour, but was more like three minutes.

What amounted to a few Olympic swimming pools worth of dark fluid dropped out of the entire third-floor ceiling. It came down like a solid wall of water, crashing down onto everything and filling the hallways. Blakely was slammed onto the floor then thrown and spun around like she'd bailed on a huge wave at the beach.

A distant part of her that still grasped at reality remembered Saunders and she panicked, thrashing for a surface she only hoped was there—she couldn't find one. She beat at the ceiling of the hallway, already out of breath. Through the murky liquid, she could see tiny blinking lights.... *Strip clubs!* Blakely swam toward the lights with all she had and reached a third-floor window. She pulled her legs in front of her and kicked down repeatedly as air depravation made her vision fade.

The window shattered and the fluid rushed out, slamming her against the window and almost impaling her on the larger glass chunks. She sucked in air greedily as she held herself away from the glass with the last of her strength. She could hear Saunders coughing and sputtering somewhere back to her left, then sirens approaching.

When the fluid was low enough, Blakely pushed off the wall and trudged through it back to the long hallway. Saunders was half conscious and moaning, but looked okay. Ganesh was halfway down it, liquid cascading off his bulky form as he waded to a large hole torn into the hall ceiling by the creatures. He seemed to examine it a moment before tucking his weapons and climbing up into it out of sight.

Blakely knew a trap when she saw one. She hurried through the last of the liquid, finding Saunders's shotgun before her own carbine, swooped it up, and ran for the stairwell they'd come up earlier. Jerry opened his door as she passed, looked at her drenched and dripping form, and said, "Jesus, did you hit a fucking sewer main?"

"Yeah, *totally!*" was all she could think to say as she booked past.

She reached the stairs and hopped up them two and three at a time, reaching the fourth floor and hearing sounds of fighting and catching eerie light flashes from the corner of the long hallway the creatures had forced their way up to. She remembered Saunders had pumped and primed the shotgun earlier and just hoped the water hadn't messed it up.

There were less than ten creatures left in the hall by the time Blakely reached it, but in the process of killing several more, Ganesh had begun to lose. The Witch was also cutting smaller sigils in the air and bolts of weird light were streaking toward Ganesh, cutting and piercing him.

Blakely advanced into the hall and fired the shotgun, aiming as far wide of Ganesh as she could. She peppered his right shoulder and haunches a bit, but hit a few of the creatures hard and bought Ganesh a few steps of retreat—but it wasn't enough and with another wail, the Witch sent every creature left standing on a mad rush at the bleeding, tired hunter. Blakely couldn't fire the shotgun without hitting Ganesh too. In the melee, his hood was shredded and his mask was thrown off his head. The name he'd been given became clear to Blakely now.

The big man's head was a chilling mix of deformity and mutation. His big shark eye was the only natural looking part of his face and head. His other eye was under layers of speckled translucent flesh, which also made up his most obvious abnormal features—bulbous growths under the eye that drooped down, obscuring most of the mouth and curled into a bunching of tendrils, the thickest one resembling an elephant's trunk.

Blakely knew she was profoundly out of the loop—on an almost cosmic level, apparently—but from what she'd seen in the last ten minutes, she knew Ganesh was her horse in this race. She aimed the shotgun at the Witch and fired, pumped, and fired again until it was empty. The Witch swatted the pellets away each time like glowing gnats.

"Shit!"

Empty but heavy, Blakely grabbed the shotgun by its hot barrel with her gloved hands and used it as a club of her own, stepping to the closest creature and beating its head. Amazing herself more than anyone, she'd killed it in a few angry *thumps*. Before she could do that again, another of the creatures backhanded her, throwing her back down the hall.

The creatures descended upon Ganesh, using their sharpest limbs to gouge and impale him over and over. Ganesh tried to fight, but soon dropped his weapons to the hallway floor and went limp. Blakely saw something like a smile spread on the witch creature's face.

"No!"

The Witch made a clicking noise to her underlings and they turned their attention to Blakely. She dragged herself back down the hall away from the creatures on her butt—but hit the south hall's wall sooner than she expected to. The creatures undulated and chittered and glared at her with three big eyes as they approached. She knew she was dead....

Until strange sounds and vibrations came out of Ganesh's body. The Witch clicked at her brood and they turned back toward the fallen hunter's form. The body shifted, rising and falling from side to side—then seized up and began convulsing.

Ganesh's body bulged strangely, the abdomen growing huge like big balloons of viscera straining to hold their contents—and burst open, spilling muck and organic chaos all over the hall. Dozens of eyes and jagged-toothed mouths opened all over the spreading amorphous mass of animated glop. It was a living blob of madness.

The thing that was Ganesh spread, pouring and throwing itself onto the rest of the creatures near Blakely. It enveloped them and ate them away into itself so quickly.... If Blakely hadn't been so frightened and confused, she'd probably have vomited on herself.

Having consumed the brood, the Ganesh blob fluttered then stretched and pulled itself toward the Witch—who seemed frightened now too. It backed down the hall away from the oncoming mass, then seemed to think of something and started to create one of the glowing sigils in the air. The hallway ceiling above Ganesh's blob form started to glow with haunting light and when Blakely looked up, she knew that whatever was coming was bad all around.... She could see another place through the light, with alien moons in an unknown sky, and swaying, towering spires all around made of what looked like fused black bones.

Blakely remembered the .45, still in its holster against the small of her back. She propped herself up against the wall, took out the pistol, thumbed off its safety, and took aim. She could barely see the Witch due to the weird light bathing the whole hallway. She decided Ganesh could obviously take care of himself, blob of madness he'd become, and fired all seven shots in quick succession toward the rough area she thought the Witch's head was.

Blakely pulled up to the tent city in the light of the early morning and parked. It had taken all night to get Saunders sent to the hospital in an ambulance, then endure six different VIPs' questions, *then* the altered versions of the questions, meant to trip her up. By the time they were done, her own highly altered version of the truth—which she'd stuck to expertly—had kept her from knee-jerk imprisonment.... But she wasn't sure she was a federal agent anymore.

Ganesh, whatever it was, had taken the opportunity to eat the Witch upon Blakely providing distraction with her pistol shots, breaking the sigil—or concentration needed to create it—and closing the hallway ceiling portal—*or whatever it was*. Ganesh's meal was messy and mean, and Blakely almost— *almost*—felt bad for the Witch.

She turned the car off and stepped out, then walked through the tent city toward the support Ganesh's trailer had last been resting near, an object wrapped in her hoodie and tucked under her arm.

Of course the trailer was gone....

But the smoking woman wasn't. She looked up from another boiling can of something on her camping stove and lit what was probably her fifth cigarette of the day already.

The woman said, "You realize the wisdom in my advice yet?"

Blakely unwrapped her hoodie and showed the woman what it had been covering—

Ganesh's mask.

"Sure...but I'm choosing to ignore the fuck out of it."

TOO MANY EYES

San Diego, California—Present Day

Sylvie finished rolling a cigarette and ran her tongue along the adhesive strip on the paper, facing mostly away from Margot in the box office behind her but hoping the other young woman was looking her way. Twenty or so feet separated the two of them and Sylvie was sitting on the edge of the sidewalk, but she knew Margot could see her well enough if she wanted to. More than anything, she just needed Margot to still want to watch her at all.

After rolling the prepped adhesive over and smoothing it along the smoke's length, Sylvie lit it and took a long drag. As she exhaled, she scanned the east- and westbound traffic for anything resembling a delivery vehicle.

Sylvie looked back at the box office over her shoulder and caught what could've been Margot looking back down at one of her beloved manga books after gazing longingly in Sylvie's direction—_could've_ been.

Margot read book after book of those Japanese comics, from super-gory horror stories and dark fantasy epics to the cutest and silliest ones. One of the few Sylvie had flipped through was about adorable little frog people in some kind of opposing faux-Soviet military forces, with cold weather hats to match. Fun but really odd and wacky.

Sylvie had been called a blerd more than once, but more in the eclectic music taste, grindhouse-obscure-cult movie way, and less so in the comics and anime way. She wondered if that made her more hipster-y and less nerdy. Either way, after high school, she hadn't kept up with many of her friends. She'd never felt entirely comfortable with their various expectations of her. The

112

minute she felt like she was unimportant to someone—or worse, an amusing novelty— she was done.

A rusty old van swooped out of the eastbound lane and broke Sylvie out of her speculation, coming her way fast enough on the sidewalk edge that she pulled herself up to her feet and took a few steps back onto the sidewalk until she was almost under an unlit theater marquee that hung over it. She'd dropped her smoke in the evasive maneuver and saw the van's front-right tire roll over it as it came to a stop in front of the theater.

Mirrored aviator sunglasses over the driver's eyes glinted through the dirty windshield and side window, making it hard for Sylvie to tell if he'd even seen her. He put the van in park, got out, and went around to its back doors.

Something about the look of him and his movements kept Sylvie from complaining about his driving. He also wore dark coveralls, boots, and a trucker hat with an LA movie studio logo on it, but something seemed off. She approached the back of the van as he was opening the doors there.

"Hey, man. You droppin' off our print?"

Instead of answering, the man took two heavy octagonal metal ICC film shipping boxes out of the van and slammed them down on the sidewalk. They looked ancient. Sylvie was no stranger to old metal print cases in her line of work, but these had layers of old info stickers, none of which were readable at this point.

Sylvie looked for anything like a recent tag on the cases.

"Should be called *Too Many Eyes*...."

The delivery driver took a clipboard from inside the van and handed it to her without saying a word. Sylvie took it and scanned the info—*TOO MANY EYES*, it was. The slip was a sign-in/sign-out setup with several signatures above their theater's scrawled name—the Rem, short for the Remington District it was at the heart of—to the left of the in/out columns.

The driver handed her a pen. She took it and ran her hand down the page to line up with the sign-in for the Rem.

Sylvie hesitated a moment as she noticed a subtle difference in the signatures on the sign-in and sign-out columns. Images filled her head of opening the cases in the projection booth, only to reveal improvised explosives—*bye-bye to Sylvie, bye-bye to the Rem*.

She sneaked another look at the driver over her thick-rimmed glasses and noticed intricate sleeve tattoos peeking out from the ends of his coverall sleeves, and more crawling a bit up from his collar and running up the back of his neck—both glimpses struck her as something like tendrils of black ivy vines. She pictured poisonous gas spraying from contraptions built into the film cases this time.

"Cult classic, this one."

Sylvie flinched a bit and almost dropped the pen in her hand at the sound of the driver's voice. Nothing overtly strange about it, but it unsettled her just the same. She looked at the print cases again, took one last look at the driver, then signed the prints into the Rem's temporary custody. She handed him back the clipboard and pen—his sleeves crept up a bit as he reached for them and she saw more of his sleeve tattoos. There were eyes in among the tendrils, and they didn't look so much like ivy anymore—almost like the design had changed since she'd first seen it a moment before.

"Haven't seen it."

"Oh, you are in for a real treat. Has a strong following. Infamous, almost. Should bring in a packed house."

"All weekend, we hope."

"Yeah, that's what I meant. Hey, enjoy it," he said, then slammed the van doors, walked to the front, and got in.

Sylvie picked up the print cases by their handles and turned toward the theater entrance.

She heard a window rolling down, then, "Hey...."

Sylvie turned back.

"That's a real old print. I recommended you take extra care when you build it, then only screen it when you have scheduled showings. Skip the check screening."

"Sure, man. Will do."

"Later."

She nodded and half smiled in reply. He put the van in drive and pulled away onto the two-lane strip.

Sylvie stole a glance at the box office as she carried the print cases into the theater. Margot was reading one of her manga books like Sylvie had thought, but it was possible there was a hint of peripheral side-eye being thrown her way too—*possible.*

She passed a row of five poster cases on the wall across from concessions, currently all displaying posters for their upcoming Tim Curry tribute event. They'd booked a video projector rental to show *The Worst Witch*, then prints for *Muppet Treasure Island* and *Clue* in the evening. Then later, director's cut of *Legend*, and around midnight, finished off with a full midnight performance/screening of *The Rocky Horror Picture Show*. They were all looking forward to it, especially Margot.

Juana at the concessions counter nodded toward the box office.

"She'll be okay."

Sylvie shrugged and said, "We'll see...."

Aaron, their new ticket-taker, was sweeping up popcorn near concessions—probably so he could be near Juana, Sylvie assumed, from how few pieces he seemed to actually be sweeping into his lobby broom and dustpan at a time. He looked from Sylvie to Juana.

"What'd I miss?"

Juana said, "Everything, apparently."

Sylvie was relieved to find that the cases held only film reels and couldn't be any more harmless.

She'd already compiled and placed a trailer ring around a "brain" controller module on the middle of a projector tree's three central platters and was prepping the first reel of *TOO MANY EYES* on a build table. Russ had finally replaced an aging change-over two projector system they'd always had with a less ancient tree-and-platter one-projector setup about three years before.

Sword of Doom ran from the top platter, through the projector—where it was projected onto the single screen the Rem had, for the viewing pleasure of a half-full house of cinema enthusiasts—and was collected down on the bottom platter, while also ending up ready for another showing as soon as it finished, if necessary.

Sylvie used the middle platter to build whenever possible, and she'd had the forethought to thread it so she could this fine Thursday evening.

Russ sat at a metal table in the corner of the projection booth that was the closest thing to an office he had, and went through his records. He'd grumble once in a while or say something to himself Sylvie had no context to understand, and could barely hear anyway over the clattering and whirring of the big projector system. Once in a while, he'd stop and look around at one or more of almost two dozen WWII-era prop-plane models he'd been building since childhood, now hung from the projection booth ceiling. Some people got so used to something that was always around that, even if they loved it, it just blended in after a while. Not Russ.

These things had always comforted her, and did today. But she was still a little troubled and couldn't place why. It wasn't just Margot.

Sylvie prepped her first splice, connecting the tail of the trailer ring with the head of the first feature reel, and caught herself being even more careful with the splicer than usual—then she remembered why.

"Hey...."

"Yeah?" Russ looked over from the source of his mumbling.

"The delivery guy said something weird I'd never heard before."

"What's that?"

"He said not to screen it after we build it. Said it's so old we should just be more careful, then show when we need to."

"Ha! Fuck that. Like I'm gonna spend what I spent on getting that print from them with short notice—I'd never even heard of that rental house *or* film before yesterday, and now they're a big, fat bill more than anything else. So I'm gonna get that print for more than I should've paid...then just *hope* it's all good when it's show time?"

Sylvie chuckled and said, "Yeah, pretty much what I was thinking, but I told him *sure.*"

"We're screening that damn thing tonight, like usual. The rest of the crew is expecting a free showing as always anyway. One of this place's few perks."

She made the first splice and lined everything up then started running the synced build table, sending the first reel through its own small set of angled and aligned rollers to be collected on the spinning platter.

"Why'd you have to get it that way anyway?"

Russ looked back down at his records.

"Your aunt Shondel had announced it way, way back...when she was still with us."

Sylvie blinked a couple times at the mention of that and they were both silent for a long moment.

"When I took the booking over, I guess I'd missed it hadn't been scheduled to actually be here in time, or at all. Stupid."

"Not stupid. It was a lot to t-t-take on. Especially after—"

Russ sighed. "You haven't stammered in a while. Sorry.... Let's not talk about that, alright? Hey, what's going on with you and Margot? Something seems off there."

"You'd have to ask *her.*"

Sylvie watched the print thickening on the platter as it rushed up from the whirring build table and noticed an odd shimmering to its surface. Reflections and the like were common, as projection prints had glossy protective coatings, but this was almost like a distortion of the light around the layering film—

"Don't be short with *me* about it."

"Sorry. Just not sure myself, I geh-guess."

Russ looked over at Sylvie, seeming to balance her obvious discomfort with his desire to counsel. "Well, don't push her away like you did with Chelsea."

"Wow, thanks. Really needed to think about *her* right now tuh-too."

Sylvie could tell her uncle was still looking at her and tried to fight off returning his gaze, then finally slowed the build table down some so she could look away from her work. He raised his eyebrows and nodded.

"Told you the same about her at the time too. Funny thing...."

"Okay, okay. I know. I'll try."

117

As Sylvie came down the booth stairs after *Sword of Doom* had finished and all the theater-goers had left, she heard the front doors rattling and the jangling of keys. She reached the base of the stairs and saw Margot looking out the glass doors, holding the keys in the lock. Sylvie just watched her a moment, trying to think of something cute and/or witty to say.

Juana came out of the theater into the lobby with a broom and dustpan and Margot looked back toward the sound—then caught Sylvie eyeing her. An expression Sylvie couldn't decipher washed over Margot's face before she bottled it and looked out the doors again.

Sylvie looked over at Juana, who mouthed a silent "sorry" and frowned. Sylvie shrugged it off.

"Was the new guy in there cleaning with you?"

"Nah, we sent him to the taco shop."

"New usher—new *Burrito Bitch*," Margot said from the doors.

Juana said, "Burrito Bitch is no more...."

"Long live Burrito Bitch," Sylvie finished and she and Juana chuckled. She'd made it through two *B*s back to back, so she felt like she'd gotten a handle on her stuttering again. Her uncle had just really broadsided her, and in a couple ways.

Margot half-smiled as she kept watch, but Sylvie knew she shouldn't get too comfortable.

Sylvie threaded *TOO MANY EYES* through the projector and onto a take-up ring on the top platter of the tree. Second nature. Smooth. She did not miss the changeover system they used to use at all.

She looked over at her uncle. Still poring over the theater's books and grumbling.

"Hey, did you put in a taco shop order?"

He chuckled. "I wish. Doesn't do me much good, recently, with how much hot sauce I'd want to put on it. Popcorn and a hot dog should be safe, though."

"Better go get that poppin', then. Ready to throw some light over here."

Russ looked over at her. He seemed so tired. Forced a smile anyway.

"Good call, chief."

Sylvie pressed the starter on the projector and it surged to life, whirring and clacking.

"You've got until the snipe and trailer rings end...."

Russ laughed. "Understood."

He stuck a pencil halfway over the page he was on as a marker and closed a ledger he'd been scanning. Got up and headed down to the concession area.

Sylvie watched the projector until the clear leader became the black film of the trailer ring. She threw a dowser open letting the light from the projector lamp travel through the film and down onto the screen in the theater.

She'd done all of that hundreds of times, but something about this felt different. Strange. That odd look the film had when she'd been building the print was even more obvious with the brilliant light going through it in the projector.

"Need new glasses...," she said to herself and chuckled.

Down in the theater she saw silhouettes of the others taking seats and remembered Margot.

Sylvie left the booth and descended the stairs into the concessions area. Russ was finishing up his hot dog prep and had a big bag of buttered popcorn next to him. He nodded, grabbed his popcorn and they entered the theater.

Russ took a seat in the middle of the back row. Sylvie would never understand why, but that was his favorite spot.

Margot and Juana sat a couple seats apart in the middle of the theater's middle row.

Aaron was one row closer to the screen in front of them taking a paper-wrapped burrito out of a brown bag. He squinted at it. Frowned. He turned it in his hand until light from a preview for the film *Amelie* started on the screen and made the handwriting on it visible.

"Uh...bean and cheese with sour cream, I think."

Sylvie said, "Margot's," then winced. She caught Margot giving her a side-eye, but Margot reached for the burrito that was indeed hers and took it. Was that a little smile again?

"*Pollo asado?*"

Juana leaned toward Aaron with her hand out and claimed her meal, a small buttered popcorn already squeezed into her cup holder as a side.

"*S* and *T?*"

Margot finished chewing a bite and swallowed. "*Surf* and *turf*, dude. Sylvie's."

Sylvie smiled to herself but quickly secured and contained it.

Aaron took the last burrito out of the bag and sat down.

Juana leaned forward again. "Hey, you got green sauce, right?"

Sylvie said, "Red for me."

Aaron rifled through the bag and pulled out a few small lidded plastic cups, examined them in the projected light, and distributed them, along with a few napkins for each of the young women. He stood, now backlit by a trailer for *Miller's Crossing*, and raised the last of them in the air to get Russ's attention. Russ raised a handful of his own, chewing a big bite of his hot dog. Aaron sat down and finally unwrapped and tore into his own burrito.

A trailer for the original French version of *Martyrs* showed as they ate, followed by one featuring Isaac Hayes as *Truck Turner*. Then finished off with *Vampire Hunter D*.

Aaron said, "*D* is rad and all, but we should show *Urotsukidōji* here..."

Margot chuckled. "Totally."

Russ leaned forward in his seat. "What's that?"

124

Sylvie turned back toward him. "It's like...anime tentacle demon porn, but with a story."

"Yeah, surprisingly strong story and characters, but it really goes there with the monster rape," Margot said.

Russ frowned. "And you guys aren't against that?"

Sylvie shook her head. "It's so fucking over the top and ridiculous in how it does it that I'm not offended, myself. The second series and film edit of it start with a goddamn Nazi-Demon-Rape-Machine that opens a Hellmouth and kills all the Nazis. Hard not to enjoy it, personally."

Russ said, "Would we sell a lot of tickets?"

Margot chuckled. "Probably, but we might need Aaron to mop up all the jizz."

"Nasty.... Why me?"

Juana laughed. "It was your idea, right?"

"Yeah, I guess that makes sense."

The trio of young ladies laughed and Russ sat back in his seat, mulling it over.

A "Thank You For Actually Coming To A Theater And Not Streaming TV Shows For Twelve More Hours" snipe played—at least that's how Sylvie always thought of it—then the screen went black.

After a long silence with no changes in the uniform darkness, tiny dots and glinting slivers appeared in the center of the screen, pulsing and growing. As they grew, Sylvie could see they were tiny, pulsing eyes of all shapes and colors. They spread, filling the screen to the left and right in an angled way, like the audience was looking down a narrow slot between to eye-covered walls. No floor or ceiling. Hovering.

As this happened on-screen, a minimal soundtrack grew in volume and intensity. Eerie analog synthesizers and pared-down, reverberating instrumentation.

Sylvie knew it was a flat 2-D image, but it had an unsettling realism to it. It reminded her of her first time watching the Death Star run in the last act of *Star Wars* as a re-release in a theater, only darker and creepier.

Aaron narrowed his eyes and finished chewing a bite.

"This sounds like Frizzi's theme for Fulci's *Zombi Two* by way of Morricone's for Carpenter's version of *The Thing*. What year was this made?"

Russ said, "Can't remember. Sometime in the seventies, so I guess that kinda makes sense."

Aaron chuckled, "Wow, I'm impressed then."

Russ scoffed gently. "A lot of the best films are from the seventies, youngblood."

Juana leaned forward and shot Aaron a look in the flickering light and waited for him to turn his head and return it. When he did, she ran a finger across her neck and pointed at Russ, then him with it. He laughed and shook his head.

The walls of eyes on the screen came together, as if to squeeze the viewer, then it went totally black again. Music faded.

Cut from black—young woman jolting out of a nightmare.

Aaron snickered. "Main character wakes from nightmare—never seen that one...."

Juana threw a few pieces of popcorn at him. "You're not a film student, are you? You sound like one. I can't stand that over-analyzing bullshit."

Aaron lost his smile and went silent, focusing on the movie.

Margot chuckled. "That's a yes."

"So?" Aaron said.

Juana leaned back into her seat. "Just don't act all smart and shit. We know how movies work too, you know?"

The young woman in the film was now in a college classroom, sitting next to a friend. "The Paranormal in Film and Literature" was written on a whiteboard next to a digital projection of an ancient-looking book. The elegantly designed embossed-calligraphy-style title was *"ESTHURS AUGEN"* and just below that in smaller letters it read, *"die Geisterhafte Königin."*

The professor in the film told the story of Esthur, a disgraced queen of a small conquered nation called Marposa in an unnamed area of medieval Europe. She turned to witchcraft and black magic to take revenge on her also-unnamed conquerors. It worked too well, the evil magic consuming her and causing her to torture and slaughter not only her enemies, but all of her own people as well.

He explained that there were only ever eight copies of this book—the original Spanish novel, reproductions of it in French, Italian, Portuguese, and Romanian, and three German copies made from the French translation, written by hand and masterfully illustrated. Authors and artists unknown. They were shared around aristocratic circles, and most of what was known about their contents was from secondhand accounts. A student in the class jokingly asked if they were written in blood.

After the on-screen class's half-hearted laughter died down, the professor said they don't know because the only known copy to have survived to the present—that this projected picture was taken of—disappeared before it could be fully examined and translated into English. Another student made a mock sound like a ghost moaning and the class laughed again.

The main character ignored her classmates and stared at the book, the camera slowly zooming in on the title.

The professor continued, skimming over fringe theories that the Romanian copy was the original, the Portuguese was, or that there was an original they were all copies of, language unknown. Also, there had been argument among some scholars about the content of the book, as there had been widely varying accounts of what happened in it that couldn't be explained by possible mistranslation. One particularly superstitious take on it was that the book's contents changed at random, or by some arcane and ghastly will of its own. The professor and other students laughed.

The main character seemed transfixed by the fine detail of the cover's calligraphy.

The professor could be heard in dramatically lowering volume—cross-faded with the theme from the title intro rising up—explaining that he'd picked this book due to his own fascination with its legend, and because a film based loosely on one of the more generally agreed upon accounts of its story was being released that coming Friday....

The surface of the book cover in the image began to warp and bulge in a few places. Then the projection screen itself seemed to. Curved slits appeared along the rounded bumps—

Piercing, odd-colored eyes snapped open in the surface of the cover, staring right at her—the main character let out a yelp and stood up from her seat.

The eyes vanished. Just a book cover again. Students stared. Professor asked if she was alright as she sat back down.

Sylvie raised her eyebrows and gestured toward the screen with her hot sauce holding hand. "Say *whaaaaat...?*"

The woman in the film went about her daily life and things seemed normal. The next day while working on an essay, she noticed a bump on her left hand. She scratched it a few times, but then ignored it and moved on. Later, she noticed it was the size of half a marble and she scratched it harder. She looked at it closely and a close-up shot revealed a fine ridge over its center—

An odd-colored eye snapped open and locked its view on her, just like her vision in class the day before. She lost it.

Aaron said, "Those practical effects are well done so far, I'll give them that. And I honestly don't get how they even pulled off those eyes in the book cover without CG."

Juana chuckled. "Hey, at least you can admit when you don't know something."

Aaron shook his head and smiled.

Russ snapped his fingers. "Cut it out, y'all. This is getting good."

Sylvie raised her hot sauce cup in a playful salute like a tiny goblet, before tipping more of its contents onto her burrito's exposed contents and taking another bite.

The film's main character tried to keep her sanity as more tiny eyes appeared on her body, some growing larger while others stayed tiny and multiplied. She tried to show the eyes to a friend, calling them a rash. Her friend saw nothing abnormal.

Later, she opened a phonebook and looked up a local hospital's psychiatry department. Picked up the phone. Hesitated. Hung it up.

Several eye bumps of various sizes appeared in an asymmetric grouping on the kitchen table she was resting her elbows on. They opened, rolled around, and locked onto her like all the others.

She picked up the phone again. Dialed. Returned the piercing gaze of the unblinking eyes as long as she could. Then looked at the ceiling and closed her natural eyes tight, tears forming at their seams. Someone answered at the psych wing. Startled, she hung up. She returned the table eyes' stare again for a few seconds—

The phone rang.

She jolted on-screen, joined by most of the small audience in the Rem.

Russ chuckled and shook his head. "Gotcha...."

The young woman on the screen picked up the phone with a shaking hand.

It was her friend who'd been sitting with her in the *ESTHURS AUGEN* lecture. She wanted to take the main character to the movie version that had just been released. The main character winced, then seemed to think about it more and decide something. She agreed. Said goodbye. Hung up. Said something to herself about maybe better understanding what she was facing.

Cut to Main Character looking at herself in the bathroom mirror, groupings of eyes all over her arms, chest, neck—some staring at her physical eyes, some her eyes in the mirror, and others going back and forth between them.

She said, "Other people might not see them...but I sure as hell do."

Another cut and she was waiting outside a small movie theater under a lit marquee, wearing a turtleneck, a big sweater, and gloves.

Juana said, "Huh...that kinda looks like the Rem."

Russ grunted. "Sure does...."

Main Character's friend showed up and they got tickets, then headed inside.

The shot of the ticket booth had a shallow depth of field, but the blurry actor playing the box office person helping the characters struck Sylvie as resembling Margot—Margot with a 1970s hairdo and clothes, but still.

Main Character's friend got some popcorn and a drink from another blurred theater worker and they entered the theater itself. There were only a handful of people in the theater. Main Character fidgeted and looked around during the grindhouse-level trailers. Then the film started.

TOO MANY EYES appeared on the screen in stark white letters on deep black. Faded out, then slivers and dots pulsed into view, just like the intro they'd seen. Main Character watched the alley of eye walls grow on the screen and squirmed.

Sylvie chuckled. "Hey, this reminds me of the time we showed *Stir of Echoes*...."

Russ chuckled too.

Aaron twisted halfway in his seat to look back. "What happened?"

Sylvie went to speak—

Margot said, "So Sylvia builds up the print of *Stir of Echoes* and goes to screen it...."

"Wasn't that a Harlan Ellison book or something?" Aaron said.

Russ shook his head. "Richard Matheson."

Sylvia said, "So I'm sitting there watching this film like we are now, for mistakes in the build, but I was alone 'cause of scheduling or something."

Margot nodded, "And this scene comes on...."

"Kevin Bacon is the main guy, I think he got hypnotized or something. So, he wakes up and he's alone, sitting in a movie theater. The hypnotist or whoever even says something like *you're alone in a movie theater* or something similar and describes it and I just get this super weird feeling."

Margot mocked looking around. "She's like, *wait*—I'm *alone in a theater*...."

Aaron laughed. "Woah. Yeah, that would be pretty fucking eerie."

Sylvie and Margot laughed and shared a look in the flicker-lit darkness that was long and pleasant enough that Sylvie didn't want to look away. But she did, and looked back at the movie.

The dialogue was overdubbed, the Spanish and Italian actors all having British accents. The main character in the film Main Character was watching was a young woman who lived in a village at the base of some mountains in medieval Spain.

Her grandmother told her about an abandoned castle town and castle in the mountains that had been forbidden to go to, even since her own youth. The young woman asked how she'd never stumbled onto it, having grown up hiking all over the foothills and mountains. Her grandmother told her it had been abandoned so long that everything had grown around it and the paths to it, and the castle could only be seen from special spots because of where it was built and its remoteness. The young woman asked how to find it. Look for black ivy in the mountain forest, she said.

Her mother overheard this and told the young woman's grandmother to stop filling her head with lies. Time passed, and of course the young woman in the film Main Character was watching took a basket for collecting flowers and such and hiked up into the deep forest.

She searched until she found some patches of ivy among the regular ground-clinging ones that were a strange bluish-black and stood out some. She followed those until they clung to the face of a short, tree-topped bluff with a ridge ascending away from its base—which she now saw was an overgrown mountain path that curved up and around the mountainside. It could've been a road for horses and carts before, but now it was only wide enough for walking.

The main character in the version of the film Sylvie and the Rem crew were viewing watched this fairytale-like imagery and seemed almost relieved as the character on screen progressed.

The path was choked at points with drooping branches that hung over it like frozen claws, and a mist gathered the farther she ascended. Farther still, the branches were webbed with more and more ivy. As she continued on, the mist grew thicker and the vines' heavy growth darkened the path. When the vines and branches had become almost ink black, the darkened path opened up some and she came to a stone wall with a badly rusted iron portcullis. The clinging mist and some leaning ancient trees kept the castle town's entrance from being much brighter than the tunnel-like path she'd followed to reach it.

Main Character in the Rem's *TOO MANY EYES* had lost her look of relief in shots of her intercut with the film she was watching.

The young woman set her basket down, hiked her simple peasant's dress up, and started climbing the portcullis, hooking her hands and feet in the square openings in its latticed structure.

Juana chuckled. "That girl's gonna get fuckin' tetanus."

When the young woman Main Character was watching reached the apex of the stone arch it was firmly seated in, she climbed the black ivy vines that grew in layers all over and through it. She reached the top and stood on the castle town's outer wall, looking up the town's sloping main thoroughfare. Its stone structures were webbed and layered with the black ivy too and the crisscrossing streets ended at another stone wall. That wall surrounded the town-facing side of the castle itself and was almost twice as tall as the town's, its looming form seeming to be in no need of a wall on its other side. The castle looked to be built on the edge of a cliff.

The young woman said to herself, "That must be the cliff over the lake. How have I not seen this? The trees must obscure it...."

Using the ivy and portcullis method again, the young woman climbed down into the graveyard stillness and quiet of the castle town.

Main Character looked anxious, the film's imagery no longer having a fairytale feel. The stone, vines, and mist gave everything an ominous, ghostly feeling now. She looked around the theater for distraction. Her friend from class was totally sold, staring at the screen. The few others in the theater were similarly entranced. Then Main Character noticed someone sitting in the front row that hadn't been obvious in the shots before. A dark figure that barely stood out against the theater's black matting below the screen.

Margot said, "Oh, that's no good. What kind of a *madman* would sit in the front row of an almost empty theater...?"

They all chuckled. Even Russ.

But then Main Character's attention was pulled back to the film in her theater as the young woman in it realized she was being watched. A tall figure stood in the shadow of the castle wall's open gate up in the distance. The figure was silhouetted but by its shape seemed to wear a black shroud and something around its veiled head glinted, even under the shadowy arch.

The young woman seemed to lose all curiosity and crossed to the rounded corner of a stone structure and tucked herself behind it. She looked back up at the castle gate and the figure was gone. She looked around—

The tall form—now more obviously female—was just down the cobblestone walkway, standing in the shade of a narrow alley between buildings to the young woman's right.

She wore a very dark shroud, its translucent fabric wrapped around her head and body as if she were being buried. There was a delicate and simple crown around the top of her head that looked like black ivy vines flowering with several elegant but odd-looking pearls.

Sylvie noticed that, through the translucence of the shroud's veil, the ghostly noble figure's features were almost skeletal, her face muscles, mouth, cheeks, and chin dimly showing skull and teeth through them. The darkness of the skull's eye sockets could be seen through the figure's tightly sealed eyes—which gave a mummy-like appearance to her face.

"Great makeup effects."

The young woman in the film Main Character was watching slid her foot across the stone walkway in preparation to retreat from her hiding spot around the corner, and the ghastly, frail-looking figure cocked her veiled head and turned an almost see-through ear toward the corner.

Margot said, "She's not watching, she's listening."

Juana groaned. "Oooooh...that's so fuckin' spooky looking. Honestly, freaky."

The young woman turned and ran back down the castle town's main street, reaching the portcullis and climbing without looking back until she reached the top and started climbing down its other side. The figure was already at the bottom inside the castle-town walls, listening to her rustling and the portcullis creaking as the young woman climbed down.

The young woman yelped, her hands being grabbed at by the black ivy. The ivy now had a life of its own and the vines looked more like tentacles.

She wrenched her hands free and dropped the last few feet, twisting her ankle and crying out. The figure's head snapped toward her on the other side of the latticed openings of the portcullis and wind howled through the leaning trees above.

The overhanging claw branches of the trees shook in the strong gusting as the young woman limped back down the misty overgrown path.

The ivy and branches came to life, swiping and grasping at her.

The ivy tentacles pulsed as they arrested her movement and closed in around her, also draining the light in the increasingly tunnel-like path. They wrapped around her like living ropes and soon she couldn't fight them. She cried in fear and frustration as the ivy and branches held her firm.

Bumps appeared on all the tentacles, then broken open with dozens—soon hundreds—of strange eyes that all stared piercingly at the young woman. She screamed—

131

The film Main Character was watching cut to black and she noticed the person up front again, just sitting motionless in the front row of the theater.

The film faded back up and the young woman's mother and grandmother argued about where she could be. The father came in and demanded to know what they were going on about.

In the light of this scene, the person in the front row of Main Character's theater rose up, very tall and darkly dressed. Like a funeral garb. In silhouette, the person walked down the row and turned up the aisle.

Main Character watched this, transfixed. She was frozen with terror, actress really selling it. As the person from the front row came closer to theirs, it became clear—

It was the figure from the castle in the movie.

Esthur.

Main Character lost it, standing and stepping past her friend the opposite direction of the ghastly, veiled figure's approach, murmuring something about using the restroom as she half-stumbled down the row to the other aisle and rushed out of the theater. She looked back and Esthur had stopped at the end of the row, eyes shut and head cocked, listening to her shuffle away.

She left the theater and crossed to a restroom under a stairwell up to the projection booth, entering and shutting herself inside. She sat on the closed lid of the toilet and shuddered, eyes wide open. Ran her gloved fingers through her hair and her sleeves came down some. The eyes on her arms were closer to her hands now. She started wild-eyed sobbing.

To her side, a bulge appeared in the small restroom's wall. A large, three-pupiled eye flapped open, oozing a thick fluid from its wall-fused lid and glaring at her. Dozens of smaller warped eyes opened in the wall around the first one and spread up to the ceiling. More opened on the other walls, then the ceiling itself. Then the floor, ogling her from between her scuffed combat boots. Eyes opened on the restroom door as she reached for the knob and opened it—

Esthur was waiting. She loomed just outside the door, ear-cocked toward Main Character.

The actress screamed and Esthur's eyes snapped open and locked on her. Clouded, pearl white where the pupils and iris would be, jet black where the whites would.

When those eyes opened, others followed.

Like the main character's body, her apartment table, and the restroom, eyes opened all over Esthur's translucent flesh. Dimly glowing. Staring. Even in the thicker layers of the shroud, haunting luminance from the eyes could be seen piercing through from all over Esthur's rangy, gaunt body underneath.

The main character shrank away and slapped her back against the far restroom wall in her haste. Then slid down it until her legs buckled and she collapsed onto her lower legs quaking in sheer terror.

The film cut to a close low-angle shot tilted up at Esthur looking down with her two milky, vacant eyes, along with dozens of the glaring warped ones of various sizes and grotesque, fearsome deformities. All but the most clouded or empty of Esthur's many eyes stared into the camera.

But it didn't stop.

The shot kept going and a shiver ran through Sylvie—the longer the shot continued just fixed on Esthur glaring, the more it felt like the movie's monster queen was looking through the screen at the Rem crew in the theater.

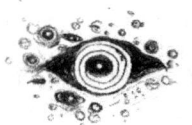

The shot of Esthur in the film should have cut back to the main character, sniveling and crying in a heap in the restroom. It didn't. The audio of her catching sobs actually faded out, room tone of the theater set and popping from a popcorn machine like hyper-natural background sound as the shot lingered uncomfortably on the ghostly queen.

Aaron chuckled nervously. "Well, that's super unsettling."

The eyes on the screen shifted, seeming to focus on Aaron.

"Hey, what the fuck?" Juana said, and the eyes shifted toward her.

Margot leaned forward in her seat. "Waaait a minute...."

Esthur's eyes looked at Margot now.

Sylvie shook her head. "Cute trick, but the story can keep going now. The four of us are sitting right in the center of the theater, so the illusion is easy. Hey, Esthur! Let's keep this going, okay? It's late here."

The eyes locked on Sylvie and it didn't feel as much like a trick anymore.

"Look up here!" Russ said from the back row a little above them.

The eyes tilted up just a bit, right at him.

"Baby Jesus...."

Sylvie stood and threw up her middle finger at the screen, still unconvinced and joking around. "Hey, Esthur—Go fuck yourself, you spooky *bitch*!"

The power abruptly cut off, dousing the projection and walkway lights and cloaking the whole theater with deep darkness.

A few of the Rem crew gasped and Russ groaned.

"Hell of a time for a blown fuse."

They took out their phones and tried to turn their screens and flashlight apps on. They worked but were far dimmer than they should've been.

Sylvie looked at her weak, barely there display. "It says I'm roaming. There's a tower two blocks from here. Bullshit."

As their eyes adjusted, a dim light from the projection booth window became more obvious. Sylvie looked up at it and shuddered—it was a very odd hue. It had a haunting, eerie feel to it and seemed to be shifting.

"If it's a fuse, how is there a light up in the booth, Unc?"

Russ stood and leaned and supported himself on a seatback to look up at the booth window. "No idea...."

136

They all looked up at it, except Aaron.

"H-hello?" he said, but not to them.

They looked back at his dim shape, then what he seemed to be focused on—

There was a dark figure sitting in the front row of the theater.

It took Sylvie a moment to see it, but there was a silhouetted figure just sitting there.

Russ finally saw it. "Shit! You all aren't playin' a trick on old Russ now, are you?"

Margot said, "I wish."

"Sylvie?"

"Not me."

Aaron stood and sidestepped to the aisle on their right, then started toward the front row.

The silent figure cocked its head, like it was listening.

Juana stood up from her seat. "Aaron, *don't.*"

"It's just a homeless person who slipped in the exit door or something."

Russ scoffed. "Not possible, kid."

Sylvie stepped over to the aisle but didn't follow Aaron.

Aaron got closer to the front row of seats, his weak phone the only light in that part of the theater. "Hello? Ma'am?"

The figure seemed to follow his progress with a cocked ear, but the outline was vague like it was wearing a hooded parka or robe.

When he got to within five feet of the person, she stood but didn't turn toward him.

The silhouetted form had to have been at least seven feet tall by Sylvie's estimation. She knew who it was but couldn't accept it.

"Aaron...."

He ignored her and stepped around the looming, shrouded visitor. The head was angled, its right ear area toward him. He stepped around a bit more. Hand shaking, he raised his dimly lit phone screen toward the person's face.

Simple, elegant pearl-topped black ivy crown. Shroud-veiled head. Tightly sealed eyelids. Grimacing skull dimly visible through translucent facial features.

Aaron's breath caught in his chest and he stepped back.

Then he cringed and shook his head.

"This is one fucked up promo campaign, you guys. Are there cameras on me?"

He turned around, looking for some sign of a setup. Hoping for one.

Esthur angled her head forward and shifted her closed eyes toward him. He stopped and stared up at her.

Sylvie raised her hand toward him. "No cameras. Aaron come h—"

Aaron screamed and stumbled back.

Eerie glowing eyes opened all over Esthur's lithe, shrouded body and Sylvie knew she must've snapped her own milky, clouded set of them open at Aaron the way she had at the main character in the movie.

As if on cue, the odd, dim light from the projection booth intensified. It flickered and pulsed, haunting and ominous now.

Esthur stepped toward Aaron and layers of her shroud raised then parted, producing an overlong arm. The wrong-looking appendage ended with a large gnarled and malformed hand that glinted with long, warped talons.

Sylvie realized it looked so wrong because it was like a layered stalk of tentacles and pus-filled cysts covered in glowing eyes of different sizes, all formed together to imitate an arm. Something started splintering in her mind and she could only watch.

Esthur took Aaron by the neck and picked him up off the floor. She held him above herself turning his sputtering, screaming head and looking him over. Examining.

Her shroud parted again, the new limb it revealed from her other side even less defined in shape. This one was a jumble of spasming tentacles around malformed bones. The bones grew impossibly, snapping and cracking as they formed into something like a jagged, roughly curved blade with tumorous growths pulsing in pockets of exposed marrow and holes pocked all over its surface. Only just formed. Petrified and living.

Esthur stuck the weird blade appendage up into Aaron's gut from below. Slow insertion, then she drove it upward with enough force that his belly opened around its base and spilled blood-laced entrails on the theater floor as he screamed—

But his screams stopped when the blade changed inside him.

Aaron's torso cracked and bulged outward asymmetrically, Esthur's limb seeming to become a huge foreign abscess. His ribs, sternum, clavicles, and spine snapped as it grew, forcing him apart from inside. Then his neck and throat bulged in her other limb's talon grip and his jaw snapped as Esthur's tumescent penetrating limb broke free and pulsed from his stretched, overlarge mouth. Aaron's eyes were wild from the pain.

Esthur deflated the abominous appendage and pulled its newly limp sack-like form out from his gaping belly. It slapped down on the floor in an accumulating puddle of Aaron's blood and ichor.

Then she held him toward the theater screen—that was glowing now, from the booth lights—and stepped or otherwise ambulated that way.

Aaron's eyes went even wilder as the back of his head and upper body made contact with the glowing movie screen—and kept going. Esthur pushed him into the screen. Not against it, but through it, like it was a huge slab of glowing gelatin. And now it was translucent and Aaron was a vague, blurry writhing shape in its malleable recesses. The mass that had been the screen took the young man, pulling him farther away from its murky surface and into the viscous darkness deeper in. As if he was sinking into a deep, benighted lake.

138

Then his entrails followed him in like someone slurping up noodles in soup and the surface sealed again, around Esthur's outstretched arm.

Juana screamed.

Esthur wrenched her limb of cysts, eyes, and tentacles back out of the screen's yielding muck, and it sucked closed again while retaining its uncanny translucence. The wraith-like giantess looked toward Sylvie and the others, clouded eyes trying and her dozens of others succeeding.

Sylvie was transfixed by those milky blind eyes. So many others piercing her with their gazes, but she couldn't look away from the clouded two that must have been Esthur's own real eyes at some point...

"Sylvie, what the fuck? Come on, *move!*"

Margot had hooked her arms under Sylvie's from behind and was pulling her toward the theater doors to the lobby. Russ was somehow between them and Esthur now and backing away in pace with their retreat. Esthur had stopped halfway up the aisle and seemed to just examine Russ with all her dimly luminous eyes.

Looking into Esthur's clouded eyes had caused Sylvie to lose time.

The theater walls, ceiling, and floor were undulating and there was a growing haze forming all over, making it even harder to see. Eyes started opening all over the walls, some almost three feet in diameter—and smaller eyes opened on those.

Margot hauled Sylvie to the swinging theater doors and pulled them through. Through the darkness and growing soupy mist, Sylvie could see Juana was already at the Rem's entry doors. She yelled curses as she desperately kicked at them with no results. There were black vines and tentacles growing in thick layers around the door-release bars and wreathing the frames. Juana had no chance of damaging them but kept trying anyway.

"Let me out, motherfuckers!"

As Margot took her hand and pulled her toward the one at the entrance, Sylvie saw the movie posters had unnatural depth to their imagery and the actors in them were growing eyes all over their heads and bodies.

Then Margot stopped and gasped. Sylvie looked at her, then where she was looking—out through the doors and windows:

The sidewalk, street, and shops across the way now looked something like the theater screen—like that thick fluid or translucent sludge with a haunting glow to it had been poured over everything, and they were at the bottom of the lake or ocean of it. It was pressed against the doors in a way that made Sylvie afraid Juana *would* break through, filling the lobby and submerging them all in its mucky awfulness.

Russ busted out of the theater behind them. "Sylvie!"

Sylvie ran back to him, trying to ignore the Tim Curry movie posters becoming more disturbing in detail and lifelike by the second as she passed them.

"Help me with this!"

139

He grabbed the popcorn machine and pulled it toward the theater doors. She grabbed it and helped. They tipped it over, slamming it down in an explosion of glass and popcorn.

The theater doors bulged outward some and the seam between them sprouted eyes and black tendrils. The tendrils became tentacles, pulsing and spreading. The doors began to glow and took on the appearance of veiny, diseased flesh.

Russ grabbed the sides of his head. "What's happening here?"

Sylvie started for the projection booth stairs.

"Whatever it is, I think it's in the *film*! We have to stop it!"

Margot started toward them. "Sylvie, wait!"

Sylvie stopped halfway up the booth stairs and looked back. Margot's expression was protective and concerned, making Sylvie want to survive this even more. Margot reached the stairs, started up them, and extended her hand to Sylvie. Sylvie took it and squeezed, then pulled Margot up to her and they embraced.

Russ went behind the concessions counter and knocked over condiments and supply boxes as he grabbed four of their big usher flashlights, then crossed to Sylvie and Margot and handed them each one.

"Better than nothing."

He turned and extended one toward Juana. "Hey, we should stick together! Juana!"

Juana looked back at them through the dense gloom now collected in the lobby. She kicked the doors one more time.

"Fuck!"

She started toward them, passing the glowing movie posters—

Eye-covered tentacles, malformed arms, and heads burst from the poster cases, the negative spaces around the Tim Curry characters now translucent like the theater's screen and sea of muck outside the doors. Warped, ghoulish parodies of Dr. Frank-N-Furter, Wadsworth, and Long John Silver in the posters lunged out of them and grabbed Juana. Sylvie could see mangled caricatures of Darkness from *Legend* and the Grand Wizard from *The Worst Witch* past the others, lashing out from their posters but unable to reach her.

Sylvie, Margot, and Russ hurried toward Juana—but Long John Silver had latched onto her with the most tentacles and several deformed hands, the Muppets in the poster having become an amorphous sludgy mass merged with the pirate's form.

As Frank-N-Furter and Wadsworth the butler clawed into Juana's shoulder and back—opening deep lacerations that sprayed blood and poured it on the floor—the ghoulish pirate held her in its many appendages. Juana was being fish-hooked, scalped, and lobotomized all at once, the many hooked tentacles and claws seeming to compete at doing damage to her.

The others tried to get hold of her and pull her free—but razor-sharp tendrils that weren't directly involved in mutilating Juana whipped at them.

The monstrous pirate and its vicious Muppet blob pulled Juana into their glowing, gelatinous poster-frame portal while she gurgled and screamed. Her bleeding head, arms, and upper body were already halfway into the poster, and her friends could do nothing.

Frank-N-Furter swiped at Wadsworth to gain an opening, then latched onto Juana's left leg. It clawed and wrenched at the limb, tearing it free and spurting blood from the newly exposed femoral artery. They pulled the parts of Juana they had into their poster portals, which sealed, then the other creatures recessed into their frames, bountyless.

Margot dropped her flashlight and beat at the surface of the glowing sludge in the poster frame most of Juana had just disappeared into, almost slipping in the small puddles of blood around its base.

Russ leaned against the wall and stared into the dim glow of the one that had taken her leg. "What is.... *Why* is this happening?"

Sylvie fought off her own feelings of sickness, confusion, and dread. She almost started crying—then kicked the wall next to the poster case Margot was at and stormed toward the projection-booth stairs. "I think I know...."

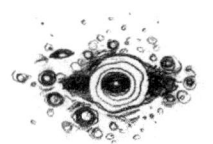

They followed Sylvie, Margot picking up her own flashlight and turning it on to cut through the mist that was still getting thicker. Russ held his like a truncheon and caught up to his niece, grabbing her hand and pulling her behind himself.

"Not letting you open that door alone. And what do you think you know?"

Sylvie readied her light like a weapon too as they started up the stairs. She could hear wet sounds of slippage, crunching, and something like moaning from the booth through the closed door. Her momentary toughness faded at the thought of what they would find on the other side, but she still forced out her answer.

"That fucking delivery guy did this—that's why he didn't want us to screen it. There were supposed to be dozens or even up to a full house of three hundred seats filled, *tomorrow* night. Filled for the fucking ghost monster queen in there to...consume? Take? I don't know."

Sylvie looked away from Russ and Margot, hoping they wouldn't see how quickly her determination to storm the projection booth had shriveled. She noticed the walls, stairs, and lobby floor below them had started to have a touch of translucence to them now too. Their surfaces were starting to look like diseased flesh, the studs and beams and joists supporting them taking on a strange black coloring, and appearing as bones in the living structure's skeleton. In past the flesh it was like gelatinous, putrid fat or the inside of a decaying internal organ.

Margot noticed it too. "Yeah...this is really bad."

"You think?" Russ said, gripping his flashlight in both hands, also seeing his theater's encroaching weirdness.

Margot slipped the fingers of a hand between those on one of Sylvie's and she squeezed. Sylvie returned it, wishing they were anywhere else.

Russ put his hand on the booth-door handle. "Okay, we ready?"

Sylvie squeezed Margot's hand this time. When Margot returned it, Sylvie let go and readied her flashlight. "Let's go."

Margot gripped her flashlight. "Okay, ready."

Russ tried to pull the door open but it wouldn't move. Tried again. Nothing. He handed his light to Sylvie, who held its glowing circle on the door. Russ took the handle with both hands and pulled. Nothing. He lifted his foot onto the jamb where it met the increasingly see-through wall. Through it and the door they could see vague dark shapes where the projector was still clicking away. But the clicking was muffled and echoing strangely.

Pulling with his arms and pushing with his leg did it, the door slowly coming out of its frame. It made a sucking sound and viscous fluids oozed down into the open threshold as more gushed out onto the landing from inside and flowed down the stairs like putrid syrup. They gagged and coughed as the smells from inside assaulted their senses. Margot tried to hold back a retch.

The projection booth was alive.

The walls were breathing through dense groupings of holes in their surfaces, ceiling the same. The floor could have been, but was obscured by several inches of the thick liquid drooling down from the ceiling all around out of clutches of clouded, murky eyes. The mist was thickest here too and had collected like a noxious miasma. But the projector was the worst of it.

Two of the three platters in their support tree were rotating and whirring, projector clicking away like before—but now they were doing that in a large, pulsing sac. It reminded Sylvie of a mineral-oil-cooled computer tower she'd seen at a hardcore gamer friend's apartment. The projector was fully functioning, even completely immersed in the translucent weakly luminous fluid in the sac. It had the same look to it as that impossible sea outside the Rem's entry doors and the place past the malleable film screen Esthur had pushed Aaron into. The projector inside was also that otherworldly black the building's support structures had become, in past the diseased-flesh walls.

The sac was big enough that some of Russ's WWII plane models had been crunched up against the oozing, breathing ceiling and looked broken. Others had fallen into the muck, and those that were left dropped intermittently, splashing into the fluid and snapping apart. Even with everything happening, that still caused Sylvie a momentary ache of sadness.

Russ stepped in and reached back for his flashlight. Sylvie put it in his hand. He swung it around in front of him and scanned all around. In the focused light, eyes were visible in surfaces all around, and the building's translucence was even more obvious.

A P-51 Mustang detached from the ceiling, breaking into pieces and causing the eyes it landed on to blink and roll around confusedly.

He then trained it on the projector in its sac. "Christ Almighty...."

Sylvie stepped in and added her light's beam to his.

A Brewster F2A Buffalo dropped from the changing ceiling.

"I think we have to stop it somehow."

Margot shook her head. "But how?"

A Douglass C-47 Skytrain fell.

Russ raised his light and brought down its unlit end against the sac, hard—it bounced off and fluids inside churned a bit, but no damage. He front-kicked it. Bigger swirl that time, but still no damage to its surface. He took a folding knife he always carried out of a back pocket on his jeans and flicked it open.

"Wait!" Sylvie said, sure she should but unsure why.

Russ raised his knife. "You said yourself we need to stop it...."

He brought the knife down, plunging it into the sac—

In the beam of her flashlight Sylvie saw the blade of the knife disintegrate almost instantly in the sac's fluids. Not registering that at the angle he was to it, Russ pulled it down to cut at the sac. The bladeless handle slipped down the sac surface, already being burned away too—the fluid from inside spurted out, splashing all over Russ's chest and face.

Sylvie's uncle started screaming as he dropped the half-disintegrated knife handle. That hand was already half gone too. He stumbled back, more of the fluid squirting out and spattering all over his legs.

Russ's clothes and flesh were even more yielding than the knife had been. Sylvie watched in stunned silence as his eyes, skin, muscle, and bone were being eaten away. Margot screamed and backed away as his legs collapsed, unable to support his burning body. His upper body slapped down into the muck on the booth floor, his screams thickly bubbling out from his corroded, eyeless living skull.

A Goodyear F2G "Super" Corsair painted as a postwar racing plane dropped from the ceiling, slapping down on his back and snapping the props and part of the rear stabilizer off.

Warped eyes opened all around him below the surface of the muck, then rudimentary appendages swelled between those that unfurled and grew into tentacles. They wrapped around him, destroying the rest of the plane model and pulling him down into the living floor—which now grew jagged teeth that were black like the building's bones. The gaping maw slapped closed, its fleshy layered seam as obscene as it was maddening. The floor bulged and undulated as sounds of crunching and piercing were audible. It was chewing. The floor thing ate what was left of Sylvie's uncle, his muffled screams only cutting off when his form had been swallowed.

Sylvie stood over the huge closed mouth, whole body shaking and her mouth gibbering wordlessly. The functional eyes visible in the murky sludge covering the floor glared at her.

The flow of liquid down from the ceiling and walls got stronger, as if in reaction to having consumed Russ. The thick, putrid fluid went from ankle deep to halfway up their calves in a hurry. More tentacles grew and unfurled out of the fluid near her feet but she couldn't make herself move.

Margot grabbed Sylvie's hand and yanked her from the spot that was about to be her death. She pulled Sylvie toward the open booth door and stepped through—

Esthur was at the bottom of the stairs. Her cloudy eyes were closed tight again, her head cocked and ear pointed up at them at the top. But the hundreds of eyes on and in her body were still glowing enough to be visible through the translucence of her shroud and flesh.

"Oh, hell no!"

Margot pulled Sylvie back into the booth and tried to slam the door. Its fleshy structure closed, but wavered in the squishy frame around it. With the door closed, the nasty fluids pouring and streaming down all around filled the room even faster.

"That won't stop her."

Sylvie shook her head. "Nothing's gonna *stop* her—she's doing all of this! Russ...is...d-dead. My uncle is dead! Juana and Aaron too! We're next and there's nothing we can fucking do. This place is g-going to *eat* us."

"*Sylvia*—don't just shut down! Please...."

"Wh-what?" Margot's tone was pleading and vulnerable in a way that struck a chord deep inside Sylvie.

"You always just give up or shut down to get out of being real—stay *here* with *me*!"

Sylvie studied Margot's face and realized what had gone wrong between them all at once. With that realization, her psyche clawed back to the outskirts of sanity. Tentacles slithering up out of the already thigh-high viscous putrescence on the projection booth floor around them also helped refocus her.

"Okay! What can we do, though?"

"I don't know...."

They looked around—Margot yelped when she caught sight of Esthur's tall form in silhouette just outside on the landing through the eerie translucence of the booth door. Sylvie knew what Margot's reaction must mean but didn't look. She could see the haunting glow of the screen/portal down in the theater through the booth wall in that direction.

"Maybe the exit door by the screen isn't blocked like the front ones."

Then her eyes landed on something atop a desk just above the rising sludge and glinting in the preternatural glow of the projector and its living sac that she realized she could use.

Sylvie splashed through the muck and picked up a film-print-moving clamp. The two sections of it were long, thin strips of metal that slid together to form a long rectangular channel that held a section of the film from the central circle of negative space to the print's outer edge. You could move a whole built-up print from one platter to another, or even from one projector's tree to another. They had two of them, but they'd rarely used them, being a one-screen theater.

Margot tore her eyes from Esthur's shape on the top step past the door and looked at Sylvie. "It probably *is* blocked."

"Either way, we should get out of this fucking booth, right?"

She unscrewed the securing system and slid the two pieces apart. To get the clamp around the print, the bottom side was very thin so it could slide under the heavy print unhindered—almost like a blade. Or like two blades in parallel, one sharper. She picked up the other clamp and offered it to Margot.

"Right."

Margot trudged over through the waist-deep fluid and took the clamp, then separated it so she had a two-bladed tool of her own. Sylvie started hacking away at the screen-side wall of the projection booth, so Margot did the same. They had to grip the tools in both hands, and in only a few strokes their hands were bleeding from the effort.

Sylvie looked back—

Esthur was walking through the door, literally. She seemed to be materializing through it, but in a messy way that pulled the door's diseased skin surfaces with her. Almost like a second shroud.

"Got it!" Margot yelled, dropping her tool and pulling the vile flesh of the booth wall apart like a mortician might. The fluids started pouring out through the big gouged slit they'd made but were being produced fast enough that they were still at wading depth.

Sylvie pushed at Margot's shoulder. "Then go—now!"

Margot started through, making Sylvie think of it as an obscene waterslide entrance.

The second skin of the door sloughed off of Esthur and she turned an ear in Sylvie's direction as she advanced, molasses slow now through the rising fluid. Most of her many eyes seemed confused and lolled around, unable to focus and glare like they usually did.

Sylvie raised her blade tool, not sure what she was thinking. But she needed Margot to get away.

From behind and below her, Margot grabbed Sylvie's ankles and pulled them out from under her, plunging her down into the muck and brushing her hard against warped eyes and forming tentacles like some kind of otherworldly ocean reef. Then Margot used her weight to pull Sylvie out of the booth opening, climbing down the mutated short wall above the theater's back row near where Russ had been seated earlier.

Submerged in the murk, Sylvie could only strain to look up through the fluid as she was dragged out of the nightmare version of their projection booth and Esthur regained what you might call her composure. A good amount of her eyes found Sylvie and locked on, following her progress through the muck across the slime-submerged, living floor—

Then they were out, Margot falling onto the back row of seats and Sylvie coming down with her. The fluids poured out of the big slit they'd cut and rushed down like a small waterfall of foul pus and ichor. They collapsed across the back row, clawing out for handholds on the tops of those seats and those in the next row.

But the seats weren't solid like before. They'd become almost see-through like the structure of the theater, and there were pulsing organs and arteries in them of unknowable purpose. The seats had too much give and that same eerie glow—but the floor was worse.

The theater floor was like the projection booth but bigger and more grotesquely transformed. Eyes, tentacles, malformed limbs, jagged mouths.

Fluids started pouring down all around and from the eye-covered walls and ceiling the same way too.

Margot and Sylvie helped each other get propped on the perverse caricatures the theater seats had become.

Sylvie pointed to the exit light, still working but an odd pale blue now.

"We've got to get there before it fills up!"

They started across the tops of the squishy seats, feeling for holds as they went. They'd made it about halfway to the front of the theater before Margot slipped and screamed.

Sylvie looked back and saw Margot being pulled down between two rows of seats, clawing at their tops. She climbed back to her and took Margot's forearms in her slimy, bleeding hands and pulled with everything she had.

"Sylvie!"

Margot's arms were slipping, her hands too slick to stop them.

"I won't let go!"

She tried not to look at the eyes and mouths down in the muck—and the tendrils and warped limbs trying to take her lover—

Then they took her.

Sylvie was almost sucked down with Margot as she was wrenched down out of her grip, but she lashed out and clawed her fingers into the seats.

Margot's eyes burned into Sylvie as she was swallowed, screaming, by the living madness of the putrid sea and theater floor.

"Margot, *no!*"

Sylvie held herself there, transfixed on the murky darkness in the muck where her Margot had disappeared. The muck was rising, though, the seats in the front rows already submerged and only the incline of the theater keeping those where she was perched exposed. The muck rose around her until she was half floating, still positioned atop the tops of the theater seats halfway down the theater's length.

There was an odd sound of vibration and Sylvie looked toward the back of the theater—

Esthur was pulling herself down out of the theater's back wall like she had the booth door, only this time she was stepping out onto the surface of the dimly glowing sludge.

With her uncle, Margot, and her friends gone, Sylvie had lost her will to fight.

Esthur rid herself of the wall shroud and crossed to Sylvie on the surface of the rising sludge. Sylvie just closed her eyes and waited....

But then a new sound came from the theater screen, and the whole theater began to shake.

Sylvie looked at the screen:

The translucent murk of it cleared and locked like a normal movie theater filled with people. Like people watching a movie screen on the other side of theirs. Watching *them*. She looked back—Esthur had stopped in place on the surface and seemed something like confused too.

Sylvie hauled herself up in the muck and started across the theater-seat tops. In just a few rows, they were too deep—so she swam. Awkwardly, but she made progress toward the screen.

She wasn't sure why, but she knew the screen was her only chance.

Esthur's impossibly buoyant steps made *slish*-ing sounds behind Sylvie, but she couldn't look back. She just kicked and clawed at the muck.

When Sylvie was within reach, she stretched and touched the screen—

It sucked her in, but not to the other side.

Sylvie was suspended in a channel between two malleable vertical surfaces. As if she was being vacuum packed in thick, glowing plastic with the muck in between, almost like a meat's juices. Then eyes appeared in the surface at her back and she heard unearthly shrieking behind her—it sounded like Esthur had lost her prey and wasn't happy about it.

The surface in front of Sylvie tightened around her and the fluid rose above her head.

Sylvie held her already strained breath as long as she could, but started to writhe in panic and opened her mouth against her will—

The muck filled her mouth, throat, and lungs.

Sylvie was drowning in putrescent, glowing sludge, trapped between layers of what seemed like smashed together planes of reality.

The moviegoers were already running for the theater exits when Sylvie's squirming, gasping form started growing out of the hauntingly luminous screen. If the terrified patrons had chanced a look back, they'd have seen a young bespectacled black woman held tight in a thick translucent blister pack, almost like heated-and-pulled plastic in a vacuum-forming machine.

But they were running from something bloodthirsty and vicious, through a place going through the early stages of a similar structural weirdness to what had befouled and warped the Rem—only worse. Madness was becoming flesh in this unknown place, and drowning Sylvie couldn't see any of it, bound and displayed exactly where, normally, the audience would be gazing.

As the last patrons desperately escaped the more sharply inclined stadium seating of this strange theater, the glowing, living screen re-birthed Sylvie. The second skin holding her split open. She spilled out, dropping and slapping down hard onto the theater floor near the recently vacated front seats. The vile sludge that had been fuming and bubbling around her—that wasn't still in her throat and lungs—poured down around and onto her.

Sylvie coughed, spat, and vomited the glowing sludge out, adding to the spreading puddle of it around her.

She curled up in the fetal position and broke down. She sobbed for Margot and Russ, the people she'd loved most. Sobbed for her dear friend Juana. Even for Aaron who she barely knew, whose biggest crime had been just days before getting a job at the Rem. She shook and shuddered, her breath catching in her chest. In less than an hour, she'd lost the few remaining people she really cared about and thought of as family, along with her grip on reality. She hoped for a moment she was maybe hallucinating somehow from an unknown illness, or maybe stuck in a horrible nightmare. But she knew she wasn't.

This was real and she was alone.

She could hear and feel the theater still changing around and under her. Eyes opened under the shallow pool of muck she was curled up in. Some just lolled around in different directions, others were clouded or unfocused like those of a dead or brain-dead person. But several found Sylvie and stared at her with piercing black dot or unnaturally shaped pupils.

Screams outside the theater reminded her she wasn't actually alone.

Sylvie had only one thing left—herself. But there were other people out there, and maybe they could help. Even having lost so much, she wanted to live. That meant getting out of this place, wherever it was. She got up and looked around.

There was blood sprayed and splashed on several of the seats in an area right in the first few rows across from where Sylvie had spilled out. Popcorn and candy had been dropped and tossed aside everywhere, some of it landing in wide, wet streaks of thickening blood that trailed down a theater entry hall to the right. It looked to Sylvie like something had come out of the screen just before she had, attacked, then dragged bodies out with it while most of the patrons ran for their lives.

The theater's transformation to chaotic living matter and haunting, sickly translucence was taking over this place now, but not as quickly as it had the Rem. Maybe she still had time. She saw her glasses in the muck near her feet, broken. They were mostly for astigmatism anyway, and she didn't mind seeing the warped changes a little less clearly, she decided.

Whipping slime off her hands and arms, Sylvie crossed to the theater entry hall on her left. The screams and shouts got louder as she approached the swinging double doors out to what she assumed would be a theater lobby, but the confusion in the screams and amount of them really struck her. She placed her hands on one of the doors and took a deep breath, trying to find a focused center. Just get *out*, she told herself, and exhaled slowly.

"Don't shut down, Sylvia...."

She opened the door and saw that she was in a multiplex. Above terrified people running and trampling each other to get out of theaters she could see theater numbers and animated film title cards. She saw "13" above the doors of the theater across from hers, an abandoned concessions counter in between. Smashed glass on a candy display. Blood splattered all over. Popcorn still popping, hot dogs still rotating on rollers, even as the structures around them became a touch see-through and those spooky black structure bones became more visible.

Down the hall, through a growing haze like back in the Rem, she saw theater markers for "12" and "11" then "10" down at the end—and between the panicked people trying to escape down the lobby corridor, she saw escalators going down. So she figured she was on an upper floor of a building. She knew it wouldn't do her any immediate good to stop to think about how any of this was possible, so she started down the wide hall.

She caught glimpses of the title animations in the ceilings above the theater doors—*The Things in the Storm, THAT!, Morgan Ashpoole's Menhirs of Madness.* Classic cult horror films. She'd seen the last two a few times, and scenes from the first on the internet. Really gruesome, disturbing old school creature features from the 1970s and '80s. Then her head filled with images of the monsters in them—and what they could do if they came out of their films as Esthur had.

153

The theater doors of house 13 back at the end burst open and more crying, yelling people poured out from between them. She hadn't caught the title of that movie, but she knew the theme of the others was amorphous, maddening, barely-seen abominations—and didn't need any more encouragement.

Sylvie broke into a run toward the escalators and the last packs of blubbering, wild-eyed people running from houses 14 and 10-12 and climbing down them. The wave of house 13 escapees wasn't far behind. As she came around the escalator entry side of a long open-air octagon of handrail topped glass barrier walls, she saw how high she was.

It was murky looking down through the eerie, thickening mist, but she could see there had to be five or six escalator flights between the ground floor and this top level she was on— switch-backing down the center of the entire vertical stretch of the octagonal shaft. Long vertical banners were hung from two sides of the octagonal opening that stretched almost down to what had to be the ground floor, covered in titles and images for the film festival this insanity had interrupted. Horror on the top theater floor, noir films on the middle, and what looked like science fiction on the lowest. From the layout, Sylvie realized there must be projection-booth floors staggered vertically with the showing floors with no public access.

She started down the escalator, following dozens of others—they were frantic and hysterical. Tripping, stumbling. Mumbling to themselves or eyes and heads swiveling around in fear of more monstrous dangers. One young woman was stumbling down in five- or six-inch heels, seemingly unaware she could just take them off and not risk a sprained ankle every other wobbly step. Sylvie almost laughed. She felt more numb now than afraid. She was still scared but after her hard cry, shock and its residual comedown and survival instincts had crept in and must've taken over. She just hoped she'd seen the worst of it already.

Sylvie had made it down about a flight and a half when the escalators started to change even more.

Their translucence became more pronounced, all the internal mechanisms and machinery that ran below their ridged metal steps visible through their exterior surfaces, black like the structure bones. Worse, though, they seemed to be warping in ways she hadn't seen. The large gear systems and motors at the top and bottom of each flight moaned—but more like something that was alive than machine sounds.

Sylvie had seen more of this than the others on the escalators, so she slowed her descent and started looking for any possible way of getting off. Panicked people from house 13 shouldered her aside and stepped down past her. She was letting the handrail slide through her fingers on both sides so it didn't pull her with it, and now she felt it changing too. She looked down and saw eyes forming and opening in its smooth black surface.

Then she caught a much slower, more deliberate movement from down on the second floor. He was just strolling down the lobby carpet through a pea-soup-thick miasma in the air on that level, ignoring the few panicked stragglers coming out of houses 5-9—

Harry Lime, from *The Third Man.*

Orson Welles had played him, of course, but if Esthur was Esthur, this was Harry Lime.

Black overcoat with high flipped-up collar, wide-brim black fedora, face shrouded in darkness from the hat's angle and failing lobby lights. But she knew. It had always been Russ's favorite older film. They'd shown it at the Rem probably five times since she'd started working there off and on in high school. He stopped near a flickering light and looked up at it, then toward the escalators. She must have been the only one looking his way, because his eyes quickly found hers.

Just like the midpoint reveal in the film, this Harry Lime gave Sylvie that enigmatic, playful smirk.

Then his face collapsed into and against itself, and his head swelled asymmetrically until the fedora fell off. From that crushed-up, bulging mess grew eyes and writhing flesh to the left and right, until the head resembled a hammerhead shark's in shape—only warped, mottled, and unnatural. Stretching even farther apart, eyes kept opening on and between the layered horizontal flaps of it. The mangled, broken-toothed mouth snapped open in a long, angled gash that kept growing too—and it let out an ungodly wail that shook something deep in Sylvie.

She looked away from the thing that was Lime and up at the first flight she'd come down from the top theater floor—the machines and insides under the escalator steps had grown bulbous tumors and pulsing organs like the theater seats in the Rem had. The steps running under the ones the people descended took on very strange shapes as they circulated back up to the ominously warped gears and machinery at the top. Sylvie listened to her instincts and stepped onto the warped edge above the steps—

Just as the escalators opened up.

The steps the people were on split into long chasms filled with black teeth and tentacles. Dozens of people dropped into the opening maws, which bit into their legs and anything else that got between their powerful chomping. Screams of terror were joined by those of slaughter. People with roughly chewed and severed limbs sprayed and pumped blood out onto each other as they clawed at the handrails and other bodies for safety. Those who escaped the worst of the initial feasting were either pulled down by the tentacles or they'd climbed onto the ledge above the steps Sylvie was on, forced to watch the others being eaten by the distorted abomination the escalator had become.

Sylvie looked back up at the first flight again—the pulsing organs that were visible through the escalator's translucence could be seen squeezing and shifting around the still bleeding and spasming limbs and body chunks of the people that escalator flight had consumed. They were already disintegrating, swirling fluids in the tightly filled, undulating chambers and sacs eating away at them with something like caustic digestive fluids.

"Jesus *Christ!*"

Sylvie was struck by a wave of nausea and her fear was back badly.

She looked down and saw that the woman with the tall heels had lost her right leg below the knee. She'd climbed over the railing and was clinging onto the outside of it as blood pulsed out of the shredded gore of what remained of her leg. The woman's face was drained white, the blood loss causing her eyes to lose focus and her motor functions to fail—

The woman lost her grip and dropped from the railing, falling three or four flights' height to the marble floor below. Her back snapped and head cracked open on impact, her other high heel shooting off her foot as something burst open in her lower body, blood spraying after it.

Some tried to scramble down to the second theater level at the base of the flight Sylvie was stranded on about halfway up. Others tried to climb back up the railing to the top floor—tentacles snatched their feet and legs, dragging them back to the waiting mouth chasms.

To get away from the ever-groping, lashing tentacles, Sylvie climbed over the railing. She gripped the pulsing, eye-covered handrail and dug her feet into the ever softening exterior of the escalator's outer structure. She could see the pulsing digestive sacs drooping down some below her from the flight she was on and tried not to think about it. Then a disintegrating head atop what was left of a torso and neck with still-living, pain-maddened eyes locked onto her from inside one of the taut acid-filled chambers.

She gasped and looked away, then saw what could be her only hope—the vertical film festival banners. The one on her side was only about five feet away. She'd just seen what the drop could do to her if she failed, but she had no other options. She readied herself, extending one hand toward the banner and shifting her body, prepping her legs for a jump.

"Oh, J-Jackie Chan, please smile upon me...."

She heard shrieks, then thumps and cracks from below and chanced a look down.

Thin black spines like quills or knitting needles were shooting out of clusters of holes forming in bulging sacs on the handrails below. They shot out, piercing through hands and arms of everyone who'd clawed their way up and over the railing, then retracted. And then the people dropped, one after another. The ones falling from lower flights mostly only broke bones. But the spine bulges were growing on the handrails from the lower levels on up. Sylvie couldn't help thinking of anti-bird spikes, but not in a way that was funny just then.

Sylvie readied her jump again, knowing she had just one chance—

The handrail bulged in her hand sooner than expected and the black quills shot out through it. She screamed in pain, but instead of wrenching away, used their anchoring of her hand to finish readying her spring. The long moment she waited for the spines to retract was agonizing, but when they did, she jumped. She whipped her bleeding, pierced hand toward the banner in rough parallel with her other.

Sylvie crossed the gap between the escalators and banner—but started dropping faster than anticipated and desperately flailed her arms as she made contact with the banner. She grabbed it, wrapping both arms around it and squeezing as hard as she could, sliding down several feet at almost freefall speed before her desperate gripping slowed her—

And her weight detached the banner from its cheap securing hooks on the top, dropping her to the ground floor.

Bodies of the dead and dying moviegoers who'd jumped off in a panic or been forced off by the black spines broke Sylvie's fall. It still hurt bad and knocked the wind out of her, but she was alive. Hurt. Shaking. Chest shuddering. But alive. Others who'd dropped when she did weren't as lucky, and she had to block out all the low moans and cries of people dying from their injuries.

Through her pain and lack of breath, she caught a glimpse of the Harry Lime creature leaning over the railing from the second-floor-lobby banister. Atop its neck was a horizontal plank of fleshy layers and eyes that had to be several feet across now, and still growing. It just watched her struggle on top of and surrounded by the deceased and mortally wounded through the myriad eyes along its crossed-*T* of a head, then leaned back out of sight.

After fighting for breath, she rolled off of the twitching and writhing bodies and hauled herself to her feet. She backed farther from the first escalator flight and its whipping tentacles. A few people dropping from above had landed close enough that they'd been immediately pulled into the escalator chasm and chewed up.

"Why...?"

Even faced with living, slaughtering madness less than ten feet away, Sylvie's thoughts strayed to her uncle, friends, and lover. Their dying faces. Their screams. She couldn't handle any more of this—and she still had no idea what *this* really was.

Fresh screams from above snapped her back into the moment. The first theater level was up only one flight from the ground floor and just after hearing more screams and sounds of exodus from another theater, she saw groups of people running for the escalator.

"Don't! Stay away!" Sylvie cried out, waving her arms back and forth above her head like a frantic aircraft marshaler, blood flinging off her wounded hand. She couldn't think of what to say that would make sense, because none of this made sense.

The first few people who made it to the escalators had no way of knowing what she meant, and the first person's eyes went wide and they tried to stop—

157

but the people behind them pushed forward and they all fell into the top of the long, jagged maw.

"No...!"

Seeing the carnage of the first few being horribly chewed up as they screamed—and Sylvie desperately trying to divert them—many of the others up on the first floor avoided the escalators, instead climbing over the railings to the sides of them and dropping down to the ground floor. Some of them stopped and stared at the dead and dying who'd dropped from above, but others just ran away in either direction down an intersecting perpendicular corridor the escalator rose away from.

Pulsing pain reminded Sylvie her hand was an oozing pincushion. She pulled a folded orange bandanna out of a back pocket that was still remarkably dry, considering all the things her jeans had been through tonight already. She flapped it open and wrapped her bleeding hand tight, the pain dovetailing with her memories of the square of thin cloth being one of Russ's ancient ones. He'd given a few of them to her to wrap into sweat-sopping headbands for projection booth shifts in the summer when the AC was out and fans were the only thing making it bearable.

She looked around at the corridor's far ends, half to stop thinking of Russ and half to find any signs of where she really was. Parking area to her left, something like a lobby to the right. The structural layout seemed odd to Sylvie, like the multiplex had been built into a much older building, then modernized—

Odd-colored flashes and crackling zap sounds came from somewhere up on the first floor out of sight, followed by more screams. She remembered the sci-fi images on the vertical banner posters and knew there must be some evil space man or alien up there, really murdering people with its fictional weaponry and whatever else was in those movies.

She didn't want to see any of that for herself, so she ran away from the escalators down the corridor to the right.

Sylvie ran past video-game cabinets and claw-game rip-off machines. She passed a couple glass-enclosed modern boutique stores, then came out of the corridor at the end where it opened up into a larger space—and she became more convinced of her old building, new theater impressions.

The building lobby area had to have almost a twenty-foot-high ceiling with ornate coffers recessed across its entire surface, windows almost as high around three open sides of the building's whole base, white pillars, and an antique-looking staircase built into one wall that seemed to rise to some clashing modern offices or maybe a nice restaurant, unrelated to the theater farther inside the building. The theater ticket office was to her right at the base of one of the tall-windowed walls, and stood out as a modern anachronism in what looked like an Art Deco–era designed structure.

Sylvie bolted across the lobby toward the big glass-and-brass double doors and what looked like a gently sloping, busy city street outside—still nighttime too, so possibly somewhere not too far from San Diego, she hoped. The big lobby hadn't warped or changed much visibly, but she could already see a hint of translucence to the surfaces.

Several theatergoers had already made it out through the lobby doors and out onto the sidewalk, and Sylvie followed them out with another group. But she knew immediately that this wouldn't save them.

Cars passing by out on the street and people walking on the sidewalks became slow-motion silhouettes, the vehicles' headlights blurring and leaving trails. Neon signs and blinking lights on store exteriors faded out. Then all the moving, lit-up signs of life faded away, leaving an unnatural and growing darkness that made everything outside look like a matte silhouette.

A young guy in a three-stripe tracksuit and sneakers stepped onto the street, spinning slowly as he looked around at the almost frozen shadow cars. "What the fuck *is* this, man?!"

Everything started to shake and rumble and Sylvie could see what few stars in the sky the city lights hadn't washed out becoming obscured by a huge, growing darkness. But the darkness also had its own haunting internal glow, and Sylvie realized what she was seeing just before it came pouring in, spilling and rushing to submerge everything—a sky-high tsunami of the luminous sludge like she'd seen out through the Rem's windows and doors.

Sylvie bolted back toward the theater doors, followed by a few others at first—then all of those who'd made it out onto the street rushed back too as the glowing sludge gushed out of the channels the streets made between the buildings across the street. Then the whole street darkened as it poured down from above.

Sylvie and most of the others had made it back inside—but the few stragglers were picked up by the wall of muck filling the street and slammed into the lobby doors and windows above, cracking them.

In seconds, the entire city area visible out through windows and doors was filled with the dimly glowing sea of churning muck, giving everything out there a ghostly pale and dark green monochromatic look and outline. The churning slowed to a swirl as it must have finished its spread or flow.

"This...isn't possible...." a middle-aged woman in the group who'd made it back in said.

A young man in a nice suit scoffed. "Oh, *this* was what caught you up?"

The guy in the tracksuit reached toward the shuddering lobby door but hesitated. "We have to help them!"

The people trapped against the glass and the sea of glowing liquid started screaming, the backs of their heads and bodies being eaten away like Russ had been in the Rem's projection booth. As the sea settled—bathing everything that could be seen outside in that same murky, haunting glow like she'd seen before—the glass cracked more. The fluid seeped in through the cracks in the door's frame and broken parts.

Sylvie turned back toward the corridor they'd come from and ran, booking across the lobby without looking back. She could hear others following, but didn't care anymore—

The glass collapsed inward, breaking all the way up to its arch-topped frame and rushing in with the gushing, churning fluid.

Sylvie heard shattering and screams behind her but didn't look back, pumping her legs harder and hoping there was a stairwell or something past the monstrous escalator down the corridor the other way. As she made it into the corridor, she chanced a look back:

Not only were people being disintegrated alive by the fluid, but there were dark shapes in it too, pulling others down into it and attacking them even as they were burned away.

She snapped her attention forward again, desperate for an unlocked stairwell or maybe an interior parking garage with levels she could ascend away from the sludgy acid sea—

A small group of people in black coveralls, boots, gloves, backpacks, and something like ski masks or balaclavas were advancing in a tactical formation from the parking area past the escalators carrying strange guns at different levels of readiness.

The woman in front and two others had earpieces poking up from half balaclavas—covering from the nose down—and all of them wore semi-reflective bubble goggles, like the old sideways peanut style Sylvie had seen in some of Russ's old motorcycle-riding footage with his buddies from way back. One of them in the rear wore a hood over their half balaclava, an opaque black bubble mask, a ratty old dark trench coat over their coverall, and didn't seem to be carrying a gun.

Sylvie looked back as she reached the still-lashing and chewing start of the escalators and saw a wave of acid sludge and formless dark creatures in it rushing after the handful of those who'd survived following her out of the lobby—

"Oh shit!"

The sight of how fast the rising liquid was moving, and how close it was behind them, drained all of her will and strength and she tripped on her own feet, slapping down on the blood-strewn marble near the hungry escalators. She sprawled and flipped over, expecting to be overtaken by the fluid any moment.

But the leader of the group raised what looked like a short submachine gun with a vertical slit at its business end—instead of the usual cylinders of barrel and such—and a fat rounded cylinder where its magazine would be. She aimed down the corridor toward the lobby at the wall to the right, just behind the last lobby escapees and in front of the fluid and fired it:

The gun's slit barrel flashed and a glowing floor-to-ceiling vertical bolt cut through the air, hitting the wall—then that glowing line stretched from where it had hit the corridor horizontally to form a visible barrier across the corridor. The fluid struck the membrane the slit gun's bolt had formed, causing it to bulge in some as the glowing muck poured higher and higher against it, but the instant surface held like super-strong plastic wrap. In less than three seconds, the entire other side had filled, the membrane a dam against the acid sea.

Then the creatures came, flapping, pressing, and brushing hard against the surface. Sylvie caught glimpses through the hazy murk, but they were just flashes of clumps of many clouded eyes, semi-decayed slippery flesh, hook- and talon-covered tentacles and misshapen appendages, jagged crimson teeth.

Their movement against the membrane stirred up some detritus that had already collected along the muck-side's base from the fluid pouring in through the lobby. Sylvie yelped and her stomach turned as she saw it was the still-disintegrating parts of the people who hadn't been fast enough—and that the creatures had missed in their haste.

One of the grotesque acid-sea beasts noticed a piece floating up near it—a mangled hand with only a pinky finger and part of a thumb still attached, connected to a forearm that ended in a gnarled stump with parts of the elbow joint exposed in the disintegrating flesh around it—and greedily took it into its mouth, layers of teeth pulling it in with two rhythmic, undulating bites.

The leader snapped her gloved fingers and there was a flash of bright white light and maybe flame in the air against their side of membrane. The creatures narrowed their many unearthly eyes and swam away—or at least out of sight in the murk.

162

The leader flipped the retreating abominations off. "Begone, carnivorous acidophilic dickheads!"

Up this close, Sylvie could see the team's balaclavas had something like dark air tubes running down their necks on both sides from jawline down into the coveralls. Also, their bubble goggles looked old, but seemed to have little electronic additions on the insides that projected info and diagrams on their interior surfaces.

The leader pulled down her mask and even with everything going on, Sylvie was struck by her beauty. She had a short, messy bob of auburn hair ending in blue-black tips speckled with bright multi-colored spots from what looked like an elaborate prior dye job. Freckles under and around big eyes with some sort of special contact lenses over them Sylvie could see even through the bubbles goggles. She also seemed to be multiracial, white with some East Asian, probably.

The woman collapsed the membrane gun to half its full size and stowed it in a slit of holster between her backpack and the small of her back. Then she leaned over and extended her hand to Sylvie as most of her team took up positions around the base of the escalators.

The one with their hood up, black bubble mask, and trench coat just stood in one place, looking around as if in a daze.

"Girl, you look a little overwhelmed, which I'm sure is understandable if you're here."

Sylvie took her hand and let the surprisingly strong woman bring her up to her feet.

"Wh-who are you?"

"You can call me Charlotte."

"S-Sylvie."

Charlotte nodded, then noticed something in her bubble-goggle interior readouts and narrowed her eyes at Sylvie, confused.

The young man in his nice—but now ruffled and blood-sprayed—suit from the lobby broke her concentration.

"That's fucking charming...but who the hell *are* you people?"

"Like I said, I'm Charlotte. That's Jn'drah...," and she nodded toward one of the two others that wasn't trench coat guy.

Jn'drah looked over, her eyes a little too big and far apart, and what looked like a vertical scar bisecting the sepia skin on her whole buzzed head starting at what could be seen of her nose above her half-balaclava. She caught Sylvie staring at her and narrowed her weird eyes—that also seemed to catch light strangely like they were hollow. She was gripping what looked like an old AK-47 with strange modifications all over, like fluid ampules and metal tubes.

"...Shasta..."

The one with the biggest pack nodded and flashed a peace-sign gesture without looking away from the bulging, gore-filled escalator-underside sacs visible through the dense miasmic mist above. She had clumpy black white-girl

163

dreads with bright blue and green roots pulled back in a loose ponytail, and carried something like a short-barreled AR-15 style carbine with its own little fluid tubes and ampules built into it.

"...and that's Mumbles."

She thumbed back toward the one in the trench coat who was still just looking around—then Sylvie saw that their mouth was moving behind their half balaclava, and there was a sound of murmuring or something coming from them, but really low.

"No, you idiot bitch—what is happening here and who the *fuck* are you with? CDC? CIA? FBI?"

Charlotte smiled and shook her head—then pulled a large revolver out of a holster on her right thigh Sylvie hadn't noticed, cocked its hammer, and put the end of the barrel against suit guy's forehead. He went wide eyed and froze, as did the other lobby survivors behind him.

All humor drained from Charlotte's face.

"Hey, Stucky—we're not here for you. Your taxes don't pay our salaries, get me? We're more like freelance Spooky Shit SWAT, if that makes it easier for you. And usually, we try to be preventative. The asshole cult who started this party was more secretive than usual, so we got the tip way too late."

She nodded her head toward the escalators.

"But seeing as how we *are* late, a lot of people are already dead. One lippy yupster prick who's keeping me from doing what I'm here to do just maybe joining them wouldn't keep me up at night—*understand?*"

Suit Guy nodded, his eyes crossed from staring at the barrel with its end pressed above and between them.

Charlotte lowered the gun, held the hammer back as she squeezed the trigger, then gently eased it back into place before re-holstering the big pistol.

Suit Guy said, "Yeah, I understand...that you're a fucking *psychopath!*"

Her hand went down to her thigh holster again—but when it came back up, she just flicked the guy on the nose.

Suit Guy yelped and recoiled. He spun and gestured toward Charlotte to get sympathy from Tracksuit Guy, Middle-aged Lady, and a hollow-eyed, blood-spattered high-school-aged couple who looked like Internet Kids on a rare IRL theater date. They all seemed too dazed to care.

Jn'drah chuckled and shook her head.

Charlotte unslung a bullpup combat rifle Sylvie recognized as a FAMAS F1—from watching too many action and war movies with Russ—with odd additions like the others, and primed its charging handle.

"Affix s'more roasters, ladies."

Charlotte, Jn'drah, and Shasta detached foot-long devices from the sides of their packs and attached them to their guns, then pulled hoses from their packs and socketed them into the backs of the devices. They looked like compact under-barrel flamethrowers but when they ignited their little pilot burners, the short flames were a pale fluorescent green.

"Shit, Sylvie.... You're leaking."

Sylvie realized Charlotte was looking down at her soaked bandanna-wrapped hand.

Shasta looked over and noticed too, then crossed toward her. She slung her carbine and reached back with both hands. The top of her pack that made it larger than the others' was a densely packed first-aid kit. Shasta took out a pair of scissors to cut the soaked bandanna off, but Sylvie slipped it off and tucked it into her also-soaked back pocket. The team medic nodded in recognition of it having some meaning to Sylvie and set the scissors down, then went to work cleaning, medicating, and wrapping Sylvie's hand with skill and care.

"Thank you."

Shasta nodded again, packed her kit back up, and attached it to the top of her main pack.

"No worries. I rarely get to patch anybody up. Mostly I just put chewed-up folks out of their misery."

There were flashes up on the first floor, then *zap zap* noises like before and Jn'drah took a couple steps back while aiming up that way so she'd have a better shot if a target presented itself.

Charlotte tapped a few commands into a small terminal on her wrist that was stitched into her coverall's arm. She looked at Sylvie again and frowned.

"Sylvie, do you know where you are?"

"I really d-don't."

"San Francisco. Well, a kind of shadowy imitation or replica of it, but the City's where you started before it went warping the lateral fantastic. You're tripping my sensors 'cause you're a little out of sync with this location. Where did you come from, sweetie?"

"S-San Diego...."

"And what happened there?"

Sylvie sighed but it caught in her throat. "We were screening a m-movie to show tomorrow...and the theater turned into a fucking nightmare like this—"

"Was the film called something like *Too Many Eyes?*"

"Yeah, exactly that—and this monster witch queen c-came out of it."

"Esthur.... And you were the only one who made it."

Sylvie just nodded, hate and sadness burning in her eyes.

"No small feat, as I'm sure you know from having met her."

Charlotte exchanged looks with Shasta and Jn'drah and nodded.

"We've been waiting for a break like this. Where did you come out, Sylvie?"

Sylvie looked up through the murk at the escalators in the octagonal shaft.

"I think it was house fourteen, at the t-top."

Jn'drah whistled. "Figures...."

As Sylvie lowered her head, she saw Mumbles look up, still mumbling quietly.

Charlotte nodded again. "Right, okay. Change of plans. Shasta—get these people ready."

Shasta detached her whole pack, set it down flat, and opened it lengthwise. She took out several wrapped rubbery packages, then flapped each open and handed one to each of the lobby survivors, including Sylvie. They were clear mask-and-hood-topped coveralls of thin rubber or plastic. Or maybe biosuit was more accurate, she thought, seeing integrated air canisters in the suit's backs with clear tubes running up the mask areas. The masks also had sets of small integrated filters in the mouth and nose areas.

Suit Guy scoffed. "What's this shit for?"

"Protection. Where we're going is a little...dicey. These suits aren't much, but they're the minimum needed for that environment to be survivable. Breathing too much of this rot dust miasma junk, or even just getting scratched or something, can turn you into something like that," Charlotte said, nodding at the living escalators again.

Middle-aged Lady said, "What do you mean?"

"Yeah, where are we going?" the female Internet Kid chimed in.

Tracksuit Guy just shuddered as he stared, mouth agape, at the shifting limbs, body trunks, organs, and heads still being digested in the hanging underside sacs running up a nearby escalator—looming over them like huge, pulsing human-meat sausages being formed.

Charlotte said, "We're going to Marposa, Esthur's own little slice of unreality. I don't have time to explain all of this to you, but Esthur is always our ultimate target, and now we can get to her. Marposa is a very dangerous, very strange place. They did all of this—killed all of these people—to charge her up, and she was supposed to be summoned tomorrow in San Diego, from what Sylvie is saying. The portals got crossed 'cause they screened the movie a day early...and now we can get to her."

Suit Guy screwed his face up. "*And?*"

"And you all are coming with us because without us, you're fucked. Won't be fun doing our thing either, but you're better off with us than here on your own."

He looked around, trying to think of a comeback, but gave up and started putting his clear suit on. The other lobby survivors did the same, including Sylvie, with shaking hands and a twisting stomach. Marposa sounded nightmarish and awful, but if it kept her with the experienced, armed people, she'd take it as something like a lesser evil.

Charlotte continued, "No arguments? I like that. Okay, what are your names? Fun as it might be, I'm not calling you yupster prick all night. I mean, I guess I could...."

Suit Guy narrowed his eyes and clinched his jaw. "Dylan."

She pointed at Middle-aged Lady. "Edith."

Tracksuit Guy said, "Ignacio."

"Odessa," and "Tim," said the Internet Kids.

166

"Thank you."

Charlotte watched Shasta get all their suits and masks fitted and sealed up.

Sylvie was surprised how well the light biosuit moved with her, having already forgotten she was wearing it until glinting from the small rotating filters over the mouth and nose area of the sealed hood and mask caught her attention.

Shasta finished with the last, Odessa's, and gave Charlotte an OK gesture before starting to close her pack back up.

Charlotte nodded. "Smashing. All right.... I'm not going to lie to you. You are not ready for this. Stay behind us and out of our way, but stick close. You have to trust us. Once this starts, we can't stop until we reach the rift in house fourteen. Understand?"

The lobby group all nodded sheepishly.

"Okay, group up behind us."

167

PATRICK LOVELAND

Shasta finished getting combat ready again and took position just out of tentacle range of the left escalator that would've traveled downward, her carbine readied. Jn'drah was to her right, ready to take the upward right one. Mumbles just watched and mumbled. Sylvie and the other lobby survivors stood in a loose bunch.

Charlotte said, "Okay, on my mark...."

Dylan cleared his throat. "Hey, don't *we* get guns or something?"

She chuckled. "No."

He shook his head.

"Three...two...one, cook 'em."

Shasta and Jn'drah triggered their under-barrel flamethrowers, streams of bright green liquid fire scorching the smacking, wailing mouth chasms and their limbs and tentacles. The fire made them glow as they shriveled and closed tight. They tilted the flames up and down, sealing the toothy openings all the way to the first theater level by some form of cauterization.

Jn'drah took the lead, hot-stepping up the right escalator. She reached the top and went into a combat crouch a few feet from it, popcorn crunching into the carpet under her knee and boot as she aimed down a wide corridor to the left that led to the theaters, perpendicular to the paths the escalators took in their switchbacking ascent. She aimed through the soupy miasma-filled air of the first theater level's lobby hallway and saw several burned and blasted open bodies strewn about and big scorch marks on the walls and ceiling. Muffled sounds of sci-fi ray-guns and such going off down the hallway in theaters and the occasional scream. Nothing in sight. She raised a hand and made a thumbs-up gesture, then brought it back down to support her rifle again.

Shasta saw the thumbs up and followed, reaching the top of the left escalator and pivoting around, then cauterizing the lower of the two flights up to the second theater level that zigged off the outside of the one she just climbed up. When she reached a landing the next flights zagged up from—directly above and parallel to the very first flight—she stopped and took up an overwatch position down the corridor Jn'drah was aiming down, intermittently looking up toward the second theater level.

–Clear,– Shasta's voice said low over a comms system Sylvie hadn't realize all of their biosuits shared somehow with Charlotte's team.

170

Charlotte pulled her half balaclava back up and shouldered her rifle. "Okay, follow me up this flight and I'll cover you to climb to Shasta."

She hiked up the left escalator, burning the long, angled gore sacs under the next flights up on the left and right as she went. Where the sacs weren't shriveled, boiling inside as they were sealed, they burst—making Sylvie thankful her biosuit's filters negated the smell. She still had to watch the disintegrating human remains squirt out and slap down amongst the bodies of the fallen from before.

Charlotte stood to the side of Jn'drah and scanned down the lobby hallway to the left as Dylan took the lead up the stairs with Edith, Ignacio, and the Internet Kids close behind. Sylvie took a last look at the acid sea to her right, held back only by the barrier from Charlotte's weird gun, deciding to take that as a sign that she could get at least some of them out of this awful situation. She started up behind Tim and Odessa.

When Sylvie made it to the first theater floor and started up the flight to the first landing, she saw Mumbles just watching them from down by the bodies of the people who fell. She had no idea what their deal was, but she figured Charlotte kept them around for a reason and just kept climbing.

Dylan made it to the landing and crouched behind Shasta, away from the writhing, chomping escalator flights she hadn't cauterized yet. Edith was slower but stepped onto the landing and past them, then held a handrail as she caught her breath. Ignacio made it up and put a hand on Edith's shoulder.

"You all right?"

She nodded that she was but looked frazzled and panicky.

Sylvie was halfway up to the landing climbing behind Odessa when space-gun sounds and crashing were heard down the first-theater-level hallway—

A human in an armored spacesuit was thrown out through one of the theater house's splintering doors and slammed into the wall across from it, crumpling to the carpeted floor. They got to their feet in time to raise a beam gun at a big bipedal robot that lumbered out of the theater after them.

Charlotte spoke low over comms. –Let these two fight and keep going....–

Sylvie watched the fight as she climbed the rest of the way to the landing, hoping the living sci-fi-trope characters wouldn't see them.

The human got some good shots in, but some small insectoid space creatures dropped from the ceiling onto their suit—and the robot took advantage, repurposing what looked like mining or geological surveying rotating saws and pickaxe limbs to eviscerate the screaming spaceperson.

Shasta made an open-handed "stay" gesture to Dylan and the rest, then stood and went to work on the left side of the next flights up. After she'd fused the first several feet of wailing, gnashing maw, she cauterized as she climbed— having to pause here and there to dodge whipping tentacles or malformed, barb-covered limbs coming out of the still-open maw chasms above.

The murderbot down the first-theater-level hallway turned its attention from the split-open-and-severed human and remaining bug creatures it was

171

mulching to the sounds and blasts of green brilliance around the escalators down the hall from it, and started toward them—

A meteor shower or particle beams shot out through a different theater's wall and doors almost parallel to the floor, pelting the far hallway wall and leaving sizzling baseball-sized gouges—also hitting the robot in a few vital spots and dropping it to the floor, a smoking, glitching wreck.

Charlotte chuckled softly. -Works for me.-

When Shasta reached the top, she took up a watch position like Jn'drah had below.

Shasta looked all around. -Woah....-

-What is it?- Charlotte asked.

-I think the closer we get to Esthur's portal, the more this place is changed by the possessed-ass movies these things are coming out of. Never seen it quite like this....-

-Peachy. Ah, yeah. I see some spacy shit down here, now that you say it.-

Sylvie noticed with just that suggestion that what she'd taken as vague suggested forms caused by the misty darkness of the hallway was also a hint of layered depth—parts of the sci-fi films' different settings dimly visible through the theater walls, floors, and ceilings. The whole place was becoming more and more translucent and showing the skeletal black understructures the Rem had, but this was different. It was like the overlapping film settings were bleeding through into this already shaky husk of reality. A fleet of ships in the distance, creature-infested space mines, the interior of a damaged orbital station, the glowing lights of an ocean base built under the ice-crust outer surface of maybe Europa or Enceladus.

Charlotte reached over and patted Jn'drah's shoulder, so she retreated to the flight leading up to the landing and hurried up it. When she made it to the landing, she took overwatch.

Jn'drah said, -Moved.-

Charlotte turned and crossed to the upward flight, then burned more gore sacs as she climbed up it.

When Charlotte reached the landing, Jn'drah started up the flight to the second theater level. She patted Shasta's pack then turned and started burning her way up the next flight toward the next landing, halfway up to the third and final theater floor. When she'd finished, she burned halfway up the last flight to the top from where she stood, then stopped and took overwatch on Shasta's position.

-Clear.-

Charlotte leaned down to the side on the landing to make sure nothing else on the sci-fi floor had taken interest in them.

"Okay, head up," she said to the lobby group on the landing.

Dylan and Ignacio didn't hesitate, climbing up the odd fused surfaces the under-barrel flame units left after fusing the monstrous parts together. Tim followed, pulling Odessa up after him.

Edith was shuddering, stuck in her crouched position with teary, panic-filled eyes.

"I can't...do this."

Sylvie crouch-walked to her and took one of her hands in both of hers.

"Edith, I'm scared too. But we c-can't stay here. We have to move if we want to get out of here."

Edith squeezed Sylvie's hand like a vice.

"If I stay with you, would that help?"

The woman locked her eyes on Sylvie's and she nodded, desperate not to let go. As Sylvie stood and helped Edith to, she glanced toward Charlotte—who was watching her. Charlotte gave her a little nod of acknowledgement Sylvie couldn't quite decipher, but she returned it and started climbing to the second theater floor. It was slow going with Edith behind, but Sylvie got them both to the top of the flight—then Sylvie saw what Shasta was talking about.

The sci-fi settings Sylvie had seen on the first theater floor were hauntingly vague, more like slowly forming suggestions. The noir-level settings looked almost real, and their overlapping layers and intermingling with the black skeletal diseased-flesh walls confused Sylvie, like all the places were there at the same time, impossibly. And some of the views would change periodically in size and orientation as if to match film cuts, really disorienting her.

Offices with light cutting in through horizontal blinds, the interior of a lavishly decorated train rushing through the snowy dark, a funhouse hall of mirrors Sylvie remembered from *The Lady From Shanghai*'s climactic showdown—and probably the inspiration for the same setup in *Enter the Dragon*, another of Russ's favorites. A shadowy bus terminal, overlapping foggy, lamplit streets—and the Wiener Riesenrad Ferris wheel in Vienna, Austria, that she knew from her favorite scene in *The Third Man*—

Sylvie remembered the Harry Lime creature from before just as she saw it again, leaning on a wall ahead near the start of the lobby hall that led to the theaters.

Its body was still a normal size, but its legs bulged asymmetrically in the suit trousers and its arms had stretched, now dragging on the floor, pulsing and glowing eyes growing all over them. The horizontal plank of flesh and eyes that had been its head had become so long that Lime had leaned against the hallway wall, about half the head flush against it going down to the floor and the other stretching up along it and following the corner formed by the wall meeting the ceiling and flopping down and drooping some as it continued to grow.

Charlotte came up behind and saw what they were looking at.

"Leave that nasty, weird fucker alone and move."

Sylvie tried to take Edith toward the next flight up but she wouldn't budge.

Edith's eyes were glassy and off. "That's Orson Welles.... I love him in the movies."

PATRICK LOVELAND

The creature seemed to notice her and tried to right itself, but the weight of its long head had other plans and sent it tipping over and sprawling across the scattered popcorn, drink cup, and candy-box-covered carpet.

Sylvie tried to pull her along again—Edith wrenched her hand free and took a few steps toward the lobby hall.

Charlotte sighed. "Shasta, grab her."

Shasta rose from her crouch and took hold of the left shoulder of Edith's blouse—

Edith whipped her arm up and around, breaking Shasta's grip, then ran toward the Harry Lime creature.

Shasta and Charlotte aimed at the thing but Edith was directly between them.

The mesmerized woman reached the grotesque abomination and helped it to its warped feet, then ran her fingers through the folds in the layered, translucent flesh between its many eyes.

"I've always wanted to meet you, Mr. Welles...."

The jagged, angled mouth that ran up the entire neck stalk that held up the flesh-plank head split open as one of the overlong arms grabbed Edith's back and pulled her toward it.

"Edith!" Sylvie cried out.

Both of her caressing arms disappeared into the darkness of its jagged maw—then the mouth snapped closed, roughly severing both arms as blood sprayed and squirted out of them.

Edith screamed as she finally seemed to see what the creature really was—

Then it bit most of her head off, part of the neck and one side of the lower jaw all that remained, flopping down as more bright red fluid surged up out of the torn arteries.

"No...," Sylvie said, meek and powerless.

As the monster feasted on her shoulders and chest, Charlotte and Shasta opened fire with their assault rifles.

The spent casings came out of the ejector ports as long strips of light that blinked out and vanished a few feet from the guns, and the muzzle flashes were too bright and looked wrong—like if shutting off a light had an echo.

The creature let out chittering shrieks as softball-sized chunks were subtracted from its form where the bullets struck it. It tilted its meaty head forward to form a kind of shield. When that didn't stop the small spheres eating away its form in flashing, vanishing clusters, it howled and threw its arms wide, standing straight and lifting its head parallel to the floor—

As an eerie glow emanated from the underside of its fleshy plank head, it floated up, almost brushing the hall ceiling as it started toward them. In time with its advancement, the Ferris-wheel layer of the movie settings began to tilt up, like a ghostly apparition viewed through a fisheye lens's forced distortions. The structure loomed higher and higher and stretched, curving away as the mushroom-shaped man-creature hovered toward them.

174

It also looked like the small spheres they'd taken out of it were reforming.

Charlotte scoffed. –Just our luck, stronger than usual. Jhn—get us to the top.–

She took Sylvie's shoulder and guided her to the next flight and Sylvie took the hint and climbed. Jn'drah was already most of the way to the top of the last flight up as Sylvie reached the landing. Dylan, Ignacio, Tim, and Odessa were watching Charlotte and Shasta hold off Harry Lime the abominable floating monster man below.

The duo had given up on their special rounds and switched to their under-barrel flamers, which seemed to hurt the hovering thing more.

–Got it, top is open,– Jn'drah said over comms.

–Copy that—get the rest of our guests to house fourteen and hold there.–

–Wilco.–

Jn'drah gestured down to Dylan and the rest on the landing to come up after her, but Sylvie saw something in her eyes she didn't like. As she crested the last escalator flight she ever planned to be on, she saw why:

They'd reached the Amorphous-, Maddening-, Barely-Seen-Abominations level, as she'd thought of it before, and boy did it sell the part now. Since she'd first spilled out of the screen in a theater down the long hall, the whole floor had been taken over by competing layers of infestation and living weirdness, somehow all visible at once. Each setting became the focus if Sylvie looked directly at part of it, the others still visible but like blurry near-silhouettes.

Then an invisible cloud of comingling smells assaulted her senses. Brine, rot, fungal stench, and other less-recognizable foulness.

Through the ever-thickening miasmic haze, she saw clutches of pulsing egg-shaped sacs. Secreted resinous structures forming on the walls, floor, and ceiling that made the lobby halls resemble the interiors of a huge misshapen ribcage covered in sea coral that was like quill-covered tumors. Fluid pools and undulating growths everywhere. Blue-black spheres of different sizes embedded partway in the walls like they'd grown there. Moonlit fields sporadically dotted with strange statue-like asymmetrically bulging and rounded obelisks of frozen innard-slop madness that jutted up from the floor at odd angles, some reaching the ceiling or disappearing into it.

Sylvie remembered the last from Morgan Ashpoole's *Menhirs* novella and the movie adaptation that brought it here, and shuddered at the thought of those obelisks waking up in real life—not that anything from the movies they'd been showing on this floor was something she ever wanted to actually be in the presence of. She could also see a tall lighthouse and a partially submerged shipwreck out past crashing waves from *The Things in the Storm* through the theater structures near them and her stomach twisted even more. "We should just g-go...."

Jn'drah looked back at her and narrowed her odd eyes. "No shit, really?"

"Sorry."

"Whatever. Okay, you all stay on my ass, got it?"

175

They nodded and followed her down the layered, disorienting lobby hallway. Even through all the spooky weirdness she was walking on, Sylvie could see suggestions of the noir level below through the floor and she tried to imagine what it must look like from the base of the escalators now, gazing up, as the layered translucence of the theater and all the film settings seemed to be accelerating. She decided it must look like a tower built from overlapping chunks of many places bleeding into each other, each level up disparate from the one below and all trapped in the ghastly decayed-flesh-and-black-skeletal-theater-building structures as a scaffold-like framework.

She tried not to look too closely at the menhirs of frozen chaotic flesh as she passed them, instead scanning all around for signs of other creatures from the monster films—

"Shit!"

A large dark form dropped onto Jn'drah up ahead from the dripping tumorous ribcage ceiling, pinning her to the conflicted layers of floor as it attacked her. It slashed and stabbed at her with glinting talons as she struggled, opening up her back. –Need help...up here!–

–Copy.– Charlotte said, sounds of flame being thrown and inhuman wails Sylvie could hear down by the escalators mingling with the background of the comms feed.

As it thrashed and struck, Sylvie recognized it from its movie—one of the amphibious sea beasts from *The Things in the Storm*, human as a starting point but mutated into a semi-amorphous mess of tentacles, fins, extra limbs—and all that covered in sporadic sections of armor-like coral growths to match their infested secretion-altered grotto habitats. Warped head with two bulging clouded eyes that looked sightless and huge multi-jawed mouth with what had to be hundreds of shiny blue teeth jutting out from putrid mouth flesh.

Tim and Odessa shrank away as Dylan and Ignacio rushed to help Jn'drah—

Another one of the creatures camouflaged up in the ribcage coral ceiling swung a malformed arm and a few tentacles down and snatched Ignacio up by his head and arm, pulling them up toward its gnashing mouth.

Dylan froze in terror, just watching the creature prepare a death strike of a bite.

Sylvie knew Jn'drah was their only hope and needed her. She looked around for a weapon and spotted a line-dividing stanchion. She hurried to it, pulled its connecting belt out, then splashed and crunched over to Jn'drah and her attacker hefting it over her shoulder.

Ignacio grunted and breathed hard as he struggled with the creature hauling him up toward his death and started swinging his legs back and forth. He flung them up and wrapped them around the thing's arm and tentacles, hooking them in a way that locked its head and mouth away from him in some sort of upside down jiu-jitsu arm bar. The creature tried to chomp onto his thigh but he desperately grappled with it, keeping it held tight.

176

Another creature came out of the curved, bumpy wall of ribcage coral to the side of Dylan and he screamed as it lunged for him, taking him to the floor and splashing into a fetid puddle of some unknown faintly luminous fluid.

Odessa stepped toward Dylan and the attacking beast, but Tim wrenched her back by her wrist and she yelped. Tim scowled.

"What the fuck, are you *stupid?*"

She pushed him hard with her other hand and her wrist slipped out of his grip.

"Fuck you!"

Tim stumbled back and slapped against one of the leaning menhirs near the hallway wall. It started vibrating and shifting—then parts of the frozen organic chaos that made up its statuesque structure started to soften and pulse as a haunting glow grew inside and around it.

He reached his biosuit-gloved hand toward the changing surface of the menhir, his eyes wide and transfixed. Odessa tried to pull him away from it but he was stronger and shrugged her off.

She slapped his shoulder from behind. "Who's being stupid now?!"

"Fuck *off....*"

When his fingertips made contact with the squirming surface, it pulled his arm in up to the shoulder and a panicked chirping cry came out of his mouth.

Odessa grabbed his other arm with both hands and tried to pull him away—

But it sucked him in all the way. She held on until the last possible moment, then let go so it couldn't take her too.

Odessa collapsed onto her knees and hands, wide-eyed gibbering as she looked between the awakening menhir and Dylan's desperate struggle with the sea beast.

Jn'drah had fought her way to being on her side, one raised arm guarding her head when Sylvie made it to her, the creature savaging her bent appendage. Sylvie set the stanchion down then heaved it up from the floor and slammed its heavy base into the creature's head. It collapsed away from Jn'drah, writhing and dazed, so Sylvie dropped the stanchion to help her up. The creature righted itself onto its limbs and tentacles before she could and loomed over Jn'drah, who was still on her back—

But she'd retrieved and readied her AK and stuck its barrel up into the monster's mouth. She fired a burst and its head was shredded—then the gore imploded, vanishing and leaving a mangled stalk atop a thick, blood-spurting neck.

She rolled over and fired two aimed shots into the creature Ignacio was struggling with, careful not to kill him in the process. Her shots hit home, Ignacio and the mostly headless creature dropping to the hallway floor.

More shots rattled off from back by the escalators and Sylvie saw Charlotte and Shasta had made it to the top.

177

Charlotte's strange bullets had peppered the creature that was on Dylan, subtracting several spherical chunks and killing it—but as it collapsed to his side, Sylvie saw it had already eaten most of his face, then through his forehead and one of his eyes to get to his brain—which was mostly gone, what remained of his skull giving it the look of a quivering bowl of gelatinous porridge.

Sylvie looked away and held down a retch as she helped Jn'drah to her feet. Jn'drah had open wounds all over her back and arms, but the dark fluid around and streaming from them wasn't red.

Shasta and Charlotte started down the corridor toward Sylvie and the others just as the abominous Harry Lime monster floated up out of the octagonal escalator shaft behind them, its underside glowing brighter now as it glided over the lobby carpet and its strange added layers. The dangling eye-covered arms had kept growing and come apart, forming asymmetric groupings of tentacles that ended in oozing black tips it dragged on the floor below and behind it.

Shasta stopped and fired back at it to slow it down as Charlotte ran. Then Charlotte stopped, turned back, and fired so Shasta could catch up—then do the same for her.

Sylvie and Jn'drah crossed to Ignacio and helped him heave the dead sea monster off of him, then up to his feet.

Charlotte and Shasta made it to the undulating menhir and grabbed Odessa, who was sobbing with wild, lost eyes now.

Charlotte looked at the menhir and said, "House fourteen—now! I'm gonna play matchmaker...."

Shasta pulled Odessa along with her while Jn'drah covered, Ignacio and Sylvie already hustling toward the busted concessions stand Sylvie had seen earlier. They all bunched up at the drooping, translucent house 14 doors. Shasta and Jn'drah each grabbed a warped, fleshy handle and pried the mottled flaps the doors had become apart. Ignacio helped Odessa inside.

Sylvie looked back down what remained of the lobby hallway, the encroaching other places blurring the borders of their confinement more all the time.

Charlotte had slung her FAMAS and had backed about fifteen feet away from the menhir, watching the Lime creature hover down the hall in her direction. When it was almost next to the pulsing, bulging menhir, she took her big revolver from its holster on her thigh and shot a few rounds into the living obelisk—

The thing swelled and burst, living chaos exploding outward as it was freed from its statue-like form. Putrescent animate madness filled the hall in an instant, pouring all around the Harry Lime thing as it tried to slash with its many tentacles and float away. Dozens of appendages formed out of the writhing muck—some rudimentary, others covered in warped but effective digits—grabbing the Lime creature and pulling it apart with quiet ease as its victim wailed, then the wretched, spumy-slick mass absorbed them.

The spawned amorphous matter of the menhir's rebirth made no sense and Sylvie couldn't look directly at it—it couldn't exist as it was. Something between liquid and fleshy solid or shifting from one to the other on such a basic level that her head swirled with confusion and doubts of reality just from glimpsing it. Malformed limbs became innard-and-concentric-fractal-bone slop that became tentacles and so on. And it all quivered and vibrated so fast you'd have trouble looking at it, maddening or not. Then it started spill-climb-crawl-striding toward Charlotte.

"Fuck *that* noise!"

Charlotte backpedaled down the hallway toward house 14, holstering her pistol and firing blasts of green flame from her FAMAS's under-barrel at any part of the menhir thing that got too close. She turned and ran toward the concessions stand and saw Sylvie.

"Dammit, girl—*go-go-go!*"

Sylvie bolted for house 14 and into it, with Charlotte right behind her. The theater had become a drooping, oozing mess of eye-covered translucent walls and gloopy seats.

The burst blister she'd slid out of was glowing and she saw that Mumbles—who she'd totally forgotten about—was staring up into it, the others waiting around him. Even covered and bundled up, Sylvie decided that Mumbles seemed to be a him.

Charlotte pointed to the big oozing blister. "No dawdling, motherfuckers—I don't scare easy but that standing-stone blob thing on our asses just filled my nightmare bank for a while!"

Mumbles stepped around and took up a classic stooped-with-interlaced-fingers boost stance. Jn'drah took point, making use of Mumbles' assistance to climb up and in. The light coming from within the blister fluttered as she entered and there was a crackling sound. Shasta aided Mumbles and Ignacio in helping Odessa up and through, then Ignacio himself. Crackle. Crackle. Then Shasta used Mumbles' boost. Crackle.

Sylvie hooked her foot in Mumbles' fingers and heaved herself up to the saggy opening.

"Shit...."

Charlotte was looking back at the theater doors—the menhir spawn was pour-crawl-roll-walking into the theater through it. She slung her rifle and took out a baseball-sized grenade with a cartoony skull-and-crossbones stencil-sprayed onto it. She gripped its spoon lever and pulled the pin.

"Never watching your movie now, you sloppy, creeptastic bitch—but here's my review anyway!"

She released the spoon and it flung off and flipped away with a tinny sound, then she threw the grenade toward the creature spill-crawling through the theater doors. The ball disappeared into the vibrating and shifting flesh and fluid surface but the thing just kept pulling its way in—

The grenade exploded, shredding everything around its radius then freezing for an instant—before imploding and vanishing into where the grenade had been, taking a forty-foot-diameter sphere of matter with it.

A huge scoop had been taken out of the flesh and black skeletal structure of the theater floor and what remained writhed and quivered like a huge wounded body. The ex(/imp)losion also left curved sections of partially severed seats behind and the entry doors were gone—and the creature out in the hall had lost everything that had been in the big ball area of the blast—

But it hadn't stopped growing and there was much more where that came from.

Charlotte had been smiling since the grenade went off, but that drained away as she saw how large the creature already was—and the hole she'd made had just given it easier access.

She turned toward Mumbles to climb out and saw Sylvie still there, raised up, bent over, and holding onto the blister opening.

"This isn't the time for you to put your ass in my face, you tease! Get *going!*"

Even with everything going on, Sylvie blushed as she climbed into the glowing opening. Then with a fluttering of lights and that crackle sound, it closed around her, squeezing until she couldn't move or breathe—

—and Sylvie was born into a storm.

She was squeezed through and spilled out of the portal like an easy birth then dropped into the arms of Shasta on the way down, who helped her get footing. She breathed in and out deliberately to recover from a strange feeling the transfer gave her and looked around.

They were under a storm-darkened sky filled with layers of rushing, wind-blown thunderheads above that seemed in competition to be the most ominous and looming. They'd come out of the portal into something like a broad, gently sloping meadow dappled with glowing pools of different sizes and bordered by odd-shaped trees that thrashed about in the storm. But the tempest swirling and blowing around them made it hard to see anything clearly. She couldn't even see the ground very well, and it seemed strange too. Banks of sickly colored thick miasma or fog or both blew quickly over and above the ground, the wind too violent to allow clinging or lazy floating.

Jn'drah was on watch ahead, rifle ready and a hood secured over her half balaclava, as Ignacio tried to comfort Odessa—who still looked half-mad at best.

Charlotte came through next, tucking and slapping down into a crouch before standing and readying her rifle.

Mumbles tumbled out and landed on Charlotte's shoulders and the top of her pack, hooking his legs down over her chest like a clown might.

–Agh, get off, you goofy prick,– she said and chuckled. The storm was so loud they could only hear each other through the comms link.

He kicked his legs up and rolled back off of Charlotte, landing behind her and mumbling as he looked around.

Charlotte pulled a hood over her head that hooked onto the half balaclava and came together under her bubble goggles, completing a full-head covering like Jn'drah had.

–Welcome to Marposa. Not a resort spa, but we've got a purpose,– Charlotte said.

Jn'drah shook her head. –I fucking hate this place.–

–Oh, come on. It's at least a *bit* marvelous,– Charlotte said.

–It's a depressing, awful nightmare place.–

–I mean...I'm not saying I'd like to build a summer home here, but the trees are actually quite lovely.–

Sylvie couldn't help chuckling at that, a line from a favorite movie of hers. The relief of escaping the multiplex had her a little more relaxed, even though she knew that would probably change soon.

Charlotte looked over at her and winked. -Oh, you know that one, do you?-

Ignacio said, -And as for the Rodents of Unusual Size?-

He, Charlotte, and Sylvie all said, -I don't believe they exist.-

Ignacio and Charlotte chuckled.

Sylvie laughed and it felt good to let go of some tension, but then remembered watching that movie with Margot and sobered. She let the wind blow her around a bit and the rain pelt her face under the clear biosuit mask.

Charlotte took a revolver out of a concealed cross-draw holster on her right hip and extended it grip-first toward Ignacio. It had a small glowing ampule built into it like the bigger ones on the modified auto rifles her team carried.

-Ignacio.-

-Yeah?-

-Fired a gun like this before?-

He nodded. -At bottles in the desert, yeah.-

-Take it. Marposa is a whole different thing from that hellish multiplex and you should have some way to defend yourself. Worse things here than bottles, though.-

He nodded and accepted it. She took some quick-load cylinders out of a pouch on her harness and tucked them into a couple of pockets on the front of his biosuit that Sylvie hadn't noticed they had.

Ignacio examined the gun, nodding. -Thanks.-

-No problem. Ever fired a gun, Sylvie?-

-Went to the range with my uncle here and there. Not a great shot, but I know the basics. Don't aim at something unless you intend to kill it, trigger discipline, et cetera....-

-Better than I expected. Shasta, give Sylvie the Squirrel.-

Shasta seemed to frown behind her half-mask. -You sure? It's pretty squirrelly.-

-Show her how to de-squirrel it.-

-Gotcha.-

Shasta slung her carbine and took a semi-automatic pistol out of a holster on her left thigh that had an oddly long guard around its trigger and what looked like a thin metal handle running under its barrel. Sylvie recognized it, a Beretta 93R. Looked cool, but like most machine pistols, had limited use. Pretty, though. And it also had those little glowing ampules installed each side of its slide, but they looked designed to make racking it easier, instead of being a nuisance.

-Okay, we call this the Squirrel 'cause it's hard to control and fires fast. Three round bursts, if you set it that way...-

Her dreads were flopping around in the heavy wind, so she pulled up her hood and secured it. She had nice eyes behind those bubble goggles, Sylvie decided, and probably wasn't bad looking all around, under that balaclava...or coverall. Then Margot's face popped into her mind again and she shrugged the blossoming thoughts off.

–...but we ain't settin' it that way. You should use it like a little rifle or carbine. The special rounds do most of the work anyway.–

She adjusted a selector switch above the grip.

–This would actually be easier for you, as I'm left handed and have to tilt it to flip the switch. I don't recommend it, though. Anyway, you're better off keepin' it single shot, experienced or not.–

Then she unfolded and attached a thin metal stock to the base of its grip and slotted a long magazine into it.

–The stock is more like a brace in burst, but should help in single. Always use this, though.–

She flipped the metal piece under the barrel down and showed Sylvie how the thumb on her forward hand hooked into the long trigger guard, then wrapped her fingers around the little handle the metal piece became.

–Lean your body forward some, and pull this down some if you fire bursts. But like I said....–

–You *really* wouldn't recommend it.–

Shasta gave a curt nod. –Right. Oh and here's the safety. Don't forget.–

–Understood,– Sylvie said, and gave a little three-fingered Girl Scout salute.

Shasta chuckled and shook her head.

Charlotte cleared her throat. –There will be no frivolity in my presence, thanks very much. Job to do, and all that. Also, Sylvie, as a payback for arming you, I expect you to be more proactive, accordingly. Take some agency, as it were.–

Sylvie nodded. –I understand.–

Shasta produced a few long 20-round magazines from different spots on her harness and right thigh holsters, then tucked them into self-securing pocket-sleeves around the midriff area on Sylvie's biosuit.

Ignacio nodded toward Odessa. –She get a piece?–

Charlotte tapped her wrist interface a few times and Sylvie saw the words COMMS BLOCK appear over Odessa's head through the mask of her own biosuit—which she had apparently underestimated, augmented reality tech somehow embedded into its thin, clear structure in some invisible way. She had noticed groupings of shiny things like little round watch or hearing-aid batteries in a few areas when she was putting it on, but for those to be actual tech themselves tripped Sylvie out.

Charlotte said, –I've seen that look before. If I gave her a gun, there's a good chance she'd put it in her mouth and, well, yeah....–

–I get you,– Ignacio replied.

She keyed the COMMS BLOCK off and said, –Nah, no more guns available.–

Ignacio nodded in an obvious way in response so Odessa could see.

Odessa's eyes shifted around like she heard them talking about her, but she was too far gone to care.

Charlotte pointed down the gentle slope of the meadow. –Okay, for real this time. Let's move, y'all.–

She started down, passed Jn'drah, and took the lead spot. The rest followed, Shasta taking up the rear with her carbine angled toward the ground and to the side—unless you counted Mumbles, who just kind of meandered and popped up here and there, Sylvie had noticed.

As they came out of the meadow, Sylvie saw they were on a sloping hillside that continued down into a wide flat-floored valley with large patches of forest—barely visible through banks of fog and clouds of particles being blown around by the raging storm. The tops of buildings poked out from the woods in a few areas, steeples the most obvious. From the vague, dark silhouettes in the distance, there seemed to be a mountain range that rose up in the direction Charlotte was walking. A bit above and from afar as they were, the valley almost looked inviting and even beautiful, in a solemn, melancholy kind of way.

Something about all of it just felt wrong, though.

Charlotte led them down one of a few road-like paths between violently swaying trees that led in the rough direction of the mountains in the distance. And then Sylvie saw the trees, and what was under their fiercely thrashing canopy, more clearly. Sylvie remembered a feeling she'd had seeing Esthur up close—that she looked at once petrified and alive. That was what this place looked like.

The so-called forests here were made up of translucent, skeletal leafless trees, only in place of the missing leaves were glowing sacs and obscenely layered colonies of sickly looking miasmic fungi. The understory was similar, only more overtaken by the fungus. Some of it looked like lively luminous coral, outstretched tentacles blowing around and intermingling here and there in a way that made her think maybe they were communicating. And the forest floor was bioluminescent living shag carpet, anemone-like tendrils of various lengths curling and climbing on each other. These grew longer and more densely layered around the edges of puddles of bubbling muck, some the size of small ponds. Concentric layered auroras wafted up off of those pools, dispersing as the lesser winds blowing through under the canopy kicked up intermittently.

Charlotte said, –Don't touch anything here but the ground. But even that's a bit dicey....–

Sylvie looked down through the miasmic fog blowing over and around them and saw that the ground was translucent. Looking down through the gauzy mottled-skin surface, she glimpsed black skeletal interconnected structures like molecular models she'd seen in school science classes but fractal-ized and

185

warped, pulsing diseased looking organ-like sacs, and what looked like pus or some other sickly fluid flowing through a gargantuan subterranean circulatory system.

She looked away to quell a rising panic from gazing down into the ground and instead took in the view of the ominous, dark mountains looming even larger on the far end of the valley over the forests. She'd thought the anemone layers where you'd expect grass to be were weird—but at least they covered up the hauntingly strange ground.

Their path widened and broke a few different directions, Charlotte taking them down the one that seemed to head toward the mountains. Its snaking-but-roughly mountainward path had encroaching patches of the anemone carpet creeping out of the forests that flanked it, and at one point it opened up to their right into a large meadow.

Near the far end of the forest lining the meadow, there was a farmhouse. In keeping with the forest around it and what Sylvie had seen of Esthur's effect on matter, the farmhouse—and everything else from its low rock walls and fences, to its animal-drawn plow—had the same eerie, glowing translucence and skeletal black-inside structures. Thankfully, there were no animals in sight, as Sylvie didn't want to know what this place would do to them.

This was definitely Esthur's realm.

Just as they were reaching the edge of the meadow and its swaying tree line met the road again, Sylvie got her unwanted glimpse. From behind the skeletal farmhouse, somewhat visible through the structure's translucence, a creature stumbled and strode into view. Stumble, stride, stumble, stumble, stride—like a misshapen newborn giraffe. It was almost as tall as the house, a warped, asymmetrical trunk of head and body atop several rickety, long legs—and all of that sharing the translucent, black-skeletoned Marposa ghost rot, as Sylvie had decided to think of it. The haunting otherness of this effect wasn't the rot of something that had died, but something so weird that it couldn't. Not naturally, anyway. She almost felt sorry for the creature, until she realized it would probably gleefully kill and consume her it if noticed her and the others sneaking through the storm.

They continued down the road, the mountains growing steadily above the forest ahead.

At another fork in the road they passed through, Sylvie noticed a village down one road that must have been home to one of the steeples she'd seen from back at the canyon mouth. Like everything else here, it was fully consumed by Marposa's warping effects. The storm wailed over and through it, the malleable ghost-rotted buildings shuddering and swaying sometimes. Through the windblown fog and forest miasma, she could see more decaying, semi-gelatinous looking black-boned beasts loping around. She only saw two, but assumed there were more meandering about town, or maybe off in what served this place as "the woods."

Charlotte chuckled. –Can you imagine what their Halloween festival would be like?–

–In a place this spooky and fucked up, I bet they dress up as normal, boring things and trick-or-treaters are given furniture catalogs and shit like that,– Jn'drah said.

–Exactly! Like, *I'm dressing up as a bookcase from IKEA.*–

Jn'drah laughed. –*I am a fresh new sealed package of socks.*–

–*I am a frying pan containing sizzling egg whites and turkey bacon,*– Shasta added.

The banter reminded Sylvie of sitting in the Rem with her uncle and friends so recently—only just hours before and she fought back tears that kept trying to well up.

A little ways ahead the road inclined into a bend lined with the ghastly trees, starting into the foothills around the base of the mountains. Sylvie noticed the trees were somehow weirder and less similar to each other, the farther up they went. More varied tree sizes and shapes. More amorphous and aggressive fungus. Much more irregular growth of the anemone things that made up the forest floor—some overgrown so much they covered what served the trees as trunks. And an even thicker, denser miasmic mist clung to everything.

Charlotte said, –Ah, getting closer now.–

She pointed at some clusters of what looked like blue-black malformed, undulating batwings with veiny translucent membranes between their spreading tentacles. They grew in among the anemone layers, some even up on the lower areas of the endlessly dying trees.

Charlotte followed the densest black tentacle-wings growth like a tracker until they came across a bluff with trees atop it and a choked path that started curving up and around into the forest to the left of its base.

Seeing the bluff was surreal for Sylvie, even more than the inherent horrible strangeness of this whole place. It was different, but close enough that she realized the bluff with the trees was a lot like what she'd seen in the film the main character went to see in the film they had watched in the Rem. They'd come up a living, desiccated, poisonous-storm-blown version of the foothills that medieval European girl had traversed searching for the black ivy—and then it struck Sylvie what the black winglike and tentacular growths in the madness forests were: Marposa's version of the ivy, or what had inspired it to be thought of as that. And they were all over the area at the base of the bluff and the choked mouth of the mountain path to the left.

Charlotte stopped at the easily missable opening into the curving ridge path so the rest did, all scanning the area with weapons ready. Other than Odessa and Mumbles, who was over in a thick patch of the wriggling black ivy lying down, letting it carry him around like a crowd surfer at a concert. She took off her pack and took a few things out of it:

Two odd-looking vambraces that she secured under her forearms, then around her wrists and secured around her thumbs. Then she took out what

187

looked like a T-ball bat–sized pointed rod in a holster and connected it to her harness in a way that she could grab its handle over and behind her right shoulder. She sealed her pack up and put it back on.

–All right, *ikimashou ka?*–

In the film Sylvie had watched at the Rem, it was normal ivy, trees, and bushes that had overgrown, concealing the ancient road that curved up around the mountain. Here it was the ghost-rotted trees, pulsing fungi, and tentacle wings choking the way. She shuddered just looking at the opening, but she knew it was what they'd come here for.

Sylvie felt a tugging at her feet and looked down. The glowing anemones that covered the forest floor were crawling and squirming on and around her biosuit-covered shoes. She lifted one foot up and drooling strands of slime followed, the tentacles writhing around in search of their lost curiosity or prey. She set her foot down in another spot and it was hungrily accepted.

Jn'drah chuckled. –Aw...they like you. Very special moment.–

–Yeah, wish I had a c-camera.–

Charlotte started toward the narrow smirking sideways mouth of the choked path.

–We better get a move on. If those happy little buddies make it to where your legs meet, you might not want to leave. Gettin' all anime on your privates and such....–

Sylvie blushed in her mask and hoped it wasn't too obvious from her expression.

Charlotte reached the path opening and squeezed into it, having to pry and pull at the overgrowth to make it through. Sylvie approached, careful to keep her Beretta up at an angle and her finger out of the trigger guard as she worked her body into the crevice. Charlotte reached a hand back through to her, and Sylvie let her take the Squirrel. Sylvie worked her way through and pulled herself out of the drooling slit the fungus and trees had formed.

The storm couldn't reach this place, the sounds of it out on the layers of trees that formed the path's concealment and protection muffled but ever-wailing. It opened up to about the width of an old horse-cart road, a curved, angled tunnel formed around and over the anemone-covered ground by inosculated skeletal trees—and everywhere, the black tentacle-wing ivy. It grew on and around all the trees and snaked through the undulating carpet of tentacles all over.

The tunnel was faintly illuminated by intermingling layers of eerie glow— otherworldly bioluminescence of the anemones and fungi or some light dimly

190

penetrating the translucent parts of the curving fused trees—but Charlotte activated a light near one of her shoulders on her harness anyway, and lights came on in the same area on her team and the multiplex survivors. Their cones of brilliance burned forward, miasma particles filling it with a dense, whirling haze. The lights tracked with their head movements, burning toward wherever they looked.

She turned back and gave Sylvie her Beretta, then trudged forward through the wriggling tentacles that were almost knee high in some places. Sylvie looked back to see if Jn'drah needed any help, but she had already made it through and was straightening up, her rifle in a low carry position down her chest and angled toward the living floor. Shasta helped Ignacio and Odessa in, then squeezed in herself.

Sylvie followed Charlotte, keeping her Beretta's business end low and toward the trees forming the left tunnel wall.

Above the sounds of the others' wet steps behind her, Sylvie heard a low humming sound and looked back. Mumbles was now taking up the rear behind Shasta again. He wasn't a small man, but he'd just had less trouble getting through than the others, she assumed.

She focused her attention forward again, then at the grotesquely formed structure of the tunnel itself. At any moment she feared the ivy would overpower them, or the grown-together trees would close around them, like the scene the character watched in the movie they'd watched in the Rem. All that still seemed so far away—and she realized it literally was. She was in another dimension or something and her life was in the hands of these capable but odd people she'd really just met. She feared their mission would be cut short by this confined space deciding to smother, crush, and/or consume them.

But the tunnel didn't close around them or acknowledge their presence at all. The anemones and ivy wings groped at them, but more out of seeming curiosity than malice. They hiked mostly unmolested with slurching, sucking steps up and around the mountainside in their tunnel, muffled sounds of apocalyptic storming outside. Their overlapping hazy cones of light bobbed around, but found no new abominations.

They came around another bend and the tunnel opened up wide and its ceiling broke open into a thrashing together of trees up in the storm—tall, leaning trees whose skeletal forms evoked thoughts of great claws. These tall, violently whipping trees hung over the upper edges of a dark structure that loomed ahead. It was different but Sylvie recognized it immediately....

They'd reached the outer walls of Marposa's castle town and its gatehouse.

These structures were twice as tall as those in the movie's movie, much darker, and even more ominous. As they approached, Sylvie saw that the structure was made of something between pitted rock and bone with only a thin, tight skin of sickly translucent flesh stretched taut over it. There was an ivy-tangled thick lattice of a portcullis, also much taller than the movie version—and on closer inspection, it seemed to be a set of interconnected lattices several layers deep.

Sylvie shook her head. "I don't know if I can climb that, even with all the weird ivy all over it."

"Good thing we're not climbing, then."

Charlotte whistled and Mumbles took the lead, trudging up to the portcullis before stopping. Without turning back, he extended his hands behind him. Charlotte took one. Jn'drah adjusted her three-point harness and slung her AK, then took the other. Mumbles started walking toward the portcullis and the other two kept his pace—

Just before they reached the ivy-choked lattice of it, Mumbles became entirely see-through, clothes, goggles, and all. Then starting from where their hands met his, Charlotte and Jn'drah did the same, all three of their bodies' insides becoming visible and glowing. Mumbles and Charlotte's bodies were visible in layers of muscles, fat, organs, etc.—Jn'drah's took on the same translucence, but Sylvie noticed something was fundamentally different about her insides. She couldn't make out what she was seeing, but she realized Jn'drah must really be inhuman in some way, especially when she remembered the weird fluid that seeped out of her wounds back in the multiplex.

And then they all went through the portcullis, like it wasn't solid. She just stared at the portcullis in a state of awkward wonder. Then she realized it wasn't the portcullis that wasn't solid—Mumbles had made them able to pass through the matter it was made of.

–Hey, guys. He's coming back, so get closer....–

Mumbles came back out, still translucent and leering—through his phased balaclava and bubble mask, she could see his big eyes and his teeth through his mumbling mouth. He turned around and stretched his hands back again.

Shasta guided Odessa and an obviously reluctant Ignacio to take them. They did and went translucent and glowing like Mumbles.

Ignacio shook his somewhat see-through head. –I think I'm gonna puke, man....–

Mumbles walked through with them in tow the same way and they all vanished through the portcullis.

–Okay, one more time.–

Even expecting it, her pulse jumped a bit when Mumbles' translucent glowing hands materialized out of the solid matter of the portcullis. She could see his currently insubstantial form glowing inside its lattice layers through the few small gaps in the wing-ivy layers too. One of his wide eyes was burning a hole in her own through his now see-through bubble goggles from within a black wreath of squirming "leaves."

Sylvie fought off her hesitation and took Mumbles' hand. Shasta took his other one and nodded to her.

She had gone through a lot since this began, but this was the strangest thing she'd ever felt in her life. Her hand tingled, pulsed, and vibrated, going see-through in layers and spreading from there to take over her whole body. Mumbles pulled her with him and she was terrified but went with it, fearing what would happen if she let go before coming out the other side even more. She just kept walking, unsure if her steps were making contact with anything or if he was just pulling her along over the surface.

Mumbles pulled her and Shasta out into a gale-blown tempest, let go of their hands, and let himself become solid and opaque again.

The storming in the valley and above the trees of the foothills had been furious, but it seemed even stronger here. She knew they'd entered the castle town, but through the hurricane-strong winds that blew banks of thick fog, rain, and miasma through, she could barely see it.

What she could see twisted her stomach with dread, which wasn't helped by a queasiness Mumbles' phase-shifting ability caused.

Marposa's actual castle town was three times the size of what had been in the movie version she'd seen, as was the castle itself, looming in the distance at the end of a gentle slope. From the vague shapes Sylvie could make out through the rolling maelstrom, many of the structures were two or three stories tall in contrast to the squat buildings in the film's set. If this had ever been a real place in an Earthly setting, it would have been a bustling hive, full of life.

The Marposa they were in now, whatever it had been, was the opposite. Desolate. Empty. The eerie faint glow of its uninhabited streets was seen only in haunting glimpses between waves of the thick fog and whirling rain.

Not only were the pitch-roofed structures here translucent with the black skeletal underframes Sylvie had become almost used to seeing, but what she thought of as this place's ghost rot appeared to become even worse the closer they got to the castle. These buildings didn't look fragile like the tainted village and farmhouse in the valley. Their exteriors had hardened in many places into a kind of solidified pitted crystalline resin that gave many surfaces an added bone-like, ribbed appearance. Blooms of the local nightmare fungus grew all over in many varieties, as did the wing-ivy. In places, the ivy grew in dense, layered patches around shiny opaque black spheres that had formed in walls, streets, roofs. The worst things were parts of the walls that hadn't hardened being see-through enough to expose groupings of purposeless organs and malformed limbs within them.

–Don't let the lavishly posh, Alps-like exteriors fool you. This place really is fucking terrible. Let's move like we're here for a reason. Also, pay close attention. Nothing's ever quite right about this place....–

She took the lead, walking through ivy and anemones that covered the town's main thoroughfare. Jn'drah and Shasta followed, heads on a swivel. Sylvie and the rest took up the rear, as Mumbles seemed to be doing his own thing again after being momentarily quite useful.

The road inclined gently at first, then became steep enough that the lanes jutting off from it sloped down and curved away or up to the sides, creating long switchbacks. In a normal place, this would've been a pleasant, scenic effect. Here it was disorienting, lending credence to Charlotte's warning.

Then the main road curved up to the left and the trio hiked up it, Mumbles somewhere close by but not always visible. Sylvie could see the walls around the castle itself through gaps between the angled roofs on the next level up, and even through the storm she could make out a huge circular stained-glass rose window high up on the castle exterior. It was the kind you'd see built into a cathedral. As if in response to their approach, a glow from inside seemed to fade up and backlight the design—an ornately intricate and beautiful butterfly. There was an ineffable strangeness to the design, but its beauty still contrasted its setting so much that Sylvie was almost sad to see it here. The glow appearing behind it could've been a trick of the light and storm. She hoped it was. Hoped that Esthur wasn't aware of everything in this place, and just waiting for them.

Charlotte led them up to an intersection where the inclining main road met the next flat level, an avenue that ran along the gradual curve of the castle's outer wall. The last regular town sections ran along in curving parallel, the buildings on the group's left backed by the high wall. She took them to the right, toward the center of the wall and its gatehouse.

The glimpses she got of the castle as a whole drove home how much the rose window clashed with it. She was no architecture expert, but it looked like a few styles fused together, leaning mostly toward the Gothic. But the butterfly window was in a huge rounded cylinder of a tower that the rest of the more hybrid Gothic and Norman sections seemed to radiate out from. And all of this was very vertical, that central tower much taller than most castles would need to be. She wondered if it was a kind of castle keep.

The thing that really gave Sylvie shivers, though, was that, architecture and style aside, all of this looked decayed and petrified as most things here did—but also, much of the structure's surfaces were covered in layered, clawing black veins. She couldn't see if they pulsed with fluid, but they gave off that appearance as an illusion, if nothing else. Then it struck here that they could be related to the tentacle-and-wing ivy—

–Hold up.–

Charlotte, Shasta, and Jn'drah were standing stock-still just ahead, Jn'drah aiming her AK at some shapes on the street about thirty feet ahead that were only vaguely visible through the storm in their overlapping suit lights. Ignacio had his revolver ready. Odessa cowered behind him. Mumbles mumbled.

Sylvie gripped the Squirrel tight and pulled its thin metal stock into her suited shoulder as she tried to get a good look at the squat forms. The vague things were all grouped around the mouth of the castle gate for the interior wall, which seemed to be open from the angled view she had.

They looked like mounds a couple feet wide and three or four long, covered in ancient threadbare cloth. Maybe twelve or thirteen of them. Some were longer and closer to the ground, but they had all been there long enough that black veins covered with winged ivy leaves had grown all over, in, and

194

around them. The glowing anemones that covered the streets had even grown up into and onto several of them.

Charlotte cocked her head. –These are new....–

–What are they?– Jn'drah asked.

–I really don't know. Marposa's always different, but strongly similar. And every new version is already ancient somehow. But I've never seen anything like these.–

Sylvie said, –You've been here b-before?–

Charlotte nodded. –Believe it. Every time Esthur's defeated, her cult spends years, sometimes decades, bringing her back. Marposa is like a sub-realm pocket dimensional extension of her self that she generates unconsciously or something, so it's different every new version, but has parts that are always the same basic thing.–

One of the mounds near them fluttered and shifted.

Sylvie swallowed hard. –C-Can they hear us?–

–No. I muted external comms.–

Another of the closer mounds moved under its cloth and flora bindings. Then another and another. In seconds, all of them were rustling in place.

Then one of them moaned.

–That's *no bueno*...,– Charlotte said.

She looked around, then Sylvie saw her face in profile through the helmet link as she looked to their side—

Mumbles was standing where she glared, mumbling away and he'd unconsciously raised his odd voice to be just loud enough to be heard through the storm.

One by one, the mounds all began letting out wails that were muffled by their coverings and the layered ivy and anemones that seemed to trap them against the writhing street. The closest one that had moaned first bulged, straining against the ivy veins and tentacles.

–Mumbles! Did you put your earpieces in?–

Mumbles turned his head toward her and nodded, still mumbling away.

–I know it's hard for you, but if you can't cut that shit out, do it quieter! Like, phase out your vocal chords or some shit!–

Mumbles did do something like that, because Sylvie couldn't pick out his mumbles in the sounds of the storm anymore.

She saw that the first mound wasn't really bulging as much as trying to rise up. Again and again it fought its bonds, pulling itself up a little more each time. Then she realized where she'd seen something similar to the mounds—deeply religious people prostrate in prayer.

Fitting her impressions, the thrashing mound was a humanoid draped in a cloak or shroud that had become a net-like trap of disintegrating cloth. Desiccated, ropey flesh barely contained atrophied muscles and tumorous growths glimpsed through the thin, gauzy layers of the garments.

The tentacles and vines held strong at first. Then the creature's struggling began to rip those around it apart and pull the ones that had grown into its body out, like a disoriented person in a hospital violently yanking out their catheter and various intravenous tubes. The vines sprayed black fluid that instantly corroded the flailing, wriggling anemone tentacles.

More of the creatures fought at their bonds, moaning louder and louder as they tried to tear free. Many of them didn't have the strength and their unholy wails remained muffled as they writhed against the tethers keeping them eternally captive. Four or five of them were making real progress following the first.

Sylvie didn't realize the first creature's eyes had been closed until it stood tall, turned its hooded head toward where Mumbles' mumbles had last been heard, and opened them. The whites were almost normal, but the pupils were clouded gray and the irises were a glowing off-white, all this glinting strangely in the light.

Even stranger sounds from a few of the translucent buildings lining the thoroughfare on their flanks began, as if in response to the praying creatures' moans. The walls of those began to quiver and shudder.

Jn'drah looked back and forth at the changing surfaces.

–What do we do, Shiv?–

Charlotte drummed her fingers on the pistol grip and under-barrel of her FAMAS.

–I don't think they can actually see us...so if we snea—–

With a cracking report, the first white-eyed zealot creature's head collapsed inward from a gunshot. In a brilliant spherical flash that sucked inward, a cantaloupe-sized chunk of the silenced thing's head vanished and the rest of it crumpled to the street and was greedily accepted once again by the tentacles and ivy.

Charlotte, Jn'drah, and Shasta looked at Sylvie, who was still holding up her smoking Beretta toward the creature she'd just killed.

Jn'drah scowled. –What the *fuck*, girl?–

–Charlotte said to be more pruh-pruh-proactive....–

The wails from the rising hooded zealots redoubled and the responses from buildings could be heard from all up and down the streets now.

Charlotte took another of the skull-and-crossbones grenades from her harness, pulled the pin out, and held the safety spoon tight.

–Oh, honey. Your heart's in the right place...but if you live through this, we're really gonna have to teach you to be more tactical.–

She turned, released the spoon, sending it flying off with a tinny sound, and threw the grenade into the center of the moaning creatures. After splatting down and being fondled by tentacles, the grenade went off—

The explosion made it twenty feet from the point of the blast spherically, froze—shredded, mangled zealot parts hanging the air of a split second—then sucked into the spot where the grenade had been.

The ghastly praying wretches had vanished instantly and a crater as deep as the explosion's kill radius was gouged out of the street where they'd been. Due to Marposa's attributes, it looked like a huge ice-cream scoop had taken the top layer off a bowl of living Cherry Garcia—organ slop and layers of tentacles and malformed limbs severed in smooth curves, pulsing as they slowly gushed and seeped thick fluids.

Then the castle town came alive.

Amorphous creatures clawed, climbed, spurted, or spilled out of the street and building surfaces all around into the storm, dozens of them—and no two exactly alike:

Pseudo-insectoids revealed their forms by unfurling from the boney hardened wall sections Sylvie had seen before, camouflaged until the moment they moved. Multi-limbed beasts similar to what they'd glimpsed at the farmhouse and village were disgorged and righted themselves on rickety legs like newborn forest creatures before loping toward them with purpose.

Sylvie watched as vaguely suggested warped organs and appendages—like she'd seen in the town walls before—formed together, then poured out of the building surfaces to become walking, misshapen vague humanoids like the slimy living embodiment of Marposa's ghost rot. Deteriorating muscle-strung skulls suggestive of different animals—but none of them quite right—would come to the surface of the walking organ-bone-tentacle-slime soup, fighting to form a recognizable shape.

Some monsters took flight from the roofs, but not with wings. More like necrotic, malformed, eyeless octopuses undulating through themselves to achieve an airborne state, their smooth tentacle-like arms ending in something like bent talons.

Jn'drah's odd eyes darted around from creature to creature. She ejected her AK's banana magazine and swapped it with a drum from her pack, then primed it. From the looks of it, Sylvie realized it could probably hold between seventy and eighty rounds.

–Okay, now that you started this, *Sylvie*, do what you just did…a *lot* more times.–

Charlotte slung her rifle, then twisted and tucked her vambrace-covered forearms together as someone putting on cufflinks might and flung her arms wide. A ten-foot length of thick cord or rope unspooling from each to drape down from her hands and wriggle in the anemone and ivy on the street. The ends tapered for the last few feet like whips of some kind. Then she realized it wasn't just the weird flora doing the squirming.

Sylvie looked closer and saw that the whips' structures were something between snake- or wheat-style chain material and living segmented *Glycera* bloodworms she'd seen in high school biology class.

Jn'drah and Shasta started firing their auto-rifles at the converging monsters all around.

Jn'drah fired on the closest converging abominations, taking them apart in clusters of null-orbs, while Shasta fired on the airborne creatures.

Between shots, Jn'drah glanced over at Sylvie's dumbstruck face.

–What did I *just* say, fresh meat? *Shoot!*–

Sylvie remembered herself and the Squirrel in her hands. She put it to good use, firing quick groupings of single shots into the most vital-looking parts of misshapen things nearest to them. After killing a few of the ghost-rotted slime-kind and going to reload, she caught sight of Charlotte starting to use her strange whips. She only got glimpses through the fog-blowing gale, but they were enough.

Charlotte wielded the bizarre lengths of living chain like the whips they resembled as she ran toward a group of shambling creatures. She swung her left arm up and around her head sending that worm-whip thing curling around above her, and then she cracked it—

But instead of cracking, it cut horizontally in a conical slice—so fast it blurred and became invisible.

The creatures within its reach came apart along the plane the whip had created passing through their bodies, but unlike the dramatic pause-then-collapse-apart Sylvie had come to expect watching anime with Margot, the monsters were immediately cleaved into neatly separated sections that spilled organs and fluids as the tumbled to the street.

The left worm-whip went limp and chain-like again after completing the devastating cut, and then Charlotte let it keep flinging around to her right side with its diminishing momentum as she pulled the right one forward and up out of the anemone-and-ivy street—

She cracked the right worm-whip up at an angle, bisecting two of the nightmare octopuses that were swooping down at her with its flashing blade phase.

–*Freshmeat!*–

Jn'drah's shout—and an added directional gesture—focused Sylvie again and she fired into an unrecognizable mess of a horror that was beelining for her from her right flank. It hit home, neg-balling a chunk big enough to floor that one—but another was close behind. Sylvie focused and dropped that one too.

She looked back at Jn'drah, who was aiming her AK at the creature Sylvie'd just downed, possibly to save Sylvie if she'd missed. The odd-eyed young woman gave a curt nod of recognition with her helmeted head and almost seemed to start a smile in the helmet link—then the frown was back.

–Don't make me cover your ass again, girl.–

Sylvie nodded in acknowledgement and she and Jn'drah started firing on more converging abominations.

Charlotte was doing her worm-whip thing, cutting down dozens in quick succession.

Shasta was also an efficient killer, sometimes dropping creatures with a single well-aimed burst from her modified carbine.

Ignacio guarded the whimpering Odessa, firing only when he needed to with the limited revolver ammo he had.

Sylvie caught the tail end of Mumbles grabbing a big, warped tentacle-y insect-man-thing—with what looked like a heavy infestation of the local glowing fungus having eaten away large parts of its malformed body—and phasing himself and it down into the wriggling street, like he'd done to get them through the portcullis before. This time, he dropped down far enough that only the creature's head and upper body were above the translucent street and—

Mumbles let go, severing his connection to the thing's body and where it met the writhing stones. Mumbles just lingered there, mumbling in his face coverings and watching it die. He and his victim looked almost like they were having a one-sided conversation in a surreal swimming pool.

Charlotte came over comms as she continued slice-whipping:

–Well, folks, we woke up the whole fucking town, so that's fun.... We need to get to the castle keep—go through the inner gate and I'll cover!–

Jn'drah and Shasta fired on the closest creatures as they advanced toward the open gate. Sylvie did the same, trying her best to cover anything they missed and picking her shots carefully because the Squirrel needed reloading far more often than the AK, with its drum mag.

Sylvie watched Charlotte's worm-whips flashing out in the murk of the storm—which seemed to be getting stronger all the time. She couldn't see Mumbles, but figured he could take care of himself.

Jn'drah and Shasta entered the gatehouse opening with no hesitation but as Sylvie followed, she looked up at the arched ceiling and saw that the layered portcullis was like the one Mumbles had pulled them through—and at the bottom of each strong iron bar was a mean-looking spear tip. She hurried through the gate, expecting the severe points to drop down into her at any moment.

They made it through and Sylvie saw that the castle's outer wall bordered a moat of bubbling sludge between it and another thick wall, and they were on a lowered drawbridge that ended at an even larger gatehouse and another raised portcullis. The moat was filled with bubbling madness made flesh almost like the menhir thing back in the multiplex and she had to look away so as not to be nauseated and disoriented by its living chaos.

Jn'drah's AK went off right next to her and Sylvie's ears rang as she spun back, raising her Beretta toward the open gateway. Charlotte was retreating, flinging her worm-whips around as she backpedaled. Jn'drah fired bursts to the sides of her to aid her falling back, but Sylvie knew she wasn't that good with her gun and just waited in a low-ready position.

Shasta covered the air above the castle wall as Ignacio pulled Odessa in by the hand.

Charlotte ignored a few fearsome monsters coming up on her rear as she turned and trotted through the gatehouse opening, spreading her arms wide and letting the worms retract into her vambraces. She stepped onto the bridge and turned back toward the castle town, standing just past the closest portcullis end.

–Do it.–

Only then did Sylvie see Mumbles' glowing form in the lowest layer of the portcullis, clinging to its underside like some grotesque version of Spider-Man. Somehow, he tripped its release—

The multi-speared portcullis dropped from the gate ceiling, impaling and crushing the monsters that had chased Charlotte in.

She watched the things bleed, spasm, and writhe. Listened to their unearthly yowls and chitterings. Instead of a playful one-liner or something like Sylvie had come to expect, Charlotte watched until she'd had her fill, then turned toward the castle and continued on across the bridge toward the inner gatehouse. Mumbles materialized out of the portcullis and followed her. Those two had a connection Sylvie didn't understand, but that was true for all of this.

Jn'drah backed across the bridge, AK raised. Sylvie looked up and saw that the many of the eyeless flying octopuses were fluttering and pulsing into themselves as they hovered just over the castle-town side of that wall. Shasta watched but didn't fire.

Charlotte glanced back and saw Jn'drah, Shasta, and Sylvie aiming up as they moved.

–They won't come this far. The ones that chased me into the gate were bloodthirsty and/or horny enough to forget why they don't come here. Esthur made them what they are...and Esthur enjoys her privacy.–

The interior of Esthur's castle keep was not at all what Sylvie had expected—as opulent and beautiful as it was haunting and empty. If everything in her land up to this point had felt chaotically and ferociously alive—even petrified and desiccated as it appeared—the keep interior was clean, still, and cold.

They'd met no resistance crossing into the castle grounds, a connected grouping of tall, smaller castle-tower structures that radiated around and connected to the central cylinder that was the keep. The black-veined, awful exteriors belied the elegant, almost austere inside chambers.

Lit candelabras, dark and lush tapestries, impressively rendered paintings, finely crafted rugs, and exquisite statues adorned the dark interiors. Mirrorlike black marble floors, ornate but tasteful banisters, beautiful chandeliers, etc.

As they crept through the ground floor, Jn'drah and Shasta scanned all around.

–I feel like we should be in, like, formal attire...,– Shasta said.

Sylvie said, –Yeah, in an Addams Family or Dracula kind of way.–

Jn'drah chuckled, which Sylvie took as a small victory. Then Jn'drah rubbed her hood-covered head.

–Hey, Captain. Can we take our masks off? Starting to get a little claustrophobic, you know?–

Charlotte stopped and raised her open hand so everyone else stopped too, weapons ready.

–I forgot you and Shasta are new here, like our guests.–

She fiddled with her wrist terminal. Their shoulder lights went through a few different colors and effects, stopping on one that brought back Sylvie's feelings of sick dread.

Outside of their cones of light, everything was still clean, tasteful, still.

Inside the eerie light beams Charlotte had switched them to everything was petrified, translucent, diseased—and even worse than outside. The lights were like glowing cones of ghost-rot vision, miasma and other particles drifting through them in a dense haze that made seeing the oozing putrescent reality harder and more unsettling. The air in the unlit majority of the corridor looked particle free, other than maybe a little dust.

Sylvie angled her helmeted head down, her light tilting in response, and saw that the entire corridor floor was wriggling tentacle bat-wing ivy. A *wake me up* yearning momentarily consumed her, but she fought it off.

–The lights now show you what's *really* real. When it comes to Esthur, trust nothing. Helmets stay on.–

Charlotte continued on, and they followed. Mumbles could be seen here and there, examining paintings and sculptures and such before vanishing again in his way.

They found a large staircase that curved around the cylindrical keep's thick interior wall, ascending to another level and stopping. At the top of that, there was a flat stretch of landing that connected to a curved descending staircase that must have led down to the other side of the level they'd climbed from.

They made their way down a long central hall that split off in irregular increments to the left and right, Sylvie's light barely able to penetrate the chaos-filled murk down what otherwise looked like a dark, silhouetted corridor.

At the end of the long hall there was another curved staircase, so they ascended.

They followed this pattern several times, and Sylvie knew they must be getting very close to the tower's highest chamber, and its beautiful, out-of-place butterfly rose window. As they climbed, traversed, and climbed, Sylvie noticed changes in the ghost-rot lights. Outside of their cones, everything was the same mix of elegant dourness.

In their beams of glowing truth, she saw what looked like black piping and conduits that were snaking in and out of the walls. The pipes were so dark they looked like silhouettes, even totally lit up as they were. They became more densely layered as they ascended, and in the last few levels, she saw the black, pulsing veins encroaching from out on the exterior walls too, with the same jet-black, silhouetted look. The veins ran through walls and ceilings, but also the floor, where they made the black ivy-wings much denser and more active. When they reached the final staircase that led upward, the veins, ivy, and pipes were so prominent Sylvie could barely see the ghost-rotted surfaces between them.

As they crested the top of the final stairwell, Sylvie was awed into stunned silence.

The ceiling had to be fifty feet high, and it was transparent, along with the curved walls of its rounded cylinder top interior shape. The otherworldly storm blasted and slammed as it whirled around the keep's exterior almost silently. The huge butterfly rose window was all the way across the cavernous chamber. Between the window and the staircase was a silhouetted machine of some kind with ghastly glowing parts that could only be glimpsed in the distant periphery of their lights. The pipes and veins snaking across and out of the floor all around fed into it—or out of it, or maybe both, like some awful heart.

Outside of their lights' spooky glow, it was an enormous empty ballroom with a marble floor that had an intricate pattern that complemented the butterfly window—and was also designed to be reflected in the high ceiling.

Coming up onto the landing, Sylvie's attention was drawn down to what lay beyond the castle that they couldn't see from the way they had come.

Marposa Castle sat atop what looked to be about a six- or seven-hundred-foot sheer cliff above a large, mountain-flanked lake of oddly beautiful and serene blue-black liquid.

Charlotte saw her examining the lake. –One time, I transferred into that. Surfaced and looked up at the castle looming up so high. And that damned butterfly....–

Sylvie looked up and realized there was another rose window atop the landing, this one with different colors and subtly different design.

–Anyway, let's get this done, y'all. I joke, but I really can't stand this place either.–

She started across the ballroom floor, stepping between or onto the pipes that didn't seem to be there outside of their lights, and Sylvie and the rest followed.

As they approached the strange machine with its many tubes and chambers and unknowable workings, they saw a dark figure standing near it that appeared in their lights and out of them—they readied their weapons.

It turned—revealing itself to be Mumbles, and he all but ignored them. He went back to examining the machine, apparently fascinated by it. Sylvie angled her head up, her light illuminating the machine that couldn't be seen outside of its miasma-filled eerie cone.

Esthur's machine was something like what Sylvie had seen referred to as 'biomechanical' in appearance. Somewhere between roughly pear and eggplant shaped, the many glowing chambers seeming to grow out of it in a grotesquely biological way between layered silhouette piping and other pulsing and thumping machine sections. The machine itself was about twenty feet tall, but there was an array of tall, pointed antennae sprouting up out of it that stretched up toward the ceiling another ten to fifteen. They had the same silhouette effect of the pipes and energy crackled around them, distorting the already hazy air.

They came closer and in their lights the chambers built into the machine at odd angles became clearer. Most of the chambers had various amorphous horrors suspended in their fluids—along with arrays of articulated arcane surgical equipment that poked and prodded at them in some automated process—as if Esthur was studying them. The creatures rarely moved and when they did it reminded Sylvie of a slumbering pet animal reacting to a dream. A few of the tubes contained beings that looked more humanoid. Sylvie stepped closer and froze—

Two of the chambers held Margot and her uncle Russ, suspended naked in the murky fluid. She didn't see Juana or Aaron, which caused an ache of loss in her chest, but this was more than she could've hoped for. Without thinking, she dropped the Squirrel and ran to the machine, placing a hand on each container.

–That's my uncle and girlfriend! We have to get them out!–

Charlotte frowned, her light sliding from Margot to Russ and back. She seemed troubled, but said, –Mumbles?–

Mumbles nodded, then crossed to the machine and placed his hands on it. In less than thirty seconds, the fluid in the chambers drained and the tubes slid apart.

–Shasta, biosuits and masks,– Charlotte said, then scanned around the chamber, nonplussed.

Shasta opened her pack and pulled out some compac bundles.

Russ and Margot came to, choking and puking out the chamber fluids before screaming and shrinking back into the tubes.

Sylvie said, "Russ! Margot! I can't explain all of it right now, but we're here to get you home...."

Shasta approached and started fitting Russ and Margot with thin transparent masks that covered their faces and had shiny ampules running up their jawlines that looked a lot like little Whip-It! nitrous-oxide canisters to Sylvie. With a little hiss from each, they blinked and seemed to calm down some.

Sylvie tried to help them both out of the chambers and Shasta focused on Russ so she could get Margot out. Russ was coughing hard and Jn'drah needed both hands.

Shasta helped Russ into a biosuit as he looked around in a daze. She handed the other to Sylvie and she got started getting Margot into it.

Margot blinked a few times slowly and said, "Sylvia...where the fuck are we?"

"It's like a nightmare dimension but we're going home. It's where that scary woman from the movie at the Rem lives. This is so fucking crazy, I don't know how to explain better. Do you remember that? The Rem and the monster witch...thing?"

"I remember.... I thought that was a fucking nightmare I was still having! Everything after I got pulled down—"

"I held on as hard as I.... I c-couldn't...."

Margot squeezed her upper arm. "I know, Sylvia. I know."

Russ grabbed her shoulder and, between coughs, said, "Sylvia!"

She put her gloved hand over his and squeezed.

"I'm *so* glad you're here too!"

He tried to smile through his coughing.

Charlotte said, –Loved ones all suited up and ready? We need to go. Something's different this time....–

Hearing Charlotte sound a little worried made Sylvie a lot worried.

–Wh-what's...?– Sylvie started then paused, realizing Charlotte had set her back to internals. –I don't understand—–

–I'll turn their ear pieces on in a minute—let's *move*.–

Sylvie gestured to Margot and Russ, then her mouth and ears. Margot seemed confused but nodded. Charlotte handed Sylvie her Beretta from the wriggling floor, then started back toward the stairs, the lake-facing butterfly window looming above and storm quietly raging all around them. Jn'drah and Shasta followed, then Sylvie, Ignacio, and Odessa did the same. Sylvie gestured for Margot and Russ to stay with her. Mumbles was still studying the machine.

The group was nearing the stairwells at the base of the butterfly when Charlotte stopped, so the rest of them did. Sylvie, Shasta, and Jn'drah scanned around, weapons ready. Ignacio had his revolver ready, one hand keeping Odessa behind him.

–Sylvie.–

–Y-yeah?–

–You said all the people where you came from died. Which ones did you actually see dying?–

Sylvie had to think back. –They all died, what do you mean?–

–Which one's actually died while you were watching? I know it hurts and you might've blocked some of it out, but think back.–

Sylvie frowned. –I.... I can't remember. It was so....–

–Never mind. Ready your weapons...,– Charlotte said.

Sylvie saw Charlotte tapping on her wrist terminal again and fiddling with something. Their lights all changed subtly. Charlotte turned around—she'd already raised her FAMAS and she sidestepped the group to aim it back at—

Where Charlotte's light hit Sylvie's uncle who had just been standing behind Margot in the line near Ignacio and Odessa, it revealed a beautiful young woman with long black hair and deep brown eyes. She was wearing the biosuit and mask Shasta had put on Russ, but above those, she wore a simple, lovely crown of black ivy and pearls. Bemused, she half smiled at them. She looked like she was waking from a dream.

Before the real immediate horror of what she was seeing could sink in, Sylvie's stomach sank and twisted up as she realized that she had already seen her uncle for the last time, and in the worst possible way. In an instant that profound feeling of loss washed over and through her and became something else. Sylvie raised her Beretta, flipped the fire-selector switch, and aimed it at Esthur's face. Margot took the hint and dived away to the side—

Sylvie fired a few three-shot bursts, fighting the strong recoil and neg-balling the witch queen's head and shoulders away and dropping the rest of her blood-spraying body to the wriggling ivy of the floor.

Charlotte raised her eyebrows. –Dayum....–

Esthur's body surged and convulsed as the chamber began to shudder and vibrate.

Charlotte lowered her head. –Ah, there it is.... I was almost disappointed.–

Jn'drah looked at her, gun locked on Esthur. –What is it?–

Charlotte said, –Children...here comes the suck.–

Esthur's head and upper body began reforming and she screamed long and low, the sounds of it changing as she was rebuilt in some unknowable way.

Then she stood, reforming the rest of the way and looking young and beautiful again, except now she had the clouded ghoulish eyes of the monstrous form Sylvie was more used to.

She formed a long, bony scythe arm like she had at the Rem, drew it back, and in one angled strike skewered Ignacio and Odessa together. They screamed then let out choking moans as it changed and ballooned inside them, cracking their bones and bursting their organs as it bulged their forms out from inside. Blood and other fluids spurted and seeped out of every orifice as the scythe blossomed and twisted inside them. Then Esthur flung them away like soulless ragdolls and Sylvie heard the sickening sounds of their mangled bodies slapping down.

Charlotte raised her rifle and fired a few rounds, hitting Esthur's head above her left eye—

Charlotte's masked head disappeared in ball-chunks right where she'd shot Esthur. Her comm-link blanked out as she collapsed.

Jn'drah cried, -*No!*-

Jn'drah and Shasta fired their guns at Esthur, her body disappearing in a flurry of flashing neg-spheres—

It reformed instantly this time, and now she'd taken on her truer form. Twice as tall, shrouded, at once petrified and putrescent, clouded eyes in her crown-topped head. Then dozens of eyes opened all over her body.

Sylvie fired her Beretta at Esthur's head again, this time her burst-fired rounds glinting and angling off to the side as the witch made it miss.

Suddenly powerless to fight, Sylvie grabbed Margot's hand and pulled her toward the stairs. Just before they reached them, she could see in her cone of light that the ivy-wings had spread into them, the black wriggling tentacles choking the stairwell and making escape impossible.

She looked back and her breath caught in her chest—

Esthur was ignoring Jn'drah and Shasta's ineffective gunfire, and coming after *them*. She moved with a blurred suggestion of many ghostly appendages and tentacles ambulating under the layers of her gauzy, threadbare shroud. Several overlong arms came out from within the folds too, one a huge bone-and-diseased-flesh scythe like she'd used on Aaron, then Ignacio and Odessa just now—only much larger.

Sylvie tried to back away, but the ivy had latched onto her boots and lower legs. Margot's legs were almost bound too. She aimed her gun in shaking hands, knowing it wouldn't save them but having no other way to.

Just as Esthur loomed over them, Margot ripped her legs free and stepped in front of Sylvie, hands raised.

"Stop!"

And Esthur did stop, her ghastly face taking on a confused expression.

Then they heard loud gunshots and shrill wailing.

211

Jn'drah was firing on Esthur from behind, her shots now flashing a brilliant pale green. The rounds entered Esthur's body and haunting lights blazed out of the wounds from deep inside, causing Esthur to howl in pain.

Shasta backed her up, firing her under-barrel flame unit.

Jn'drah said, "I never carry just one type of ammo, bitch!"

All light drained out of the room but the lights from the team's suits, Esthur somehow cloaking the huge chamber in inky darkness.

Esthur evaded, dodging low to the side out of Jn'drah's beam of light, and appeared on Jn'drah's flank just as she turned her light that direction—

"Hngk—"

Jn'drah was lifted high off the ground, impaled by Esthur's scythe arm with such force a third of it came up out of the young woman's suit streaked with dark fluids.

Esthur flung her away, tearing her into pieces—the left-arm-with-severed-torso-and-legs section colliding with Shasta and knocking her out cold, while Sylvie heard her head, upper body, and right arm flopping into a rough roll as the connected cone of light flipped around.

That light, the one on Charlotte's body a ways away on the ivy floor, Shasta's glowing upward from her supine form, and Sylvie's were now the only lights in the huge chamber, other than a dull, eerie glow coming from both of the butterfly rose windows. Sylvie fumbled with her light, desperate to shut it off and hide, but also with a sick feeling Esthur could see them anyway.

"Sylvia...." Margot said in a meek voice and reached back to grip her arm.

Sylvie looked up and her light tracked with her head—

Esthur was right there in front of them, oozing eyes piercing into them as her limbs and scythe arm retracted, ready to strike.

Sylvie caught something move in her peripheral vision and looked that way.

Charlotte's harness light was moving. Just as Sylvie realized it was probably just the ivy wriggling around and that she was about to die horribly, the light came up off the floor like Charlotte was getting up—

There was a finger snap in the dark from that direction and a ball of white flame rolled over Esthur's back, like Sylvie had seen at the membrane wall in the multiplex. The monster squealed strangely and spun around.

Two more snaps—left, right—and Esthur's face and torso burned for a moment.

In those flashes, Sylvie could see Charlotte's form. Just before the flames extinguished, Sylvie saw Charlotte raising her arms wide away from her sides, then darkness again.

With the sound of those hands slapping together, Esthur's arcane machine in the center of the chamber burst into white flame, lighting up the room like a huge, haunting bonfire. In the long shadows cast by the flames, Charlotte ripped off her shredded balaclava and dangling remnants of her bubble mask.

"You've always been a tricksy bitch, Esthur...but I admit, I didn't see that mirror attack bullshit coming, my dear. Would've worked on someone a little less...long-lived and *durable*."

Esthur let out a harrowing howl with a layered chittering backend.

"Yeah, yeah—let's go, you old fuckin' hag!"

Charlotte flung her arms wide again, loosing her worm-whips at an even greater length than before—and she raked the ivy floor with them and let out a banshee-like shriek that set the whips aflame with white fire.

Esthur lunged across the chamber and Charlotte feinted away, slicing with one whip's flashing blade phase and burning into Esthur with it as she dodged.

Charlotte stuck her landing and twirled, cutting Esthur again with one whip, then the other. Limbs flew off and sickly glowing fluids sprayed out of the witch queen as Charlotte went to work.

Esthur's remaining limbs all cracked and grew, giving her multiple bone blades and tentacle whips to match Charlotte's.

Sylvie and Margot watched Charlotte and Esthur trade strikes, dodge, and circle each other as they fought. Sylvie wanted to help but didn't know how. Then it struck her. She picked up her Beretta and beat its sharp metal stock against the ivy on her legs, then ripped the ivy away from Margot's and handed the Squirrel to her.

"Take this. It won't hurt her, but might distract her or something."

With Margot not far behind, Sylvie trudged across the wriggling ivy and wings toward Jn'drah's body and picked up her AK. Those last bullets she'd used on Esthur seemed to do something, and that was way better than nothing. She looked down at Jn'drah's lifeless face within the still-working comm-link and cringed.

Charlotte came over comms, Sylvie assumed through a throat mic or something.

–Jhn, quit playing possum—you're gonna bum out the noob.–

Sylvie said, "Wh-what...?"

Then Jn'drah's voice came over comms, but her masked mouth wasn't moving:

–Ha! I thought you'd maybe really moved on that time, Captain. Don't scare me like that....–

Then the hood burned away and Jn'drah's head opened along the vertical seam Sylvie had noticed before, crumpling like accordion layers down away from a grapefruit-sized spheroid chamber full of clear liquid.

Inside the chamber was a small creature that looked almost like a baby dumbo octopus with a cross between zebra striping and cheetah spots on its bright multi-colored pastel skin. It was in a support harness with a tiny equipment panel in front of it and several electrodes attached to its head like an EEG rig.

The little thing wagged a tentacle-arm at Sylvie. –Take good care of my chopper, all right?–

213

Sylvie looked down at Jn'drah's AK in her hands.

–Will d-do.–

The real Jn'drah pressed a tiny button above her little equipment panel and all the electrodes and support harness detached from her body as a little mask came down on an articulated arm and was fitted over her eyes and gill ports.

The fluid drained from the chamber and it opened. Jn'drah climbed out and slithered across the ivy-covered floor, fighting off its prying tentacles with her own as she made a beeline for Shasta's limp form.

–Coming at you, girl!–

Shasta came to and shook her head, then she hauled herself to her feet, carbine ready.

A curved, capsule-shaped chamber formed horizontally along Shasta's suit back, shoulder to shoulder. Jn'drah the little octo-person hopped up onto Shasta and climbed up her body, then into the chamber on her suit's back. The capsule sealed and filled with fluid, Jn'drah watching Charlotte fight Esthur, now with a front-row seat on Shasta's back as she removed her little fluid-breathing mask.

Sylvie detached Jn'drah's ammo pack from her surrogate-body thing's shredded suit and attached it to her own, then aimed the AK at Esthur as she crossed the chamber toward the fight.

As Esthur and Charlotte lunged, whirled, dodged, and whipped at each other, Sylvie and Shasta waited for an opening. Charlotte rolled away and Esthur showed her back—Sylvie and Shasta fired their weapons into it, lighting her insides up and causing the monstrous witch queen to shriek, spin, and retreat into shadows at the edge of the chamber.

Charlotte said, "Thanks for the support, ladies."

She heard sizzling and looked down—some ivy-wings were sizzling and being eaten away in circular patches on the chamber floor—

Charlotte looked straight up—her light tilting too—in time to see Esthur standing on the chamber ceiling—just before she dropped.

Her gigantic, many-limbed form descended upon Charlotte, but she dive-rolled away just before certain impalement and evisceration.

Esthur let out a maddening howl and all of her dozens of eyes locked on Charlotte rolling away as she rose up, almost as tall as her machine now. The ghastly giantess was now a towering mess of those eyes—hundreds now, more accurately—layered tentacles, overlong arms and legs, and flowing layers of her disintegrating shroud—which was glowing now on its own and had seemed to have grown with the rest of her, as had her ivy-and-pearl crown.

Sylvie fired her AK at Esthur, but with diminishing results.

–Shit! It doesn't hurt her anymore!–

Shasta said, –The catalyst tube is *dry*—switch it out!–

Sylvie rifled through the ammo pack she'd taken from Jn'drah's body but found no long liquid-filled tubes.

–Shit, they must be on my busted exo-armature.–

–On my way...,– Sylvie said and trudged back toward the pieces of Jn'drah's destroyed false outer body.

Charlotte stood and retracted her worm-whips, the flames extinguishing as they slid into the vambraces. She reached back and grabbed the little T-ball-bat thing from its sheath on her back, then pressed a button just above its gripping handle with her thumb—

The lance grew instantly to about twelve feet in total length, becoming a shrouded two-handed, foot-thick jousting-style lance with angled holes up and down its length almost to the end of its last several feet that tapered to a severe point.

Esthur lunged, her huge main scythe arm slicing the air on its wide path toward Charlotte.

But Charlotte angled the lance parallel to the floor and dived toward her, within the closing arc of Esthur's strike.

Charlotte rolled up to her feet and into a thrust-ready position, then used all her strength to bring the lance up into Esthur's chest—it plunged in deep, a few feet of it coming out the other side. She pulled a trigger in the handguard shroud—

The holes along much of the lance's length fired—glowing, barbed stakes exploding outward and piercing in dozens of places, shredding as they went.

Esthur's scythe arm and several other limbs detached and were flung or dropped to the chamber floor, others dangling at the ends of what strips of tissue remained. The entire right-shoulder region of her giant body was mangled and mulched, the strange flesh and shroud pitted and spurting fluids where the stakes had come out.

"You got fuckin' lucky on that one!"

Charlotte pulled the lance back out, spilling buckets of ichor and black blood from the open wound. Before she could try for another attack, Esthur smacked her away with a bundle of limbs and tentacles from her other side. She held on to her weapon as she flew, but landed in a hard tumble and lost it.

As Charlotte was hauling herself up, Esthur clenched a few of her big, talon-tipped hands while staring at the ivy-wings around Charlotte—they whipped around her and the lance and she couldn't pull free.

"Cheatin' bitch!"

Esthur mewled as she clawed at her destroyed right side with several hands and a few tentacles, her eyes scanning the chamber—

First a core set then all of her eyes locked on Sylvie fumbling to get one of the catalyst tubes she'd found on Jn'drah's armature into the AK's under-barrel port. The huge witch queen moved with incredible speed, and she'd crossed the chamber and was almost ready to strike before Sylvie finally got the catalyst tube in and flowing.

Sylvie raised the rifle to fire, futile or not, as Esthur's left side was snapping, bubbling, and forming new scythes to go with its tentacle whips.

215

Esthur pulled back her scythes and went to strike.

Images of Aaron, Ignacio, and Odessa being broken outward from the inside filled Sylvie's mind, paralyzing her—but Margot grabbed Sylvie's shoulder and threw her out of the way, then raised her arms toward Esthur's own—

Glowing black eyes opened all over Margot's arms as those in her head closed—impossibly black like the pipes and veins of the machine—and her limbs bloomed, becoming translucent amorphous interlaced branches of black bones and living petrified flesh.

Margot's arms stopped Esthur's death strikes and flowed around the abominable queen's own amorphous limbs. Esthur struggled against her bonds, a momentary Goliath to Margot's David.

Margot's eyes snapped open, the whites all black like her eye arms, the irises and pupils clouded and haunting like those in Esthur's own head.

Sylvie didn't know how to feel, having seen what Margot had become—somehow infested or infected by the Marposa ghost rot—but knew it didn't matter at the moment. She raised the AK and fired into Esthur's head and chest area, getting the shrieking response to the internally flashing rounds she wanted once again—

Until her magazine emptied.

"Fuck!"

Shasta shot at Esthur as Sylvie searched in the ammo pack for the right rounds, then fumbled to switch them out. As she chambered the fresh mag's first round and raised the AK again, she caught something in her peripheral vision on the machine at the chamber's center:

Mumbles was standing on the top of the machine, his hands around the antenna array.

The antennae went translucent as he did the same, and he descended into the machine, the antennae following him down—

Just as he vanished down into the machine, the antennae dropped out of the clear chamber ceiling—as if the violent storm outside had birthed them—just above Esthur. The long, spear-like rods dropped, Mumbles appearing near the top end out of the ceiling as they fell.

Esthur was impaled so forcefully by the antenna rods that they sparked upon striking the chamber floor after coming down through her. Margot barely winced at them passing through her ghost-rotted arm trees that had arrested the witch queen. Mumbles used his strange abilities to pull Esthur down the antenna rods she'd been penetrated by, and Margot adjusted to allow the monster's descent to the wriggling ivy floor.

Esthur wailed as she bled out her vile essence, her strength waning.

Sylvie didn't hesitate, firing the AK into Esthur's head until her magazine emptied again. She reloaded and emptied again, chittering howls coming out of the giant abomination.

Charlotte had pried and ripped herself free from the ivy, and was sauntering up to the restrained and dying Esthur holding her lance.

216

She looked at Margot. "It's a thing of beauty to witness beings with potential really...*becoming* something...." Then she locked her icy gaze on Esthur.

"Especially if it's to royally fuck up a used, tired has-been of a monster queen."

Charlotte reached Esthur, then hauled back and thrust her lance deep into her. Pinned as she was, the lance went into her neck just under her jawline and penetrated deeply before firing off its stakes, bursting and ventilating her huge body.

A long, reverberating and chittering death rattle came out of Esthur as she let go—her corpse immediately dissolving into putrescent matter and fluid around her huge, misshapen, and grotesque skeleton.

Charlotte pulled her lance out, collapsed it to T-ball-bat size, then re-sheathed it.

Margot cringed and retracted her bloomed multitudinous limbs from the fuming cesspool, becoming her normal-seeming self again, two arms, two legs, natural eyes. She blinked a few times and backed away from the fresh kill scene, confused.

Sylvie crossed to her and took one of her hands.

"Hey, we're gonna be okay. You did what you needed to d-do."

Margot looked at her with mortified, teary eyes.

"What am I now? What did she *do* to me?"

Sylvie thought for a moment then said, "Honestly, I don't know, Margot...but from what I've seen tonight..."

Margot stared at her with desperate, streaming eyes.

"...you are nothing like her."

Margot wrapped herself around Sylvie and they both cried and shuddered as they embraced.

Charlotte chuckled. "Yeah, let's hope...but we have more pressing matters."

Sylvie looked at Charlotte, then where she was glaring:

Esthur's body wasn't just dissolving—it was eating away at the floor. But worse than that—as it fell away, it was pulling everything else with it.

Charlotte raised her eyebrows. "Usually, she dies and the place sticks around a while before disintegrating or something. I don't know what's different, but it looks like Marposa's going down with its queen this time...."

Sylvie and Margot looked at each other, then back at Charlotte, Jn'drah, Shasta, and Mumbles—who was crawling up out of the warping, sagging chamber floor.

Charlotte chuckled and said, "Well, this should be a fine fuckin' hootenanny...."

217

PATRICK LOVELAND

Sylvie could see vague impressions of multiple tiny black eyes under the gauzy skin of Margot's hand in hers, as they rode in the back of a pop-up campervan toward a place east or maybe southeast of San Francisco in some sparsely-forested grassy hills.

Shasta drove the van, which smelled like a patchouli graveyard. She had asked them if they'd met Wahrheit, and they said no. She said that was a shame, but where she was taking them they'd meet Polish Stan, and he was like a brother to Wahrheit.

They smiled and nodded, as she was obviously stoned out of her fucking mind from the bowls she'd burned through after they'd made it back to what Sylvie thought of as the Real World. But she was a competent and defensive driver, as well as being a fearsome interdimensional monster hunter, so Sylvie wasn't too worried.

Shasta had a bag of Bali Shag on her dash and she'd let Sylvie take it to roll a few, nic-fitting as she was after all the excitement had subsided. Sylvie took one of those rollies out, lip-slicked it, and lit it, all one-handed. She took a long drag, held it, and let it out, blowing smoke out into the Misfits-, Leftöver Crack-, and Crass-stickered-and-sprayed van interior.

Margot looked over and caught Sylvie looking at the eyes under her skin. Sylvie could see more black eyes just beneath the surface of Margot's otherwise lovely neck.

"I love you, Sylvia. I don't know what's coming...but I'm with you."

Sylvie squeezed Margot's eye-filled hand.

"And I'm with you."

A rusty old van pulled up in front of the Rem theater in a nice, hipster-clogged suburb near San Diego and parked. A tattooed driver got out and crossed to the theater doors. With little effort, he broke in and made his way up to the projection booth.

He used the still-functioning projector, tree, and build table to break down *TOO MANY EYES*, the film he'd delivered there before the whole debacle up in SF. If they'd just listened to him, it would've worked out. Well, not in the Rem crew's favor, but it would've gone as the Black Ivy Collective had planned.

The projectionist-delivery driver exited the theater with the metal hex-boxes containing the film and opened the back doors of his van—

A strong kick sent him slamming into the back of the van's passenger seat, causing him to drop the reel cases along the way.

Someone climbed into the van behind him and slammed the rear doors closed.

He struggled to flop around and get a look at the intruder—

Just in time for her to place the tip of a gently forward-curving butterfly knife she'd just fanned open under one of his sunglasses-covered eyes.

It was a lovely woman with odd contact lenses over her eyes, wearing a hooded plastic coverall that immediately turned his stomach with a twisting dread. He recognized her from a PowerPoint presentation they'd had at a BIC gathering about legendary old hunters to watch out for—Charlotte O'Shea herself.

"Hey, zealot dickboy. You wanna drive me to Esthur Cult ground zero...or you wanna die today? I'm way, *way* past over her and Marposa coming back. And if you're wondering..."

The woman smiled, a glimmer in her eyes as the blade broke the skin under his.

"...your life means fuck all to me."

7

TOMORROW AND BEYOND

The Bulb

Northeastern United States—2051

A city-sized bumpy sphere of pale-green luminescent flesh dangled hundreds of tendrils the length of highways as it glided northward over the Hudson River near Hoboken, New Jersey.

Rachelle "Hyna" Sandoval and her team watched it float high above from inside their powered-armor suits on the deck of a small cloaked ship on the river. If the almost noontime sun hadn't been obscured by dark, pouring clouds, the huge thing would have blotted it out from almost any point underneath.

The tendrils were covered by thousands of clouded eyes or sensors the size of halved basketballs, and they gracefully picked over any remaining energy sources in a three-mile radius, as if they were under individual or guided automatic control. They slithered and caressed buildings, machinery, long-abandoned vehicles, and any other possible source of whatever energy it sought.

Electricity had been the obvious early assumption, but it also absorbed heat and radiation, as was discovered when the Bulb hovered above Chernobyl and Fukushima for days just caressing the meltdown sites. It had also fondled the ground above the Lucens underground test facility partial meltdown, which had been sealed for decades, and examined Three Mile Island, before moving on and meandering from one functioning plant to the next. After that it had refocused on major population and infrastructure centers, and at present, it was picking back over the ones it had started with after appearing initially.

228

Sandoval looked back and forth in her shell-suit's head case, a sideways egg of thick, opaque armor on the suit exterior. It was nestled atop the suit's twelve-foot-seven-inches of roughly human-shaped—but boxy here, too smooth there—bleeding-edge military tech. Its real-time exterior feeds allowed her to see the decimated remains of the industrial areas and the West Village lining this stretch of the Hudson as if there weren't five inches of plasteel armor physically obscuring the natural view. The only things breaking the illusion were an AR heads-up display showing translucent readouts of tactical information and her suit integrity and weapon statuses, and those of her team members' suits. Also, the pouring rain slapping and running down the armor exterior was vaguely visible as a kind of curved surface several inches from her face, which was comforting in an ineffable way.

She contemplated for maybe the fiftieth time what the creature might need the endlessly sought energy for. Most of the planet lay quiet and dark, sucked dry by the monster, and with absolutely no answers as to why. Actually, many had put forth the possibility that it wasn't a huge monster at all—it could be a ship, and maybe needed to recharge, they said. Sandoval had a guess it was a mix of both, but in a way humans couldn't relate to—but also maybe neither by the same reasoning. Some even thought it was some form of god.

"The Bulb" was what most everyone called it due to the colossal ball on top, the tendrils clinging to its lower hemisphere before draping almost straight down and fanning out, plus its eerie glow. Billions dead and the remains of humanity a scared, desperate mob.... Sandoval didn't care what she should call it—today, the monster would be brought down for good. It had been traversing the northeastern United States for days now, but this was the first time it had been over a body of water viable for their purposes.

She looked back and forth again, this time at two other shell-suits on her left—Reilly, Quaker—and two more on her right—Beech, Laidlaw. Her team. They were ready—as ready as they could be, considering their very possible impending death. Most of them had children they knew they wouldn't see again—actually, Sandoval remembered, Reilly's wife was pregnant now so, in a way, they all did.

Sandoval's only solace was that after today, their grieving spouses and partners could raise their children in a world without this monster...and hopefully one united by a cosmic truth it almost certainly represented. As the acting prime minister of the North American Coalition had said in her most recent speech, "We are not alone...and all of our manufactured problems and stubborn selfishness have kept us from becoming one global humanity for a greater good."

The five power-armored warriors were secured leaning back at an angle atop special apparatuses installed onto the deck of a Coast Guard Fast Response Cutter they had repurposed for this mission. A relatively small, fast water vessel had been settled on because all attempts to approach the creature by air directly had failed.

Manned helicopters and a succession of drones had been obliterated by its whipping tentacles in impressive and terrifying shows of defensive awareness. After this violence and continued lack of any communication, they had also failed to harm it with orbital particle beam platforms. The Bulb had drooped a bit in the air after the beam successfully penetrated its entire vertical girth, only to float up into orbit and destroy the offending platform, then go on about its business.

This would probably fail too, thought Sandoval, but she tucked it away in her mind.

Beech had an extra cylinder of metal on her suit's back—a six-foot bomb they hoped would be enough to end this—which had necessitated a different apparatus design for her suit. Sandoval had wanted them each to have a bomb to increase their chances, but with the world in the state it was in, there had only been enough resources globally for the one. She just hoped it worked when it came time.

At least as far as the instruments and sensors were concerned, everything was in fact functioning as designed and intended, so the decision came down to her discretion.

Sandoval said, "Okay...suits, 'pults, and bomb look ready...but are you guys?"

–Ready,– Quaker said, always eager.

–Ready,– Laidlaw said.

–Sure,– Reilly said, casual as possible.

Silence from the bomb carrier.

"Beech?"

Sandoval heard a long intake of breath, controlled exhalation, and some form of murmured prayer from Beech over the squad comms feed.

She watched the Bulb sliding through the air high above the river and noticed it changing direction somewhat to now pass over the river at a slight northward angle. Soon, it would be back inland over New Jersey then probably Upstate New York, and the operation would be a wash.

"We can wait another minute maybe—"

Beech said, –I'm ready.–

"Okay, good. 'Cause I can't think of anything *I'd* rather be doing," Sandoval lied. Beech started to chuckle, but it caught in her throat.

Sandoval said, "Alright, no speeches. Once this starts, it's gonna happen fast. You know I love you guys...*and* you know why this needs to happen."

–Word,– from Reilly.

–Awww, shucks, girl. Love you too,– Laidlaw said.

Quaker took his time for once and just hummed a tune. It had become a running joke for them since the bar brawl during his bachelor party that they hadn't asked for but *had* won.

Beech sniffed, obviously holding back tears, and said, –Dammit, Quaker....–

"Amen...," Sandoval said, then keyed over to global comms and said, "This is Sever-One, Sever Team. Commencing Operation Lights Out on my mark. Warm up all actors." She made a thumbs-up in her suit, and its big multi-tool and weapon-flanked bionic hand did the same. The ship operators turned over the engines, and everything powered up from stealth trickle level to full.

She raised her synced suit arm and held it as she said, "Five...four...three...two...one...."

Sandoval swung her suit arm down and said, "Blitz."

As the modified cutter ship heaved forward and picked up speed toward the slowing—confused?—Bulb, the sky was set ablaze. Artillery batteries and mobile platforms fired from all over a five-mile area. Drones filled the sky as they ascended toward the massive creature, firing Vulcan cannons and rockets with no hope of doing real damage—but that wasn't the point. This was without a doubt the largest, most potentially destructive, and most expensive distraction in human history. Especially when its utter harmlessness to the focus of its assault was taken into consideration.

But that was exactly what Sandoval and her superiors were hoping for when they devised the plan—a distracted, annoyed Bulb might not focus on a small ship on the river.

So far, that seemed to be the case. The artillery battered the Bulb's lower half and even reached higher sporadically. Quad-rotor and VTOL drones buzzed and flew around it like hummingbirds and hawks, peppering the Bulb with their own weapons. If this attack had been focused on anything else in this human world it would have been utterly decimated. Anything. The Bulb was at best irritated.

Unimpressed as it seemed to be, the monster still took action, whipping and slicing some of its tentacles from on high. They cut through buildings and streets and all other infrastructure with no great effort, throwing up clouds of dust and sending rubble and debris flying as far as the eye could see. High-rises, skyscrapers, office buildings, etc., collapsed and tumbled down—some diagonally cut sections of large buildings were thrown with the rubble, taking out any flying drones in their paths.

In a small part of her mind not focused on the planned task at hand, Sandoval was glad that she had demanded the artillery be manned by remote-controlled bipedal Hüm drones. The Hüms were a bit twitchy in "rehearsals," but they were performing just fine, and she knew only plastic, rubber, and metal were being shredded and disintegrated in the Bulb's attacks.

The task at hand dangled and slithered ahead, below the looming sphere—the tentacles that weren't attacking. Sandoval broke motion-sync and keyed a code into a pad within her suit's shell arm. The apparatus bases extended and bowed, forming into the arms of what amounted to five high-tech catapults with a shell-suited human in each harness.

Sandoval used a contact pad to focus a glowing box in her AR overlay on her choice for ascension. Once she confirmed it, it locked on. The ship pilot crew received her selection, locked on the shifting coordinates, and steered the cutter upriver toward it. She re-engaged sync between her shell and real arms and readied herself.

In the periphery of her eyes, Sandoval registered the shores of the river blurring by through the streaking rain on the head-case exterior. The heart rates of her team members were high, but that was to be expected—what they were about to do was worlds away from what they had spent their lives training for before the Bulb arrived.

The AR box began flashing in their overlays.

Sandoval said, "Fail-safes...released."

The cutter captain said, –Now within optimal range....–

"Copy," Sandoval confirmed, then to her team said, "Prepare for launch."

Four small green lights winked on then off to answer affirmative on her team-suit readouts. That along with all the technical systems in the green sealed it.

Sandoval ordered, "*Launch.*"

Hydraulic clamps holding Sandoval and her team members in place on their catapults released, and each shell-suit was flung in an arc toward the huge tentacle, sailing over the river and outpacing the cutter through momentum mixed with sheer kinetic release. Just before the shell-suits reached the apex of their ascent, jump thrusters on each of their rear upper exteriors fired and sent them flying straight for the writhing sensor-covered appendage.

"Go to manual thrust control!" Sandoval barked, surprised at their speed of approach. They didn't actually want to make contact with the tentacle if they could help it—their suits had every kind of shielding humanity's scientists could layer in below the shells themselves, but they still didn't know if it would save their suits from being sucked dry.

They each steered just to the left side of the vertical length, all but Quaker succeeding.

"Fire tethers!"

Each suit raised its arms, and tungsten-carbide harpoons on unbreakable lines fired out with puffs of compressed gas, then their own small thrusters engaged, closing the gap between the suits and the tentacle and sinking into its surface.

Sandoval, Reilly, Beech, and Laidlaw flew just wide of the tentacle's left side and let the harpoons reel them in until they were within about fifteen feet of the surface. Upon reaching this distance, nonconductive spears of something like rubberized plastic telescoped out of the suit's rough shoulder and hip areas. The spears plunged in, and then smaller spears shot out of their main shafts like barbs under the surface. This all held the four shell-suits in place away from the energy absorbent surface and its cloudy-eyed half basketballs.

Quaker's spears didn't shoot out, because he came up on the tentacle's surface too fast and was still trying to veer away when he fired his harpoons. As he was trying to trigger the spears, he hit the surface.

"Quaker, jump off and engage spears!"

Quaker fought the harpoon-line tension as he tried to follow Sandoval's instructions. He got his suit's feet onto the surface, squatted toward the surface to jump, and disengaged the harpoons—Quaker's suit power and vital levels went flat in Sandoval's AR overlay.

"Quaker!"

The shell-suit fell to the river.

Sandoval blinked a few times and just stared at the spot where Quaker's suit splashed down before she remembered the situation—they needed to keep on task or they would all die for sure. She fought herself hard to sound cold and professional....

But instead she belted out, "*Exam!*" in a sorrowful moan.

The "Exam" was something they had observed on only a few occasions when the Bulb caught a tentacle on something or vice versa. It would raise the offending tentacle to a nondescript grouping of the sphere's bumps nearest the tentacle's tether point.

The lower tentacle area they were speared to started to curl and rise toward the sphere midsection.

Sandoval succeeded in mastering her tone this time as she said, "Prep for *Flick....*"

After they were dangled in front of the huge hemispheres of the bumps along the sphere's equator, the tentacle was flicked up and away from the bumps. At the moment before it finished its upward climb, the shell-suits retracted their spears and flew upwards. If she hadn't been so close to possible death at any moment, Sandoval might have been able to appreciate the spectacular aerial view of what was once the thriving New York / New Jersey area as they spun up and away from the Bulb.

"Parachutes."

Several large parachutes popped from the upper sections on the shell-suits and flapped open.

"Reorient."

Small thrusters all over the suits fired, using the tension of the suits against their parachutes to place them back on a Bulb-ward course.

"Cloak."

They each engaged a visual cloaking system developed during the last global conflict—it was imperfect and at best odd looking in overcast daylight, but close enough to invisibility for their immediate purposes. Sandoval just hoped visual sensory input was what the Bulb relied on most.

Sandoval and her three remaining team members forced themselves to remain as calm as possible as they descended toward the upper half of the Bulb at the end of huge, fluttering, invisible parachutes. In her mind, she kept seeing the moment Quaker's signs blanked but knew his wouldn't be the last to do so and tried to force the images out with thoughts of her son growing up without fear.

Most of the artillery was destroyed below, but the flying drones were still distracting the Bulb well, and Sandoval was thankful for that.

Sandoval, Reilly, Laidlaw, and Beech touched down on the mottled, meaty surface near the Bulb's apex. The Bulb's exterior bumps surrounded them like half domes in a curved, rain-battered desert of flesh. With the help of nanotech in their weaves, the parachutes became like fine nets and retracted into their storage compartments.

"Okay, guys, focus...."

Three tiny green lights winked on for a moment in her overlay.

"Lasers."

Four sets of three beam-throwers extruded from rings around the shell-suit midsections and pointed down at the surface. They warmed up, shot down, and rotated, cutting circles just wider than each suit's bulk in the surface. Sandoval couldn't decide if the surface reacted like organic or manufactured material, but maintained that maybe they just didn't have a frame of reference.

Either way, the suits plunged through meat, frame, and fluid as their lasers cut farther and farther into the Bulb. As their suit re-breathers kicked on, Sandoval was also grateful she had demanded true pressure and air seals on the suits. As their lasers cut downward, they dived deeper into the bowels of the Bulb—

They stopped abruptly, connecting hard with a thick ball of something the lasers couldn't penetrate. Sandoval gathered herself and examined her readouts—they were deep but not at ideal projected bomb depth.

She couldn't see a thing.

"Thermal...." The internal makeup of the Bulb made that a mistake, blowing out their internal views with bright nonsense.

"High-contrast sonar!"

Their suits started pulsing with a layered audio ping system, showing on their head-case interiors as rough visual information. Sandoval studied the visual abstractions: they were on some form of skeletal internal protection sphere. Organs and/or machines pulsed and pumped all around, some seeming to malfunction due to their violent penetration.

"Okay, let's move—we need to find a way down—"

-Shit!- Laidlaw yelled, then screamed—

A pod of several bumpy spheres—six to ten feet in diameter—descended on his suit and pierced it somehow. All Sandoval could see was his suit pressure being lost, followed by bio flat lines.

Reilly shambled through the fluid toward Laidlaw and the spheres and started firing concussion shotguns in his suit's forearms—the closest sphere took it point blank, collapsing inward almost halfway. He fired at the other spheres as they attacked his suit, peppering and denting them, but they worked in unison to pop and open his suit. Sandoval could only guess as to what had actually killed Reilly when his readings went flat.

"Beech...," Sandoval started, unable to voice what she was thinking.

–I know, I know—we have to....–

"Do it, Beech!"

Sandoval primed her concussion guns and fired on all the approaching spheres while Beech detached and armed the bomb. Sandoval danced and rolled through whatever the Bulb's interior fluids were, pulping and disintegrating all comers.

Beech started, –Okay, it's set! Let's—–

Sandoval looked back at Beech, whose body was exposed in the fluid and being taken apart by the spheres.

"No!" Sandoval fired on the spheres until her guns ran out.

More bumpy spheres swam to meet her, replacing their fellow shipmates or antibodies. Sandoval knew they wouldn't be able to stop the bomb now that she could see its countdown in her overlay. She considered just letting them take her....

Then thought better of it and hit her suit thrusters. They clogged quickly but gave her the push to sail away from the skeletal sphere surrounding whatever the Bulb's core was.

When Sandoval was clear of the internal sphere's outer edge, she re-engaged the laser system and set all mini-thrusters to push her down toward the direction of the circular cut.

Sandoval cut all the way out of the Bulb's lower, south-facing curve and dropped into the sky above New Jersey, followed by a river of the internal fluids. After falling away some, she hit her parachutes and felt their welcome pull against her descent. She reset her visuals to normal view and rotated to look up so she could watch the explosion when it came—

Instead, she saw the outer surface of Bulb pulsing and swirling in a psychedelic fashion.

She looked down in time to watch New Jersey disappear....

The sphere of psychedelic distortion had swallowed the Bulb and enough area around its exterior to swallow Sandoval's suit with it. The weird swirling sphere collapsed toward the Bulb's surface, and Sandoval saw that she was somewhere else entirely—she was in deep space, her view a daunting maw of black, glowing planets, and a field of bright pinpricks stars.

The suit's parachutes collapsed in front of her and shriveled in vacuum due to the air filling them abruptly not existing, and they obscured her view. She keyed in their detachment, and as they floated away from her egg-shaped head case, she was met with a sight she had trouble comprehending....

"The" Bulb glided through space toward what could only be described as a *family* of Bulbs, of which it would have to be considered the runt. If it was huge, these dwarfed it, the largest few easily the size of Earth's moon. The larger Bulbs' tentacles caressed and prodded the smallest Bulb, maybe diagnosing its recent injuries.

Even with her basic knowledge of the stars, she knew she was screwed. This wasn't even her solar system from what she could tell....

As Sandoval watched the bomb count down and pictured it in the Bulb's gut, she mustered all of her remaining energy and will to curse the Bulbs from her airtight suit interior:

"Watch your child die and *understand*.... Come to Earth again, and *my* son will kill every fucking one of you...."

As the bomb counter ticked down to zero, Sandoval raised the shell-suit's right hand with its middle finger extended and closed her eyes, picturing her baby boy.

7

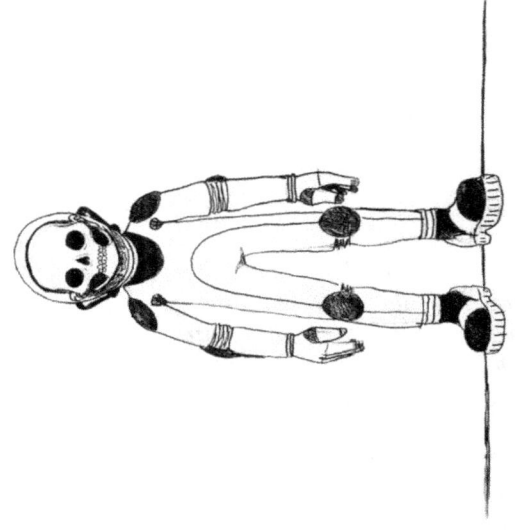

Ghosts of the Spires

rigs. Spire-Two's tether point was only a few hundred feet deep, but "better safe than sorry," Bianca figured. The sub eased down and locked into hydraulic clamps.

A hatch popped outward with a hiss, detached, and rolled away on a guide arm, revealing Dr. Danish Haamid.

Bianca said, "Uncle!" and smiled as she approached and hugged him, her dread momentarily forgotten. "I thought you were at Spire-Three."

He returned her affection and said, "We're closer here, or I would be."

"You're sure?"

Danish said, "Come, I'll show you."

They started down a pressurized industrial tunnel toward the main facility. Danish said, "You don't have to call me uncle forever, girl," and chuckled.

"You and Dad are like brothers, right?"

"How is he?"

"The same...."

Bianca followed Danish through the main prefab complex of the facility, then another tunnel across the sea floor. This tunnel had a transparent ceiling and, once again, Bianca had trouble taking her eyes off the Spire towering in the murky waters as they neared the forward research prefab.

The forward facility was a chunk of torus with rounded ends, affixed around a quarter of the Spire's base. Bianca could see the bare Spire through a sealed chamber with thick acrylic windows.

Bordering the Spire chamber were large airlocks and a central control room. Across from the control room, a ten-foot circular plate in the Spire's surface was visible due to a subtle seam.

The dread crept back....

A row of auto-guns on tripods and roll-down pressure shutters helped, but only so much.

"Dr. Haamid!"

An ebullient young man with a lock on the back of his head similar to a Hare Krishna's *sikha* approached Bianca and Danish. He also wore what had to be century-old equipment in a harness over his chest and abdomen. A set of cords like what you'd use for an old electric guitar dangled almost to his knees, along with others she didn't recognize, and all kept together in a bundle with a Velcro strap.

"Bianca, this is Asher Pettigrew, a specialist of sorts. Asher, this is Bianca Moody."

Asher shook Bianca's hand a bit too earnestly and said, "Hi, they talk a lot about your dad here. I'm Asher—"

"I just said—"

"Doctor Haamid, I think I'm close!"

239

Danish put his hand on Asher's shoulder.

Asher said, "Sorry, I'm trying."

"It's fine—just relax. We'll head right in, don't worry."

"He is stim-freak, Haamid. He *can't* relax."

Bianca looked toward the voice and saw the intimidating build; scarred and grim visage; and dark eyes of some sort of merc. The severe-looking man scoffed and walked toward the control room.

"Who's he?" Bianca asked.

"Vuković, our 'safety coordinator.'"

Bianca chuckled—but then she saw *him.*

Dr. Udo Jäger.

She approached him.

"Hello, Udo."

The gaunt, dour man turned only partway toward her, perhaps not feeling she was important enough to give his full attention as he scanned a readout bank at a lesser researcher's terminal projection.

"Bi*anca.* How pleasant. I thought you were studying your ancestors in Ethiopia. You could have easily joined us remotely from Spire-One without so much dreadful *travel,* communications being what they are, yes?"

"Mali, actually. Spire-Two is where I was *told* to report. Maybe you should check your records."

"Still brash as ever, eh?"

"And you're still a pedantic racist, I see."

Jäger sneered, glanced at her, and said, "I fail to see how I'm a racist for pointing out you needn't have come so far away from home."

"Proving my point, yeah? Oh, and I'm from Cincinnati, thanks again."

Danish hooked her by the elbow, led her toward the control room, and whispered, "Already, Bianca?"

"How could I not? He—"

Danish pleaded, "I know, believe me. But we won't succeed without him."

Bianca heard Jäger order Asher into the control room as well and they all entered it and sat down among several research assistants. Asher sat cross-legged on a wide, padded stool and plugged his cables in.

Bianca said, "Hey, Asher. What's your 'specialty'?"

"Oh, I'm an abstract holo-constructionist and noise artist."

Danish said, "We found young Asher performing in Berlin."

"Yeah, much more understanding there. I'm from Alaska."

Jäger sneered and said, "We were just fortunate that this nonsense 'art form' exists."

Asher just looked down at his lap and said, "Wow, thanks, Doctor."

Bianca said, "Don't listen to him," then to Jäger, "If you have Asher, why am I here?"

"You are here to do what your father, frankly, did better. When it was just his Empathy, we had no chance. Also, Asher is capable enough, but it took us a bit to realize that we needed his noise and light, *and* Empathy."

Bianca said, "So, you need me to, what, *feel* what he's doing?"

"Essentially. He is the lockpick, and you are the ears, yes? You feel and listen for the pins to fall on the shaft, so to speak," Danish said.

Jäger's basilisk eyes locked onto Bianca.

"How is your father, by the by?"

She just returned his cold gaze for a moment, then said, "Still in the behavioral hospital you put him in with all this...."

"Yes, well, his level of sensitivity and talent proved to be misfortunate. Hopefully your meager abilities are just enough to do the job without such issues."

Bianca hated that Jäger's expression didn't change while delivering his retort, but there wasn't much about him she didn't hate.

Asher said, "I'm ready."

Bianca took Asher's cue and reluctantly forfeited the staring contest to look at him. "Okay, so what do we do?"

Danish said, "React to Asher. Guide him."

"Okay."

Asher's hands assumed a poised position over the small knobs, buttons, and pedals of his patchwork, round-ish synthesizer setup.

Danish and the other researchers looked at Jäger patiently. Jäger said, "Commence combined-element attempt one."

Asher started slowly as the researchers became a murmuring hive of data-analyzing activity. Bianca knew almost nothing about making music—which was fine, because that's not exactly what this was—but as she understood it, the intro was like a layered arpeggio of clicks and pulses.

Pitch was shifted, squawks and blips were sifted in. Heavy, low bass was generated as thick, shifting tones with no rhythm. The visual accompaniment came from holo-projectors in the plate chamber, and looked like a psychedelic 3-D light show at first.

Intricate patterns emerged in the visual and noise output in the chamber. Bianca watched Asher manipulate a swirling maelstrom into calculated iterations and loops to build intricate geometric shapes above the holo-projectors amidst the light show.

This is where Bianca got her first real feeling of what they had to do—she could feel something from the plate itself.

"That *shwoopy-ping* thing. Do that a little slower...."

Bianca used onomatopoeia and free association to get a small level of synergy with the madly focused artist. It took some trial and error, but as their communication synced them more and more, Bianca reacted and focused on what felt like nodes in the door—three focal points in an upside-down triangle formation.

Danish inhaled sharply and said, "There!"

The points began to glow visibly *within* the plate. They could all see the glowing spheres just past the Spire plate's surface, though, as if in AR overlay.

Bianca knew they were almost right on, but a feeling began to compete with her excitement and desire to show Jäger up.

She felt a presence fighting their progress.

But then Asher aligned his iterations and tones with her advice once more, and it happened—

The glowing spheres in the circular plate pulsed in a sequence, then receded from the surface, fading from their view.

The circular plate broke apart in complex prisms like a puzzle. It collapsed from its center outward until it was gone, leaving a gaping circular maw of inky blackness the ceiling floods could barely penetrate, and filled the chamber with clouds of dark blue dust and, if their readings were right, air that could probably kill.

Bianca hated pressure suits. Orbital-station research stints had caused that. These helmets were less claustrophobic, at least.

After checking and rechecking each other's suits, they assembled in the airlocks and waited to be let in. Bianca noticed two maglev hover skiffs about eight feet by four—one at each lock.

Jäger signaled and the control room popped the lock doors. Bianca followed Jäger and Danish into the Spire chamber, her boots crunching in what she had thought was dust. Now it seemed like pulverized coral or bone.

The mercs entered first—amped, ready, unceremonious. Vuković carried a large shotgun but also had a splash-shock gun slung against a tactical pack that he wore over his combat pressure suit.

She was pretty sure the other mercs were called Wilks, Stevens, and Crenshaw.

It was silent for a few minutes and Bianca started to worry.

Over comms Vuković said, –Clear.–

Jäger stepped through the threshold. Danish followed, then Bianca and Asher did the same.

Jäger said, "We've entered Spire-Two, Base-Two."

Asher had his holo/noise rig adapted to fit on the outside of his pressure suit, along with amplifiers, speakers, and a small holo-projector.

Even with their suit lights, the first Spire chamber was so dark it felt like it absorbed light. The floor and walls were made of some form of grooved black metal.

The chamber was a hundred feet across and, other than scattered patches and small dunes of the blue coral dust, empty. The swooping groove patterns in

242

the floor and coral sand within them made Bianca think of Japanese rock gardens.

They advanced toward its center. A tech called Jules took up the team's rear, placing small balls on the chamber floor that sprouted antennae.

Danish pointed a flashlight upward and there was an obvious ceiling to the chamber about fifty feet up.

As they approached the center of the murky chamber, the floor curved upward and met in a cylinder, forming a thick floor-to-ceiling column about thirty feet in diameter. Instead of curving into the chamber ceiling the same way, it cut off abruptly.

"I admit, I'm unsure what our next step should be...," Jäger said, examining the column.

Bianca almost couldn't believe that he'd said it, but before she could chuckle or make a snide remark, she was struck by a presence.

She said, "I feel something."

Jäger just turned and eyed her coldly.

She said, "Asher, play the same patterns you did before."

Asher warmed up his portable rig and did so. The dazzling shapes and psychedelic sea of light they rotated in gave the chamber an eerie glow to add to its already spooky atmosphere.

Bianca let the sound vibrations and empathic resonations guide her to another triangular arrangement of glowing orbs within the column base's center. Once again, they could see them even through the matter somehow.

"Almost the same, but...."

She and Asher coordinated until the orbs synced, glowed, and rose through the column into the ceiling, vanishing. Most of the team members were standing near to or on the curved base of the column—they were lucky—

A form of paragravity engaged and the central column became its source—and its circumference the floor.

Those nearest the column's curved base fell forward, tumbling onto its surface.

Those farther from it dropped and slid or were thrown into a rough roll down the curve. The maglev skiffs smoothly slid down the curve onto the column, upending Danish and knocking Asher away as he tumbled to one side, and causing Crenshaw to grab a rectangular support railing that jutted up around skiffs' edges.

Jules got it the worst because he was farthest away. Because of the lack of transitional gravity, he fell at an angle toward the column from twenty feet up. Both arms snapped on impact and he was knocked unconscious in his suit.

The dark-blue pulverized coral showered down from what was the floor, covering the team and the column surface.

Crenshaw laughed as he rode the skiff—until he realized it was speeding up and wouldn't stop. He hopped over the railing and pried a panel open and flipped a master toggle. The skiff maglev cut out and dropped onto the column, skidding into the surface of the ceiling that was now a huge circular wall.

Stevens and Wilks hauled themselves up first and slung their weapons as they hurried to Jules. After a quick check, Wilks hurried to the scientist skiff, got medical packs, and went to work on him. As Wilks worked, using large, ribbed quick-wraps to set the bones, Stevens grabbed a compact gurney. He unfolded it to full man size and set it down next to Jules.

After patching and drugging Jules as much as they could, they activated a set of sputter-thrusters on the gurney's underside. It rose and guided itself back toward the plate opening.

Wilks opened comms and said, "Base-Two, Jules coming back to you—prep for hot landing due to...adjusted orientation."

–Wilco.–

Stevens said, "You guys patch Jules up good, alright?"

–Wilco.–

Wilks said, "Okay, there's only like five more of these hover-gurneys, so don't everybody go for a high dive."

Stevens and Crenshaw chuckled but Vuković grunted and they stopped. Danish said, "Well, what now?"

Crenshaw turned the skiff back on and it resumed normal function.

Bianca and Asher helped each other up and dusted off a bit before approaching the wall. They started their lockpick back-and-forth and the wall responded. Similar to the plate, it collapsed into itself away from the column, and there were gasps and oohs from most of the team. Vuković whistled.

At this new orientation, the Spire was a huge tunnel into the distance, stretching so far they couldn't see the end. They could only see its interior at all because the Spire material had an effect similar to one-way mirrored glass—what looked opaque on the outside was translucent on the inside. They couldn't see clearly, but the shifting of the ocean and the lights of the prefab base chunks could be seen. Only, all of that was pitched vertically behind them. The tunnel was also crisscrossed with smooth, curved structures like flying buttresses.

Jäger said, "Truly marvelous. Advance please."

The team continued down the central column walkway with the skiffs on auto behind them. The view out of the one-way Spire surface gradually brightened and swirled more visibly. Bianca realized they were near the ocean surface.

When they crossed the threshold of the ocean surface outside, the translucence of the Spire exposed a hidden beauty—the tunnel was lit now almost as through stained glass. The thick, translucent cylindrical walls of the Spire contained intricate, layered patterns that enhanced, diffused, and distorted the light. Combined with the buttresses, it was beautiful and magnificent.

So why did Bianca feel that dread again?—it twisted her stomach, and worse than before.

Near a crossing of several buttresses Bianca felt more than saw an amorphous swirl of distortion—then it was gone and her stomach relaxed some. In the strange light, it could've been her nerves and not her gift that caused it....

The team came across a sphere about four-foot in diameter, resting or installed on the column. A quick walk around the column revealed two more, creating a triangular formation like those they had seen a few times now.

Jäger said, "Well, activate them."

Bianca and Asher quickly succeeded. With no doors to open, she was curious what would—

They were somewhere else. More accurately, they were much farther along the column and Spire's length/height. Still on the column, still in the Spire...but they had been transported a great distance.

They marveled at the view of clouds, ocean, and land masses they could see all around from a great height "behind" and below them.

Danish stammered, "We're in the.... I—I think we're in the upper stratosphere...."

Jäger said, "*Teleportation*.... Think of what this means...," but he seemed almost sarcastic to Bianca.

Jäger hastened along the column and the team and skiffs followed. He slowed soon, though, as they approached the vertical terminus of the Spire—an outward curve that formed a "plate." They could see it through the one-way outer cylinder of the Spire, looming amidst the stratosphere ceiling.

They approached a shiny, translucent wall ahead.

Vukovi approached the wall and knocked—or tried to. His hand went through it and he recoiled.

"Not solid...."

Jäger snorted softly and said, "Well, obviously." He entered the chamber beyond with no hesitation and became a vague, man-shaped blur.

Vukovi followed, then called back, "Clear."

The rest of the team passed through after them.

The column ended about fifty feet ahead in a circular wall covered in dimly glowing domes with weird machinery moving inside. It looked alive to Bianca...like pulsing organs and bones repurposed into pumps, gears, pipes. The column's surface within about thirty feet of the dome-covered wall was raised a bit.

Jäger approached the raised part and stepped onto it, then continued to the wall of domes.

"I have a feeling that whatever this does, you should all join me on this strip."

The rest of the team joined him and Bianca and Asher went to work.

The skiffs tried repeatedly to join them too, but seemed to be resisted by the dome-adjacent ring.

Danish said, "I suppose we will be fine without them...."

245

The domes glowed brighter and their almost obscene internal workings became faster and more elaborate. A visible plane like a laser field cutting smoke appeared in front of the undulating, blurring domes, and another formed behind the team.

When the dome wall activated, Bianca's vision became a blur of organic matter, darkness, and streaking lights.

The group appeared on a column like the other, but this dome wall was behind them.

The vertical fields lingered for a moment then disappeared. The moment after they did, something clattered to the column floor—a wobbling round object that rolled away fast enough to come back over the cylinder and clink into Danish's boot. It was a grenade and Danish jumped backwards.

Stevens chuckled as he crossed to where Danish was. As he bent to pick up the grenade, he said, "It's not live, man."

Vuković crossed to Stevens and grabbed the back of his tactical pack. "Jäger was right.... Next time, stand closer to center," and handed him a spray can with FOAM-THERMITE printed on it vertically that had fallen out as Stevens had walked to Danish.

Stevens's pack was missing a perfectly cut vertical chunk of its furthest rear compartment. He detached his pack and patched it with a medical wrap from inside it.

Jäger murmured, "See that you do...," as he stormed forward with purpose.

Instead of smooth flying buttresses, this section had some form of piping or ducts. The conduits snaked asymmetrically between the column and outer Spire wall. Heat and moisture swirling off the conduits filled this stretch with hazy steam.

Bianca didn't like this place. The Spire behind them was haunting but beautiful—this was unsettling. The dread was back now and bad. She had to stop and almost doubled over.

Danish and Asher came to steady her.

She breathed through her teeth as she said, "Let's get this done and go. I hate this place already."

"Me too...," Asher agreed.

As they followed Jäger through the Spire's boiler room attraction, the column went through another closed wall/ceiling. The conduits also went through this wall into whatever was past it.

Bianca signaled Asher to start and they quickly triggered the door lock. As the wall collapsed away between the conduits, they were met with a vision of cosmic wonder that disoriented them all.

From between the conduits they could see the moon and stars. The former was huge compared to what they were used to seeing. There was also a subtle distortion to the outward view that bothered Bianca.

Jäger hurried onward.

246

Danish said, "This is.... How far...?"

Jäger replied, "From the size of the moon, I'd say approximately sixty thousand miles from Earth."

Danish said, "That's impossible—a structure like the Spire couldn't extend anywhere near that far. And we've seen the terminus for years."

"I don't believe the last teleportation was through the structure...not strictly, at least. A force connected to it maybe...."

They kept discussing as the team continued along. They were far enough ahead that Bianca only caught bits—"climbing...," "geosynchronous...," "center mass...," and "counterweight."

The column and Spire abruptly curved outward, creating a ball within another ball, the actual end of the Spire.

As they walked across the column-ball's outer surface, Bianca heard tortured moans ahead.

Then she saw the trees...if trees were made of bone, covered in mold with innumerable tiny black eyes in it, and had...lungs. Bianca shuddered because of their grotesque appearance, but also from a deep sorrow and intelligence she sensed from them. The mold—if that's what it was—also seemed to expel a kind of miasma or pollen that made the air in this ball-in-ball area even harder to see through. The miasma settled on their pressure suits and Bianca brought some up to her face plate—it seemed to vibrate, even as it rested.

Bianca also noticed that while the tree creatures seemed to sprout from the column-ball surface, she caught glimpses of glowing machinery similar to the dome wall bio-mech devices peeking from under the curved floor between their roots. There were also two-foot diameter plates or plugs at the bases of each of the grotesque trees.

The team slowed now, creeping around the ball and through the murk of this horrible orchard—all but Jäger, of course. He strutted through the orchard like he didn't see the tree beings at all.

At the far end of the ball from the column proper and the ultimate endpoint of the Spire, there was a larger tree that ended in a liquid-filled translucent sphere. The miasma clung to its warped-bone branches and the sphere underside.

Inside the sphere was a different being from the trees, it seemed. What Bianca could make out through the thick liquid in the sphere and miasma between them suggested limbs, tentacles, a misshapen lump of a body, and many eyes with no real pattern to their natural placement. It appeared to be in stasis...or dead.

"Begin!" Jäger commanded as he stared out at the stars. He seemed truly uninterested in the astro-biological wonders on display, and Bianca had no idea what he was thinking.

Vuković and his safety team scanned all around as Asher and Bianca warmed up. She didn't even know what they were activating in this place, but Jäger seemed confident there was something.

The dread came back and strong as she caught the first impressions from nodes within the liquid sphere's bio-mech tree base. It seemed like these nodes were linked directly with whatever the Spire's function truly was. Asher was lulled into some kind of trance as he worked and she was sure it had something do with the nodes.

The dread twisted at her insides, and the presence returned—the thing that had observed them before.

It was nothing more than a distortion in the air, but she felt and saw its many eyes. She didn't know how, but the thing in the liquid was approaching her.

It filled her head with images—fluid, quick, changing. She was on the verge of vomiting as she guided Asher to the last node shape and tones. She stopped in mid description and Asher went into a trance loop.

"Jäger, we have to stop! This thing is a doomsday machine!"

Jäger didn't look away from the stars as he said, "No, you simple, ignorant beast.... It is *ascension.*"

Vuković looked over at Jäger, brow furrowed.

"What are you two talking about?" Danish asked.

Jäger said, "Bianca's father showed me the truth. He connected me with the stoic angels we just passed through."

"Those messed-up trees?" Wilks asked.

Bianca held back bile as she yelled, "These things killed the fucking *dinosaurs*, Jäger! The Pilot couldn't stop the orchards in time, but just after, it called the machines back to their sockets and trapped the Spires in static phased pockets of space-time! Something related to their space travel that it repurposed...." She was overcome for a moment by all of the images in her head and the implications of them.

Confused, Danish pleaded, "How could you know that, Bianca? And...if they didn't want us to use the Spires, why did they appear?"

"Because the lower phase-shift cores failed. They weren't in full off-phase and degraded over millions.... Jesus, Jäger, they've been hidden for *millions* of years, and you want to wake them up?! We weren't supposed to ever find them!"

Jäger unzipped a large pocket on the front of his pressure suit and produced a short Orbital-Ops semi-auto pistol. He crossed to her and placed the gun against her faceplate.

Vuković and his crew aimed at Jäger.

"Finish it."

Bianca said, "We all die if I do," and closed her eyes, ready for the worst.

After an excruciating moment waiting for death, Bianca's eyes fluttered open to see Jäger looking genuinely torn. She remembered a tenth birthday gift from him almost two decades before—an AR science lab taught by adorable animated creatures—and wondered how much humanity was left in him.

But then he proclaimed, "Then *I* will!"

248

Jäger, apparently paying more attention than Bianca had thought, used Bianca's rough method, sans Empathy. Asher finished the performance with a bit of trial and error, and suggestion from Jäger.

The Pilot howled to Bianca as its tree descended into the ball's surface out of sight.

The bio-mech trees' moaning became a high-pitched squealing and chittering. The stars and moon blinked out, replaced by huge versions of the pumping, glowing bio-machines all around, their inner-workings free from domes and pumping and undulating all around like a sky of obscene madness around their tiny column-ball planet.

Asher snapped out of his trance and murmured, "What the actual fuck?"

Bianca said, "I saw a distortion before.... I think we just woke up a cloaked seed ship.... We were looking out *through* it."

Seeing the bio-machines surrounding them changed something in Jäger. He seemed to be released or was jarred loose by the disgusting display surrounding them. His gun arm went slack as he tried to process what he was seeing—

With a distinct *fwap* sound, Jäger's body and head flashed and he dropped, seizing up as he fell. Bianca looked toward where the flash had come from.

Vukovié was still aiming his splash-shock gun.

"I heard enough to know—we go now."

Bianca nodded and started back through the orchard. Wilks caught up, taking point. Vukovié took up the rear after Asher and Danish passed him. Crenshaw and Stevens took the flanks as they hustled through the miasma, kicking it up even more.

Danish said, "But, Udo...."

Bianca snapped, "Let him *ascend*, Uncle."

They made it about halfway back across the ball's outer surface before the ground started vibrating. One of the odd plugs at the base of the bio-mech trees popped up half a foot—then rose up with a metallic screaming sound about six feet from its base.

The six-foot cylinder detached and hovered for a moment before starting to change—

Vukovié shot it with his splash-shock gun and it dropped to the ball surface.

"Faster—now!" and now the scary merc sounded scared.

They made it to the start of the conduits before another cylinder popped out. Vukovié shocked it and it dropped, but another two popped out. He fired at them—three more.

"Crenshaw, Stevens—with me." They stopped and prepped. "Wilks, Moody, Haamid, Pettigrew—go...."

She didn't need to be told twice and rushed on ahead with the rest.

Vukovié called after them or maybe her, "Leave door *open!*"

Vuković's hands were shaking. He'd made a career dealing with humans who either deserved to die or whose lives were worth less to him than a new boat or something. But this was next-level crazy alien shit.

The plugs kept popping out and he fired until he had lost charge on his splash-shock, and his men had only brought projectile weapons. He had a feeling those wouldn't cut it.

As Vuković hurried to detach his pack and throw a new charge into his gun, one of the cylinders had a chance to change into its functional form.

Crenshaw and Stevens fired.

Their powerful but useless hot metal bounced off or was deflected by an energy field and the cylinder went from smooth to angular and distorted. Its top and bottom collapsed toward each other and met, squashing the shape into a disc, then pulling back apart. Like maybe an impossibly complex Rubik's Cube solving itself in a few more directions, the plug became an ever-changing rough ball of swirling geometric shapes—it pulsed between multi-compound dodecahedrons to things Vuković had never seen.

Before he could reload his splash-shock, the plug ball projected a glowing cylinder through Stevens, lighting his body up where it went through in what looked like a full-color X-ray—

The projection pulled back into the plug ball, taking everything that its cylinder had lit up. Stevens's legs toppled over, one with a chunk of suited hip left.

Crenshaw made a sound like a baby chick.

The ball pulsed, then used the materials Stevens had given it. Three feet off the surface of the shifting geometric shapes, a hard weave of flesh, organs, bones, pressure-suit material, guns, med supplies, and body armor started forming like a curved, spindly shell. It was fed from the ball in strings of matter as a spider might spin a web of the same materials, but with no limbs used.

Vuković finished his reload and fired the splash-shock at the newly armored ball—it shifted the bulk of the almost finished Stevens-shield toward the shot, absorbed it, and sent it toward the Spire's outer wall.

More plugs popped out.

"No!" Vuković bellowed, his emasculation nightmares made real.

Crenshaw had picked up on Vuković's waning stability and prepped a grenade, ready to throw.

"Flank it!" Crenshaw yelled as his arm went forward. The grenade left his hand just before the plug's glowing cylinder lit him up X-ray-like from his lower jaw to his upper thighs—then took his materials.

As it started to weave more shielding from Crenshaw, Vuković hustled through the tree beings to its side, ignoring the new plugs.

Crenshaw's grenade blasted hard against the shifted bio-weave shield—

Vuković maxed-out the splash-shock and fired at the exposed flank—he struck home and hard. The plug ball and its shielding dropped, its ball form shattering and the majority of his team members' remains and gear slapping down to the grooved floor with a sickening sound.

Vuković watched the other plugs changing into geometric-ball shapes as he rushed toward the column proper—

Three shots rang out and he dropped.

Jäger limped past Vuković's prone, still form.

"Turnabout is fair play."

Bianca could barely see through kicked-up miasma and the humidity of where the conduit chamber met the orchard ball section. Asher eagerly waited to help her close the door. Danish was staring at the column surface, hunched over with his hands on his knees—almost unhinged from what he had seen. Wilks was as tucked into the cover from a column-close conduit as he could be, dead-eyeing the fully open attack area from the conduit chamber.

A vague upper-body arose around the curve of the column cylinder in the murk to his left and Wilks tensed. Before Wilks could decide if it was one of his comrades, Jäger fired his pistol twice and with surprising ability. Wilks fired wide in reflex as he dropped dead, his cracked helmet hissing from its new openings.

Jäger limped up to Bianca and Asher, gun drawn. Danish approached him but Jäger pointed the gun at his faceplate.

"Close the door!"

Danish yelled, "Where are the others?!"

Jäger pistol-whipped Danish, cracking his helmet and dropping him to the floor. Bianca came to his aid.

A *fwap* was heard down the column and they could see the vague shapes of a combat pressure suit and vague ball dropping and shattering.

Vuković yelled, "Keep it open!"

Jäger fired his pistol until it was empty, sending Vuković behind a close conduit. Jäger reloaded and pointed the gun at Asher, so he began the locking process. With no choices left, Bianca helped.

More of the dim ball shapes appeared in the distant murk. As Bianca worked, she could hear more of Vuković's shots and tinkling crashes of his success. Each time a chittering, squealing ball dropped, she hoped one of those awful tree beings died horribly—though, she was afraid the balls were expendable and would regenerate forever, from what the Pilot had shown her.

Vuković ran from his cover, splash-shock readied. He couldn't see Jäger, but he had no choice—he was almost dry and with no more charge packs, he would have no way of fighting what seemed like an endless onslaught of those terrible ball machines.

The psychedelic light show and forming geometric shapes were all he could see in the dense miasma and conduit output.

Jäger could see him better due to the miasma being thicker where Vuković was, and rose the pistol to fire—

Danish kicked into Jäger's right knee, almost bending it into his left, and Jäger went down.

But the wall started reforming toward the column.

"*Please no!*" Vuković begged.

The wall closed and Vuković pounded against it, still pleading for mercy.

On the floor, holding his busted knee and shaking, Jäger raised his pistol and fired one clean shot into Danish's faceplate.

Bianca screamed and shook.

Jäger aimed at Bianca again and said, "Help me up!"

Bianca choked up as she hooked an arm under one of Jäger's and hauled him up, then just glared at him, sniffing as she awaited more orders. Jäger slapped her helmet with the pistol barrel and pointed it down the conduit tunnel toward the teleporter.

"*Auf geht's!*"

They started forward, but Jäger was heavier than she expected and going was slow.

"Asher! Help her!"

Asher scowled but the pistol helped him work past his misgivings. The three of them limped along the column.

A rattling sound started above them in one of the conduits, then an added hissing to the conduit's own.

"They're coming! Get us to the transporter!" Jäger cried.

A circular outline flashed in the conduit, and a curved plate dropped from where it was instantly cut, along with a thick, nasty fluid, a spray can, and one large, cursing safety coordinator.

"Vuković!" Jäger pulled his pistol arm over Asher's head and aimed at the muck-covered merc—

Bianca lifted then jammed her lower leg down hard into Jäger's already injured knee and grabbed the pistol barrel, causing him to fire wide of Vuković. She wrested the gun from his grip and let him drop to the column, then pointed it at his faceplate.

Bianca said, "Hey, let's go!"

They hurried down to the grotesque dome wall and Asher started performing with no hesitation. Bianca guided him as she watched a crying, sniveling Jäger hobble his way toward them, cursing them all the way in a few different languages.

A look of triumph lit up his face as he started to cross the plane of the raised transporter ring.

As the transporter activated, Bianca smiled and said, "*Bis dann!*"

As the murky tunnel was replaced by the pumping domes, Jäger's wide-eyed form shrank a bit. As the swirling laser-smoke plane cut out, the front half of Jäger's suit and body curled away and slapped down onto the column, sliding around its curve a bit. Bianca and Asher looked away—even Vuković did after a moment.

They hurried on toward the shiny barrier, passing the skiffs they'd had to leave behind.

Asher said, "I'm never leaving Berlin agai—"

Then Asher stepped through the barrier in front of Bianca and Vuković and fell forward/down into the newly returned Earth-oriented gravity of the Spire's "stained glass" chamber.

He stopped somehow and dangled, his head pulsing with blood as he watched wave after wave of tree plug cylinders form into complex geometric shapes below. A sphincter wall started collapsing toward Asher along the shiny barrier's path.

He looked down/up and saw large gloved hands on his ankle and foot. They started to heave him back up into the transporter chamber and he looked back down in time to see circular shapes opening in the Spire's outer surface....

Vuković hauled Asher back up onto the cylinder just before the sphincter wall closed—

Gravity returned to Earth here too and they fell onto the wall's surface. The maglev skiffs slammed down rear-first and teetered over, then fell against the wall/floor's surface.

Circular ports like those Asher had just seen—and Bianca had seen before—collapsed away, causing the upper stratosphere to suck and pull at their suits as they struggled to their feet.

Asher said, "Those fucking machines are down there—thousands of them!"

"How do we get down?!"

Bianca looked around, searching for a solution....

Her eyes landed on an overturned maglev skiff. She stormed over to it and tried to turn it back over.

Vuković yelled, "What will that do?!"

Asher crossed to Bianca's side and helped her tip the skiff over. Bianca realized maybe their synergy had transcended puppetry.

Vuković shook his head, saying, "They fill the lower chamber.... We can't go down there!"

Bianca and Asher looked at each other and in rough unison said, "Not on the inside...."

Vuković's eyes darted back and forth behind his faceplate as he tried to comprehend what they meant.

When it clicked, he said, "That's *worse!*"

Asher and Bianca threw some equipment off and freed some securing straps, then guided the maglev skiff toward one of the open ports in the Spire's outer surface.

Bianca said, "We're going. Are you?"

Vuković looked genuinely pained as he searched his mind for an alternate solution.

Plug ports they hadn't seen popped up into their chamber, possibly as an internal security response.

As the cylinders started to reform, Bianca and Asher pushed the skiff toward the open port, climbed onto it, and secured themselves as tightly against its surface as they could with the newly free straps.

Vuković ran behind them and jumped, grabbing the safety rail just before the skiff emerged from the Spire's interior....

The skiff went far enough out of the port to break contact with the Spire for a long moment, then fell and glommed back onto its outer surface hard and started descending.

Vuković almost lost his grip when it slapped back against the Spire's surface, but held on, and started to climb to Bianca and Asher.

The skiff kept accelerating downward and Vuković had to fight it with everything he had, climbing over secured equipment boxes and canisters. He released a stack of medical drugs and bandages and secured himself with the free straps.

The beauty of the blurring Earth rising to meet them would have been breathtaking, if the Spire hadn't started discharging otherworldly death machines from every open port they sped past, filling the sky. Bianca didn't have time to think about what the machines were going to do, but she knew enough from what the Pilot had shown her....

They were descending so fast that the skiff was vibrating badly. The ocean surface was getting bigger by the second. They were going to black out soon.

Asher yelled with all he had left, "*How do we stop?!*"

They all shook internally, the realization of their folly cutting deep. Vuković laughed at the madness of it seeming like a good idea.

Bianca craned her neck down at the skiff contents and laughed a different laugh, kicking a stack of strapped-in boxy shapes marked HOVER-GURNEY....

As they made their way south to New Zealand in the stealth boat Bianca had arrived on, she injected some painkillers into Asher's arm. He'd told her the best dose not to speedball him (too hard)—he'd landed his gurney hardest, cracking a femur.

Vuković asked her from the helm, "Why there? Australia has better defenses."

Bianca watched a rear video feed of the Spire as they got farther from it and said, "My father's hospital is in New Zealand...and I think he's the only human being on Earth with any real idea what we just woke up...and maybe how to fight them."

7

254

PIE

Hong Kong—2071

The spooky hooded bastard's eyes shifted down and reflected neon Chinese calligraphy from a puddle on the narrow Hong Kong market street's empty walkway, giving them a haunting glow.

Arjun realized the syndicate reaper must've been wearing AR lenses, since naked eyes wouldn't have looked that way. And this reaper liked to play the part, didn't he? Black-on-black boots, pants, gloves, and big, puffy hooded jacket over a dark-skinned head and a thick black scarf over his face too. Those creepy eyes were the only thing Arjun could make out in the depths of the draped, puffy hood.

Arjun was sitting where the reaper had laid him out—with a surprising amount of ease considering the reaper's average size and slight form—and his legs were near the standing reaper's. He considered kicking the reaper's legs out from under him and running, but after the walloping the bastard had given Arjun already, he doubted his ability to execute.

Then he remembered the Triad thugs the reaper had used to clear the market of patrons and shop owners—the latter forced to close and lock their storefronts and not come out under pain of death—and decided he'd be dead before he could run to the next intersection.

<<*Bring me the children,*>> the reaper said in Cantonese. Arjun had been in Hong Kong long enough to pick up a decent amount of the dialect, but if he had understood it or not, the way the reaper said "children" would still have

256

given him the same chill. Arjun watched Triads wheel two large cases from a white lorry that was parked nearby.

The dark purplish cases resembled comically large luggage hard cases on four wheels. Arjun noticed some block letters stencil-sprayed on the sides of the cases that read PIE in construction orange.

<<*How are they?*>> the reaper asked.

A Triad inspected the cases and said, <<Tired and anxious.>>

<<*Let's make it easier on them then.*>>

The reaper took out a small semi-auto pistol with an integrated suppressor. He chambered the first round and fired two rounds down into Arjun's right leg. Arjun cried out and clutched it.

The reaper re-holstered the pistol and walked back to the cases. The Triad who had checked the cases stepped back and lowered his gaze, seemingly as disturbed by the reaper's appearance as Arjun had been. The reaper pressed some buttons and the cases popped open a bit at each vertical seam and hissed like air was escaping.

As the cases came apart, what Arjun saw stretching and rising from them hastened him to his feet. He desperately limped away from the reaper and his monsters.

It's cold and dark here, Daddy, Boy said in his mind—*Daddy doesn't have to hear with meat ears.* Boy looked over at Girl, her pink skinclothes reflecting what little light this boring place had as she stretched and yawned. She agreed it was cold and said she wanted to go back to sleep.

Boy felt pinches in his neck, then warmth—Daddy was letting them see things the pretty way. With a pulse and beep, the dark place swirled with color and turned soft. Boy looked over at Girl and could see a yellow bow on her smooth pink head now, which made him smile.

Cascading pinpricks of light coalesced into glowing flowers, butterflies, snails, birds, bunnies, and kittens all around. Boy could see the warm sun among huge, fluffy clouds.

Daddy told them to look at a gingerbread man who was running away from them in a funny, stumble-y way.

That gingerbread man is full of cake and candy! If you catch him, you can have it! Daddy said.

Boy became excited—*Oh! Is he like a piñata?* Boy and Girl looked at each other, ever so excited now.

Yes! Exactly that! Go get him—get all that cake and all that candy!

Boy and Girl rose up and bounded after the gingerbread man, feeling so happy now out in the sun with all the cute and happy things. Gingerbread man wasn't very good at running, though, and Boy and Girl were almost sad when they caught him so fast—that is, until they opened him up and got their yummy prizes.

A quail egg burst at the center of a *siu mai* dumpling in Naoko's mouth, the intense yolk mixing with the minced pork and chopped shrimp just right. Naoko loved Hong Kong dim sum and it made up most of her diet on these little meet-and-greet field trips—she could get it in Osaka, but it wasn't the same.

She slurped some of the tea—mostly to cleanse her palate, as she much preferred Japanese tea—and went for the largest *cha siu bao* pork bun on its plate, snagging its plumpness with her personal stainless steel chopsticks. The metal utensils were black with bright pink blossoms appearing to swirl around the top third of their lengths.

Naoko moaned and hummed sing-song noises of approval as she chewed, not worried about being rude—her sounds were easily drowned out in the cacophony of the busy establishment. What wasn't lost on her in the din were snippets of conversation about her appearance, nationality, and/or mixed heritage.

It probably didn't help that she was wearing a T-shirt with cut off sleeves and her Second Skin tats were so new on the market—her hands, arms, upper chest, back, and neck up to her jawline were covered with slowly animating abstract graffiti in all major written languages, and all with a subtle glow effect.

If they knew what other bleeding-edge tech she'd had installed *under* her skin, they would be even more confused and worried, she had thought.

Her dark-green faded pompadour and pink eye shadow seemed to be another topic of discussion, taking it into territories of sexuality.

She did her best to ignore all the talk about herself as the "weirdo," "dyke," "gangster," girl—and possible high-end niche prostitute?—and filled her mouth with a big hunk of crispy rice-flour shrimp roll.

An obvious fellow Yakuza with long, straight hair squeezed his way as politely as possible from the door to her table. He tried to act cool as he asked in Japanese, <<Is your name Naoko *Alexeyev*?>>

She nodded and gestured for him to sit across from her with her chopsticks and he did.

<<What kind of name is Alexeyev?>>

"You speak English? I doubt many of these fine folks do. They strike me as old school mainlanders mostly."

"I do, yes," he said.

"Father was Russian and Chinese—mother was Zainichi Korean Japanese."

"I see. And...why is your hair so...<<boyish>>?"

"You're pretty forward. Are you asking me if I like men or women? Might as well join the discussion...," she said and nodded toward a group of gossiping men at a nearby table who'd been at the core of the sexuality debate aimed at her. "I never decided—didn't see a need to."

He scrunched his face a bit and asked, "Okay.... Why is it so short like that, though? Longer for women is better...."

"Ah, you're a neo-traditionalist...." Naoko closed her chopsticks at the center of a fist as she said, <<Let me show you.>>

258

Without leaving her seat, Naoko kicked one of his wooden chair's front legs, snapping it, and he collapsed down onto the table, trying to hold himself up as the chair teetered under his weight. With one swift motion, Naoko leaned forward, gathered his long hair into her free hand, and yanked his head down onto the table as she pushed the sharp steel chopsticks against his throat.

Some of the other patrons feigned shock but didn't seem that shocked, truth be told. Most didn't even look over. Naoko decided they found her more interesting when it wasn't as obvious how dangerous she was.

Naoko leaned in close and said, <<See? Your hair is a tactical weakness. Also, you're very rude. You haven't stated your name, affiliation, or purpose here, and I have been patient, I would say.>>

<<I apologize! My name is Kuwabara Takehiko! I was sent for you!>>

<<By who, Kuwabara? Who are you with?>>

<<Inagawa-ikka! We need your help with a murder!>>

Naoko let go of Kuwabara's hair and pulled back her chopsticks, using her other hand to return them to eating position. She dipped them in the hot tea pot to sanitize them, then replaced its top and snagged another cha siu bao bun and dug in. With a half-full mouth she asked, "Murder? Aren't you boys mostly into running local porn-game arcades?"

Kuwabara tried to look natural holding himself up on the three remaining chair legs.

"W-we were taking protection from Indian tailor...," Kuwabara looked around the room for listeners before lowering his voice and saying, "and he was also feeding news on the...*locals*—the ones we don't deal with already."

Naoko said, "I'm not police. I don't solve murders. I fix things."

"That is what we need. This no ordinary murder—this method was...<<unnecessary>>."

"I was in town for a meeting—not my normal duties. Why should I—"

Kuwabara interrupted, "This is for you," and took something from a pocket in his suit jacket, lowered his head, and offered it to her with both hands—by balancing and sliding on his elbows.

Naoko took the item—a small tea bowl. It had been broken at some point and repaired in the *Kintsukuroi* method—the pieces were rejoined with gold dust in the resin to call attention to the repair.

"Takeda-sama said it means—"

"I *know* what it means," Naoko snapped back. "Takeda gave you this—Takeda himself?"

Kuwabara nodded and bowed as much as he could while holding the table.

Naoko carefully pocketed the small bowl in a thigh pocket on her satin cargo pants. Then she dipped her chopsticks in the hot tea bowl again before securing them in a slender black case and tucking them in the other thigh pocket.

Naoko said, <<You should have given me the bowl first.>>

Naoko had seen many grizzly things in her career, but this was near the worst. The Indian tailor had been taken apart, then the limbs and viscera had been spread and draped around the shopping street, partially eaten, and...played with. The last part bothered her most and as she studied a life-sized animated plastic stand of a popular Chinese singer with the tailor's large intestine wrapped around its neck like a feather boa, she shuddered a bit. The singer continuously smiled and winked in a loop, the boa blood smeared across her mouth area, giving it a macabre feel.

Local police had allowed them into the cordon, a favor to a local Triad group that Inagawa-ikka had had dealings with, Kuwabara had explained. He had driven them here along with two of his underlings, a buzzed-headed thug named Murata and another named Higuchi who had messy hair, a translucent eye patch with a Jolly Roger on it, and something wispy resembling sideburns on the sides of his face.

Higuchi sneered, <<I did not know there was this much blood in a human body.>>

Kuwabara said, <<I have seen bad things...but this.... There is no honor in this....>>

Naoko said, <<Whatever did this has no use for honor.>>

<<'What'? Don't you mean who?>> Murata asked.

<<'Who' implies a person did this—a human. Seems like human is becoming a fuzzy term, though, so I guess both work....>>

"What do you mean? Wait—not important. May I ask...?"

Naoko looked at Kuwabara, curious why he had switched to English again. "What does the tea bowl mean?"

Naoko sighed and said, "I guess I was already pretty hard on you—I'll let your continued rudeness slide...." Kuwabara couldn't help rubbing the marks on his neck left by Naoko's chopsticks as she said this. "Someone called in a marker...an old, big one. Even with how awful and shameful this is, I don't understand why it was called in myself. That one was reserved for...," she trailed off as she noticed a police-car light glint off of something on the powered hinge system on one of the closed shop accordion shutters.

Naoko walked toward the closed-shop exterior and looked closer. The glinting object changed some and she knew she was right—it was a camera. It was the size of a marble and secured in the workings of the security shutters. Its autofocus and exposure were making its aperture change in size and move very slightly as she approached. She couldn't see a microphone but didn't want to take chances so she acted like she had decided the camera was nothing important, turned around and walked back to Kuwabara.

Naoko lowered her voice and said, "Does one of your boys have scanning equipment handy? I thought I'd seen something promising on Murata's belt under his jacket."

"Yes, for confidentiality sweeps during important meetings—why?" he started to look around nervously.

"Stop—just look at me." He did. "There's a camera behind me. I think this was a setup to see who would come looking. I say we look for them instead, right?" Kuwabara nodded. "Okay, go to Murata and turn him away from where my back is facing then have him zero any camera signals in the area that aren't official. Scrub all the frequencies—"

Kuwabara frowned and said, "'Zero'? 'Scrub'?"

She sighed and said, <<Look for location, search through....>>

He nodded his understanding and crossed to Murata, turning him away from the camera as she had said. Murata fought his obvious curiosity and from what Naoko could tell from his blocked movements, he had started searching upon request.

Naoko strolled around casually, trying to give the impression she was still just trying to make sense of the messy scene. In her peripheral vision she noticed Murata nod to Kuwabara and then to her.

<<Okay, time to go,>> Naoko said to Higuchi, who was using a stick to poke what looked like part of a lung hanging from one of many ornamental trees that lined the shopping street. He looked at her and flicked the stick down into a dried blood puddle then joined her.

They left the cordon and got back in the car before saying anything else, then caught Higuchi up. He was confused and angered but ready for what he knew Naoko was planning.

Naoko asked, <<Do you have another pistol?>>

Kuwabara said, <<You don't?>>

<<I had one for use during my stay, but I was supposed to leave a little after you came to find me so I had already turned it back in. I don't travel with firearms on me—imagine that.>>

Higuchi opened a compartment in the console and produced a large revolver for her, as well as a few quick loads that she tucked into her cargo pant pockets.

<<Thanks. Okay, let's follow that signal, shall we?>>

Kuwabara drove while Murata kept on the intercepted signal and watched a small video screen that showed the feed from the camera back at the murder scene. As long as that feed was still live, they were in business.

So, of course, a few blocks away and with a very strong signal source, the live feed cut out and they were blind.

<<Pull over and stop,>> Naoko said and looked all around as Kuwabara did as she said. There was nothing obvious around and she almost decided to move on, but a white lorry parked down an alley to their left caught her attention—mostly because it didn't seem like it should, and there was no one in the cab. Nothing about it stood out, but she had learned to trust her instincts in her current employment and they were definitely talking to her now.

<<That's it—the lorry over there.>>

Kuwabara didn't want to question her so he asked Murata, <<Seem possible?>>

Murata grunted in the affirmative as he switched his scanner off, set it on the dash, and took out his own pistol, chambering the first round with the slide. Higuchi took a machine pistol from under the front seat, loaded a magazine, and put it under his jacket.

Kuwabara asked, <<Should I be ready to drive?>>

Naoko tried to gauge how many thugs could be in the back of the lorry then said, <<No, come with us but leave the car locked and running.>>

Kuwabara took out a semiautomatic pistol of his own, chambered it, and engaged the parking brake. They all re-tucked their weapons and got out of the car, Kuwabara locking the car remotely.

The quartet entered the alley, Naoko and Kuwabara taking lead—one on each side of the lorry as they passed the empty cab—and Murata and Higuchi waited by the cab to watch the street behind them. Naoko and Kuwabara took their pistols back out and readied them as they reached the closed rear cargo doors.

Murata and Higuchi looked back at them and they both nodded, so they slipped down the cargo section's length and took up positions a bit behind Naoko and Kuwabara, guns readied.

Naoko gestured for Kuwabara to open the cargo-section doors and aimed at their center. Kuwabara extended his hands but hesitated, then in one quick motion, threw the latch and swung them open and pulled his gun back to the ready—

Triad thugs inside the cargo box fired Taser pistols into the quartet's chests, their prongs piercing just enough to make good contact before huge surges of electricity went through their bodies.

Before Naoko fully seized up, two things struck her—there was a creepy fucker with glowing, reflective eyes sitting in the cargo box between two weird cases near its rear, staring at her intently. And second, as smart as she thought she'd been, she'd had no reason to expect an actual trap, which she almost had time to be troubled by.

Naoko came to from being dropped into a puddle of now pouring rain. She blinked and tried to shake the thick treacle of forced unconsciousness out of her head as she watched the Triad thugs that had shocked them drop Kuwabara, Murata, and Higuchi down as well. They weren't bound in any way—which made her more nervous than she already was—but they had taken all their guns, of course.

She glanced around and saw that it was night already and they were in a narrow alley in one of the poorer districts—one of many jagged, snaking alleys between densely packed high-rise low-rent apartment estates. These alleys were like a maze with few unblocked entrances/exits, due to their use in local crime and conspiracy. The local thugs were nowhere to be seen, though.

The alley was narrow enough that she could see the lorry had been parked a ways down at the mouth of the artificial slot canyon they were deposited in. Another set of Triads led by that creepy reaper—Naoko decided that's what he had to be, with that spooky getup—rolled those two large cases she'd seen before toward them.

Naoko had dealt with reapers before but this one was especially strange—their origin was unclear but their appearance and tactics had risen from certain Southeast Asian Triads needing to instill terror at a level only supernatural implications could on their more superstitious competitors. It was so effective, many groups had started using them as enforcers and Naoko had personally had to neutralize several in her time. But this one was something else. Something about his eyes and movement bothered her.

The reaper gestured for the thugs wheeling the cases to stop. Naoko noticed orange Roman letters on the side that said PIE. The reaper approached the captive Yakuza and stood at their feet, examining them. He nodded as he decided something about Kuwabara, Murata, and Higuchi, then lingered on Naoko and narrowed his glinting eyes some as he sized her up.

<<*How are they?*>> the reaper hissed in Cantonese with a strong accent—Naoko decided it was Indonesian.

One thug checked the cases and said, <<Sad and confused.>>

Naoko watched the reaper tuck the tips of his fingers into his puffy black jacket and rub the palm up and down on the material like he was considering something. She could see the bulge of what had to be a pistol in that pocket and she prepped herself for an attempt at a disarming move, but the reaper pulled his hand back out and said, <<*They have grown well and learned much—let's make it* fair *for once....*>>

The reaper turned away to walk to the cases.

<<What is this?>> Naoko asked in perfect Cantonese.

The reaper stopped, but only turned his head in his puffy hood so that she could see mouth movements in his face covering—which were also off.

<<*These unlucky boys are...*>> "collateral damage" <<*...but today you die, Naoko Alexeyev.*>>

Kuwabara, Murata, and Higuchi looked at each other, then Naoko, but she didn't take her eyes off the reaper as he walked to the big purple cases. The reaper keyed a few things into a panel on each case and they popped a bit with a hiss and opened fully.

Naoko had never seen anything quite like what was in the cases—they had been human at one point, but now they were seamlessly fused with artificial extensions and enhancements. They each wore combination armor and body suits—one blue and the other pink—and big, round helmets that covered all of their features besides their jagged-toothed mouths. Their glowing eyes could be seen through the translucent bubble on the faceplates above their mouths and the helmets had many cables running to spheres of some sort on their backs that had thick plastic antennae sprouting from them.

Higuchi said, <<Are you serious?>> apparently unimpressed.

His expression changed when the creatures stretched and rose from the cases—they had to be eight or nine feet tall, and their artificial legs bent the wrong way and also had more joints than was natural. Their arms were also overlong and ended in curved foot-long talons of pattern-welded steel. They had been butchered and surgically fused with the most lethal parts of the US military's Hüm bipedal humanoid drone program. The *why* of that was something she would consider later, if she survived this day.

The blue and pink cyborg monsters hunched back down and looked at the reaper. From what Naoko could see of their faces, they looked miserable as they seemed to communicate wordlessly in some way. The reaper caressed their helmets, then pressed something on them and their glowing eyes went mostly dark—it looked to Naoko like internal augmented-reality goggles had come down over them, similar to modern combat helmets—and after a moment, the monsters smiled big. Ampules in their neck armor plunged something into their bloodstreams as well and the cyborgs vibrated with excitement. They smiled even bigger, showing more of their decayed, broken natural teeth, and what looked to Naoko like translucent artificial canines and molars—all in a power-assisted jaw.

<<Oh...shit...,>> Naoko muttered as she got to her feet. She couldn't remember the last time she'd actually been scared...but she was now.

The cyborgs stretched once more then started running toward the Yakuza, the blue one so excited that it tumbled as it ran, rolling then flowing back into running seamlessly.

The others were frozen in place, so Naoko grabbed Kuwabara and Higuchi by their jackets and pulled them stumbling to their feet as she started running down the alley.

Naoko looked back as she rounded the first intersection into another alley offshoot and caught a glimpse of the two abominations taking a screaming Murata apart with ease in a swirling mess of blood and other fluids, the pink one wrapping his intestines around its hands like a rough cat's cradle while the blue one whipped them around like streamers, loops of him catching on fire escape–ladder hooks. They started biting into them as Naoko ran around the corner and lost sight of them.

Daddy's so nice, Girl thought as she played with the bright, colorful piñata man and ate his juice-filled candy rope. She watched glowing butterflies flit about all around and thought, *We have so many friends to play chase with today.*

Boy laughed and hummed a happy song as he ate the cake from the piñata man's tummy and laughed at a cartoon puppy stumbling around near them.

Girl said, *We'll get too full—we should catch the others too now!*

Kuwabara kept saying, <<Shit-shit-shit-shit...,>> as they all ran down the tight alley. He was in the rear as the pink creature came around the corner, sprayed and laced with blood—and teeth wet with it. She tumbled and rolled now too, the fresh kill exciting her even more.

Kuwabara almost came apart in one slash of the pink cyborg's talons, and his howl was cut short by the next. The blue monster somersaulted around the corner and joined her.

Naoko knew they were dead if they didn't change the rules somehow—as she ran, she looked up and it hit her. She used her own—comparatively modest—internal enhancements to help her jump up to a bundle of phone, power, and TV cables that were rigged in zigzag patterns above all of these narrow stretches of the maze of alleys. She swung up and climbed onto a dense stalk of the bundles, then whipped one arm back down for Higuchi but he couldn't comprehend why she had in the haze of fear and madness he was in.

<<*Grab it!*>> she yelled.

His head cleared enough to understand and he grabbed her arm. She used his momentum to swing him up onto the lattice of crisscrossed cables, then climbed up the side of a vertical air duct. She jumped for another, grabbed, and climbed, then up to the next and the next.

Higuchi couldn't do the same things she could and he had to make do with scrambling up a thick pipe as the people in their apartments closed metal security shutters all around, also dousing the only light sources beside layered neon signs all around. At least she had given him a chance, she thought.

The cyborgs didn't seem fazed by verticality or darkness and used their unnaturally long limbs and agility to climb up the walls, air-conditioning units, and fire escapes with even less trouble than Naoko. She was chilled by the reality that they seemed even faster this way than running. They reached Higuchi with no obvious effort and opened him up—the pink one pulled his right arm off and sucked on the blood spurting from it and the severed brachial artery in his exposed shoulder interior.

She considered breaking into one of the apartments and trying to fight them in close quarters, but quickly reconsidered when they finished toying with Higuchi's bulk and cackled and giggled as they eviscerated and strung his insides around the high alley walls.

Naoko kept climbing but knew she had as little hope of escaping them as she did fighting them hand-to-hand in a fair fight, even as skilled in multiple deadly martial arts as she was. She felt the tightness in her thigh pockets, registering for the first time since she came to—they had let her keep her chopsticks and the small bowl.

After consuming their fill of Higuchi, they seemed to be taking a rest before they would inevitably climb up after her. Naoko tried to master her fear as she saw the cyborgs' blood-smeared helmets and talons glistening in the dark below. Strings of indirect reflections from neon at far ends of the space between the buildings gave the blood-slick creatures a subtle, haunting glow in the dark as well.

Naoko turned her attention upward and climbed the air conditioners, ducts, and shuttered window frames with spiderlike efficiency. As she climbed, she used a backup control system she'd had implanted to navigate her AR overlay—a metal bead in her tongue against the treated inner surfaces of her teeth. With adrenaline pumping and quick movements necessary it was difficult, but she was able to initiate a diagnostic on her body's implanted systems. AR self-check: glitchy but functional. Strength and endurance enhancements: functional and in use. Targeting assist: semi-functional. Stun field: non-functional—due to being shocked earlier she assumed—and possibly dangerous to her as well in all this rain. Sonic mid-to-high-frequency emitter: functional. *Better than nothing*, she thought.

She ascended to what would have been the roof of a normal building, but in this part of Hong Kong there was another level to these dense tenements: the rooftop slum. They ranged from shanty towns with corrugated metal walls and roofs to more complex, quality constructions. As Naoko hoisted herself up over the edge of one of these "houses," she saw this rooftop neighborhood was a combination of the two major styles. She heard shuffling and confusion down in the home she had just mounted. She could also smell chicken curry through the rain and rust. That made her hungry—hungry and mad.

Things weren't going Naoko's way today, and she much preferred when they did. She needed to change something else about this situation, and quick. She scanned the rooftop neighborhood, the pouring rain giving the whole jagged rectangle of makeshift abodes and gardens—and what looked like a bar— a shine that her AR overlay's filters had to adjust to. Dynamo-powered camping lanterns at varying levels of dimness were strung in several places, and candle-powered in others. Wet paths weaved between rows of buildings and someone had patched into the building electrical and powered an old neon San Miguel Beer sign outside the DIY rooftop local's bar. There was her chance—but she needed to even up the teams first.

Naoko peaked back down over the corrugated-metal-roof edge and saw her pink and blue pursuers, still glistening and grinning as they ascended. She lined herself up with the pink—*female?*—monster in the lead. She sat down, then laid her back down onto the metal and raised her legs, tucking her knees toward her chest. She extended her arms and used her after-market heightened strength to clutch the metal roof, then dig her fingers in like claws with a chorus of tiny shrieks. She only had to wait a long moment.

As the pink monster clawed up over the edge, Naoko slammed her boots into its armored chest, sending it back off the shanty roof and down between the buildings. Naoko ripped her fingers out of the metal, rolled over, and heaved herself up into a run. Sounds of the pink one slamming into air conditioners and such down below were reassuring. She looked back in time to see the blue monster climbing onto the roof of another shanty home. More sounds of confusion and anger were heard from down in that home.

Naoko dropped to the roof surface and slid off it and down onto the roof slum walkway. She ran the tight maze from memory and neared the glowing sign outside the bar. As she passed it—ignoring a few sad sacks inside arguing about how many man-made chemicals were in the rain—she retrieved the chopstick case from her thigh pocket. She popped it open, took the utensils out, and gripped them both in her left hand. She tossed the case aside and slowed to a stop as she turned around.

The pink cyborg was dropping onto the walkway in the distance behind the blue one that was charging at Naoko. She decided this could go either way. She engaged her high frequency emitter and warmed it up with a pulse—good to go.

As the blue monster neared the neon San Miguel Beer sign, Naoko raised her right hand and aimed it at the sign. Tiny surgically installed plugs filled her ears as she pulsed the emitter out on ultra-high. The neon sign vibrated, shuddering hard on the bar exterior. Naoko maxed the pulse level out and hit the sign again, just as the blue monster passed it—

The neon sign exploded into a brilliant cloud of colored light and showered the confused blue cyborg with glass. He staggered and ducked away from the blasting particles, covering his helmeted head as a child might in a sprinkler. Naoko bounded toward him, keeping the pink one's position in sight as she neared them both. As Blue lowered his arms to see and prepped a slash at her, Naoko dived into a roll. She rolled just under the slicing talons, then up into a half-crouch. She gripped the metal chopsticks tightly in her left hand, pressed her open right palm against them, and used all of her enhanced and natural strength to slam the sharp eating tools back into the armored but exposed ball of electronics on Blue's back.

The blue monster howled and shook, seeming to lose control of his artificial parts some as he tried to turn and face her. She sidestepped with him, raised the heel of her booted foot, and kicked the still half-exposed chopsticks in the rest of the way, causing Blue to jerk and spasm.

Naoko caught Pink still coming in fast in the corner of her overlay. She dug her enhanced fingers into the underarms of Blue and hefted him around toward his barreling companion, just as Pink was striking—

It worked. Pink slashed down at an angle across Blue's armored throat and chest, her talons far too efficient at opening them up for Naoko's liking—but in this case, she approved. Pink's big smile finally drained from her face, in time with Blue's fluids, as she tried to understand what she had done. Naoko kicked Blue into Pink, Blue's weight causing Pink to collapse backward and down, his lifeless overlong arms tangling up with Pink's own. Naoko climbed onto the pile and used her tongue-on-teeth interface to direct all artificial strength to her upper-body.

Naoko's first punch broke Pinks helmet faceplate—and the still-natural parts of Naoko's left hand. Her second broke it further, along with her right hand. Three-four-five broke Pink's AR goggles—six and seven, what was left of her natural face. After that, Naoko counted in inches as she beat the human head inside the monster machine's helmet down to the brains, then those down into the rear of the braincase.

Naoko hadn't appreciated being made hungry and angry in the same evening.

After she finished, she just breathed heavily and held herself up atop the mess of blood, brains, and electronics. She heard shuffling near her and looked toward it. A few old Chinese men were staring at her from the makeshift bar doorway, mouths hanging open. She ignored their dumbstruck horror and nodded toward a wheelbarrow filled with bricks that she'd just noticed past them at the doorway.

<<That spoken for?>>

The man that seemed like the barkeep shook his head.

The reaper had cut his relay feed after Boy's vitals had drained and Girl's enhanced eyes could see her own head's contents. He figured Alexeyev was well out of the area by now. They'd have to reach the roof and clean up the rest of his failed children....

There was a creaking and thumping sound above in the high alley walls. The reaper took his pistol out and pressed its priming button.

A large AC unit dropped from above, crushing the reaper under its substantial weight. A moment later, the pink monster's body landed on a few of the Triads, killing two instantly and crippling a third.

Naoko swung down on a bundle of cables then dropped, rolled to the reaper's side, and grabbed his pistol. She rolled again, sprang up into a crouch, and, in a sweeping motion Takeda had taught her years before, fired precision fatal shots with her broken hands into the confused Triad thugs that Pink's huge body had missed. She aimed at the crushed gangster under Pink but decided to let him suffer some.

The reaper was still alive so she stepped back over to him, gun pointed down into his hood between those eerie eyes. She looked around for more thugs and her eyes landed on the bright orange PIE stencil-sprayed onto the big cyborg cases.

<<Hey, reaper.... Before I kill you, I'm curious—What's "P-I-E" stand for?>>

The reaper chuckled, his demeanor unsettling for someone who should've been moaning in agony. As he pulled his hood away, revealing *its* robotic head on articulated shocks with antennae and synthetic tendons and tubing, it hissed,

"Perception Is *Everything...*," and laughed as it pulled its jacket open—its torso was packed with plastic explosives.

Naoko took three steps and dived behind a dumpster just as the remote-controlled reaper exploded, decimating the lower outer sections of surrounding apartment buildings and almost flipping her cover over.

Pain from shrapnel that had caught her lower right leg throbbed, but she used it, hauling herself up to her feet and limping down the alley toward the lorry.

After she hot-hacked it and got away from this mess, she decided, she was going to find Takeda and make him tell her what this was about and, someday, she would find whoever had made those cyborgs and dummy reaper, and hurt them real bad.

Somewhere in there she was going to squeeze in some more of Hong Kong's finest dim sum, though, no question about it.

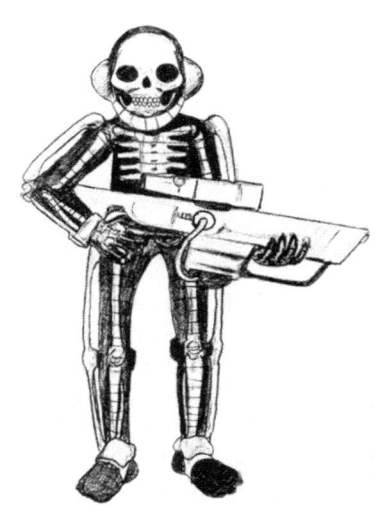

R-Day for Mr. D

New Jonesport *station—2142*

The Earth loomed over New Jonesport like a huge moon...but Mr. D knew if anything was a moon, it was New Jonesport. It was actually an orbital platform in geostationary orbit, and his father had built it.

Paragravity kept the inner, Earth-side surface of New Jonesport's gently curving oval shape the "ground," which in turn kept Earth a constant fixture in the sky above the platform's gleaming buildings, smooth streets, and artificial lakes. All of this was encased in a ten-foot-thick clear plasteel covering, sealed, and pressurized.

His father had wanted New Jonesport "anchored" over Jonesport, Maine— but the physics of that didn't make sense, not to mention the politics. It was built in a locked orbit over Singapore.

Mr. D looked down from the view to see his underling's progress on his cocktail, if you could call it that. Tommy, the new barkeep, limped through finishing the drink while Mr. D watched, seated atop a padded stool at the bar in what amounted to an automated limousine the size of an old airplane tow tractor, but tall enough inside for people to stand up straight with a bit of headroom. The interior walls and ceiling of the moving VIP lounge were almost clear—camera paneling on the large vehicle's exterior transmitted a feed uniformly to the interior surfaces, creating an illusion of translucence.

Mr. D finally got his drink and he took a sip. He watched other automated vehicles driving on the black conductive metal roads, and he imagined how much every single person within twenty-two-thousand miles owed to his father and him. It amused him for a moment, then a wave of dread tightened and spoiled his stomach. It was "R-Day," after all....

"Scenery—relaxing-type...three."

The streets and cars faded away and were replaced by a simulated panoramic feed of dark, rolling waves in a stormy open ocean. Sounds of this scene rose in volume as well, howling wind and waves sloshing and crashing.

Mr. D sipped more of his drink.

The stormy ocean views blinked out when they reached his personal estate—a ring of posh buildings under a clear dome at the center of the orbiting station's sealed Earth-side surface. The highest part of the dome was a bump on the clear station seal exterior, and the dome's life support and gravity could be cut off from the rest of New Jonesport if necessary. On his worst days, Mr. D had considered locking the dome down and popping the seal casing off the rest of the city.

The lounge moved through the pressure lock's doors and drove onto an elevator platform that ascended diagonally up an artificial hill that the estate ring was built onto. Mr. D watched his estate security people seal the vault pressure doors and check their weapons, as he'd ordered in his R-Day memo. The elevator crested the hill and the vehicle drove to a wide staircase that led up to the estate entry doors. The lounge doors opened.

"Wait here. I'm gonna need a couple-three more of those drinks and a ride to the best sex club we got when this is done."

Mr. D stepped out without waiting for a reply and walked up his estate stairs, currently flanked by over twenty bio-augmented mercs. He waved his neuro-chipped hand at the large front doors to slide them open. Some of those mercs were over seven feet tall, with bionic arms almost to the ground. *Good.*

Over his shoulder Mr. D said, "Remember—stay out here! You're *backup!*"

He went to his chambers on the second floor, changed into a special armored biosuit, and entered his walk-in vault. He opened three different locks on a smaller safe on the back wall of the vault, and removed an insulated rubber case about thirteen by thirteen inches and two inches thick.

Mr. D held the case in his hands and said, "Revenge Day...."

At the center of Mr. D's estate ring was another, smaller dome. He walked down a lush garden path to the translucent hemisphere, then waved its doors open. He stepped in, holding the thirteen by thirteen square case in one gloved hand, and unslung a large particle beam rifle in the other.

At the center of this dome, there stood a circular plastic table topped by a wide, squat cylinder with integrated panoramic speakers and a needle-tipped arm resting on a small rest support. A rare throwback turntable from around the 2050s—it had taken many of his best connections and markers to get a hold of it...but he needed it, even if today was the only time he'd ever use it.

At the center of this turntable was a spindle. Mr. D propped his beam rifle against the table and code-released the locks on the square case. He removed a twelve-inch vinyl record. It was a faded mix of sickly colored splotches.

Mr. D placed the record on the spindle, slid it down onto the platter, then picked up his beam rifle and walked to a control panel near the outer edge of the sealed dome. He pressed a sequence of commands into the control surface, then raised his rifle toward the turntable.

The platter began rotating and the tone arm swiveled over to the record and gently down onto the start of the groove.

The music sounded wrong and reverberated off the dome interior strangely. The record started to glow, casting an eerie light and darkening the view out through the dome. A luminous mist now poured from the record platter, spilling to the chamber floor and spreading across it.

The turntable disintegrated as it erupted upward in a geyser of glowing sludge that cascaded down to the cylindrical table, eating it away to nothing. The sludge poured out more of the mist as it melted the floor, leaving a mottled depression covered with baseball-sized gouges.

There was a flash and Mr. D blinked a few times as he tried to focus on the deepest part of the depression—

In the center of the depression, a figure had appeared, prostrate as if in prayer. Where its head touched the sludge-eaten surface, an intricate glowing sigil flashed, then came apart like ashes and vanished. The figure hauled itself up onto one knee—although, it seemed to have several. The figure's all-white robes and adornment were of impossibly beautiful materials.

Mr. D aimed the beam rifle at its head area.

"This is for my father...."

Its smooth mask or helmet snapped toward Mr. D's voice, a strange apparatus fused into the mouth and nose area. There were no obvious eyes, but deep within its multiple skull-like ocular openings a haunting light burned, glinting as it moved.

In a gravelly rasp, and like the sounds were formed backwards it said, "*Ah, a Delamarre....*"

The hollow but piercing eyes locked on Mr. D(elamarre)'s own.

"*This seems to be a duel, so I will state my—*"

Delamarre fired his rifle, the brilliant beam perforating the air and entering the ghastly figure's torso, then slicing up, severing its misshapen body open and cleaving its helmeted head at an angle. Cauterized cross-sections of inhuman organs, bones, muscles, and arteries glowed and the figure teetered, almost coming apart all the way as the separated parts slapped down on the scarred depression surface.

"Fuuuuuuuck you! That's the *end* for us!"

The raspy backwards voice laughed, coming from both sides of the flapped open figure's severed helmet head and throat. The open parts rose off the floor and their viscera slapped back together in one motion, the two parts sizzling back into one with a flash of ghoulish light.

"My name is Thri'sst'uhl—to finish my obligated duel announcement.... Honestly, though, we'd thought your line was extinguished," the voice rasped and gurgled.

Delamarre just stared at the re-formed figure, his hands shaking and his insides shuddering in his special suit. He went to Plan B. He pressed a few commands into the control panel.

Big Gatling beam guns came out of sealed cases all over the dome interior, hummed up, and fired into Thri'sst'uhl, shredding it.

The pieces reformed even faster this time, and before the dome guns and Delamarre could fire again, Thri'sst'uhl jumped up toward one of the Gatling setups. One of its appendages disappeared into the gun, and Thri'sst'uhl aimed the weapon down toward Delamarre, firing a stream of beam bolts at him. Delamarre dived away, dropping his gun.

Delamarre sprinted for the dome's doors. They slid open and Delamarre stumbled out, Thri'sst'uhl laughing in raspy taunt behind him.

The lush garden that lined the path Delamarre ran down burst into blue and violet flames as every surface of his estate ring darkened and seemed to pulse with malignant, festering boils.

Delamarre threw his warping estate doors open and used his special suit's built-in exo-assist to advance through his home's first floor with long, quick hops. He didn't stop to open his front doors—he exo-lunged fifteen feet and busted out through them, rolling down his stairs as the bionic mercs readied for their fight, stims and implant-heightened reflexes and muscles giving them confidence.

"Kill that fucking thing!" Delamarre yelled as he bounded down the steps to his waiting lounge vehicle.

The doors opened and Delamarre threw himself inside so fast he slammed into the vehicle interior wall. He waved his hand to seal the vehicle and said, "Go-to, dome exterior, New Jonesport armory...."

The vehicle vibrated as its batteries whirred up. The vehicle walls went clear, and he watched the long-limbed killing machines flail and swipe and shoot at Thri'sst'uhl back up on the stairs, only to watch them come apart, torn open or heads crushed spraying blood and maintenance fluids.

The lounge started rolling away from the steps toward the hill elevator—but Delamarre watched the last few mercs fall quickly and with sickening brutality. He watched Thri'sst'uhl scan the area and see the vehicle they were in.

"Tommy—you got a strap?"

"Fuck yes, sir!"

Tommy reached under his bar and pulled out a flak-shotgun, then a plasma auto-pistol, which he threw to Delamarre.

Thri'sst'uhl crouched and jumped, sailing from the stairs in a high arc. Delamarre followed, aiming through the vid-feed plasteel. Thri'sst'uhl landed on top of the lounge—

Delamarre ordered, "Disregard safety mesh—bypass elevator—A to B— destination pressure door!"

The large lounge vehicle broke from its path to the elevator platform and drove toward the hill edge. As it rolled down the hill ring, its minimal shocks and suspension caused it to shake and rumble violently.

Even otherworldly as Thri'sst'uhl was, it had to crouch and grab a hold of the vehicle to stay on top of it. They barreled down the hill, Delamarre's estate guards firing at Thri'sst'uhl on the descending lounge's roof—but the lounge drove straight through the bulk of them, only a few diving away in time.

The lounge vehicle crashed into the pressure doors, bending and damaging them. Delamarre and Tommy were thrown around inside. Delamarre looked up through the vid-feed walls to see Thri'sst'uhl staring down at the interior. It slapped a few of its hands onto the outer roof surface. The vid-feed of the outside cut off and went black, and Delamarre could only see Tommy trying to haul himself up by the glow of his bar. They heard screams outside from the last of the estate door guards, then nothing.

The interior feeds of the vehicle glowed back to life, and what they displayed was impossible—pumping, undulating biomachine creatures with too many glowing eyes slithering through an ocean of filth and diseased organs.

Tommy said, "B-boss...?"

"It's not real, Tommy! Don't look at that shit!"

Thri'sst'uhl's glowing white arms swung down from the ceiling—through the solid surface—and hooked toward Tommy—but he rolled over his bar, knocking everything down with a crashing and shattering of metal and glass. Tommy lit the ceiling up with his flak gun until the spot where their otherworldly attacker's arms had swiped down was pocked and glowing, and the maddening horrors had cut off of the interior feeds.

Delamarre stood back up, chuckled, and said, "Hey, maybe you got it—"

The glowing arm swiped down again, slapping onto Tommy's head. Thri'sst'uhl made Tommy aim at Delamarre and fire his flak-gun, mulching everything in the gun's path. Delamarre exo-dived to the farthest spot in the lounge floor he could and fired quick plasma bursts across Tommy's torso and head area, popping them open and forcing Thri'sst'uhl to pull his arm back up out of the lounge.

Delamarre said, "Oh you don't like plasma?!"

Knowing he was dead if he stayed in this big, dark coffin trying to avoid Thri'sst'uhl's swipes, and emboldened by the creature's recoiling from the plasma bursts, Delamarre crawled to the lounge doors. He took a deep breath, opened the doors, and dived out. As he rolled out of his dive—

Thri'sst'uhl slammed down onto him, snapping his pistol arm and pinning him to the ground.

Delamarre tried to claw at Thri'sst'uhl's helmet with his power-assisted free arm, only to have the creature grab that arm and snap it against one of its too many knees. Delamarre fought off sobs and just moaned through his agony.

Thri'sst'uhl got close to Delamarre's face.

"What now, Delamarre?"

Delamarre closed his eyes tight, tears spilling out.

"Estate—bubble pop!"

The highest part of his estate dome released its explosive bolts, detaching its apex. The dome interior violently purged its pressure.

"Helmet!"

Several pieces formed out of his suit's neck support and encased Delamarre's head in a clear ovoid.

Delamarre and Thri'sst'uhl were pulled upwards, tumbling through the escaping air as they approached the open maw out into high orbit.

Thri'sst'uhl laughed and taunted, *"Was that supposed to save you?"*

Delamarre said, "What c-can I give you so you stop?!"

Thri'sst'uhl just watched the dome's opening get closer.

They were pulled out into space and Delamarre watched his family's legacy and his beloved playground get farther away, Thri'sst'uhl's iron grip guaranteeing he was never coming back.

Thri'sst'uhl forced a big hand down into Delamarre's space helmet and clasped it over Delamarre's face. Its horrible voice vibrated into Delamarre's skull.

"To expect mercy was...foolish."

They tumbled farther and the heat became unbearable. Delamarre realized Thri'sst'uhl was forcing them into an atmosphere entry burn...but its words burned at Delamarre as much as his body did.

Thri'sst'uhl watched the last of its sworn enemy's body burn away in its many hands. It considered allowing itself to burn up with Delamarre and return to its home, then realized how long it had been since it had frolicked on "Earth"— and decided to drop to the surface and entertain itself.

7

R-Day for Mrs. D

Undisclosed Location—2144

Thirty unconscious prisoners stood in an inky dark, high-ceilinged cylindrical chamber, their bodies secured against eight-foot metal poles that held them upright by their backs—shackles on them locked around their necks, wrists, and ankles. Electricity coursed through the poles, jolting the hapless men and women awake. A chorus of confused gasps, groans, and yelps filled the hundred-foot-diameter chamber and faintly echoed, due to their concentric circular placement closer to its center.

More gasps and cries were let out when the neck shackles injected the prisoners with a fluid that felt cold as it entered and strange as it pulsed through them. It was more nauseating than inebriating, and one of the prisoners thought of it as if maybe his blood was vibrating.

The shackles opened, releasing the prisoners, and the poles slid into the floor, disappearing. Some of the captives collapsed onto their hands and knees or haunches, while others stumbled but kept their footing. The more active of them groped in the deep darkness, desperate to find some way out of whatever this place was.

One silhouetted man said, "F-fuck, man.... I mean.... What the _fuck?_"

"_We're_ fucked, is what I'm thinking," a young woman said.

An older woman said, "I have one more appeal.... This better not be—"

A circular section in the ring of wall around the chamber interior vanished. The one who felt his blood was vibrating realized it must've been a nano-solid section. They could see it had dematerialized because it was one end of a long

tunnel or corridor—which ended in a bright opening that seemed to howl with
whipping wind at its far end.

The unshackled prisoners squinted and looked around at each other.
They all wore pale blue jumpsuits and had thin blood trails trickling down their
throats from the neck injection points the shackles had left.

"M-maybe they're letting us go...."

"Not likely. I still got thirty years in fron' uh me."

A few brave prisoners approached the tunnel opening, so others followed.

The howling wind on the far end of the tunnel threw snow around, some
of which flitted down into the tunnel near that opening.

The braver prisoners continued on, creeping into the tunnel, one of them
beckoning the others to follow—

They all stopped in place at the sight of a glowing ball floating into the
tunnel from the snow-whipped far end. The tunnel was only lit by the cloud-
covered daylight at its exterior mouth, so when the orb entered, the effect was
startling and almost psychedelic. It was a pulsing loose sphere of layered
holographic projections, like a see-through onion of runes and archaic
equations.

The orb throbbed more as it traveled down the tunnel, passing harmlessly
through the bodies of the first few prisoners it reached—who looked back to
watch it as it approached the huge empty disc of chamber they'd awakened in.
The looks on the faces of the prisoners near the disc chamber opening—and a
sudden dimming of the already weak daylight behind them—turned the
vanguard back around in time to see what the orb had led to them.

It wasn't an animal and it certainly wasn't human.

It *was* at least twelve feet tall, so it hunched over some as it entered the
tunnel.

The best that vibro-blood prisoner could do to get his head around it was
as a huge figure draped in glowing, impossibly white robes, its body a writhing
tangle of many pale and beautiful yet boney and warped humanoid and
insectoid limbs, all straining and clawing to move it forward. Its head was
encased in a helmet—or was its own biomechanical skull—which had beautiful
rune-etched tubes and transparent fluid-filled shocks disappearing into the
robes that flowed around what served it as a neck area.

For vibro-blood it was as fascinating and stunningly beautiful as it was
ungodly terrifying—even as he was turning to run back toward the disc chamber,
he couldn't look away from the elegant, monstrous thing. He also couldn't look
directly at it without swooning some and becoming confused—

Then his perception cleared some as the thing reached the now-retreating
vanguard prisoners, and took them apart.

The movements were unnaturally blurred and hard to make out, but two
then three of the closest prisoners' bodies were torn, cut, pulled in multiple
directions. Blood sprayed and burst from them, splashing across the tunnel
walls. Intestines, organs, and splintered bones were thrown all around. Their

281

screams were drowned out by those of the rest of the prisoners, now escaping into the disc chamber.

Then the beautiful monstrosity seemed to *absorb* the blood and parts of the prisoners into its bulk by way of an unknown force that resembled magnetic attraction to vibro-blood's limited perception.

The glowing orb that had brought the creature into the tunnel reached the center of the chamber and froze in place before visually disintegrating. Between that and the opening at the far end of the tunnel to the outside closing back up, the prisoners were once again swallowed by deep darkness.

In place of gasps and confused murmurs, the dark was now filled with terrified wails, desperate cries, and wet, meaty sounds of slaughter—sickening snaps, crunching, and sliding.

Begging.

After the screams and death thrashes dissipated, there were only the indecipherable sounds of this sublime, awful being consuming the human prisoners' bodies in the dark.

The sound of rustling leaves and strong wind through trees arose from all around the feasting creature, and the chamber floor glowed up to a holographic but almost real-looking dark forest floor. The ring of chamber wall then faded up as an encircling forest of warped, gnarled trees, the periphery of the disc chamber as meadow. Last was the chamber ceiling, its circular edges where they met the ring like swaying claws of the tree branches and a starry, moonlit night.

The creature stopped doing whatever its consumption process involved and looked around, a prisoner's still-spasming torso, head, and arm dangling out of part of the thing's skull/helmet—that was broken or phased open.

The holographic leaves at the center of the chamber floor glowed brighter in a five-foot-diameter circle and rose, cascading down as a very real figure ascended out of the floor.

It was a magnificent, faintly glowing woman, her dark-ringed eyes closed tightly. Even with eyes closed, she was regal and elegant, yet exuded a deep melancholy. She was flanked by two black veiled and robed female figures, both standing silently behind her—and as real as the leaves she'd just caused to flit down to their forest floor.

The woman wore a veiled crown of black opalescent spear tips pointing up to the "moon" in a rising stagger to a highest central point, like a cathedral's spires. Butterflies and thin black serpents nestled around the spire bases. She held a jet-black bastard sword with crimson etchings on its entire blade surface, her open left hand resting atop the ball of its hilt end at her shoulder level and its tip against the glowing forest floor.

Her elegant robes were white as fresh snow, but blood-soaked from the forest floor up to around her concealed thighs. Her white gloves and sleeves were also soaked crimson, almost to her elbows.

The creature shifted around to face her and leaned forward to advance—

Her eyes opened, and her gaze was enough to stop the elegant abomination in place.

The creature sensed the woman's intent from the piercing stare she had locked on him and pulled the remaining eviscerated and separated bodies into its bulk by an invisible force, also sucking the blood from all around into itself. It stood upright, over fifteen feet now, and gathered its many limbs in toward its torso and under its beautiful, impossibly clean robes. It stood at respectful attention and waited.

"I am Lucette Delamarre, and I intend to kill you."

The creature dipped its strange head area down in a nod of recognition.

In a layered voice pulled backwards out of liquid the creature said, *"I am Thri'sst'uhl.... Honorably met. You're far more polite than your...?"*

"Husband."

"That must've been difficult for you. My killing of him, I mean."

"I didn't expect basic psychological taunts from a being so legendary and ancient as yourself..."

Thri'sst'uhl dipped its head again in recognition of her accuracy, respect, and possibly its own mild embarrassment.

She continued, "...and he took *my* family name. I am—*was*—the last of the Delamarres. He was brilliant and lovely...but not at all as cultured and tasteful as my family would've liked—if any still existed, after your kind's campaign against us."

"Ah...that would explain it. Clever...for your kind. I will say 'campaign' is a strong term, though, as it was so easy to destroy them."

Lady D's eyelids fluttered a bit and they just stared at each other for a long moment. Rolling tumbleweeds wouldn't have been out of place.

"Yes, I understand females are the dominant force in your culture."

Thri'sst'uhl cocked its head a bit.

"What else do you believe you understand about my culture?"

Lady D cocked her head as well and said, "You and I both know that's irrelevant to the matter at hand."

"Yes, you're focused. You've planned this. I can see that. It must mean...so...much...to you. Even your appearance—we aren't unfamiliar with what you would call culture. You appear as your mythological figure 'Tisiphone'.... Appropriate enough, as I am to be revenged upon for what you think of as a murder."

"Indeed, you are. My husband was an awful, hotheaded fool. He gambled *poorly* and had many other women and men—I allowed it because he was mine and that was understood. Would've also been hypocritical of me to complain....

"But it *was* inexcusable that he used my family's acquired resources and techniques to summon you without my knowledge. I think killing you was to be something like a present from him to me...and he'd also come to think of my father as his own when we were but small children, so that was his personal reason to hate your kind, I have to assume. While I do not condone his methods or what he did, I *did* love him. Fathered two of my children. Lover, co-conspirator, partner—maybe even...friend.

"He was unprepared. I am not.

"You killed the beloved husband of a rich, powerful, *vile* woman. So understand and make peace.... Today, *you* die."

Thri'sst'uhl's many deep-set eyes glinted from Lady Delamarre's glowing image as they shifted in their dark recesses in the skull-helmet and settled on her weapon.

"You are quite confident.... Is this sword the reason?"

"Ah, you noticed. Well, it took a lengthy expedition to acquire it—I even had to pass through one of the myriad locks of Junction in a Sken'ghi smuggling vessel, disguised *and* hidden. Thrilling, I must say.

"But yes, this blade has your attention for a reason."

"You want this badly, don't you?"

"I do, and I will have it."

"Because you have that sword?"

"Because I'm smarter than you are."

"We'll see...," Thri'sst'uhl said and shifted a bit in its robes, readying itself.

Lady Delamarre nodded acknowledgement and raised her free hand. She snapped her fingers, which echoed off the actual room's surfaces, but was softened by the howl of the artificial wind.

The two shadowy sisters behind her collapsed to the forest floor, cascading down as something between ashes and cherry blossoms. Her robes, gloves, and crown pulsed and distorted, then became a storm of glowing particles that swirled around her, a cyclone of freeform nano-mesh. They reformed and came to rest as a sleek suit of exo-armor that retained some of the elegant robes as flourish and the soaked-blood effect, but was otherwise all high-tech battle gear.

As the helmet area formed around her head and face, Lucette said, "Shall we begin?"

"Yes, let's...."

Lucette's helmet sealed and became solid and opaque—retaining a suggestion of the crown of spear tips—and she took her long black sword by its hilt and readied it in both hands.

Thri'sst'uhl lunged with incredible speed, some of its limbs whipping out from under the robes like mantis legs of flesh and bone with talon-sharp tips.

Lucette stayed stock-still until the very last possible moment, then a cloud of holographic glowing mist exploded around her and a blinded Thri'sst'uhl struck at where she'd been, hitting nothing—

She rolled up from her escape lunge, pivoted back toward Thri'sst'uhl, and swung her long blade upward from the forest floor, disturbing a long patch of artificial leaves. Thri'sst'uhl twisted as the slash went deep into its back through the glowing robes, lessening the damage some—but not enough.

Oily black fluid with glowing green and purple bubbles and sickly brown streaks sprayed and excreted from the long wound. Eyes and pulsing malformed organs and straining untethered muscle tissues writhed and twitched in pools of this "blood" on the forest/chamber floor, eating into it like acid after a moment and distorting the forest illusion in that area.

Lucette used a ballerina's grace to allow the attack follow-through to dissipate...then kicked her suit's exo-strength in hard, swinging the sword down again—

It sunk into the chamber floor, almost to the hilt.

Thri'sst'uhl had shrunk away just as the blade started making contact a second time, and was huddled just out of Lucette's range. Thri'sst'uhl was trying to stifle raspy moans of actual pain and Lucette smiled inside her helmet, even as she struggled to wrench her sword free from the chamber floor.

Lucette caught something in her peripheral vision and looked over as she finally pulled her sword free—where Thri'sst'uhl's blood had eaten at the floor, the distortions and amorphous organic chaos were spreading. Their very-real weirdness was perverting and assimilating the artificial beauty of her beautiful dark forest setting.

"Disgusting...," Lucette said to herself.

Thri'sst'uhl struck out at her with several of its longest, sharpest limbs in a wide arc—Lucette threw herself away, then slid away backwards through the air just above the ground, integrated paragrav thrusters in her suit giving her added agility.

Thri'sst'uhl advanced, lunging again as Lucette came to a poised stop on her heels.

Lucette strafed to her right using the paragrav again just before Thri'sst'uhl would've struck her and slashed up at the creature's appendages, severing several of them.

Thri'sst'uhl howled long and gravelly as Lucette slid to a sideways stop through the nonexistent yet dramatically scattering leaves on the chamber's slick, yet clumpy, grassy-looking surface.

Lucette heard something like sizzling and looked at her sword—the surface was being eaten away by the eyes-and-organs living blood from Thri'sst'uhl, so she whipped the squirming fluid off and it ate into the floor and forest illusion there too. The horrible undulating muck seemed to be spreading from both pools of the blood in the chamber now, pulsing with a black glow of silhouetted mist and crackles of energy like electricity arcing around into the floor like fluid spider legs.

Thri'sst'uhl whipped toward Lucette and extended several of its more armlike limbs in her direction—

Now she was pulled to Thri'sst'uhl across the chamber floor, her suit's boot tips scraping against the surface with a squealing sound.

Lucette engaged her paragrav the other way hard and slowed to stop, but Thri'sst'uhl's force kept wrenching and tugging her in small increments to itself.

*"I suspect you may be...*disappointed *today, Lady Delamarre...."*

"Do you?"

Lucette gripped her sword in both hands, reversed her paragrav, and let her own propulsion and Thri'sst'uhl's unseen force pull her straight toward it.

Thri'sst'uhl realized too late, and Lucette reached its body in an instant, plunging the long, black sword into what seemed to be its densest grouping of limbs and possibly its chest—

Upon sinking the blade all the way in, Lucette said, "Bolts!"

Circles of light appeared all over the chest, shoulder, and helmet areas of her exo-suit, then shot off in short shafts of light. Where they struck Thri'sst'uhl's body all around, spherical chunks of matter two feet in diameter disappeared. One of these took a curved chunk out of the creature's head/helmet area and even stranger squirming blood-and-organ slop burst out of its confines.

Lucette steered Thri'sst'uhl's body and oozing head wound away from herself with the sword's hilt as its disgorging contents seemed to be almost reaching for her as they descended.

Thri'sst'uhl cried out and moaned with layered voices and slumped back, almost falling completely back—but Lucette held its body where she stood.

"Now that victory is assured, I won't keep it a secret any longer—I'm building a ship that can reach your artificial paradise...and I'm going to storm and splinter the gates, then destroy *all* of you."

Thri'sst'uhl lifted what was left of its head and locked its few remaining deep-set black eyes onto Lucette's helmet.

"You think I was summoned from that sad, ancient tomb? Its beauty is now matched only by its stillness.... You know less than think you do. And why would you want to wake those sleeping...'Matriarchs'—as you call them—from their dream? I despise them more than you can imagine...but they've done nothing to you...."

"You aren't...?"

"It was my *kind—those of us who would not bow and would not sleep, even in their perfect place—who has tormented your family. You should have done more research, madam. It is my kind you want destroyed...but I doubt any ship you could conceive of would survive our adopted home, let alone the journey there."*

Lucette hesitated a moment, confused and trying to process—

Thri'sst'uhl shifted and twisted its body, snapping Lucette's blade off into itself and causing her to stumble back a few steps with the useless hilt still in both hands.

She tried to engage her paragrav thrusters to retreat but Thri'sst'uhl hauled back and whipped a long, sharp raptorial leg down into Lucette's chest. It went through her exo-suit and out the other side, spraying blood onto glitching grass, leaves, and flowers. Thri'sst'uhl hauled its body forward, pinning her to the chamber floor and looming over her and oozing organic madness onto her suit's chest and neck.

"Why don't I...show you...where I came from?"

The illusory forest glitched out and the ceiling, interior ring of wall, and floor were filled with something like an ocean...

"I showed your...'beloved'...husband. He didn't enjoy it."

Instead of water, this was an ocean of madness. The discernible glimpses of anything like solids or fluids contained eyes, organs, viscous blood and discharge, oily, iridescent ichor, and warped, ever-growing and re-fusing breaking bones—and things far less recognizable, and even more chilling to Lucette as a result.

Lucette moaned and coughed inside her helmet as it darted around languidly, taking in the horrors on display.

She said, "Plea—hgk.... Please...."

"Are you going to beg, just as your pitiful husband...hnnghk—did?"

Lucette's helmet locked back on Thri'sst'uhl's wounded head area and her groveling became mirthless laughter.

"No, I just had to wait a bit longer, apparently," she said.

"For...mmnnhhngk...what?"

"Did you think those poor prisoners were a gift? An offering? I just needed more time for the cocktails I'd mixed for you and pumped into them to take hold."

Thri'sst'uhl rested back on what served it as haunches as it moaned and seemed to swoon and become dizzy even.

"You're right—I do need to do more research. You've done *so much* of the work for me just now, but I'll learn what's needed to modify my navigation charts and ship. But I *will* find this awful place you've revealed to me so carelessly. I truly hope you have loved ones there. I'm going to open them up and hurt them until they're insane from the pain I've put them through and longing for death...."

Thri'sst'uhl hauled itself up with great effort and struck down into Lucette with two more of its more mantis-like limbs, impaling her chest—but she laughed again, and harder this time.

"Did you think I was going to place myself within the quite lengthy arms' reach of an ancient, otherworldly monster? You are a*dor*able...."

Thri'sst'uhl used a few of its more dexterous limbs to pry Lucette's helmet open, finding an artificial head with brilliantly glowing cybernetic eyes.

The living liquid-horror ceiling disintegrated, another nano-solid, and Thri'sst'uhl craned its head up to take in a snowy storm-ravaged sky that was very real. A circular area of the sky was pricked with brilliant specks of light, which quickly grew in size to streaking points.

"Hey...."

Thri'sst'uhl looked down at the robotic doll it had taken for Lucette herself.

In a sing-song taunt Lucette's avatar leered and said, "Smaaaarteeeerrrr...."

Thri'sst'uhl crushed the robot's head in a shower of sparks and arcing energy, which caused her taunt and cathartic laughing that followed to shift to speakers embedded throughout the disc chamber.

Thri'sst'uhl looked up again and let out something like a raspy sigh.

A storm of particle beam shafts showered down from an orbital platform, disintegrating the disc chamber and everything in it, and eating a glowing crater deep into the surface of the snowy, mountainous area the kill zone had been constructed in.

Steam would billow up out of the crater for hours, before it would dissipate and the mottled crater would come to resemble the surrounding natural layout to the average onlooker.

Roughly five hundred miles away and deep underground....

Lucette touched pressure buttons on two outer points on her full-face remote/VR helmet's jawline and it hissed before popping open and collapsing into nano-solid holders under her head. She sat up from the VR bed's form-fitted bench and swung her legs down to touch her feet on the warmed stone of the chamber floor.

"Well, my dear, departed husband.... That is the very last time I have to finish something you so enthusiastically started."

Applewhite & Zorn: Delamarres Ascendant

Deimos Station—2153

Applewhite and Zorn rode a tram through a tube that ran between two large, reflective domes in a larger cluster of them on the surface of the Martian moon of Deimos. They reached their destination, went through secondary security, and stepped onto an elevator that began its descent toward their specified sublevel.

The elevator interior had the illusion of being transparent, and they watched advertisements play out in real time as if they were in a tube that just happened to be placed within the scenes' settings. With the aid of AR lenses and their individual preference and habit-based histories, an advertising AI chose different products and scenes to show them.

Applewhite watched as two middle-aged women lovingly caressed each other's faces and kissed. Tears filled their eyes. One of them vanished. Grief counseling details appeared. Applewhite clenched her jaw and narrowed her eyes a bit. As if sensing it had offended her, the ad AI switched tactics and dissolved from the scene of grief to one of a woman playing with cats in a summery meadow.

Applewhite nodded and the AI added cat food made by the brand shown in the scene to a shopping list that faded up in her peripheral vision.

Zorn watched a scene taken from a VR game set in a dark fantasy world. She watched from a fixed position behind a ninja-like rogue character as it stealthily moved through a gloomy ancient castle avoiding huge, armored undead knights.

Zorn nodded and the AI added spendable in-game currency to her account for the game.

Never satisfied, the AI dissolved the scene to a party setting with people drinking and dancing. Dating account preferences and attractive male and female faces in circles faded up in her peripheral view. She shook her head, backing out of the dating app.

"They're rich kids, right?"

Applewhite looked away from a fresh ad scene to meet Zorn's sideways gaze. "The Delamarre children? *Rich* doesn't do that kind of money justice. Obscene, really. They didn't get all of it, though. I dug a little deeper last night to prep. After a huge mining and research colony implosion, their mother, the widow Lucette Delamarre, used half of her family purse fighting lawsuits then settling *big*."

"Implosion? Like, figurative?"

"*Literal.*"

Zorn raised her eyebrows. "Spooky."

"That's not all. Most of what she had left she poured into some secret research."

"What kind?"

"*Secret.* No idea. But then she disappeared, so...."

"Five'll get you ten." Zorn frowned. "How'd the kids get the money then?"

"It was a space-faring accident. Some old maritime thing. Wreckage was produced and analyzed. No regular crew lived to contradict whatever the story was. Either way, there was no chance she survived it, so the heirs got their inheritance."

"So they got the money and what?"

"We don't know much, but it seems like they continued their mother's weird research."

Zorn shook her head. "I fucking hate rich kids."

The elevator arrived at their floor. Applewhite stepped out and Zorn followed her down a low-lit hallway with thick transparent cell doors. Glowing AR letters floating in the air near the hall ceiling read BEHAVIORAL WARD in soothing pale blue. The words paced the two women's movement until they each looked up at them. Once seen by both, the letters faded away.

Zorn said, "You said we'd be questioning only one of the Delamarres, right?"

Applewhite nodded. "Correct."

"Why just the one?"

"Because we haven't the slightest idea what happened to her brother."

Zorn chuckled. "We could beat it out of her."

Applewhite stopped and turned, placing the back of a hand against Zorn's chest and stopping her.

She whispered, "Cut that shit out. Let's be professionals here. She's rich. She's eccentric. She's also a human being and it sounds like she's been through a lot."

"Sounds self-inflicted to me...."

Applewhite tapped Zorn's sternum gently but firmly with her knuckles. "Be professional."

Zorn nodded affirmative. Applewhite lingered to be sure, then nodded and continued down the hallway. Zorn followed.

They arrived at one of the transparent cell doors and looked inside the dim cell. Faintly glowing letters read CATHERINE DELAMARRE until the two investigators looked at them, then faded away.

A young woman was raised up on her lower legs atop her cell bed, pressed against the nearest wall. Her eyes were red and teary, darting around toward the wall's upper surface near the cell ceiling. She pressed her ear against the wall, listening.

Zorn looked over at Applewhite, who glanced sideways but didn't make eye contact. Applewhite touched a glowing circle on the door surface and a soft pulsing started in the cell. The young woman looked toward them.

"Catherine?"

"*Lady Delamarre.* If you must be informal, my preference is *Cathy.*"

Zorn shook her head then squinted. "*Lights—full.*"

The cell lights brightened and Cathy climbed off the bed and backed into the far corner, looking all around at the walls and ceiling. Panicked. Desperate.

"No! Please...."

Zorn frowned. "What's wrong with you?"

Applewhite gave Zorn another side-eye but Zorn ignored it.

"*Lights—low.*"

Zorn shrugged off yet another look from Applewhite.

Cathy calmed some. "I'd have them off, but the servants here won't allow it."

Zorn frowned. "Servants?"

Applewhite said, "Lady Delamarre, I apologize for disturbing you. May we speak?"

"Are you not?"

Zorn chuckled to herself.

Applewhite blinked and clinched her jaw. "We need to speak with you about the circumstances that brought you here."

"I see."

Cathy examined the walls again. "Is there another place we can go? I'd rather not speak about this here."

"Of course."

The trio entered a dark, circular room with a table at its center. The walls and ceiling brightened some. The ceiling was an artificial disc of partly cloudy sky. The ring of wall around the room resembled the elevator in function, but was programmed for soothing, not advertisement. Slowly changing natural environments. Soft tones, chimes, and wind gradually became bird and insect sounds, then distant crashing waves, and so on.

Cathy examined the more advanced walls and took a seat at the table. The others sat across from her.

"What shall we speak about? Specifically, I mean."

Applewhite and Zorn each put on thin gray gloves then touched their right temple and heard two almost inaudible beeps. Their eyes scanned AR documents in a shared file application.

"Our interest here is first and final voyage of the M-C-L-dash-thirteen-seventeen-dash-A, *Cumaean Sybil*. The second *Cumaean Sybil*, actually."

"Our ship...."

Applewhite typed a quick note about Cathy's strange expression on mention of the ship, her haptic-tipped gloves giving the physical sensation of solid keys as she touch-typed. Zorn activated an AGREED icon that floated in their shared AR overlay.

She continued, "Also, the deaths of the captain, crew, and your brother—"

"Hugh isn't dead."

Zorn typed "???" and Applewhite activated the AGREED this time.

Zorn tilted her head. "How could he *not* be?"

"No other survivors were found. No bodies at all. The remaining section of ship you were anchored to was empty."

"And why were you in an emergency radiation tent secured to the *outside* of the hull?"

Cathy looked away and watched the current nature scene.

"I wouldn't have been safe inside."

Applewhite frowned and activated an icon that read EVASIVE. Zorn AGREED.

"You agreed to speak with us, but so far you are being really vague."

Cathy locked her eyes on Applewhite. "I will say what I like, or say nothing."

Zorn said, "Then why agree to this?"

Cathy looked down at her lap. "Cold feet maybe?"

Zorn shook her head and looked at Applewhite. "Lady Delamarre, we have authority to—"

"I am the daughter of two multi-disciplinarian geniuses. Along with astronautical engineering and physics, law is not unfamiliar to me. My family is not what it once was...but retainers remain in place with lawyers you would *not* triumph over."

"Why would you speak with us at all then?"

Cathy thought a moment. "I'm not sure myself...." Then she straightened up some.

"Alright, ask your questions. Though, you mightn't believe the answers."

Applewhite scanned the documents again.

"So, official records have been pieced together showing you used many different labor sources to construct the ship in Mars orbit in separate pieces, then another team to put them together. Then another to finish it and get it fully functional."

"All correct."

"Why the secrecy?" Zorn asked.

"What was its special purpose?" Applewhite asked.

Cathy rubbed the fingers of one hand with the other.

Applewhite continued, "I mean, what did you *think* your mother designed it for? Obviously, it didn't work properly."

"Didn't it?"

Zorn chuckled.

Applewhite sighed. "Alright, let's go from the start of the voyage then."

Cathy nodded.

"After testing and an unceremonious commissioning, you, your brother, and the crew left Mars orbit for as yet unverified coordinates. That was April Seventh, Twenty-One Fifty-Three."

"Correct."

"Where did you go?"

"While technically essential, where the ship traveled *to* wasn't as important as what happened once we got there."

"And what was that?"

Cathy smiled, her eyes taken on a glossy, dazed expression.

"We prepared for the true journey...."

Unverified Coordinates—April 7, 2153

The *Cumaean Sybil II* slid through the utter silence of space, an antennae-sprouting anterior half-dome attached to and followed by a narrow tube of hull that was bisected about halfway down its length by a bulging, rounded section. A large black sphere was secured in a curved structure resembling a cage, which joined the forward and aft lengths of the tube. Drive thrusters made up the last section of it. The long cylindrical hull also bulged outward in a few areas where supply cargo and life support ran in parallel to its length.

On the bridge, Captain Sockwell watched the stars from under a transparent bubble at the apex of the half-dome forward section of the ship.

She reclined in a padded bench-seat, and due to paragravity, could've been mistaken for standing with bent legs.

The first officer and pilot, Polk and Getty, radiated from a central point, the three forming a squat *Y* in their wheelhouse bench-seats. They each wore thick, translucent AR visors which displayed ship orientation and other navigation and operations data.

Sockwell said, "Slow to a stop and anchor her."

In unison Polk and Getty said, "Slow-to-a-stop-and-anchor...."

They manipulated glowing AR controls floating in front of them.

The ship eased to a stop.

Sockwell raised her visor and took in the naked majesty of space through the bubble panel viewport. "Thank you, gentlemen." She activated comms. "Lord and Lady, we have arrived at your designated location."

Inside the Delamarres' cabin, Hugh Delamarre stared out a floor-to-ceiling picture window that faced rearward, the hull foreshortening away and giving a clear view of the caged black sphere halfway down the ship's length. If the ship was a mushroom with a long, straight stem—minus black sphere and cage bulge—their living quarters were built into the cap's underside facing down, but in actual use, facing away from the direction of travel.

Nine circular scars evenly dotted Hugh's buzzed scalp in a three-by-three square arrangement and he sat on the edge of a large bed wearing only silk shorts. Cathy was lying under the sheets, her eyes on the cabin ceiling.

Over comms Sockwell said, –Should we—?–

Hugh keyed the line open. "Await further instructions."

–Of course. I apologize.–

"Unnecessary. Just wait."

–Yes, sir.–

Hugh closed the comms channel and rested his hand on the bed. Cathy tried to take it but he pulled it away. She narrowed her eyes. "What's wrong?"

"I'm sorry, I just...."

"Are you afraid?"

"Yes, but not of failing."

Cathy placed her hand on his back.

"I should be the one to—"

"No. She was clear on only a few things, but there's no question that the process requires quietude and practiced focus you don't possess. You wouldn't grasp the right words."

"How do you know what the words should be?"

"The words are there only for me. It's the way the words help me guide my *will* that's important. With your lack of training, you mightn't survive and I couldn't...."

Hugh looked down at Cathy and caressed her cheek.

"I couldn't bear that."

Cathy clasped his caressing arm to her chest. He placed his other hand atop hers.

"If I succeed, we will all arrive together."

"You believe that? Truly?"

"Yes. I know now that this is what all of our turmoil and misfortune were leading toward. The Delamarre name will be widely known and revered once more."

Cathy released Hugh's arm and freed her hand from his. She turned her head against the bed and looked toward the black sphere.

"You sound just like.... Has she spoken to you again?"

Hugh looked back at the black sphere.

"I must prepare."

He stood and left the bedroom. Cathy watched him go then looked back at the sphere in its cage.

In a walk-in closet with pressure suits on hooks between the dressers for normal clothing and accessories, Hugh pulled on a thin jumpsuit, fingerless gloves, and a pair of toe shoes. He placed an earpiece in his ear.

He left their quarters without speaking again and made his way through the ship's front squashed hemisphere section—or mushroom cap, as he liked to think of it—and made a paragrav transition to the perpendicular paragrav surface that ran through the tube section.

Hugh walked down a long corridor that ran the forward length of the tube, which intersected with short hallways that led into the life support and cargo areas. The corridor split into two curving hallways around the black sphere's cage, then met at the mouth of a long hall down to the engines-and-thrusters area. But his destination was a hatch at the center of that split. He opened it and went inside.

He pressed his earpiece. "Cathy?"

Back in their quarters, Cathy heard a pulsing sound coming from something on a nightstand. She wrapped the comforter around herself and got off the bed, then picked up her own earpiece and put it in.

–Can you hear me?–

She said, "I hear you."

Cathy crossed to the picture window and sat down cross-legged, still in the comforter, and looked out at the tube and caged sphere that stretched into the distance.

Hugh walked down a cylindrical tunnel with corrugated walls, approaching another sealed hatch with large, bold warnings printed on it. He leaned forward and grasped a handrail that was installed around the tunnel interior where it met the sphere.

–Are you in the sphere?–

Hugh stared out a small porthole window on the hatch at eye level. It was jet black and its opaque darkness filled him with anxious dread.

"Just reached the door."

He pressed a few solid keys on a panel next to the hatch and a light faded up in the depths of the sphere interior. He felt like he was looking down the smooth-bore barrel of a gun at the location of his own demise.

–I love you, Hugh....–

In their quarters, Cathy gazed at the sphere through tearing eyes.

Hugh sighed over comms. –You know I feel the same.–

She smiled and closed her eyes tight, tears trickling out.

–You'd better not be crying.–

She forced a chuckle. "I'm not."

–Okay, good. Now, I'll need to concentrate, so only use this line if there's a dire emergency.–

Cathy rubbed tears from her eyes.

"Understood."

There was a soft beep in her ear as comms closed.

Hugh pressed another key and the sphere hatch opened. He walked down the smooth, black "gun barrel" tunnel and entered the sphere interior.

Outside of the periphery of the light he'd activated, a breathing machine rested, bolted to the floor. Its tubes snaked into the light and a nasal cannula rested on a velvet cloth next to an odd veil. Next to the square of velvet were a sumi-e brush, squares of thin paper, and black ink.

Hugh crossed to the breathing machine and turned it on, then sat cross-legged in the center of the lit circle and put in the cannula. After testing it for proper flow, he donned the translucent, rubbery veil. He breathed in and out as he looked down at his gloved hands.

Hugh's vision gradually gained a shimmering effect and the surface of his hands, legs, and the floor seemed to become composed of connected psychedelic symbols or cryptic characters from a language he couldn't understand.

He lowered his hands and prepared the ink. He placed a square of paper on the larger square of velvet, dipped the brush into the ink, and made a circle on it.

Sockwell, Polk, and Getty were still lying in their bridge bench-seats, now just waiting and watching the stars.

Getty shifted his head against the headrest, looked at Polk, then Sockwell, then back out at the stars.

Sockwell said, "Question, Getty?"

"It's just...we come out of sleep halfway to the asteroid belt. Then navigate to these coordinates and...nothing. There's nothing here."

"Just ask her; damn," Polk said. Then to the captain, "What are we doing out here?"

Sockwell sighed. "Being paid quite generously not to ask that one—exact—question."

"Sure, but we all got the same contract, right? Did you actually read it?"

"I read enough."

Getty frowned and said, "I skimmed it...."

"There's some weird shit in there."

Sockwell sighed again. "Polk...."

Getty turned his head and looked at Polk. "What do you mean *weird*?"

"The hazards implied—"

"*Polk.*"

"We're earning our money, is all I'm saying."

Sockwell shook her head.

Getty looked back out at the star, eyes darting back and forth in thought.

In the Delamarre quarters, Cathy flipped through structural diagrams of the ship in her AR overlay. She studied the actual cage section of the ship that the sphere was secured in from her view out the picture window, then diagrams of it.

She flipped through handwritten notes. One read, "The best way out is always through. But the only way through is sacrifice."

Cathy frowned and brought up images of the original *Cumaean Sybil* wreckage.

"What went wrong, Mother?"

She sighed and kept poring over the diagrams and files.

In the sphere core, Hugh retrieved another square of paper and placed it atop several others on a stack of fresh *ensō* circles on the velvet. He mumbled continuously, going between almost inaudible poetry and glossolalia.

As he made another circle, the edges of it bled some and warped. He mumbled louder as he finished it, put it on the stack, and started another. He could hear a growing hum from the sphere structure. His motions distorted in his vision as if the light had to catch up to the movement.

He waved the brush in front of his face, seeing a visible warping and trails.

Hugh started painting another circle and the hum from the sphere all around him became louder and the distortions more pronounced.

In the silence of space, the sphere vibrated in its cage, then the cage did the same. The vibrations traveled down the cylindrical hull to the forward "cap" section.

Sockwell looked around as the vibrations reached the bridge. Getty raised his hands and watched them vibrate along with everything else.

Polk said, "Captain?"

"That's your *weird shit*, Polk. It's what we're here for, so calm down."

Cathy watched the hull vibrate and shudder out in the silence of space, while feeling and hearing it do the same to the cabin and her bones. She stared at the black sphere, her stomach twisting with dread.

Hugh's glossolalia grew louder and more insistent. He started another ink circle. As he progressed through the drawing, the ship shuddered harder and moaned from structural stress.

A rhythmic pulsing from the surrounding sphere began to rise above the shuddering.

Hugh got a fresh paper and started another circle. The distortions in his vision through the veil swirled stronger with his movements and all of the interlocking symbols making up the fabric of physical reality pulsed in time with the growing rhythm.

He started another circle, his movements becoming a blur of light and motion.

The navigational displays and lights on the bridge fluttered and dimmed.

Polk swallowed hard and looked at Getty, then Sockwell—who blinked a few times before returning Polk's panicky gaze.

Cathy's overlay pulsed and wavered on a view of her mother's notes.

"*The best way out is always through...but the only way through is sacrifice....*"

She stared at the word sacrifice.

"No...."

Cathy pressed her earpiece. "Hugh.... *Hugh?*" Then activated an emergency function, forcing the comms line to Hugh open.

Blurring, warped Hugh was making yet another circle. The ship's moans and shuddering were now layered with distant but intensifying ethereal tones.

–Hugh! Answer me!–

"Cathy?! I told you—"

He finished his circle and the sphere interior chamber went black.

Cathy watched a silent wave of spatial distortion emanate from the sphere, knocking out the ship's exterior running lights as it came toward her in the forward cap section. The wave reached the cabin and killed all the lights and power in it.

All of the bridge equipment, displays, and lights cut off, leaving only the dim light of the stars coming in through the clear plasteel dome.

Polk's eyes went wide. "No fucking way!"

"Polk. Why aren't the backup systems on?"

"Are you serious?"

"*Polk!* Why?"

"If I had a backup system to check it, I'd tell you!"

"Calm. Down."

Polk forced himself to breathe in and out in a controlled manner.

Getty sat up, swung his legs over the side of his bench-seat, and stood.

"Paragrav is still on?"

Polk nodded. "It'll keep going until friction slows the charged rings' rotation."

"If everything is down, what about life support?"

They all looked at each other in the murky starlight. Sockwell and Polk climbed out of their bench-seats and the three crew members each hurried to pressure-suit storage lockers that lined the circular bridge interior wall.

Cathy breathed shallow as she fought to rise from her comforter on the floor, then stumbled through the dim starlight from the window to the walk-in closet.

She grabbed one of the hanging pressure suits and clawed her way into it.

Fully suited, she came back into the bedroom, stepped onto the bed, walked over it, and hopped off on her way to the cabin door.

She looked out at the silhouette of the dark ship exterior and caged sphere amidst the beautiful stars one more time, then opened the hatch.

Hugh was bathed in fluorescent light. The ensō papers glowed, as did his veil and the whites of his eyes behind it. All of his movements blurred and warped now and he pulled the rubbery veil off and dropped it, leaving the cannula connected to the breathing machine that was still somehow operational.

The moaning and shuddering were gone and soft, shifting tones replaced them.

Cathy strode toward an intersection of corridors, the only light sources her helmet faceplate and a spotlight on her pressure suit's chest. Both lights fluttered, constantly on the verge of cutting off completely. A thick mist of some kind filled the corridors, almost like a fog.

She heard a hatch opening ahead and booted footsteps above as she reached a vertical intersection.

From out of sight she heard, "Lady Delamarre?"

"H-hello?" Cathy said as she entered the intersection and looked up. "Yes, I'm here."

Sockwell, Polk, and Getty walked toward her, but due to their perpendicular paragrav, they appeared to be defying gravity as they descended toward her. To them, she appeared to be standing on a wall in front of them, parallel to their corridor's floor.

"Is it the whole ship?"

Sockwell nodded in her helmet. "Afraid so. We're on our way to life support."

"I need to reach the sphere...."

Polk scoffed. "For what, exactly? What did your brother do?"

"If he succeeds, I won't need to explain it."

"The fuck does that even mean?"

Sockwell grabbed Polk's shoulder. "Shut up, Polk!"

Hugh meditated in the dark, eyes closed. He cocked his head to one side and the tones changed. He cocked it the other and they changed again.

"*Invictus?* Yes.... William Ernest Henley's words will guide me, as they have done for us so many times before. Thank you, Mother."

He took a deep breath and let it out, controlled and smooth.

He began it as a whisper.

"*Out of the night that covers me, black as the Pit from pole to pole....*"

The hum came back.

"*I thank whatever gods may be, for my unconquerable soul.*"

Cathy walked ahead of the bridge crew through inky darkness and the strange, ever-thickening mist that their poorly functioning lights had a harder and harder time cutting through.

Hugh's eyes moved back and forth under shut lids as he listened to the tones.

"*In the fell clutch of circumstance, I have not winced nor cried aloud.*"

The hum grew in intensity and the tones fluctuated. The chamber started to shake.

"*Under the bludgeonings of chance, my head is bloody, but unbowed.*"

The chamber shook harder.

The ship's long forward corridor started shaking too as Cathy and the bridge crew traversed its length.

Polk stopped. "What is that?"

Sockwell said, "I don't know."

Hugh's eyes snapped open and he raised his voice.

"*Beyond this place of wrath and tears, looms but the horror of the shade....*"

As Hugh glared into the shifting darkness, the tones, hum, and shaking grew stronger.

"*And yet the menace of the years finds and shall find me...unafraid.*"

301

The corridor shook and they had to steady themselves on the walls.

Cathy stared into the darkness in the sphere's direction.

To herself she whispered, "Hugh, please don't...."

Hugh shut his eyes again.

"*It matters not how strait the gate, how charged with punishments the scroll....*"

The chamber quaked and the tones swirled ever more intensely.

"*I am the master of my fate, I am the captain of my soul.*"

Everything stopped. Hugh opened his eyes. Silence. Darkness.

A fluttering sound started to his right, so he looked that way—a series of replicas of him wearing the veil appeared in succession and extended into the distance and darkness.

Fluttering sounds to his left, more veiled Hughs to his left.

Fluttering sounds above, more Hughs duplicated into the black sphere's benighted sky.

Fluttering sounds below, more Hughs into the black sphere's ocean depths.

Fluttering ahead, and Hugh looked forward again.

Hughs stretched forward into the darkness, backs to him. Our Hugh leaned to his left to look down the line. These were also veiled, except for a Hugh several Hughs down.

The back of that Hugh's buzzed head was visible.

The sounds and corridor shaking lessened, but persisted.

Getty said, "Eye of the storm?"

Polk's eyes darted around. "But what kind of storm?"

Their booted footsteps started to sound wet. Cathy ignored this and trudged on.

Polk stopped and crouched, bringing his low, flickering lights closer to the floor. His gloved hand groped through the mist toward the floor—

It looked *alive*—squirming, pulsing. Clouded eyes opened and rolled around, almost sightless but searching. Bulbous growths pumping. Slithering tentacles.

Polk threw himself up and back, slapping against the curved corridor wall. He pulled himself away from its almost obscenely yielding surface—it was made up of glistening, undulating bulbs and grotesquely organic pulsing nodules. Sickly colored fluids pumping through bundles of translucent arteries. Chaotic, oozing viscera.

"No. This can't.... What did you people *do*?!"

Cathy kept going, her light almost out of sight down the corridor through the mist and darkness.

Hugh leaned a little farther left trying to get a look at the unveiled replica of himself—

Its head jerked. It jerked again and that Hugh began to spasm and shake. Our Hugh said, "Hello?"

The unveiled Hugh whipped its head to the left in response, its profile a mess of tentacles, pulsing sacks, and a jagged-toothed, almost insectoid mouth where its face should be.

Hugh gasped and jolted back onto his hands.

Fluttering started behind him into the distance. He forced himself to look back—

Hugh screamed.

Polk raised his glistening pressure-suit gloves and stared at them, hands inside them shaking. His slick suit arms distorted as they shook.

Getty said, "Wh-what is that? Is that real?"

Polk strained to look at Getty through his faceplate.

"Which is worse? It's real or we...?"

Sockwell grabbed his suit shoulder. "Polk, we need to keep it together, get me? I don't understand this either, but we need to get life support back on or it won't matter either way!"

Polk looked at his warping gloves again, then at Sockwell and nodded in his helmet.

"Okay."

Sockwell moved on toward the Life Support section, then Getty and Polk followed.

Chittering and inhuman wailing joined the wet sounds of the living corridor.

They all looked around wide eyed but continued forward.

Ahead of them, Cathy stopped at the threshold of the corrugated tube of corridor leading to the sphere. She keyed her comms open.

"Hugh.... Hugh, can you hear me?"

Sockwell reached the intersection with the main corridor and Life Support sections first, and tried to spot Cathy's lights in the distance.

Polk and Getty stopped near the intersection, mouths agape and eyes darting all around.

Sockwell narrowed her own. "What does that girl think she can do at the sphere?"

"I don't think they knew what this awful ship was for when they built it. I hope it swallows them both!"

Getty looked ill in his helmet. "Swallows.... Won't it swallow us t-too then?"

Sockwell started to turn back toward them but stopped. She stared down the intersecting Life Support corridor at something in its inky darkness.

"What is that?"

Cathy tapped her earpiece. "Hugh, please...."

–Hello, Cathy.–

"Are you all right? What's happening to the ship?"

Silence.

She started down the corridor to the sphere hatch.

Sockwell took a step toward the Life Support corridor.

Polk leaned forward and bent some to look around the intersection's curved corner.

"What is it?"

"It looks like—"

A large, amorphous creature rushed Sockwell, its glistening body a blurring translucent mass of dripping tentacles, clouded eyes, and jagged, long-toothed mouths.

Sockwell screamed as it forced her into the dark of the other Life Support corridor and out of sight.

"Captain!"

Thrashing, tearing, screaming, and gurgling were the only answer Polk received. He twisted around back toward the forward ship sections and pushed Getty that way in front of himself.

As they both stumbled away from Life Support, sliding and several wet, malformed feet slapping down onto the corridor floor in pursuit could be heard back in the dark.

Cathy crept down the corrugated tunnel. Clutches and pods of the wet, living nastiness grew here too, but it hadn't consumed it like the corridor she'd just come from. They dripped audibly, giving her another thing to try to ignore.

–The ship is preparing for what you never understood was its true purpose. Mother has joined the Matriarchs in their self-made Heaven.–

"And you'll join her? *Without* me?"

–Not exactly.... But either way, her design is only for one.–

Cathy looked at a dribbling, pulsing pod near her hand on the corridor's ridged surface.

"Her design is *digesting* itself, Hugh!"

–You never understood. *The best way out is always through....*–

"*But the only way through—*"

–No. You never asked the right question. *Through* what?–

Polk rushed behind Getty, guiding him forward with a push and nudge when he had to. Polk slowed and listened. The sliding and wet sounds of pursuit were gone.

Getty kept going but stumbled and crumpled to the ground ahead, his back to Polk. He moaned and held his gut.

Polk caught up and grasped Getty's shoulder, trying to help him up.

Getty's moans became inhuman, and a high-pitched chittering joined the awful sounds.

"Get up, kid! It's gone for now, but—"

Getty rose and whipped toward Polk—it wasn't Getty anymore.

The pressure suit incasing the thing that was so recently Getty bulged and pulsed and its helmet faceplate was filled to bursting with guts, teeth, and shiny black sacs—all pressed against the faceplate surface.

Polk screamed as it lunged for him, the suit bursting open with flailing warped limbs and latching tentacles.

Cathy reached the sealed sphere hatch. When she looked down the gun-barrel tunnel into the sphere core, light faded up. Hugh was sitting on his lower legs, hands on his thighs and elbows out, as a samurai might.

"I thought you wanted me safe!"

–From the sphere, yes. From the rest? You will prevail, I'm sure. You are a Delamarre, after all.–

The light faded out again. Swirling, odd-colored light replaced it, illuminating Hugh but leaving the spherical core walls black behind him.

Hugh looked up at a light source Cathy couldn't see.

–*Nunc animis opus, Aenea, nunc pectore firmo.*–

The shuddering hum returned, stronger than ever.

Outside the ship, a circular void opened in space on the ship's starboard side. No light escaped its enormous, gaping maw.

Cathy beat the sides of the hatch porthole window with her gloved fists. "Hugh, no!"

As if in response, Hugh turned his head to look at her and, through the veil's translucence, she could see he was smiling.

The shaking was so strong that Cathy had to grab for handholds on the ring of safety bar around the corrugated tunnel where it met the sphere.

The sphere lurched to the starboard side of the ship and the barrel-tunnel view went with it. In the last instant before Hugh was pulled out of Cathy's sight, his eyes flashed and light poured out of them like torches.

Cathy clung to the safety ring as the sphere was torn from its cage and pulled toward the void in space, destroying the cage completely and breaking the ship in two.

The forward and aft sections spun away from the void as it swallowed the sphere and closed, completely disappearing.

Cathy held onto the ring with all she had as the rotation and vacuum tried to suck her out into space.

Applewhite cleared her throat and blinked. "And how exactly did you slow the ship's rotation?"

Cathy frowned. "I am the daughter of—"

"Geniuses. Right."

"Also, I'm an engineer myself and trained in extravehicular activity work. I found a tool compartment in the umbilicus and adapted one of the life-support tanks to spray like a thruster. Short bursts to conserve, but I calculated well enough and slowed it to a comfortable amount."

Zorn seemed impressed. Applewhite did not.

"Then I found the radiation tent in an exterior maintenance compartment and—"

Applewhite tapped the table with her fingertips. "Bullshit."

"Pardon me?"

"I don't believe you. This is some form of manipulation. I don't believe anything you just told us."

Cathy blinked and chuckled to herself. "That is your right, I suppose."

Zorn leaned forward. "Could there have been a special coolant or other leak that could've caused hallucinations?"

Applewhite shook her head. "No. I'm not entertaining this nonsense."

She deactivated the AR file-sharing system and stood, gesturing toward the door.

Cathy's smile vanished and she nodded.

After Applewhite and Zorn led her back to it, Cathy stepped into her cell and turned back toward the clear door.

Applewhite said, "You're right. There's probably nothing we can do to you. You're a waste of our time anyway. You can join your brother in Hell for all I care, *Lady* Delamarre."

Zorn chuckled. "Hey, come on."

Cathy met eyes with Applewhite. "How superstitious of you. There are far more wondrous and terrifying places than you can imagine, you simple woman."

Applewhite gave her a mirthless smile, then turned and walked down the ward hallway.

Zorn started to follow.

"Please. Can you turn the lights all the way down? My voice won't operate it and I've...I have decided it is what I want."

306

"Sure. *Lights—off.*"

The lights faded down, leaving only the dim hall light through the cell door in the room.

"Thank you."

Zorn nodded then caught up to Applewhite, who was storming toward the elevators.

"Hey, I thought we were supposed to be professional."

"That horrid girl was mocking us with that story...."

In the dim light of her cell, Cathy stood with her eyes closed. The cell walls and clear door began to hum and shudder.

Behind Cathy, an eerie light faded up within the solid wall as if it were a window and there appeared the silhouette of a man just past the wall surface. His eyes opened, pouring out light.

Cathy's eyes opened too, the same light pouring out of them.

Applewhite and Zorn heard the humming from back at Cathy's cell. They looked at each other, then hurried back down the hall.

Just before they reached the cell, there was a chittering and snapping sound, and a flash of eerie light. They reached the clear door and looked inside the dim cell. Applewhite slapped the cell door. "*Lights—full!*"

Light filled the empty cell.

Applewhite sighed and said, "I fucking hate rich kids."

Halcyon-noyclaH

SSFS (Sol System Federation Ship) Andrew Furuseth, *Vesco System—2189*

Abe Nanjiani knew there was something very wrong with the ship they'd happened upon from the moment their imagers had zoomed it, a sleek rhombus just hanging at an awkward angle as it orbited Vesco-458c. The forward sections and bridge bubble on one end of the long diamond shape were obscured, the angle dipping the front of the ship into the gauzy ice and rocks of the planet's inner rings.

"I mean...we all know what that is, right?" Science Officer Meghan Malcova said.

Abe said, "Looks like it...."

First Mate Grant Blaylock adjusted the zoom and frame on a touch panel, trying to get a clearer image of the obscured front third of the diamond.

Captain Thurgood leaned back in her padded chair and said, "The *Halcyon* didn't have markings, Blaylock."

Margaret said, "So you agree it's the *Halcyon?*"

"There were only three ships made with that diamond design, and two disintegrated just after launch when their experimental engines kicked on, so yeah...."

Grant said, "Other than some dents from debris collisions, the ship looks intact. What's it been, about fifty years?"

"Seventy, more like," Thurgood said.

Abe said, "And what if it is the *Halcyon?* We have to—"

Thurgood looked at Abe and narrowed her eyes.

"I'm sure I know what your concerns are. You're a civilian, Abraham. All due respect, but this is technically a merchant marine vessel, and we will abide by maritime considerations."

"It's peacetime. Also, I'm now a civilian, yes, but I am *the* civilian in charge of making sure the prefab structures in the hold reach the colony site on time and intact."

"Admiralty law states—"

"This is space, not the ocean."

Thurgood clenched her jaw and said, "Don't be cute. And I'll ask you to not interrupt me on my own bridge, civilian or not."

"Understood. Respectfully, though, Captain.... We need the colony structures completed before the colonists arrive, yes?"

"It was your altered course and special stop that brought us out this way and ate into our time, remember?"

Abe sighed and said, "We needed better HVAC units. That was necessary. This is not."

"I disagree. Malcova, Blaylock—grab a few crewmen from their bunks and take them over to that ship."

They nodded and left their posts and walked past Abe, who then followed.

Thurgood saw this and said, "Nanjiani?"

"I'll be going as well," Abe said.

"Why?"

"So your people don't waste any more time."

Abe, Meghan, Grant, and three crewmen—Ueda, Koehler, and Witt—sat strapped into three rows of two seats atop a ten-foot rectangular open-"air" shuttlecraft. They were secured with bent-*U* safety bars that came down around their helmets and onto their spacesuit chests. Abe was in the rear-right seat next to Ueda.

He looked at Vesco-458c—"Set" as it was dubbed in their files—a beautiful orb of milky white and swirling pale greens. The rings of ice and rock around it were violet and bluish-white.

The *Halcyon* had been swallowed up by Set's shadow on its rings. They entered the shadow as they cruised over the outer rings. Abe examined the ship's silhouette. Its aft section had five cylinders that bulged out.

Spotlights on the shuttle front came on as it glided over the *Halcyon*. A complex thruster sequence turned the shuttle around, brought it down some, and reoriented them to the odd angle of ship. The portside corner of the diamond was just to their right.

The shuttle stopped and their securing bars released and eased up over their helmets. Koehler and Witt in the front pushed off of their seats and engaged thrusters on their suit packs that sputtered with soundless flashes, the two crewmen maneuvering toward a hatch on the *Halcyon*'s slanted hull.

Grant said, "Get some more light on it, guys."

Koehler and Witt did so, then took up flanking positions on each side of the hatch. They un-holstered thick-barreled coil-pistols and waited as the rest of them left the shuttle seats. Abe felt the weight of his own coil-pistol in its thigh holster—a left-handed one he'd had to search for in the armory, as he was apparently the only lefty aboard.

Abe followed the others. Meghan maneuvered herself to the hatch, then took an omni-key—a curved pistol grip that ended in a shiny chromed ball the size of an orange—from an extra cross-draw holster on her waist. She pressed the ball to the *Halcyon*'s hatch and Abe saw readouts appear on her helmet's curved interior.

ACCESS GRANTED flashed a few times and the doors opened.

Without hesitating, Meghan maneuvered herself inside. She made it to the far door and the rest followed her in.

"Paragrav is down, but there's still power and pressure somehow...."

After the chamber repressurized, Meghan pressed the panel again. It pulsed three times and the interior doors opened.

Their lights burned through the jet black that must've blanketed the *Halcyon*'s interiors for decades. They had two ways to go. There was a sharp corner to their right—the left point of the diamond, viewed from the top—which angled off and ran down to a heavy sealed door with many multilingual warnings printed on it and ENGINE ROOM above them. To the left the corridor had a door on the right marked LIVING QUARTERS then LABS and GREENHOUSE in smaller letters, and the door at the end was marked BRIDGE.

Grant said, "Okay, three ways to go. Koehler, go with Malcova to the engines. Witt, come with me to the bridge. Ueda, please go with Mr. Nanjiani to the labs—if that's alright with you, sir."

Abe said, "Of course...."

They broke off in each direction, finessing their thrusters in the tighter spaces of the ship. Abe followed Ueda through the door into the living quarters and mess area. Past the mess was another door that opened on a metal stairwell down to the labs and greenhouse. Ueda used the handrailings to pull himself down the narrow passage. Abe did the same and followed him down.

–The engine room's sealed tight. I was able to unlock it through the computer system...but it won't open,– Meghan said over helmet comms.

Grant said, –Okay, meet us on the bridge if nothing works.–

–Wilco–

They reached the labs, a smaller diamond half the size of the ship with slanted walls. Their lights cut through dust or other particles in the air. The center of the equipment-lined lab had a paragrav inverter—an energized panel that kept its surface gravity and could flip, rotating two people sitting on simple pneumatic supported seats to a new orientation.

Abe pushed off and grabbed one of four safety bars that lined the inverter's rectangular area. He grabbed one of the clamshell seats and pulled himself onto it.

Ueda said, "What are you doing?"

"We have to check everything we can, yeah? I want this all over with."

Abe pressed a touch panel attached to the seat, but nothing happened.

"Blaylock...," Abe said.

–Go ahead.–

"Living quarters and labs are clear. I can't engage the inverter to the greenhouse, but I've seen no signs of life."

–Good enough. Meet us on the bridge. I think we figured why none of us have found anything....–

Meghan had used her omni-key to bring the core computers out of their decades-long standby loop. The lights and paragrav were still down, so they all floated in the glow of the holo-panels they were watching, between and around a set of four installed crew seats in a diamond formation. They weren't sure if their mag-boots would mess with these old computers. Meghan manipulated overhead diagrams of the ship layout, focusing on relevant sections as she went.

Meghan said, "I scanned the engine room and greenhouse with the internal sensors. No signs of life. No static, frozen, or desiccated lifeless matter—"

"As in bodies?" Koehler said.

"Exactly. And I have no idea why we can't get into those sections—the computers show them as unlocked."

Abe said, "So, we've effectively looked everywhere, and nothing. No one's here, dead or otherwise."

"Right," Grant said.

Meghan said, "No records of any foul play or boarding or anything strange at all. Except, their logs show they descended to the planet surface. But their pods are still here."

She focused the diagram views on the drop-pods, two downward pointing cones on the *Halcyon*'s underside.

Grant said, "Or they came back automatically somehow."

Ueda said, "Could they have sent them back for some reason? Could there be like a contamination down there or...something worse?"

"Oh, *please*. The ship is empty—what more are we required to do?" Abe said.

Grant locked eyes with him and said, "Captain?"

Thurgood came over comms, –We need to investigate those drop coordinates. If they obviously died down there, we're good. Have to exhaust every option. Then we move on to the colony.–

313

Abe narrowed his eyes at Grant.

Grant said, "Wilco," then to Abe, "You can go back to the *Furuseth* if you like."

"No, you all seem almost excited. I wouldn't want you to get too absorbed and dawdle."

Abe had always hated planetfall, and today would be no different. He'd seen people cheer, whoop, and holler as they fell, terminal velocity giving them a buzz like an old throwback rollercoaster. He couldn't wait for it to end.

Their shuttle used frontal retro-thrusters to slow down from orbital velocity, the six of them sitting on what felt to Abe like a far-too-open platform. He knew specialized force-fields became a focused-energy drop-cone—he just didn't want to have to watch entry burn firsthand.

He closed his eyes as he felt the reassuring grip of orbital gravity loosen, the shuttle's nose starting to dip. When he opened them again, the nose was glowing from initial entry. Their descent became more vertical, the energy cone around them set ablaze. The black of space became grays and greens as they dropped into a swirling storm. The shuttle vibrated and shook. Abe thought they might hit hard, at least sparing him from hearing any more animal calls—

The landing thrusters fired, they slowed, then gently touched down. The smoothness of it belied the intensity of the storm they'd been deposited in, and as it powered down, the shuttle rocked back and forth some on its landing gear.

Witt tried to say something but it was muffled by the howling wind.

–I guess we'll need to use comms down here,– Grant said.

Witt laughed and said, –That was amazing! Never gets old, man!–

Abe shook his head.

The shuttle safety bars released and swung up. The team stood and stepped off the shuttle but stayed close. Meghan had already brought up the *Halcyon*'s ship data and Abe could see the bright lines and curves in her helmet faceplate of its coordinates being matched to their gathered map data and surface data of Set.

She started walking and said, "Okay, their landing zone was this way...."

The rest of them followed her in single file. Abe linked to Meghan's data feed and saw a faint, pulsing drop beacon the *Halcyon* crew must've left, and a bold, glowing square for their shuttle's position. Both nodes were in a dim glowing mesh of topographical imaging based on probe bounce-back data. Abe was happy to have something to look at other than spacesuits and swirling dust and fog or gas that was probably poisonous.

–There!– Meghan said as they neared the weak beacon.

Through the maelstrom, Abe saw a rough ring of boxy dark shapes. The team made a circle around them. It was a set of prefab sensor, generator, and transmitter rigs.

-Looks like a forward operating setup,- Grant said.

Meghan approached one of the base camp generators. She took out her omni-key and touched it to the rounded box—charging it, Abe assumed. She finished and turned it on. The generator warmed up, also waking the other old equipment up. Readouts streamed and beeps and shifting tones were just barely audible, even over the storm.

A glow appeared in the distance, then a dimmer one past that one. In their data links, nodes began lighting up, tracing a dotted path about two or three miles away from them.

Grant said, -Looks like the *Halcyon* crew laid down some breadcrumbs....-

Thurgood came over comms, -We see it too. And from up here, that path seems to just stop in the middle of nothing.-

-Please advise,- Grant said.

-If you get to the end of that breadcrumb trail and find nothing, we're gone.-

Abe said, -Fan*tastic.*-

Thurgood said nothing but Abe could picture her expression.

-Okay, suit lights on so we don't have to rely on suit HUDs for locating each other. Let's keep going,- Grant said.

But Meghan was already trudging through the storm toward the first glowing breadcrumb. The rest followed, each turning their lights on.

The breadcrumbs were spikes that had been shot down into the smooth, dry ground that the dust and sand washed over due to the storms. From the top of the spike, a long, thin rod had telescoped upward and a glowing orb bobbed around at the end of that. This reminded Abe of an Earth fish he'd seen on vids that used a similar bioluminescent version of this to catch prey in the deep dark of the sea—he shuddered and looked around at the dark swirling all around, feeling for his coil-pistol again with his gloved left hand and finding it.

As they were coming to the third marker on the plateau, Meghan slowed and stopped.

Grant said, -Wh-what is it?-

-I'm not sure....-

Visibility was clearing more and he could see the last handful of lights, and where they stopped—

There were ruins everywhere. They were profoundly foreign and looked more petrified and eroded than broken and crumbled. But they had definitely been made by intelligent, living creatures. The ruins were only the first thing he saw, though....

The ruins surrounded a curved circular covering about a mile in diameter. It was like a smooth overturned plate on a desert of pale green sand.

Grant said, -Captain, I think we might be here a while.-

Abe hated the words Grant had said, but couldn't disagree.

Thurgood said, -What is it? We can't see anything up here.-

Meghan said, –I think what we're seeing is a shield that exists to provide not only physical shelter but also that lack of scanner visibility you're describing.–

After a moment, Thurgood said, –Alright.... Keep going, but please be careful.–

Grant said, –Will do.–

Meghan moved on, tromping through piles of sand and whipping winds.

The plate was on a series of large support struts that ran all around the edge of its underside. It was dark underneath, but not as dark as it should be. Abe figured the plate was thick but translucent. Wispy-tipped mounds of sand had piled under the plate's edge and outer surface some, but after they'd climbed and crawled past those, it became obvious that most of what the plate was covering was intact and undisturbed.

They'd entered what felt like an enormous hangar, only not for vehicles. There were freestanding structures all around in concentric circles from a central point. They resembled cacti in shape, but were made up of tumorous, colorful animal flesh. Some were more bulbous than others, and some approached the look of diseased spheroids on stilts or support struts. They all had what looked like organic, roughly arranged ladders—two to three vertical spines connected by bulbous growths that looked climbable.

Meghan said, –I can't think of another way to.... This is *incredible*.–

Koehler said, –Have we ever found anything like this?–

–Honestly? No. We've found microorganisms, complex extraterrestrial animals, and the Vran'Chua'lt...but they're relatively primitive, outside of their seafaring and aeronautical genius.–

Ueda said, –This is *bad*, is what you mean.–

They ignored him and continued on, following the breadcrumb lights. The dotted path kept going toward the center of the plate covering. The cactus at the center was rounder and had something more like stairs—still comprising warped bulbs and spinal columns, though. An almost entranced Meghan led the way up them.

The chamber interior was a big hollow ball of boney flesh. A complex pattern made from stacked metallic plates with intricate designs cut out of them was installed at the center of its circular floor. More sleeping *Halcyon* crew equipment was arranged around the pattern plates. The *Furuseth* team stood around one half of the pattern, Ueda lingering by the gaping entrance they'd come in from.

Meghan looked at Grant and he nodded. She turned the equipment on with her omni-key and it all hummed and glowed to life. She examined a special readout screen with odd symbols on its screen and notes with arrows in a basic user interface. She touched the one that read ON and the symbol its arrow pointed at began pulsing.

A circular panel rose up out of the floor near the *Halcyon* equipment.

Meghan placed her hand on it like a touch pad, but there was only a high-pitched whine heard. She frowned and looked at the *Halcyon* readout again.

Ueda said, "Do you really want to make this thing work? I mean, what does it even do?"

The next note said CODE.

Meghan touched this one, and the room filled with strange tones and rhythmic clicking that vibrated the entire structure. She'd never heard anything quite like it, and entered commands into her omni-key.

Witt said, "What are you doing?"

"This is something totally new—I'm recording it for analysis."

Abe said, "Fine, great.... Can we leave now?"

Grant stepped closer to Meghan and examined the readouts on the *Halcyon* equipment.

He said, "I can't disagree. This all seems pretty cryptic. We should...."

Abe looked from Meghan and Grant to what had stopped the latter from speaking—

The layered plates had started rotating. They whirred up to a blur and a translucent, reflective fluid swirled up out of the plates over the spinning patterns. The shiny fluid spun fast enough that it looked like a lumpy blob. The blob grew into a sphere and kept spinning.

Grant was mesmerized. He stepped toward the shining sphere, raising a gloved hand.

Abe said, "Blaylock!" and Meghan said "Grant, stop!"

Grant said, "I'd have thought a scientist would be more curi—"

His fingers made contact with the sphere and it started pulling him in.

Meghan lunged, grabbing his other hand. She used all of her weight to pull away.

Abe tried to grab Meghan by the waist to add his own strength—

The sphere pulled Grant and Meghan in and toward its center, the surface rippled, then it started descending.

Ueda said, "Shit!"

Koehler and Witt let out overlapping strings of other expletives.

Abe panicked, thinking they'd be pulled down into the spinning pattern—but those plates had opened from their centers and recessed to the edges of the circle. The sphere kept dropping into a cylindrical tunnel that had opened up. He was still moving forward and dived down into the tunnel—

He fell through slick, bony nine-foot-diameter rings of glowing flesh—but the sphere was descending too fast.

"*No!*"

Abe activated his thruster pack, burning it hard and shooting downward as fast as it could go, closing the gap to the ball that was taking his friends—or at least fellow humans—away.

He was almost there. He stretched his shaking left hand out, grasping for the sphere with all he had—

It took him, pulling at his arm with incredible force. The sphere sucked him in, enveloping him in what he now felt was a gelatinous, almost obscenely welcoming and eager substance.

Then Abe felt warm and safe, and he drifted off to sleep.

The three *Furuseth* crew members awoke in the room their descent had started in. They stretched and yawned as if from a long, restful sleep. They helped each other up and looked around.

The chamber was empty. The *Halcyon* equipment was there, but it was collapsed and nonfunctioning.

Grant said, "Wh-where are the others?"

Meghan turned in a slow circle.

Abe said, "What is it?"

"Something's wrong...."

"Well, yeah, I'd say s—"

"No, not like that. Everything looks right...but feels wrong. You don't get that feeling?"

Abe and Grant looked around. Abe got what she meant but couldn't place it either.

Grant said, "You're right, but what is it?"

Abe said, "For now, I think we should get back to the ship. Maybe we were unconscious for longer than we thought—wait. What if they left us?"

"Captain Thurgood?" Grant said over comms.

All they heard was distorted waves of noise.

Meghan said, "Okay, maybe the storms are interfering somehow. I agree with Abraham—let's get back to the shuttle and get above all this."

They looked at each other and nodded in their helmets.

Climbing down the strange tumor and spine steps, Abe could see the dim outlines of the breadcrumb lights leading out toward the open plateau, but they were retracted into their bases and turned off. Meghan took her omni-key out of its cross-draw holster and touched its chrome ball to one of the light bases. Something about that was odd to Abe, but he still couldn't place it.

"The power and signal links are down. Here...."

After a moment, the lights telescoped upward and began to glow again. They cut the dimness around their orbs for about thirty feet around. Everything seemed the same. Abe still knew something was off, and started walking with purpose down the line of lights between the concentric rows of the grotesque cactus chambers. Meghan and Grant hurried behind him.

They reached the edge of the upturned plate covering and entered the storm, starting toward the *Halcyon* base camp and shuttle nodes, which were still where they should be.

Nearing the base camp, Abe heard an unearthly shrieking in the distance.

–Did you hear that?–

Their faces in their dust-blown faceplates confirmed they had.

Meghan said, –The storm?–

Another screech, but closer and on the other side of them—and this one had a gurgling and ghastly chittering as it trailed off into the howling wind.

Without hesitation, they ran toward the shuttle node on their HUDs—

The shuttle was there, swaying and shuddering against the wind as it should be.

That relief mixed with Abe's grim realization that this meant their comrades hadn't left in it—but it also meant they hadn't left at all.

They climbed onto it, Meghan and Grant in the front seats, and Abe instinctively taking the seat he'd had before. His mind was on the eerie sounds of life out in the storm, but he knew something wasn't right about his seat either—

They heard more shrieking, this time in several places and all around them.

Abe wrenched his safety bar down over his chest and said, –Dammit, just go!–

Meghan and Grant pulled theirs down too and she slapped the ESCAPE BURN button hard—

The shuttle thrusters blasted downward, sending out clouds of exhaust and sand that rolled outward as they started ascending. Their helmets auto-tinted or they'd have been blinded, and the Gs sucked them down into their seats as the force-field cone formed—vertically this time and more rounded.

Abe strained to turn his head against the gravity and look down. There were dark shapes in the rolling storm, the size of elephants but far less symmetrical—and with a disturbing lack of uniformity between the few he'd glimpsed. His view was obscured by the storm as they raced upwards, and he closed his eyes and hoped their ship was waiting out in space just past the orbital pull of Set.

It wasn't.

They'd broken Set's pull and reached orbital velocity, then Meghan had eased the throttle down. They floated in orbit high above the rings, just staring at where the *Furuseth* should've been.

Grant said, "They.... They really left us."

Meghan made some adjustments on the shuttle control screen.

"What are you doing?" Abe said.

"Maybe there's another explanation. I'm searching for comms signals—there!"

They heard something but it was too quiet. She boosted the gain.

–*...an-pan, pan-pan, pan-pan.... All stations, all stations, all stations.... This is the GTC ship* Halcyon*....*–

Meghan and Grant looked at each other, then back at Abe, eyes wide. He shook his head, then looked down at the rings. He followed them around to the left and saw the small diamond nearly halfway around toward the far horizon, still floating with its forward section dipped into the rings. They'd been in such a hurry they'd lifted off at an odd angle and came up a ways from where they'd dropped.

Abe said, "It's still there," and pointed. They looked.

- We're experiencing trouble with our propulsion systems and require technical assistance or a ship large enough to hold ours and to transport us to the nearest space station....-

Then the call repeated.

Grant said, "What the hell is going on?"

Something about the rings and ship bothered Abe now. He looked down at the empty shuttle seat Ueda had sat in earlier, its safety bar down for takeoff as if it were holding down an invisible man. Ueda's seat was on his right. Why was it strange? Abe felt for his coil-pistol with his right hand—it was there, on his right thigh. He'd had to search for a right-handed holster in the armory because they were less common—

"That's not true," Abe said.

Meghan said, "What?"

"I'm left handed...."

"Not sure how that's imp—"

"I'm *left* handed! My pistol's on my right thigh, and I went to grab it with my right hand! It felt *natural*.... I was sitting on Ueda's *right* side—but this is the seat I was in, I know it!"

Meghan said, "That's it!"

"What are you two talking about?" Grant said.

She said, "This isn't our.... We're somewhere *else!* Everything's flipped or inverted."

Abe said, "Like a mirror."

Meghan pressed the omni-key to *Halcyon*'s airlock hatch, activating and opening it. Abe knew they were on the wrong side of the ship, but here it wasn't. This was the lock they'd come in before, only on the ship's right side— and the ship was also pointed to their left now. He looked back at the shuttle floating behind them, flipped but still so much the same. Its designation letters must've been backwards, but with his brain flipped too, he could read them clearly.

Grant said, "Why are we doing this again?" and chuckled, but Abe knew he was scared—they all were.

Meghan said, "We need to get back to that portal on the planet, but we have to answer this call and put it to bed."

"It's been seventy years...."

Abe said, "And we're in a different dimension that's attached to ours, only inverted. Who knows what else is different here? They could've been waiting all this time for help."

Abe wasn't sure he believed that, but he'd been forced to become far more open minded in the last twenty minutes. He wasn't sure about anything now.

Grant said, "If it's attached to ours, why is the *Halcyon* here, but not the *Furuseth?*"

Abe and Meghan said nothing.

They entered the lock and it closed behind them. She opened the interior door and they maneuvered into the ship's corridor. Abe looked down toward the engine room and saw an emergency lock installed over its door like a big metal *X*. They went right, toward this version of the bridge. Meghan opened its door and they floated inside—

Abe grabbed Meghan's and Grant's suit shoulder material and held them. They looked back at him and he nodded his head toward the bridge crew seats.

There were two people in very old spacesuits slouched in two of the seats closest to the ship controls. Their suits were more primitive. The helmets were like a fighter ship pilot's, a much smaller faceplate and the mouth-and-nose areas were covered and had thick tubes snaking out from there to a row of air canisters on their chests and abdomens.

Grant feathered his thrusters toward them and Abe tightened his grip.

"What? They're obviously dead. Let's turn off the call signal and get home—"

A raspy, hoarse coughing reverberated through the bridge and Abe saw the suited figure near the control panel moving. The other form did the same, its cough even harsher and sounding thick with phlegm.

"Lights...off. Please," the first cougher said, and Grant stepped back.

"Please...turn them...off," the other one said through his hacking. Their voices were muffled by their helmet designs.

The *Furuseth* trio did what they were asked, a hand or two shaking in the process.

Dawn was approaching, and the chamber was bathed in dim light from the local star's rays coming through the ice and rocks of Set's rings. The two *Halcyon* crewmen finished coughing but stayed where they were, more upright but still a bit slumped over in their seats.

Meghan said, "H-how are you alive?"

"What are you doing here?" The first crewman said.

Abe said, "We found the portal, down on the planet."

"Of course.... They made it past the creatures." the second crewman said.

"What are those things?"

"As far as we could tell, they're the primitive descendants of the ones that made the gates."

"Gates?" Abe said, emphasizing the plural sound.

The crewman laughed and said, "Oh *yes*, there are many...."

Abe didn't like the tone of how he said it or its implications. He tried to be subtle and tapped his thumb with his index and middle fingers in a quick sequence, activating a kind of "mute" feature their helmets had—he could be heard in the other *Furuseth* helmets but not outside. He spoke in a murmur, careful not to move his mouth too much.

–Meghan, don't answer—but can you hear me?–

She cleared her throat.

Grant almost said something but Meghan made the clearing sound again.

Abe switched back and said, "Why didn't you go back through it?"

The first practically cackled and said, "We tried! By the time we figured out we were somewhere...*else*, we'd been here too long to—"

"Wait—how long have *you* been here?" the second interrupted, shifting in its seat.

Abe didn't like that at all and said, –This might be very bad. Keep them talking.–

Meghan cleared her throat in recognition and said, "Not long. M-maybe a few hours."

The two crewmen sat up some and turned their helmeted heads toward them. Abe was pretty sure their faces were glowing.

Grant said, "Weren't there four of you?"

"There are. Cerna's locked in the engine room. Our engines didn't react well to the gate's pulse, and neither did he. Started to become...something else."

"The engines or your man?"

The other crewman said, "Both."

–Meghan, we're going to need a distraction,– Abe said, sure now.

Grant said, "And the other?"

"She's in the garden...."

The *Halcyon* crewmen hauled themselves up out of the chairs and stood, then the closer one took a step toward them. Their boots were magnetic, but seemed set to half power so they could take quick steps.

Abe could see now that he was right—not only were their faces glowing, they were almost *translucent* and a strange mix of fluorescent colors. Abe was most disturbed by the skulls—half visible under the glowing faces, but deep black instead of white. He shuddered and wanted to look away but couldn't for fear of what they'd do next.

Their name patches were visible now—the closer one approaching them was BODENCHAK, and the other was DELINE.

Bodenchak said, "You must have a ship. Was it in orbit when the gate pulsed?"

Abe noticed Bodenchak's teeth were black like his skull.

Meghan said, "No. Why?"

"The pulse that comes out imprints matter, but it's weak enough that it doesn't get past the inner rings."

Through his own black teeth Deline said, "We can use your bodies to get back through—"

"Because they're more fresh...."

"But once we're through, if your ship had been hit by the pulse—"

"The bad things could follow us—find us again."

–We're gonna need that distraction.–

Meghan took out her omni-key, turned on her own mag-boots, and sucked down onto the grated bridge floor. She crouched and pressed the device to the flooring, using its conductive pathfinding to access the bridge computers.

Bodenchak stopped and said, "What are you doing?"

Abe heard a rising whine and strong growing vibrations from behind them. Deline said, "No!"

Meghan had turned on the *Halcyon*'s engines.

Both ghastly crewmen glowed brighter and Deline said, "You don't understand!"

Bodenchak seemed enraged and he took two steps toward Grant—

Abe un-holstered his coil-pistol—which felt strange doing with his right hand, but was correct here—and fired two of its hyper-accelerated projectiles into Bodenchak's head area. Bodenchak's helmet faceplate shattered and the small spears blasted out the back of it. His face and head partly exploded too—but he seemed unfazed.

Bodenchak lunged and grabbed Grant while he was taking out his coil-pistol.

Meghan said, "Grant!"

Abe looked for another shot, but didn't want to hit Grant.

Bodenchak came apart, his suit and body becoming almost liquid—and filled with slithering, see-through tentacles. All this poured into Grant through the solid matter of his suit, and he went slack. As Grant's body slowly rotated in zero gravity, Deline came for Meghan—

Abe holstered his pistol and grabbed her hand.

"Hold tight!"

Abe leaned backwards and fired off his thruster pack, pulling them both toward the bridge entry door they'd come in through. They almost slammed into the wall next to it, but he corrected.

A hideous muffled scream was heard from the other side of the barricaded engine room door, even louder than the ever-rising engine sounds. Abe let off the thrusters and grabbed a support bar that ran the length of the corridor. He could hear the tinny steps of Deline's mag-boots behind them.

Meghan said, "Grant, no!" and a sob caught in her throat.

Deline's steps stopped and Abe looked back down the corridor—

Deline had become half liquid like Bodenchak had, and his limbs and body bulged and writhed. Amorphous glowing appendages spilled out and pulled the creature's bulk down the corridor.

Abe beat the living-quarters door button until it opened then pulled Meghan in with him. Before he could, she'd pressed the button on the other side. Once it had closed, she shot the panel.

"Let's go!" she said, above the sounds of the thing that had just been Deline pounding and slapping the door.

Abe fired his thrusters, feathering this time and reaching the stairwell down to the labs. Meghan followed and he guided her down before himself.

"Wait, you guys!" Abe heard Grant's voice from beyond the closed starboard living-quarters door, across from the port one they'd just entered. Then he heard a sizzling sound back at the door Deline had been beating on—

The Deline creature was coming through the matter of the door, phasing somehow.

Abe saw that Meghan had made it down to the labs, and he rushed after her.

She said, "Why did you bring us to a dead end?!"

"Sit here!"

Abe maneuvered to the seats on the paragrav inverter and pulled himself onto one. She did as he said, but looked unsure.

"Trust me!" he said as he pressed the button—nothing happened.

Meghan pressed her omni-key to the inverter surface and it found an *X*-shaped device on the other side of the panel. It unlocked that, and they heard it detach.

From up in the labs Grant's voice said, "Oh, you won't like the garden, guys!"

Abe slapped the button again, and the panel started rotating—and at that moment, Abe realized how similar the words garden and greenhouse could be, and what one of the crewman had said about the fourth crew member.

It was dark from the sealed blast shutters, so Meghan opened them with her omni-key. As the panels slid away, they were treated to a beautiful, glowing spectacle.

The panel flipped them over into an alien jungle.

The Earth plants that the *Halcyon* had left with had become pastel and neon living tangles, somewhere between flora and fauna. Abe was pretty sure some of the pulsing bunches also had eyes.

A tortured moan announced the fourth crew member—she'd grown into un-plants, and moved freely within their matter. She formed into a human/space-suit shape and examined the now floating intruders in her home with a black-skulled, translucent-faced head of her own.

Meghan said, "Nope!"

She holstered her key, pulled out her coil-pistol, and fired it at the clear plasteel greenhouse panels. Abe took out his pistol and fired in the same area—

The panels shattered—then immediately disintegrated, sucked outward.

Abe and Meghan were pulled that way too, but the garden monster prepared to swipe and grab at them with all available tendrils and fronds. Meghan grabbed Abe's hand and kicked on her own thrusters, sending them up and out through the growing opening. She cut the thrusters and they tumbled a bit.

Abe pointed and said, "Get to the shuttle!"

They reoriented and fired off toward their waiting vehicle. As they were pulling the safety bars down, Meghan pointed toward the *Halcyon*'s underside. Abe looked—one of the drop cones was silently shifting and prepping for drop.

Abe locked his bar and thrust downward with both of his thumbs a few times.

"Go-go-go!"

Meghan engaged the front thrusters hard, forcing the shuttle out of orbital velocity and almost flipping it around...but gravity took over and pulled them down toward the planet. Their force-field cone engaged and they plunged toward Set.

Abe looked up and saw the dark *Halcyon* drop cone falling after them.

–Shit!–

Meghan said, –We can make it.–

They dropped until the landing thrusters fired.

Abe said, –Will these packs work in atmosphere?–

–They should—wait, why?–

The *Halcyon* cone was only a hundred feet above them, so Abe pulled an emergency release on the safety bar and forced it up to free himself. Meghan did the same. They jumped from the landing shuttle that was still about fifty feet above the ground, then kicked thrusters on. Abe and Meghan came down and away from the shuttle, almost reaching the ground before the strength of their pack thrusters beat out their downward momentum—

They blasted away, flying just over the ground at incredible speed. Abe caught glimpses of the dark shapes in the swirling storm approaching, so he steered up from the ground some and Meghan did the same. The two raced above whipping, undulating forms, and Abe tried to ignore the shrieking and chittering.

The plate covering was in sight.

Abe and Meghan maneuvered down and tried to fly in right between two support struts. Meghan made it clean, but Abe brushed one of them and tumbled. Hit the floor of the cactus hangar and rolled hard as Meghan sputtered and feathered her pack to a running stop. She started back toward Abe—

"No! Just go!"

She hesitated, then started for the central portal.

Abe got up and limped after her.

"Come on.... Don't leave, you guys!" Grant's voice called from just inside the plate edge.

Abe looked back and saw the glowing, half–see–through thing in one of their own suits—but it was misshapen now, the forms inside warping and straining against the thick fabric. Abe hurried after Meghan, who was already at the tumor/spine steps.

They entered the portal chamber and crossed to the equipment. Meghan woke it up and started the sequence—but the last step wouldn't work. The tones weren't right.

"It won't work!"

Abe fought his panic to think, then said, "Your recording—play it, but can you make it backwards?"

She could and did.

The shiny portal fluids started flowing and spinning into a sphere.

"Don't worry—I'll just come in after you and bring one of you back for Deline to join with!" Bodenchak said with Grant's voice out in the hangar—but very close now.

Meghan swapped her omni-key for her pistol and shot each *Halcyon* equipment box until she was satisfied they were destroyed.

She said, "Just try it!"

Then she dived into the portal sphere.

Abe hesitated, then jumped in after her.

They were awakened on the portal pattern's other side, and Koehler and Witt helped them to their feet. Ueda stood by the chamber entrance, staring at Abe and Meghan like they were ghosts.

Koehler said, "What the hell happened?"

"Where's Blaylock?" Witt said.

Meghan said, "We're going to need a debriefing...."

Thurgood came over comms from up in the *Furuseth*, –Took the words right out of my mouth. You're gonna need to explain this one too....–

Thurgood sent a zoomed vid feed of the *Halcyon* to all of their faceplate interiors—

The ship was distorting and warping as it hung in the same orbital position. It almost looked alive. Then the engines glowed brightly and translucent tentacles squirmed and burst out of the engine housings and other parts of the diamond-shaped hull—

All at once, the engines flared and the *Halcyon* shot away out into open space. Scattered ice and rocks thrown off by the *Halcyon*'s takeoff floated off in all directions.

Meghan looked at Abe, awestruck.

Abe said, "Magical.... Can we please go now?"

Beluga

Outpost [REDACTED]—2213

Marcy's eyes fluttered open with a languid resistance she couldn't place. *Was* her name "Marcy"? "Marcy" *felt* right. Why, though? She blinked and felt her eyelids fight the same treacle-like viscosity. Was it just her muscles? Atrophy?

She tried to move her head but couldn't. She took in what was in front of her—then realized it must also be above. She had a feeling of near weightlessness, but from the vague signals her body was sending to her brain, she felt like she was lying supine. Nothing in her body felt specific—couldn't place toes, thighs, chest, etc.

Above was a swirling abyss of murky shades of gray and dark blue. The slightest hint of connected triangles in a curved surface seemed to—

Something moved in her peripheral vision but it was out of sight before her eyes could catch it. Marcy tried to strain against whatever was holding her head and moved just a bit farther, but more murk was her only reward.

Emboldened by that small success, Marcy brought her head back to center and fought the restraints with her chin and forehead.

Marcy had been taken apart.

Her chest was open, her ribs sawed through clean and the sternum and rib ends removed. The organs within had been lifted out and placed in trays of clear plastic and pin-cushioned with something like thin glowing fiber-optic strands. The strands connected to smooth, rounded pieces of machinery with rows of tiny pulsing lights. The skin had been slit and pulled away from fat and muscles—which were separated and held apart in something like clear plastic sheathes—and sections of radius and ulna opened like her chest had been, exposing marrow. Her hands had also been dissected and dismantled, but were still connected by tissues and those strange glowing fibers. The fibers and lesser machines seemed to be connected to a larger machine below her she could only see suggestions of.

Marcy screamed but no sound came out.

She didn't understand how she was still alive. However this had been done to her, it was executed with extreme care and precision—but it still seemed impossible.

It was murkier down past her navel but Marcy couldn't look at her deconstructed body another moment. She was already approaching hyperventilation—and watching her heart and lungs work through that, connected with translucent extension patch tubes grafted into arteries and air tubes—when a strange head rose up near her own. It was some kind of biosuit helmet with a curved mirrored faceplate over the eye and nose area.

The biosuit wearer rose even further with a strange slowness, and bubbles broke free from the faceplate and floated lazily upward. Marcy's panicked mind still registered that she must be suspended in some kind of thick fluid. She also caught a glowing name strip on the biosuit chest that read M. ALBRECHTSSON.

The reflective faceplate moved from her face to her open chest area and back, seeming to study Marcy's body reacting to her fear.

The murk up past the biosuit wearer lit up, the triangular suggestions Marcy had seen glowing in a sequence. Starting from the center of what Marcy now saw must be a geodesic dome structure, the triangles glowed then blinked out—either disappearing or becoming translucent.

"Albrechtsson" floated up in the viscous murk, tubes and gear attached to the biosuit's back trailing and following it up. She couldn't see where the trail led to—but then she saw the suit's bloody gloves and a long, curved blade like a warped scalpel in one of them.

Through the thick murk and past the almost lotus-like break in the dome paneling, Marcy could just make out stars...then something blocking some of them out.

Albrechtsson looked down at Marcy again, then back up at the thing that was quickly blacking out the sky.

Marcy thought she could hear something like pulsing sirens out past the opening in the dome—but her breathing reached a hard peak and she lost consciousness.

Marcy was already moaning and crying into a pillow when she regained consciousness, face down on what would've otherwise been a comfortable bed. She'd never felt so much pain—coming from all over and different types at once. Dull, deep throbbing; sharp, biting; pulsing, layered burning....

She shifted and sobbed into the bed, still clawing into the pillow with one hand as her other searched for purchase on the mattress. Instead, her fingers dug into something softer than the pillow or bed.

Marcy turned her head against the mattress—sucking in air against the pain and feeling saliva drain from around her clenched teeth and down onto the sheets—and saw that she was clutching a beluga whale doll. She threw the mockingly adorable stuffed sea creature off the bed and continued to writhe in agony.

A soft beep sounded from just below her jawline, followed by a pinch in her neck. This barely registered through the pain—until it took effect. In less than a minute, her body pulsed with soothing warmth that seemed to neutralize the acid burn of the pain as a weak base would.

Her sobs became joyous as waves of euphoria washed over her, only to subside as quickly as they'd come—but the pain stayed gone, so her relief was enough. As the pain had lessened, she'd ended up on her side, hands over her tear-clammy face. She took her hands away from her face and, even in the dim light of the room, saw the scars.

Her hands and forearms were laced with intricate, orderly patterns suggestive of what had been done to her in what she'd assumed was a nightmare—*the fluid surgery torture chamber, or whatever it was*. She hadn't felt pain in the chamber, but what she'd seen had done more than enough damage.

She couldn't go through that again. If that chamber was real—and the scars told her it was—she had to get out of this place.

Marcy tried to focus, but the comfort and relief the shot in her neck had brought were as distracting as the incredible pain they'd replaced.

She sat up on the bed, placing her feet on a warmed pale orange floor. She wore cloth shorts and underpants, and a sleeveless shirt. She looked her body over. Every visible part of her body was covered in interconnecting seams of thin scar tissue—and they weren't just thin; she could see them clearest when they caught the dim light in the room at an angle.

She touched her head and felt close-cropped hair on top, then kept running her hands back. She felt the hair turn to fresh stubble on a large area on the back of her head and stopped, feeling a new flushing chill of horror as she forced herself to inspect the area with shaking hands.

There were scars there too.

Marcy pulled her hands back in front of her face and watched them shake.

She tried to say, "Why?" but nothing came out of her mouth.

She checked her throat for scars—but a padded collar obstructed her search. The collar was half an inch thick, seamless, and had harder parts under what felt like a woven fiber surface.

The painkillers must've come from this thing.

Marcy rubbed her hands up and down her scarred thighs, mostly to stop the shaking. She couldn't stop the fluttering in her diaphragm or shuddering in her chest, though.

Why am I here?
Who would do something this...wrong?
Think.

Her memory was foggy at best. Her name was Marcy...*something.* She vaguely remembered having studied something complicated. Probably STEM related. Was this something she'd volunteered for? Like a fucked-up clinical trial or something?

Marcy looked around her room—*or cell, more likely.*

Normal things—comfy bed, clean sheets and pillows, and tasteful, minimal nightstand with pitcher of water and glass. The dim light came from glowing panel strips along the bases of three of four dark-blue walls, the one with no light strip across from the foot of the bed. The corner to the left of the bed where it met the wall had a translucent waist-high walled area with a hinged section, and what looked like a curving depression in the floor with foot-shaped outlines—she realized it must be a form of toilet.

Normal-*ish* things—stuffed beluga-whale doll she'd thrown.

Odd things—all four corners where the ceiling met the walls looked cut off with black reflective triangles. Something about that felt bad—like whoever was doing this to her could watch through those triangular panels, or something behind them. "Cameras," she thought the word was. Nothing felt definite. Everything felt new or off, but like something she *should* know.

Oddest thing—there was no door.

No door meant no escape. Marcy couldn't accept that.

She tried to stand but even with the powerful painkillers in her, her legs felt wrong and she had to slump back down onto the bed. She tried again and succeeded, but kept a hand on the bed as she limped around to the foot of it.

How does somebody escape a sealed room?
No door. No windows. No—

She looked up and saw an air-vent grate above the bed. The openings were a set of concentric circles held together by an X that ran through them. Marcy climbed onto the bed on all fours, then stood up. She did her best with wobbly legs.

The grate was a seamless part of the ceiling.

Must not trust their guinea pigs to want to stay in their cages....
Too bad.

Marcy slid her fingers into the grating and pulled down, hoping the seamless look was an illusion. There was no give. She tried again, harder. Nothing. She hung by her fingers, pulling her legs up from the bed and hoping her weight could bring it down. It was solid.

She glared at the grate in despair...then got mad.

Marcy redoubled her efforts, jumping off the bed and pulling herself up by the grate, then dropping down as hard as she could. She did this over and over, her anger growing with each failed attempt.

331

Then Marcy's fingers started to elongate—the proximal phalanges stretching down from where they met the knuckles. They pulled down long enough that her feet sunk into the bed and she teetered back at an angle. The stretching parts became almost translucent and—

She released her hooked fingers from the grating and dropped, catching the corner of the bed with her butt then rolling off and slapping onto the floor. She was conscious but her bell had been rung. She shook her head and looked at her hands—they were normal again, other than all the scars.

What was *that?*

Marcy curled up fetal and her sobs returned. Her crying only came out as tears and air catching and shuddering in her throat—she felt like she was moaning, but she couldn't. In between the choking sounds her throat was making, she heard a very faint high-pitched sound.

The wall across from the foot of the bed began vibrating—with a low *wump* sound, it became translucent. It was still closer to solid than clear, but Marcy could make out the dim suggestion of a starkly lit section of corridor. It was pale orange from walkway to ceiling, like the floor of her cell.

Marcy lifted herself up onto her arms.

A boxy, waist-high shape came into the light from the far end, moving in silence. She wasn't sure if it actually was silent, or her wall was sound-proofed—with a twisting of dread in her stomach, she assumed the latter. The thing stopped at a dark square of wall—like the one Marcy was looking out through, she assumed—did something she couldn't make out near it, then continued toward her translucent wall. The light in the hallway went out and she could see only the slightest suggestion of the corridor and the boxy shape.

Marcy got to her feet.

With the wall translucent but corridor lights off, Marcy could make out a dim reflection of her face. She had dark eyes and hair. She could make out some freckles—and faint scar lines. She couldn't remember if her face had been opened up in the chamber....

A light in the corridor ceiling above the other side of her translucent wall came on, and her reflection was replaced by a closer view of the boxy thing as it cruised up to her cell. It was a drone of some kind. Its side paneling rolled up into itself and two manipulator arms retrieved a thick plastic slab from within its bulk. It looked like a food tray.

Food delivery-bot? Maybe it has....

A four-by-twelve-inch section of the wall disappeared somehow and the drone socketed the tray into it and started to ease it in—

Marcy pulled the tray through and went down on her knees, sticking her arms through and grabbing the drone's retreating manipulators. It pulled one free so she grabbed the other with both hands and tried to heft the bot toward the wall. She couldn't move it, and switched to trying to find buttons on its surface.

If there's a door button—

332

The tray opening in the door attempted to close and sensed her arms. Lights flashed in its rectangular outline, warning of imminent closure. Marcy's desperation kept her fighting, and that brought her anger back.

The lights flashed brighter and made a pulsing sound of warning now. She closed her eyes and kept searching with one hand while she held the manipulator arm with the other.

Fuck you! Cut my arms off then, you piece of shit!

It did—or would have. The tray opening closed, lights and alarm ceasing.

Marcy could still feel the manipulator and surface of the boxy food drone. She opened her eyes and would have yelped if she could have.

Her arms were *in* the door. The chunk that had closed was solid, but the sections of her forearms that were where it had closed were translucent—and her arms were still there on the other side. The sections in the door also looked warped and pulsed strangely. Marcy panicked and let go, pulling herself away from the wall, and her arms with her. She fell back on her butt and her back collided with the firm softness and paneling of the foot of the bed.

A rotating glow—like a tiny old-style police roof light—was emitted from a spot on the drone's topside, and it continued on. The wall vibrated and become opaque again with a *wump.*

Marcy examined her arms. Once again, scars but otherwise normal. She didn't understand how it worked but she knew if that torture room was real, this warping or phasing was her only way of never being in it again. She got to her feet and placed open palms and fingers against the wall.

She pressed her hands against the wall harder and pushed, but nothing happened. She pushed over and over again, but her hands remained solid.

Why?

How does this work?

Her frustration led to fear, flooding her mind with images of her dissected, impossibly alive body in that chamber.

Her fear pushed her toward anger.

Marcy's hands went through the wall, her arms now looking cut off at the wrists. She hesitated a moment, then focused on that feeling of simmering rage and stepped forward. She caught glimpses of the door's inner workings before stumbling out into the dark corridor.

The collar started flashing and making a high-pitched alert sound.

Marcy forced nightmare images into her mind again and focused on her hands and neck. The collar vibrated as she pulled it out of her neck through the substance of her body, then she examined the interior of its ring. It had layered needlelike barbs for staying in place, and the slightly thicker injection needle.

What is this awful fucking place?

She decided to take a chance that the phasing worked both ways, and focused on the collar even harder—it went translucent along with her hands, so she pushed them through the wall to her now empty cell and dropped the collar inside.

Whatever this place really was, most of it was underground.

Marcy had sneaked through its many dark corridors, hiding from food drones a few times, to a curved hall twice the width of the rest with gray walls. She'd followed it long enough to decide it must be a circle or oval around the whole level. Then she'd tried to phase through that and succeeded, only to go a few feet through metal and concrete—and into solid rock. For a panicked moment she thought she might fall through it. She didn't know anything about how this power she had worked. As long as she concentrated, she could walk forward on the same plane...but there was nothing but rock for ten feet. She got spooked and hurried back into the curved hallway.

She knew she had to go up, but had no way to know how far.

Marcy had climbed onto a medical equipment station she'd found and went through some quick trial and error to learn to climb with her phasing ability—all the while trying to ignore that every time she used it, she saw more and weirder pulsing and warping suggestions undulating within her own natural body shapes.

She'd also had to fight the urge to use her phasing to enter another cell like the one she'd been in and see if there were more like her. She'd decided that even if she could get another person out through one of the doors, she wasn't sure what else getting out of this facility would require—and that could just get more people hurt.

Marcy's forehead and eyes emerged from the surface of a grated floor panel as if from a steamy pond, several floors up from the patient/prisoner levels she'd started on. She held herself in a phased crouch within layered sets of fluid-transfer pipes and conduits filled with shrouded bundles of electronics cables. This flooring was more utilitarian and well-used than the other floors she'd recently climbed up into and out of, and she hoped that meant she was close to ground level.

Satisfied she was alone, Marcy hauled herself up out of the floor and crept down the corridor. More conduits and pipes lined the hallway walls, and tightly enough that it almost felt to Marcy like a movie she felt she'd seen at some point in her foggy past about men on a submarine—which she also half remembered was a boat or ship that went under the water; and a ship was a boat that didn't....

This feeling of unsureness about *pretty-much-everything* would've haunted Marcy, if she'd been willing to stop and really think about it. Instead, she pushed on.

334

A porthole window in a sealed hatch-style door didn't discourage Marcy's submarine associations, but as she sneaked up to it and peaked in she saw something that didn't fit with them.

Several strange, bone-white figures stood in special stations, motionless. They were the shape of a human man, but with a hunch to the slim muscular triangle of upper body that connected two thick, overlong arms—which ended in something between hands and multi-tools. Where their hips would be there was a smooth inverted wishbone of metal or plasteel housing shocks and struts that connected to the tops of roughly humanlike legs. Their heads were on shocks and struts too, and were suggestive of a human head wearing something like a fighter-pilot helmet—only all one piece and with a murky translucence that mostly hid complex electronic workings within.

I...don't think these drones deliver food, Marcy thought, then she shuddered at the thought of what these things could do to her.

More deathbots are probably all over this level....

Marcy lifted a leg and stepped partially *into* the hatch, boosting herself up and climbing into the ceiling. She was getting the hang of focusing her fear into its own mental compartment for phasing use—and these man-drones didn't hurt that process one bit.

A few more levels up, it struck her that she hadn't seen a single other person here. She climbed up out of the floor, crept around a level long enough to get nervous and a little creeped out, then kept going up. Also, it had to be almost thirty levels she'd climbed now, and she had a feeling the one she'd started on wasn't the lowest....

Marcy's forehead and eyes came out of a floor and saw only white.

She pulled herself up out of the surface more and it took two more feet for her to see what the white was—she was climbing up onto a snow-covered roof in a blizzard at night. Wind howled and snow blew all around, sweeping across the piles thick enough to not be moved.

What is this, Antarctica? You've got to be fucking kidding....

Marcy climbed back down and searched the level for anything resembling warm-weather clothes, but found nothing. She couldn't find evidence of any other humans here—other than Albrechtsson, but at this point Marcy wouldn't be surprised if he was a robot too.

Having failed to find warmer clothes, Marcy took a chance on something and climbed back up onto the snow-swept roof. She treated the outside as she had the subterranean rock she'd walked through—if she kept herself something like half-phased, she couldn't feel the cold. She'd also noticed that if she stayed in a phased state, she didn't have to breathe. That was convenient, but also disturbed her.

Okay, what are we working with here...?

She was on the roof of what seemed to be the largest single structure in sight. It had a tall, complex tower covered in antennae, dishes, and arrays of slightly curved vertical panels in different arrangements. That communications

335

tower was at the center of the large circular roof surface. She rose from a crouch and phase-stepped through the snow piles to the curved edge closest to her. The roof was about three stories up, so her view was decent.

Flood lights here and there around the facility structures were almost obscured by the thick snow rushing through their illumination, along with all the snow blowing between them and Marcy. She could make out suggestions of shapes.

There were prefab structures on stilt supports, Quonset huts, and geodesic domes. The domes filled her with dread—their curved surfaces made up of connected triangular frames were without question the triangles she'd seen in the fluid-filled surgery chamber. She could see three of those domes on this side of the facility alone.

Lightning or something like it flashed on the horizon, the snow so dense the distant brilliance only dimly lit up the sky where Marcy was—but in those flashes she could see silhouettes or larger shapes above the ground level of the facility.

All around and looming above the facility grounds and beyond the immediate perimeter she could see, there were huge radio telescope dishes. It reminded her of something she vaguely remembered was called SETI, but the dishes and support structures here were even larger. There were other shapes too—mostly outside the facility perimeter—and Marcy's best guess was they were something like huge resting artillery guns.

An alert sounded from speakers all over the facility.

Shit—they must've figured out I'm out of my cell!

Marcy ducked down instinctively, but she wasn't even sure how visible she was in her phased state. She let herself drop through the roof a bit, and crawled through it and the snow with just her eyes and the top of her head poking out above the windswept surfaces.

But no one came for her. No spotlights. Nothing near her changed.

She progressed around the edge of the circle slowly for a few minutes, still looking for a way out. There was nothing visible in the dark blizzard, and no lights in the distance at all. If this was Antarctica or Alaska or Canada or Russia...she was in for a hell of a walk with no compass, food, or water—or clothes and boots for that matter. She knew all of these items were important, but still it was distant *why* she did.

Lights glowed around the circle edge off to her right and even over the blizzard she could hear strange-sounding voices.

Marcy crawled over to that edge but stayed hidden in the snow and roof.

A spotlight followed a strange form that kept diving and tumbling out of its circle. The form shambled between a Quonset hut and one of the raised buildings. Through the whipping snow and dark, Marcy saw silhouetted humanoid forms cut off the form's escape route in the distance—it threw itself up into the stilt structures under the building. The circle of light found it again and it flung itself through the openings between the stilts, climbing with several misshapen limbs indistinguishable as legs or arms before throwing itself some distance again.

Another group of humanoid forms approached the panicked amorphous creature from near the base of the building Marcy was on—she saw it was a team of the bone-white "deathbots" she'd seen earlier. It occurred to her from how well they blended in that the coloring was a form of camouflage. They held strange guns that looked like big assault or particle rifles, but with thick cables running from open ports in their hunched triangular torsos to the back of flat rounded-square panels on the end of the guns perpendicular to their length.

The drones took positions a few feet from each other and aimed their weapons at the escaping beast. Spotlights from their head sections came on and startled the creature, stopping it in mid climb—and Marcy saw at this distance that it was translucent, with the vague suggestion of having once been human. But now it had too many eyes, all of them deep black but clouded as if with cataracts—and those cloudy parts caught the drones' lights with an iridescence and as they darted around, they trailed an eerie psychedelic distortion of the light as well.

Its mouth broke open at an unnatural angle and a few other openings came apart within its warped, pulsing interior. From the depths of its pulsing innards, an unearthly howl rose and its haunting sound cut into Marcy's mind, even over the blizzard.

Whatever the drones' guns fired, it was invisible—Marcy thought of riot deterrent microwave emitters—but she could hear them vibrating as they went off.

The creature's howl became a shrill, chittering cry, and it dropped to the snow below the stilts. It writhed and collapsed in on itself in places, reforming different shapes as it whined—tentacles, malformed appendages of no obvious purpose, the suggestion of bones and organs growing at an exponential rate under a taut exterior layer that acted like a skin around an animal—or several—evolving in real time.

The wave-guns went off again, vibrating louder.

The interior shape-shifting and chaotic self-birthing slowed and the frightening monstrosity collapsed its shape into what seemed like a defensive posture. Then it mewled and sobbed in its own weird way, but the straining mess of flesh, fluids, and organs had lost its face and head in the process of whatever it was doing and Marcy couldn't tell where the sounds were coming from.

Then she finally saw another human.

A well-bundled human form trudged up to the half-circle of drones through the snow, followed by another drone that was different from the others—if they were bone-white, this one was dried-blood red. Its head section also seemed to contain a glowing actual head within its jet fighter–helmet-shaped translucent plasteel, which Marcy thought must be some kind of display or surface projection illusion. This red drone had a different gun too—no square panel, a fat barrel with holes along its length, and a soccer-ball-sized spherical tank near its shrouded rear pistol grip.

The bundled human approached the defeated monster as it cowered in the snow. She—it seemed to be a she—got closer than Marcy expected, studying the shuddering mound of organic chaos from only a few feet away. It reminded her of how Albrechtsson had studied her in the fluid chamber, and she realized that probably *was* her.

Apparently satisfied, Albrechtsson turned away from the creature and started back through the snow. She was wearing a breathing mask with a clear faceplate, and Marcy caught something like a nod of approval as the masked face rose and fell with a sharp motion toward the red drone.

The red drone stepped forward, raised its weapon, and used it.

Bright green liquid fire came out of the gun—not quite napalm, but it doused, clung to, and burned. It burned like fire and acid at the same time, engulfing the screaming shapeless monster and eating away at its bulk as it lashed at the parts it hadn't disintegrated yet.

Marcy didn't wait another second—she turned away from the grizzly scene and ran, still submerged in the fluidlike give of the roof and snow covering it.

It wasn't lost on her that her phasing had made her body look less and less human as she'd continued to use it. She knew that whatever that thing was, it probably started as something more like her—and she'd rather die more human than more like that.

The other side of the facility had more huts and domes—but no drones or Albrechtsson.

Marcy knew she had to be quick. She judged the distance between the base of the structure she was on and where the lights were swallowed by darkness out by the dishes and artillery guns, and past them. She focused on the phasing more intently and let herself drop through the material. Her eyes, nose, and forehead were the only things exposed, and she felt like she was on an amusement ride of some kind as she plummeted down the wall through a blizzard.

Just before reaching the snowdrifts built up around ground level, Marcy slowed herself and stopped. The feeling she'd had when she'd walked out through the solid rock from the underground facility area kept her from having any desire to disappear entirely into any other surface.

She crawled out of the wall and through the snowdrifts, keeping all but her eyes as hidden as possible. Wind howled above her, blowing snow all around as she advanced toward the underside of another raised stilt building. She sneaked under that all the way to the far side, then continued out past the reach of the facility floodlights.

About a hundred yards past the lights, Marcy climbed up out of the snow-covered ground. She stayed half-phased as the deep cold necessitated, but walked normally otherwise. She was nearing the base of one of the huge dish structures when alarms sounded again from the facility behind her.

Marcy hurried forward through the storm and stepped right past a convex circular panel on part of the dish structure. She stopped in place and stared at it—black and reflective, like the ceiling corners back in her cell. The alarm sounded from the dish now too and floodlights lit up all around its base, exposing Marcy's translucent form.

No!

She ran.

Away from the lights. Out into the dark.

At first there was only snow and howling wind. She put as much distance as she could between herself and the base before she heard the sounds of machines behind her. The storm had died down some, so it was possible the source wasn't close behind. She looked back and saw the lights from three large tracked "snowcat" vehicles. They were moving at high speed on their tank treads in her general direction about fifty feet apart.

Maybe they haven't seen me!

She was still in the dark—it was possible they hadn't.

Marcy started to phase her body more to drop into snowy ground and hide—

A ball of glowing energy traveled from the left snowcat closest to her and struck her in the chest.

She collapsed back onto the snow, her body completely solid again—and now consumed by the extreme cold she hadn't felt at all yet. Marcy curled into a ball to keep warm, but it didn't help. All she could do was shudder and try to keep her teeth from chattering together too hard as the snowcats rolled up to her.

The red humanoid drone approached holding the special energy gun she'd been dropped by, and she saw that she'd been right—the glowing form inside the translucent drone head section was an illusion. It was a real-time embedded 3-D animation of a heavily scarred face with a cloudy dead eye. The white drones followed and stopped in a wide semicircle, similar to how they had with the creature before—and two of the white drones had guns like the one the red one had used to kill it, which sent an even deeper shudder through Marcy.

The glowing head spoke in Russian, but not to her. Strangely enough, Marcy understood him, even though she knew somehow it wasn't her first language.

<<That could have been worse....>>

<<She should never have made it this far,>> Albrechtsson said as she made her way through the snow toward Marcy.

<<We had no idea she could do any of that. You didn't seem to eith—>>

Albrechtsson raised a gloved hand to silence him.

Marcy wanted to beg for her life, but her voice still wouldn't come.

Albrechtsson stopped feet from her and said, "Your vocal chords were taken out of the sequencing. You simply can't speak or make any vocal intonations. Fortunately for me...."

Marcy closed her eyes and started weeping, sure she'd be killed as soon as this awful woman stepped away from her.

"What did you think you were.... Where were you going to go?"

Marcy opened her eyes and glared at the woman—but she was looking out into the dark beyond the snowcat lights. Albrechtsson's eyes glimmered, and she looked sad. The woman turned her head and looked down at Marcy again through the clear faceplate flanked by a thick, padded hood—the light from a snowcat illuminated the woman's face and Marcy was struck deeply by something she couldn't comprehend. Albrechtsson's face was so familiar....

It was the face she'd seen in the reflection in her cell wall.

"I know you don't know much..."

Albrechtsson locked eyes with her—and Marcy noticed now it was the same face, but older.

"...but where is it you think you are?"

<<How would she know that?>>

<<*Octopus* knew more than she was supposed to—why couldn't *Beluga*?>>

<<True....>>

Albrechtsson said, <<We are so close. This kind of thing cannot happen again.>>

<<At least we have *her* back. Only two left from this cycle and they both "evolve" and escape on the same day....>>

Albrechtsson said, <<Maybe if they could transfer some *human* staff out here, we'd have less trouble with these automatons being outsmarted.>>

<<Hey, I'm human. Just less...*meaty* than I used to be.>>

Marcy looked at the Russian, realizing he must be some kind of cyborg. He met her gaze through whatever mechanism gave his still-human brain sight—as it certainly wasn't the glowing eye in the animation. He looked away, almost sheepishly.

The Russian cyborg said, <<So that's me, an army worth of drones, and you—you're human too, remember?>>

Marcy looked back toward the woman—Albrechtsson's eyes studied Marcy's face, then took on a distant stare that went through her.

Albrechtsson looked up at the sky again and said, "I wonder if that's still true."

<<Huh?>>

Albrechtsson said, <<Have them warm her and transfer her to the operating theater. It's close now...or it soon will be. I tuned your pulse gun based on guesses—make sure you hit her with it again if she starts to change at all.>>

<<Understood.>>

The woman turned away and walked back to the snowcat she'd exited.

Instead of bathing Marcy in green fiery death, the armed drones watched as four of the others guided a hovering unit toward her that was like a clear coffin with padding, restraints, and what had to be heating equipment. They picked Marcy up with surprising care and set her in the chamber as gently as they could. They closed the top—

The Russian cyborg grabbed the clear lid and the drones stopped. For a moment, he couldn't seem to bring himself to look at her.

Then he did look at her and said, <<This is more important than I could ever say in words.... Please understand that.>>

He let go and the drones sealed Marcy in the clear coffin.

At least it was warm.

This time, Marcy was taken apart fully conscious and without pain blockers.

If her mind had been capable of it, she might have found it fascinating how much incredible technology went into her instantaneous deconstruction. A symphony of incisions, pumping, flaying, sawing, grafting, stitching, sucking, pulling, transfusing....

But all she could comprehend once it started was pain.

Before starting the process, Albrechtsson had floated around her, wordless and cold. The mirrored faceplate helped this impression, but the lack of any interaction somehow made it even worse. She'd hooked up the surgery machine's tips, needles, blades, saws, etc., at their starting points as she floated through the thick chamber fluid. So precise. So gentle.

After Albrechtsson had exited through a fluid lock chamber, Marcy had been able to crane her head far enough over in the restraints to see Albrechtsson at a control terminal for the machines. She was still wearing the biosuit, and the mirrored faceplate still hid her face—the face they shared. Marcy would never get an answer to why they did.

Marcy couldn't scream or moan or cry like she thought she was doing. Albrechtsson had taken even that from her. All she could do was convulse and shudder silently.

Through her haze of maddening agony, Marcy took in experiential glimpses of what was happening outside of her personal hell chamber—

The triangle panels in the geodesic-dome ceiling went clear—she saw out through the lotus opening....

An alarm sounded, unlike the earlier ones—like a thumping pulse drawn out to sound like a slowed down air-raid siren....

The light above the facility was blotted out by a huge form that quickly filled the sky....

The closer it came down to the facility, the better Marcy felt. The pain and madness were still there, but this sky-filling thing was like her—like a moon-sized warped ball of what she was—or maybe she was like *It*. This evil human woman had made her like this huge, beautiful thing somehow...

...translucent, squirming, undulating, slithering, pumping, phasing...

...and It had come because that woman was hurting her.

As this god of a thing loomed over her, it allowed her to become her true self—her human shape, open and on display as it had been made by this awful human fool, was abandoned and she unraveled and opened once again...into her *real* self.

Her rebirth was announced by impossibly loud trumpets....

Albrechtsson watched the colossal abomination being sucked into itself, imploding at the entry wounds the facility's special artillery guns had opened in its bulging, distorted form. The thing they'd just killed was hard to comprehend. You could look at it with naked eyes and never quite see it or understand it. Through her faceplate's finely-tuned AR filters, she could see it for what it was—a gargantuan mass of monstrous insanity made semisolid.

As she watched the creature disintegrating into itself in a psychedelic lightshow of organic fractal madness, she thought—*We can kill you. I...can kill you.*

The facility shook hard enough to slosh the operating theater's fluid around, causing it to slap against the dome interior near its apex—bringing her attention back to Beluga.

The young woman who'd entered the dome tub had become something very different over the course of what Albrechtsson thought of as the "beckoning process." Albrechtsson studied the warped mess of translucent tentacles, organs, misshapen bones, mouths, and too many eyes that had so recently looked human and resembled her in her youth....

Albrechtsson keyed a set of commands into her control panel, and the fluid in the dome ignited bright green—it burned away all of the organic material in the dome, then was extinguished by a catalyst fluid before being sucked down a large drain in the chamber floor.

The entry wall to Beluga's room vanished and Albrechtsson stood in the corridor a moment, just looking around. She stepped in and walked to the stuffed animal on the floor. As she picked it up, she heard automaton steps out in the corridor—less rigid though, so probably Spichak. She walked out to the corridor and saw the glowing representation of his old, grizzled face looking happy for first time in decades.

Spichak said, <<You were right! We *can* kill those bastards!>>

<<Or whatever it is those new guns do....>>

<<Come on! Who cares what they do? If the space monster is gone, it's fucking *gone*!>>

342

Albrechtsson said, <<I suppose.>>

She flashed Spichak a half smile and walked past him toward the lifts.

Spichak said, <<Hey...,>> and she stopped and looked back.

<<Yes?>>

<<Does this ever get easier for you?>>

<<What's that?>>

<<Doing this to...parts of yourself.>>

Albrechtsson said, <<Better to use "parts" of myself...than anyone else or theirs.>>

She started back down the hall but stopped again.

Without turning back she said, <<And...no,>> then continued on to the lift.

Albrechtsson entered her dark personal quarters and walked through to a clear plasteel picture window—installed in the curved surface of the highest level of the main facility, most of which was underground—without turning the lights on. She raised the beluga doll toward a curved shelf above the window but she caught sight of one of the snow-swept operating theater domes out in the storm and hesitated. She lowered the doll and stepped away from the window and shelf.

On the way to her large, comfortable bed, she grabbed a bottle and lowball glass from her dining area. She set the bottle and glass on a nightstand, crawled onto the bed, and collapsed into large pillows stacked atop it.

She cried for about ten minutes, then rolled over onto her back and composed herself as best she could. She poured three fingers of ancient rum into the glass and downed half of that in one pull. She sucked air through her teeth as the rum she'd quaffed burned, in spite of its luxurious smoothness.

"Open comms—Spichak."

After a few beeps, Spichak said, <<Yes, ma'am?>>

<<Prep another set. Mem-plants must be immaculate.>>

<<We killed it. What good—?>>

Albrechtsson said, <<We killed *one*. I know there are more.>>

To herself she repeated, "I *know* there are."

<<Understood.>>

<<And Spichak....>>

<< *Yes*, ma'am?>>

Albrechtsson sipped her drink and turned the doll in her other hand.

<<Retire the *Beluga* subject designation.>>

<<After this many cycles through? You're honoring this one? That's new....>>

<<Call it what you like. Any other *B* animal will do.>>

Spichak sighed in a digital rasp and said, <<Yes, ma'am. Anything else?>>

<<Just wake me up when they're ready for birthing.>>

<<The gestation takes almost twenty hours—>>

<<And you can wake me when that's *finished.*>>

<<*Understood,*>> Spichak said and closed comms on his end.

She sipped her drink and looked across her quarters at the shelf above her large, curved window and the storm it sheltered her from. In the dim light from the facility external floods coming in, she could make out twenty-five other stuffed animals resting on the shelf. The darkness of the empty spot between *Antelope* and *Crab*—and the dolls that continued all the way from *Dove* to *Zebra*—threatened to swallow her.

<<"*After this many cycles...,*">> she said, mocking Spichak's words and their cruel implication.

She opened a drawer in the nightstand and took out a pressure syringe. She pushed the device into her neck and injected herself with its warming fluid. Her eyelids fluttered and almost closed. She looked at the beluga doll and sipped her drink until her arm drooped in time with her eyelids.

"*Ad...infinitum....*"

Her arm fell onto the bed, the glass tipping out of her hand. It rolled away and dribbled the last of the liquor onto the bedspread in a curved trail.

Marcy Albrechtsson slept.

ABOUT THE AUTHOR

PATRICK LOVELAND writes screenplays, novels, and short stories. By day, he works at a state college in Southern California, where he lives with his wife, young daughter, and a cat so black he seems to absorb light. Patrick's stories have appeared in anthologies and periodicals published by April Moon Books, Shadow Work Publishing, EyeCue Productions, Bold Venture Press, Sirens Call Publications, Indie Authors Press, PHANTAXIS, and the award-winning Crime Factory zine. Patrick's first novel, *A Tear in the Veil*, was published in June of 2017 by April Moon Books, and a revised version will be released in 2019 by Stay Strange Publishing.

Twitter: https://twitter.com/pmloveland
Facebook: https://www.facebook.com/pmloveland/
Blog: https://patrickloveland.com/

www.ingramcontent.com/pod-product-compliance
Lightning Source LLC
Chambersburg PA
CBHW071152100726
47908CB00002B/345